Rich Relations

RICH RELATIONS

William Wright

G. P. Putnam's Sons
New York

Library of Congress Cataloging in Publication Data
Wright, William, date.
  Rich relations.

  I. Title.
PZ4.W954Ri 1980   [PS3573.R554]   813'.54   80-15418
ISBN 0-399-12462-4

PRINTED IN THE UNITED STATES OF AMERICA

Rich relations give
Crust of bread and such
You can help yourself
But don't take too much

—Billie Holiday, "God Bless the Child"

Prologue

As they moved about the grounds of their suburban ashram, the Hare Krishnas gaped openly at the nattily dressed man—handsome, worldly, twice their age—who sat alone at the wrought-iron table on the terrace. His white linen suit and Panama hat harmonized with the sunswept lawns and the Wall-Street–Tudor mansion, but clashed absurdly with the pink-robed religious zealots.

Ignoring their stares, Brandon Hartshorne crossed his legs, shot a linen pant leg and looked at his watch. Any minute, he thought wryly, these pimply zombies will witness a vision that will make them forget me and have them ringing their bells and holding up whatever talismans Krishna permits.

He considered the gray stone house that was draped with ivy and wisteria vines. Exactly the house he would have expected of Tom Tollover—outsized, pretentious and crumbling. The grounds were lovely, unspoiled even by a vegetable garden stamped gracelessly on one side of the lawn by the Hare Krishnas. Vast expanses of untouched lawn remained, sloping gently to a ring of woods, oaks and maples interspersed with rhododendron.

And nowhere in the enclosing ring of trees was there an opening to reveal the shabby housing development that Brandon had driven past just before reaching the entrance gates to Mapleton. Except for the robed spirits, the house probably looked just as it had when Augusta and B.K. were growing up there.

As he heard the faint staccato slap of the helicopter motor,

Brandon gave a final consideration to the young devout and wondered how such people—spiritual, austere, self-denying—could be of the same species as himself and his two famous stepsisters. Not possible.

As the helicopter hovered over the estate, then descended slowly and noisily onto the center of the lawn, the Hare Krishnas abandoned any pretense of casual curiosity and stopped their strolls, their gardening and their discussion circles to stand watching the aircraft. When the motors were out, Brandon bestirred himself and walked down the flagstone steps and crossed the lawn toward the helicopter.

The door opened and a young man in a banker's gray suit and regimental tie hopped down, then reached back to assist a stunning woman—about thirty-five, stylishly dressed in a tan silk pants suit and a red silk scarf. Large dark glasses and loose-falling brown hair were unable to conceal an impressive beauty.

She moved to Brandon and kissed him warmly. "You were an angel to come," she said as they linked arms and started up the lawn, the young banker trailing behind carrying a black leather attaché case.

"I was, wasn't I? But then I happened to be in New York and Westbury is only forty-five minutes from the St. Regis. And you know, B.K., I try not to miss any of the thrilling installments in the running serial about my two legendary stepsisters."

She nodded toward the Hare Krishnas. "I know it's a sentimental occasion, but it seems too much for even your sense of theatrics to have brought the Mormon Tabernacle Choir."

"You'll change your mind when you hear them hum their rendition of 'Just One of those Things.' It will evoke the early fifties, North Shore debutante mood. Surely you knew the Hare Krishnas had bought your old home?"

"Yes, but I thought they'd be upstairs studying scrolls or something—or on street corners singing the Krishna fight song. But they're all over the place like some Hindustani garden party."

As they reached the terrace table, B.K. sighed as she took a seat. "I had planned a little alcoholic reinforcement before our plunge into the past, but I don't know if it's appropriate with all these devout eyes bearing down on us."

"If there's one thing you and your sister should have learned by now, it's how to carry on as though you were ordinary mortals, as though your every hangnail wasn't a matter of public concern."

"You're right. Besides, I need a drink more than I need their approval." Turning to the gray-suited man, she said, "All right, Higgs, if you don't mind . . ."

He placed the leather case on the table before them and snapped it open. Nestling in red suede compartments inside were four silver cocktail glasses and a silver shaker glistening with little beads of moisture.

Brandon laughed. "Good old Mark Cross has surpassed himself this time."

"Hermés. Such trinkets more or less come with the helicopter." Higgs neatly poured two martinis and placed them in front of B.K. and Brandon. They toasted each other, then drank.

"Don't look," B.K. said, "but are the spooks headed for us?"

"No. I bet they'll stand frozen like wild game until you and your aircraft take off, even if it's hours from now." He examined the cocktail case. "You know, B.K., your sister—our sister—is incredible. Do you suppose she snaps open some little leather case every time she brushes her teeth?"

"You don't really think she brushes her own teeth?"

"Foolish of me."

A pale, balding man, ageless and official-looking, came toward them from the house. "How do you do," he said without expression. "I am the assistant director. Mr. Axian has been called away. Your family things are in his office. He said it wasn't necessary for you to await his return to start going through them. His office is right through there . . ." He gestured toward open French doors.

"The music room," B.K. said absently. "Thank you. I think we'll sit here another minute."

The man nodded and returned to the house.

"Why have these items turned up now," Brandon said, "after so many years?"

"The letter Gus received from the director had some obsequious crap about 'personal memorabilia of your illustrious family' . . ."

"But think how many other occupants this house has had since you lived here. Do you have to be famous to have your possessions returned?"

"Just one more area," B.K. said taking a swallow of her martini, "where it doesn't hurt." She looked up at the house, lifting her sunglasses. "I would love to say how much better Mapleton looked when we lived here. The truth is, it's in better shape now. The lawns and gardens are more under control. I don't see any broken panes and the cracked flagstones have been replaced. Whatever you may think of your stepmother, she worked her ass off keeping us and this house together. Twenty-four rooms and only a high-school girl twice a week to help her clean. And none of those middle-class suppers in the breakfast room. Daddy insisted on the main dining room every night, with damask napkins Mummie ironed by hand. For him, we had to live as though there was a staff of six. Mummie was the six. Gus and I helped with the gardening."

"What did he do?"

"Played tennis, on Sundays polo. . . ."

"Why didn't you hate him?

"We worshiped him. You only saw him when he was starting to fall apart. When we were children, he was fun and he looked like a movie star. He always made Gus and me feel special, superior to the other kids even though we had no money and they all did. He had a lot of ploys to pump us up—the Tollover family history, his connections, our breeding. But what worked most on our snobbishness was an attribute of his that was never mentioned—his looks.

"When we go through that trunk in there, you'll probably learn some things about your stepsisters you never knew—and if anyone is entitled to grow bored with us even if the public won't, it's you. The one fact that influenced our childhood and upbringing more than any other was silly: we had a very *pretty* father. He had charm, style, panache—but the looks were what let him get away with so much, what made Kate work for him, what made everyone adore him—even the hordes he owed money to—and what made Gus and me desperate to please him, to win his approval, just to attract his notice. How many years has he been dead? Gus and I are still trying to divert him from his women friends long enough for an approving nod . . ."

"Well, please stop now," Brandon said, taking the last sip from his martini. "The world can't take too much more achievement from you two."

B.K. smiled. "Achievement is too nice a word." She stood up. "Let's not put it off any longer. When we go through that junk, you can pick yourself out a souvenir of the childhood of the two most notorious adventuresses of their time."

Part One

1 Through the French doors shot a thirteen-year-old Augusta Tollover, her dark hair flying, her strong features clouded and tense. "Hurry up, B.K.," she called over her shoulder into the house behind her. "This is an emergency." She ran down the steps and across the lawn towards the woods. Through the doors ran B.K., two years younger, her fairer hair in pigtails. Already confused and anxious, B.K. stumbled on the tall grass growing between the flagstones. She avoided falling, then chased her sister across the grass into the woods.

The tall trees all but eliminated the May sunlight and B.K. lost sight of Augusta, but she knew where to find her. Fifty yards of shadowy path brought her to a small clearing and what the sisters called the Italian fountain. The stone structure curving around a pool was an authentic nympheum—a stylized, man-made grotto of the fifteenth century which had been brought over from Italy and reassembled on Long Island by the banker who built the Tollovers' estate in the early 1900s.

Of all the mansion's vestiges of European elegance—the leaded windows, parquet floors, carved oak staircase, beamed ceilings—the fountain was the only authentic element, the only feature, ornamental or structural, that was not a replica but the real thing. If the girls knew this, it was not the reason—not the conscious reason—they picked the nympheum for their private retreat. It was separate and hidden from the house; their parents never came there and barely knew it existed. With its dripping, moss-covered stones, dark brackish water and, in the center of the curved stone facade, a statue of a nude woman whom the girls had named Miss Daphne, the grotto had an air of mystery and romance that suited Augusta and B.K.'s most serious discussions.

Augusta had already regained her breath by the time B.K. came panting into the shady clearing and collapsed on a stone bench. "Now you understand, B.K.," Augusta began, "anything we discuss here is top secret—automatically. I have something now that is super important. You must doubly swear not to say anything about it to anyone—not to mother, or any of your friends, *anyone*. Do you swear?"

"Yes, Gus." B.K. crossed one leg on her knee and stared at the overhead branches.

"Sit up. You can't swear lying on your back. Say after me, I, Belinda Knight Tollover of Mapleton, Westbury, Long Island, swear I will say nothing about what my sister is going to tell me."

B.K. repeated it.

From the pocket of her tennis shorts, Augusta pulled a folded piece of violet paper. "It's about Mummie and Daddy. We thought that maybe their fighting means they don't love each other? Well, now I've found *this*. It was in the pocket of Daddy's raincoat."

Warily B.K. said, "What is it?"

"It's a note, stupid. From that horrible mother of your friend Becky—*Fern Havermeyer!*" She spat the name as if it were veal kidneys. "She doesn't sign her name but I know it's from her because of the showy printed stationery— 'Sea Cliff House, Oyster Bay, New York.' Now listen to this. 'Tom, Dearest— Our *encounter* at the Piping Rock dance last weekend was more than I dared hope. For so long I had wanted this to happen. I thought I'd been in love many times, but you make me realize it has not happened to me—*before*. I know I'll see you at polo on Sunday, but I yearn for something more. Another "golf course"—and soon! Arrange something, I beg you. Till then, my darling, I am completely and utterly, your, F.'"

Augusta folded the note and put it back in her pocket. "It makes me want to be sick at my stomach."

[2]

B.K. looked perplexed and in pain. "But, Gus, Mrs. Haver-meyer has a husband."

"I know, dumbhead, and our father has a wife. That's what makes this so serious. I think she's his mistress. Do you know what that means?"

"Sure," B.K. said with no conviction.

"It means they take their clothes off and do things to each other, things that feel terrific . . ."

"Things?" B.K. asked, abandoning her pose of awareness.

"Different things," Augusta went on coldbloodedly. "Often involving here . . ." she pointed to the statue's crotch, "and up there . . ."

In an overload of emotion, B.K. clenched her jaws and widened her eyes. Then, as the import sank in, she burst into tears." Not Daddy. He wouldn't, I just know. How can you see all that in a stupid note? Most of the women love Daddy. Can he help it if Mrs. Havermeyer is in love with him and writes him a dumb note? I bet they all do."

Seeing her point register with her sister, B.K. stopped sobbing and watched hopefully as Augusta pulled the note from her pocket and read it again.

"I don't know . . ." Augusta said slowly. "It *sounds* like he loves her back, but you're right. It's not definite." Then with her former authority, "But we've got to do something once we find out for sure."

"Do what?"

"Something to Fern Havermeyer."

"Hurt her?"

"Maybe. Something to make her stay away from our family. In the meantime, we must keep our eyes open."

B.K. lay back down on the stone bench. "Why does our family always have to be so different?"

"You know what Daddy says," Augusta answered cautiously. "The Tollovers are special . . ."

"Other families around here don't fight all the time. The mothers and fathers like each other. They all have so many more *things* . . ."

"You know what Daddy thinks of all the new-rich families around here. They don't have our breeding."

B.K. was tired of this reasoning. "Does breeding mean you have to fight all the time? And have no maid? I'd rather have a maid for Mummie."

"I'd rather be special."

"Just Daddy saying it, doesn't make it true."

"You know it's true, fuzzbrain. Look at Daddy compared to our friends' fathers. He makes them look like goofs. If anyone was ever special, he is. And we're his only two children."

"He goes away all the time, and he doesn't . . ."

"He's sending us to Wyoming this summer, isn't he?"

B.K. switched instantly to adoring daughter. "Do you think he means it, Gus? That ranch is so expensive. Sandra told me how much it costs—she was amazed when I told her he'd let us go. I forget how much she said it was, but it's a lot."

"Of course we're going," Augusta said. Uneasily she added, "We may not stay as long as the others. But if he said we're going, then we are."

Augusta lay on her back on the other bench, staring at the small space of sky between the trees, listening to the drip of the water on the cool rocks. She was riding a spirited mare with her friends into the Black Hills, knowing they were at Eaton's, the most famous dude ranch in the West, the one where only the best families went, a ranch that even to have *heard* of it, showed you were somebody special from New York or Chicago's rich suburbs. Her father knew. Her father was making Eaton's possible. He was a wonderful man. If she could only figure out a way to hold off those terrible women like Fern Havermeyer who wanted him for themselves, who in their grasping, scheming plans were hurting Augusta and her family. If it weren't for selfish bitches like that . . .

Augusta forced her mind back to the mountains of Wyoming.

When Augusta and B.K. walked back to the house, the late afternoon sun had retreated up the lawn from the advancing shadows of the bordering trees. On the terrace Augusta could see her mother and father sitting, long-stemmed cocktail glasses in their hands, she in a flower-print dress, he in his city clothes with the suit-coat off, but otherwise shirt-and-tie impeccable.

Even knowing it was a lie, Augusta cherished the picture of a happy, prosperous family—an attractive man and woman chatting intimately, sipping cocktails, sitting before the sprawling house that, from a distance, spelled wealth, luxury and refinement. Augusta knew too well how misleading the apparition was, compared to the reality of her family life. But still she cherished it as a vision of how her girlhood might be if only a few details could be changed. She was close to living a rare and charmed existence—and this thought sent a flush of joy through her at her good fortune.

People outside her family also saw these pictures and were, Augusta hoped, misled by them. Outsiders didn't know that her parents rarely spoke to each other except in anger, that plaster fell from her bedroom ceiling, that her dresses were lengthened and doctored to look different from last year's. And these others would surely not know about notes in raincoat pockets. The world saw only the pretty pictures; her father saw to that. Augusta too was soothed and comforted by these false glimpses. When things got bad she would mentally thumb through her collection of happy tableaux—with her parents on the beach at East Hampton, riding with her father in Smithtown, Christmas morning with them all together at Mapleton—to shut from her mind the aching present.

At the top of the terrace steps the girls ran toward their father.

"Finally, the grand duchesses!" Tom Tollover shouted with gusto. "Augstrina Tomasova, Belinda Tomasova—how imperial you both look. Fresh from cantering your estates whipping your serfs, no doubt." He grabbed them both to receive kisses, then implant others. Augusta received hers joyfully. B.K. yielded more shyly, staring at the large, swarthy hand, wondering if it had rubbed Mrs. Havermeyer's crotch.

". . . And pay your respects to your mother, the Dowager Empress Catherina Petrovna . . ."

"It's not as though the girls and I hadn't seen each other all afternoon, Tom," Kate Tollover said, managing a smile.

"Did you help your mother with the gardening?"

"An hour . . ." Augusta replied.

"A half hour," corrected her mother.

"You know our deal," Tollover said sternly to his daughters. "You must do your chores and be helpful if you want to go to Eaton's . . ."

A sharp look from Kate Tollover.

"Oh, Daddy," Augusta said, "you know we'll do them, and lots more. We'll do anything you want . . ." She looked at her father adoringly—his black hair sleeked back but curling slightly over his starched white collar, his thin moustache always so immaculately trimmed, his large dark eyes that smothered with seductive warmth whomever they took in, and the tailored white shirt with the tiny "T.T." embroidered over the pocket. His shirts always looked crisp, even on warm spring days like today and after working on Wall Street, riding the New York subway and the Long Island Railroad, somehow still clean and crisp.

"Augusta," Tollover said sharply, "you've got twigs all over your rear end. A grand duchess doesn't grovel in the dirt, even in her tennis togs."

Augusta brushed the bits of leaf and grass from her seat. "We were sitting by the fountain . . ."

Kate Tollover cut in. "You and B.K. go and set the table. We'll be eating in about twenty minutes."

"In the dining room?"

"Of course in the dining room," Tollover said cheerfully. "Did you think we would dine in the garage?"

Augusta laughed and grabbed B.K.'s hand. Together they ran into the house. In the music room Augusta stopped to tie her sneaker lace, B.K. going on ahead. The room's heavy brocade curtains kept out all but a few slivers of afternoon sun, giving it an eerily majestic look. Her parents' voices rose in anger behind her. She wanted to go on into the kitchen but stood immobile looking at the large mahogany piano, grotesquely out of tune, the Victorian furniture, not noticeably shabby in the dim light. As the anger rose on the terrace, she thought how few people had a music room, not even her rich classmates. In her mind she pushed out the room's walls and

[6]

pushed back the time fifty years before the house was built and peopled the room with ladies in full dresses and handsome men in Beau Brummell dinner clothes, waiters serving punch from silver trays and a string trio playing delicate music.

Kate Tollover's voice broke into the vision. "Good breeding's not going to pay for Wyoming—or anything else. You make me sick!"

Augusta's picture was finished. She needed other pictures.

The following Sunday as she was about to compete in the trials at the Meadowbrook Club, Augusta saw a different sort of picture. As she rode one of Sandra MacNeil's mares onto the field, she passed some parked cars. Standing up against the side of a panel truck were her father and Fern Havermeyer, she looking absurdly jaunty in jodhpurs, tweed jacket and ascot. His hands were on her shoulders. He ducked to kiss her but she turned her head away with a giddy laugh.

Augusta could only see them for the instant her horse passed the cars, but the picture hit her as though someone had wrenched the back of her neck. Always when Augusta was about to compete she felt her insides giving way. She would stem the collapse by reminding herself that she was by far the best rider in her category. But this feeling of yawning disaster went beyond her fear of failure. The wins were to please her father, who had taught her to ride, to hold herself, to look down on judges. But here was this father, this reason for striving and succeeding, sneaking kisses with her friend's simpleton mother.

But who was affected? Her own mother? Augusta had a rare stab of sympathy for her mother, whose life was chore, who always did what their father demanded. She thought of her mother in the same way she thought of other nice people who ministered to her life and B.K.'s—affectionate, helpful, carping, as might be expected, but doing everything, even getting angry, within the bounds of well-bred behavior. Yet Augusta thought of her mother with no more real love than she felt for her teachers at Greenvale, Sally who helped with the cleaning, her many Tollover uncles and aunts and her mother's brother, Uncle Harry.

All of these grown-ups, her mother included, were mere attendants in the brilliant ongoing spectacle of Tom Tollover and his two paragon daughters.

As she walked her horse to the starting post, Augusta stiffened her back and threw off her feeling of betrayal. Who said the most spectacular man in the world had to be without fault? Marital infidelity, Augusta knew, was very upper class, very aristocratic. She had read books. She knew how other fathers pretended to be exemplary husbands, then sneaked off to motels on Northern Boulevard, keeping their wickedness out of sight of their wives and daughters.

As she approached the starting line, the hard lump of anger inside her wouldn't be reasoned away. Why could nothing be as it was supposed to be? As she went through her trials, an energy seized her and she performed flawlessly, effortlessly. She felt an exhilarating contempt for the girls who snickered at her father's flirtations, at her patched riding jacket, at the five-year-old Buick the stitched-together Tollover family would drive from the club. She could ride circles around every one of them.

The judges, who had seen many excellent riders over the years in Augusta's age category, were astounded by the haughty assurance with which this rather shy-seeming girl took first prize.

2 Sitting with friends at the Meadowbrook Horse Show, Kate Tollover considered the charade her life had become. The crowd milling around her—some children, some old people, but most, like herself and her husband, in their thirties and forties—belonged to a stylized and remote world that didn't happen to be hers. It was a world of large homes, servants, exclusive clubs, expensive boarding schools, of summers abroad and winters skiing in Vermont. On ritualistic occasions like today's horse show, it meant picnics from Abercrombie's hampers on the tailgates of Ford station wagons or women in de Pinna's tweed suits, their hair in arrogant

upsweeps, consoling each other about losing yet another maid to defense work, men in J. Press tweeds comparing black-market butchers and trying not to gloat about how much richer the war was making them, only turning serious over truly important matters like their children's chances of getting into St. Paul's or Miss Porter's.

Kate was not born to this world, nor had she grown up in it. She had lived in it for fifteen years and, to an extent, been accepted by it, but she knew her only connection to this exotic planet was her husband, who was now off among the parked cars with Fern Havermeyer, repeating the spectacle that had titillated at last Saturday night's Piping Rock dance. She looked around at the jolly, healthy faces. They were not bad people actually—as kind as most, not stupid, educated, with considerable tact and good manners,. and they had been generous in befriending Kate, although she never felt, except in a few cases, this was anything more than a manifestation of their enthusiasm for her good-times husband. There was an added dollop of pity for Kate now that the good times raged on behind her back.

For all their careful rearing, their conviction that certain things were never discussed, that nice people simply didn't care about material matters, each of these thoroughbred cronies, Kate thought bitterly, knew to the penny how in debt the Tollovers were, how little Tom brought in from his school-tie job with the brokerage and how much they were able to wheedle from his uncle Jack Tollover to partially support their slip-covered standard of living. These discreet friends also knew how Kate had to fight to keep Tom from spending what little there was on women or clothes for himself.

When Kate married him, none of these socialite friends could believe that Tom Tollover was giving up one of New York, Long Island's and Palm Beach's most glittering bachelorhoods to marry Kate Nobody from New London, Connecticut (north of Yale, south of Harvard), and it turned out that Tollover himself hadn't believed it much either.

Her first meeting with Tom, the quick romance and unlikely marriage, had all been too much the stuff of *Saturday Evening Post* shopgirl fiction for anyone to take seriously. Tollover had been one of the best-looking adornments of the most select East Coast circles, circles that could draw physical beauty from other social strata as they needed it, but to which Tollover belonged by virtue of his birth, his upbringing and his personal style. He was not earmarked, as were many of his friends, for a family fortune; still, there was a vague aura of money around the Tollovers. He had been taken on by the Wall Street firm of Montgomery Jackson, where he could cash in his St. Paul's and Yale connections, in time easily bringing in enough to effect a suitable living standard. And to top off this parfait of eligibility, he was adored by all of his fancy chums for his no-fail high spirits and party-moving energy.

In short, he would have made a good match for an heiress of good social position, but for a wealthy girl of marginal position—and many such were after Tollover—he was fantastic.

As a secretary in his Wall Street firm, Kate had been in awe of Tollover. She knew herself to be—by his standards—a girl with no money, no family, and looks that were considered average even at New London High School and the University of Connecticut, where she had spent a year before being forced to drop out and take a job.

As soon as she sensed Tollover's fascination with her, however, she quickly raised her self-esteem and her aspirations. When they met, he seemed bored with his high-living, spoiled cronies, and especially with the feckless women who chased him. He called them "perpetual flappers who continue to flap after their age and the economy has made such frivolity passé." As he and Kate started seeing each other, she shrewdly played up the one attribute she suspected he prized: a level-headed practicality that spelled Good Wife Material. She was careful, while contrasting her feet-on-the-ground personality with the scatterbrained debutantes he was used to, never to abuse her rivals. Instead she maintained a good-natured tolerance toward the rich and their carefree ways.

Tollover's marrying Kate was an act of contempt and irreverence, an ultimate thumb in the eye to society, the same people who had always cheered his pranks—wearing red socks to a black-tie dinner, fox-trotting his partner into a reflecting pond, driving his roadster into the formal gardens of an estate. Marrying Kate was his ultimate boyhood prank.

As a wife, she had worked out far better than he had any right to expect. It was a tough adjustment for her, despite her eagerness to adapt and despite his blunt counseling. On their honeymoon he had stunned her by complimenting her conversational reticence when they encountered some friends of his at their Bermuda hotel, then adding, "There are two types of women who marry up socially: the extroverts who hope to obscure their ignorance with a noisy display of self-assurance. These never change and remain as common as they were before their marriage. The others have the good sense to shut up for a year or so, to listen and learn. This group has a chance of making it."

It wasn't so much the charm of the advice, but rather Kate's own nature that set her on the second path. She proved to be a good learner. She had no illusions about her scrap-metal-dealing father and school-teaching mother as having any social position, but she always felt they were a finer caliber of people than their friends. She thought little of whether this stemmed from breeding, good genes or more finely developed qualities, but she grew up with a vague feeling that a social error had been committed in her family's situation, and that it would be appropriate for her to set things right. When so dashing an opportunity as Tollover came before her, she was quick to seize it. She was smart enough to realize before her husband told her that such a matrimonial bonanza would require her to subjugate her pride—to shut up and listen.

Tollover relished the role of tutor. He loved telling Kate how to dress, how to entertain, how to converse with all sorts of people, how to deal with inferiors, and how to make inferiors realize they were inferiors so they would roll over and be dealt with as such. The nuances of class and style were not automatic reflexes with him, as they were with his friends. Tollover was consciously aware of the rules and techniques and so was an adept teacher. Kate, who admitted her ignorance and was very retentive, was an ideal pupil. By the time Tollover had become bored with the game and with Kate, she had as much polish as many of the women in their circle and knew some tricks they didn't.

The Professor Higgins–Liza Doolittle phase of their marriage was perhaps the most successful. The birth of Augusta, then B.K. two years later, further established the family as more than a mere teacher-pupil combine. The trouble came from a quarter that Kate had never worried about. Her husband, it appeared, knew everything about leading the good life but how to finance it.

His parents, who had some money, had been badly hurt by the Depression and there was no assistance from them, nor any expectations. Several Tollover uncles and aunts were wealthy—particularly Tom's great-uncle Jack, who was a bachelor—but the two men had little use for each other and there was something in Tollover's nature that made him go out of his way to antagonize a rich uncle who was his only possibility for salvation.

As for his own earning record, Tollover had started out well on Wall Street—even for the twenties—certainly well enough to make him think that big earnings would return when the Depression passed. Even in the early years of the depressed economy, Tollover made a killing on a traction-company bond issue, netting him enough to buy the large house in Old Westbury.

For the past three or four years, Tollover had earned very little, the house was heavily mortgaged and the rich relations had grown bored with supporting him. As the bills mounted, Tollover became increasingly cavalier about his responsibilities and would view his family from time to time as a costly nuisance. Kate kept after him about their debts—a hopelessly middle-class trait of hers, he would say; true aristocrats never worried about such things—until eventually he would borrow cash from a friend or relative to get them through. Given their financial situation, which appeared less and less temporary with each year, their plutocratic style of living became more and more nonsensical—particularly the huge house, which needed about twenty thousand dollars worth of repairs and six full-time servants, but which Kate was expected to operate on pennies with an occasional assist from a local girl.

On the rare occasions when Tollover would permit discussing their unrealistic living, Kate would point out that many of his well-born, boarding-school friends were living simply, in small houses, some sending their children to public schools. This sort of talk would propel Tollover into a fury. His first outrage was usually over her lack of confidence in him. He professed shock at her willingness to sell them all into the terrors of the lower-middle class just because of a passing economic slump. The peace-restoring coda usually was his claim of how easily he could put his hands on money if they *really* needed it.

Kate came to realize that all of this talk beclouded the true reason for his unrealistic obstinacy; he had a horror of being the Tollover who lost his family's class gains, gains that had been won with such difficulty over their five generations in America. He was a snob on a personal level; he valued his social friendships, felt he belonged with them, that the Racket Club and the estates of the North Shore were his natural milieu. But he was also a snob in a broader sense, one that included the long line of Tollovers in American down to Augusta and B.K. and to some extent embraced Kate as well. While his own ego could have survived a temporary relinquishing of upper-class trappings, he would insist, on the few occasions he discussed a come-down seriously, his sense of family pride could not allow any such relaxing of standards. Kate often wondered, however, if it wasn't really the other way around; if his fanatical sense of "protector of the Tollover faith" wasn't a screen for a childish clinging to the privileges and ego-props of class.

But now she cared little for the deeper motivations. Her sense of irony had long since worn out over her grand-slam matrimonial "catch" netting her nothing more than a much larger house to clean and less actual comfort than the average factory worker's wife in Pittsburgh. She and Tom did have some worthwhile friends—people of cultivation and taste, even some wit—and they often were invited to splendid parties in breathtaking settings.

She was not oblivious to the advantages for her daughters—good schools, polished friends, visits to stimulating homes—but she often wondered if these advantages weren't more than offset by the embarrassment and chagrin they must feel at having so much less than their friends. When they arrived at school age, wouldn't they be happier and better adjusted, Kate wondered, if given the upbringing their finances dictated and the upbringing Kate herself had survived.

There was something unarguable about good schools, however, and by the time Kate discovered her husband's womanizing, which wiped out any personal happiness her marriage might have brought to her, she felt that her daughters were too set in their pattern for her to consider changing it drastically.

Then too, with each year she remained in her pointless marriage, Kate felt herself more a part of the rich. She managed this double paradox—neither born to money nor having it now—by her ironic breakdown of the rich into two categories: those with money and those without. The penniless rich, she called her family bitterly, too stubborn to be poor. She was too stubborn herself.

Kate certainly looked like she belonged. Her penetrating blue eyes and fine features came together in looks that, while not as glamorous as her husband's, appeared more a product of Wasp North Shore intermarrying than did his swarthy beauty. She wore her light brown hair in a soft, becoming bob in imitation of an actress she greatly admired, Margaret Sullavan.

Her only plebeian flaw was a shortness of stature. Kate compensated for this by a rigidly erect posture that, when she walked, turned into a near-athletic springiness. This feature perhaps contributed more to her well-born demeanor than any other.

Her wardrobe was meager but correct, thanks to her husband's dictum: a few good things rather than a lot of cheap things. Her friends had grown quite used to a rust tweed suit from Peck and Peck, a dressy black wool suit from Bergdorf's (the best thing she had) and two winter evening dresses and two summer ones (one dress from Saks, three made by a seamstress she had found in Garden City). For five years this had been the backbone of her wardrobe, but most of her time was spent in the cotton wraparound dresses she wore when working about her vast house.

Perhaps Kate resented more than anything the way her husband placed her in the role of spoilsport nag with her daughters. Totally captivated by their dashing father, they were too young to understand his carelessness about supporting them all. He was fun and she was anti-fun.

One day they would understand, perhaps. But now there was this new absurdity about the dude ranch—nine hundred dollars for each girl, plus the transportation to Wyoming. Kate doubted if he would earn that much in the whole year, and if he had that much cash, it would go far toward paying off some of their more immediate bills. She would stop this lunacy if it cost her marriage and whatever love her daughters felt for her.

Watching him approach now through the horse-show crowd with Fern Havermeyer—immaculate in his blazer, flashing white teeth smiling greetings to the many who hailed him as he passed their groups—she hated him for forcing her life into nothing more than a defense against his infantile behavior. Even now it was obvious that, to those who knew or cared little about his record at family support or marital fidelity, the spectacle of Tom Tollover was a huge success. And of all the many people who looked on and applauded the spectacle—including his two daughters—she was the only one hurt, the only one not amused, by these two foibles.

"Katie, dear," Fern Havermeyer enthused as she approached, "weren't you thrilled by your daughter's win? She was sensational. I heard one of the judges say they had never seen such form in a girl her age . . ."

"I heard him say the same thing about you," Tollover said slyly to Fern, who seemed less willing to push their luck with Kate and ignored him. Tollover turned to Augusta who, with B.K., was approaching, her blue ribbon in her hand. "Gussie, dear, you were wonderful. We are all so proud of you!" Augusta smiled shyly as her father hugged her. "You know Mrs. Havermeyer . . ."

"Hello," she said with a chill both Kate and Tom noticed.

"You were just marvelous, sweetie," the other woman said, patting Augusta's cheek. "I've got to run. I'll see you all at the Stehles' Wednesday."

"Aren't you proud of your sister, B.K.?" Tollover said, putting his other arm around the younger girl. "What a pair you'll both make at Eaton's. Show those Wyoming yokels how to ride. But listen, Augusta darling, one little thing. When you are receiving the prize from the judges, try not to smile so much. You looked as though you were surprised to have won. That's not the way to do it. Make them feel you are doing them a favor by riding in their little show and accepting their prize. A small smile and a polite 'Thank You.'" Then, turning to his other daughter, "We'll let B.K. be cute and girlish, but only for another two years, B.K., that's all. Then you too must turn into a duchess, cold and aloof and breaking hearts. Right, B.K.?"

She and Augusta both giggled and ran to the Buick. He turned to help Kate gather their picnic things. "I suppose," he said, "you are going to savage me about Fern? I recognize those silences of yours."

"You know I haven't cared about that sort of thing for some time now. She is really quite ideal for you. One thing, though. I think it is clumsy of you to let Augusta become aware of what you're up to. You saw how she spoke to her . . ."

Tollover's jaw tightened and he slammed down the lid of the hamper.

Kate went on. "I think we all have a right to expect a little more form and style from you, Tom. But on this ranch business. I'm going to fight you to the death on that . . ." Then, over her shoulder as she carried the folded blankets toward the car, "Even if it means losing all three of you."

3 With handsome and well-groomed Tollovers distributed over the threadbare furniture, the main living room at Mapleton looked impressive. Tom's older sister Polly and her

banker husband, there with their two sons, were harmonious replicas of the old-school types of Tom and Kate's circle of friends. The same was true of his second sister, Merle—blue suit, gold circle pin, alligator handbag—and her rep-tied husband whose family printing business earned just enough to get successive generations through the right schools and afford them sufficient acreage and club memberships to insulate them from a hazardous world.

Also blending smoothly into this *tableau vivant* of comfort and respectability were Tom's parents, a handsome couple in their late sixties with no hint of either their son's flamboyance or his swarthiness. They seemed in awe of him.

The two figures who lent most distinction to the family were Tom's great-uncle Jack Tollover and his sister, Mable Winott, the rotund widow of a one-time United States ambassador to Spain. She had been a great beauty who had made a brilliant marriage—money and lineage to spare—but had given in to a temptation for caustic remarks and overeating.

Her brother was a picture-book paragon of the old-school dandy—perfectly tailored gray suit, a gold chain on his waistcoat, an inch of white cuff, black onyx and gold cuff-links, a full head of steely gray hair. His renowned precision as a lawyer had earned the old bachelor an impressive fortune.

Uncle Jack had helped Tom financially from time to time, an indebtedness that didn't stop him from antagonizing his uncle on numerous occasions, usually over matters of form. The problem between them was not that either man made light of his social position; they both took it seriously but arrived at widely diverging conclusions on how it was to be acted upon. The old man had lost patience with his nephew's financial disorder. It was only through the most abject appeal to Tollover family honor that Tom had won his uncle's assistance with the girls' schooling, but even this lever was losing its effectiveness as Uncle Jack came to suspect more and more that he was financing his nephew's recreations.

Kate Tollover darted around the large room looking after her fifth and sixth generation in-laws. She knew they viewed her with admiration, even sympathy, for managing with so little assistance. Kate also knew there was a blind, xenophobic side to their snobbery that allowed them to condemn her to household drudgery, not because it was essential to the life Tom forced on her, but because that was what women of her class *did*.

Tom Tollover loved these family parties. For him it was a reaffirmation of who the Tollovers were. He loved, too, his role among them as trend-setting man of fashion, dazzling and annoying his tradition-bound kinsmen with outlandish variations on the upper-class code. What he lacked in capital, he would make up in style.

For today's gathering, Tollover sported a tweed jacket, a pale yellow oxford shirt and a paisley scarf. All the other men present, even Polly's boys, wore neckties. Tom made the rounds of the room filling cocktail glasses from a silver shaker, assured he was bringing a touch of movie-star glamour to his relatives' stodgy lives.

Augusta and B.K., ladylike in their best dresses, passed hors d'oeuvres, thin crackers spread with anchovy paste and cheese sticks that Kate had baked at eight that morning. Their father, approaching everything like a theatrical presentation, had given them his usual coaching on dealing with the family. "Address them by name," he said, "'Great-Uncle Jack,' 'Great-Aunt Mable.' Speak distinctly when answering their questions. Don't be shy. But worse, don't be full of yourself . . ."

Augusta enjoyed this feeling of being on stage. It was a controlled, no-surprises situation in which she knew she would shine and win the approving notice of her father. There were few other occasions where they worked together at anything.

She also liked the family gatherings for the inevitable family history that even the smallest occurrences evoked from the older members. Someone would light a cigarette and Mable Winott would say, "Your great-grandmother, in her brownstone on Twenty-eighth Street, never permitted smoking in any room except the library—and of course the conservatory for large parties."

Someone else would mention the war in Europe or the Pacific, and Uncle Jack would say, "This is the country's first war that didn't have at least one Tollover representative—and don't explain again, Tom, about your perforated eardrum, you're too old to be a malingerer." Then to Tom's father, "And you, George, a mere lieutenant in '17—the lowest rank the family ever sank to!"

The endless litany: "This is who we are, this is who we are." It was all presented with a coating of self-disparagement and modesty. They would not have bragged about how big a fortune old Jesse Tollover had laid up in the 1880s any more among themselves than if there had been strangers present. Occasionally the reminiscing would prompt raised-eyebrow references to a family scandal or to a Tollover whose eccentricities would be considered insanity in anyone less protected by family name and money.

"This is who we are. This is who we are."

"Have another cheese stick, Great-Aunt Mable?"

Years later Augusta and her sister would look back on these family parties as long exercises in self-congratulation, pathetically bourgeois. But for the young Augusta and her sister the pageants succeeded in instilling a much-needed sense of having some advantage, at least, over their wealthier classmates. Tollover's aim of imparting to the girls a sense of superiority was successful, but it rankled Augusta that the basis of *her* superiority, upbringing and breeding, had as one of its basic tenets that these attributes could never be referred to or pointed at. Her friends' assets—clothes, cars, exquisite homes—were laid out for all the world to reckon with.

Her father had drilled into her that dignity, self-containment, aristocratic reserve would be noticed and admired, even among children of her age. Wasn't the horse-show victory affirmation of this? But there were many times when such intangible advantages struck her as empty, invisible, worthless. Then Augusta would give herself up to paroxysms of unaristocratic envy.

Later, at the dinner table, as Kate was ladling out a shrimp bisque, Uncle Jack said, "Things must have livened up for you down on the Street, Tom, with the war effort . . ."

"It's still a bit slow in our area, Uncle Jack," Tom replied. "But a few signs say this is finally changing."

"Odd," the older man persisted. "I understood that with Pearl Harbor, Roosevelt had brought an end to the Depression."

"The prosperity is not quite as widespread as his propagandists would have you believe. Did you enjoy the Bordeaux, Jack? It's a prewar case, of course . . ."

"You always manage to live well, Tom," his uncle said with unabashed malice.

"One way or another. A grateful client sent me this case," he lied nonchalantly.

As Augusta and B.K. cleared the table, their great-aunt Mable picked up a clean butter plate of an ornate blue-and-gold Victorian pattern. "It's so strange when we visit each other to see this same china at all our houses. It's like not quite dining out."

"When Jesse Tollover admired something, he admired it," George Tollover put in.

"You told me," his wife said, "that he was in London and tried to buy this pattern and was told it was no longer in production. To make it again, they required an order of at least five complete sets and in those days a dinner service was about forty-eight places . . ."

"So now we all have the same china," Aunt Mable sniffed. "It's like Schrafft's or some restaurant chain . . ."

As Augusta pushed through the pantry door with her hands full of gold-and-blue china, she thought how wonderful it would be to order five dinner services because you wanted one. Then she thought how furious her father would be if now, a hundred years later, she or B.K. broke one of the dishes. In the household of Tom Tollover, such a mishap would be an unbearable symbol of the slow, steady attrition of Tollover prestige under Tom's stewardship.

About nine that evening, long after the guests had left and Augusta and B.K. had finished helping Sally clean up, Augusta was passing through the dark entrance hall on her way to her room. From behind the closed library doors, she could hear her parents' angry voices. She stopped to listen, staring at the crack of light under the door.

"How like you," she heard her mother snap. "To accuse me of bitchery because I'm jealous. I gave up caring about your Fern Havermeyers years ago. I don't mind going through with our sham marriage if you would for once act responsibly toward the girls. I'll put it as bluntly as I can. If you don't behave sensibly about this ranch thing, I'm taking the girls and leaving."

"Oh, that again," he said thickly. "Let me again remind you that you could get nothing to live on if you left. Not that the courts don't have a soft spot for a mother fighting the world alone on behalf of her two tots. But even the courts can't get blood from a stone, you know. There's not a court that could make Uncle Jack cough up. Not his concern. Only mine. I'm afraid you're locked in, my dear."

Kate was silent for a minute. "We'll see." More silence, then she went on quietly, "You've given me a closeup view of all your worst qualities, Tom—irresponsible, immature, vain, unfaithful . . ."

". . . Let's not get operatic."

"Arrogant, frivolous—I could go on and on . . ."

"You usually do."

"But you are not crazy. You know you do not have the two thousand dollars to send the girls to Eaton's, and you have no hope of getting it. Even if you could get Uncle Jack or one of your friends to let you have it, it should go to any of a hundred creditors who have been patient out of nothing more than pity. If they hear you're sending your daughters to a ridiculously expensive dude ranch, and they will, they'll be down on you like the furies—and I wouldn't blame them. You know the girls are not going, so it's simply a matter of will you tell them or will I? And I'll be damned if I will. You strut onto center stage, make your princely offer, accept the hugs and kisses—then leave me to explode the dream. This time I won't do it for you. You're going to tell them, and tell them . . ."

Augusta stumbled back through the hall toward the pantry, bumping into B.K. in the semidarkness. She picked up the telephone and dialed the MacNeils' number. She gave the butler her name and asked for Sandra.

"What is it, Gus? Why are you calling Sandra?" asked B.K. Augusta ignored her.

"Hello, Sandra? Listen. I've just had a long talk with my parents, and the most exciting news! My father wants us all to go and live in France for a year or two, just as soon as the war's over. He's even talking about me and B.K. going to college there . . . the Sorbonne, I guess. But he wants me and B.K. to take an intensive French course this summer. Right here in Westbury, or at C.W. Post College, I think. Anyhow, it means we won't be able to go to Eaton's with you and your family. Isn't that the dregs? Can you straighten it out about the reservations and everything? No, it's definite. I hate it, of course, but the idea of France . . ."

She hung up the phone and turned to B.K. "Well, now you know." She pushed past her sister and headed toward the stairs, B.K. trailing behind her.

"Why, Augusta? Why did you do that? That's not true about France, is it? Did Daddy say we couldn't go to Wyoming? Did Mummie?"

Augusta didn't answer. Some time ago she had told B.K. she was through with crying. Now she was too close to it to risk conversation. Let B.K. figure out what happened. Just two years younger—she still knew what to expect. Augusta only wanted to get to her room, close the door and deal silently with the betrayal, the buffeting by forces beyond her control. She knew she was fortunate compared to most girls her age. How far up did you have to be to make you immune from this sort of disappointment? Why did they tell her, this is who you are, this is how you are to live? Then they came and said, no, that's *not* who you are; that's *not* how it's supposed to be.

Leaving B.K. stammering questions below, Augusta headed up the wide oak staircase, automatically avoiding the treacherous holes in the carpeting. From the library she could hear her father: "I'm sick of listening to what a mistake you made marrying me. It's nothing to the mistake I made. The fortunes throwing themselves at me! And I had to pass them up for you! I've made some bad deals on Wall Street, but nothing like this little merger . . ."

4 In the late forties and early fifties, the Greenvale School was considered the best private day school on Long Island's North Shore. The children of the great families were represented—Whitneys, Pratts, Phipps—or their corporate relations. The school also had students from far more modest families, prosperous locals who made no pretense of social prowess. Among the local people, a small group lacked money but had scraped together the hefty tuition in response to an argument with the public schools or perhaps a nostalgia for their family's lost affluence.

The students were divided into two groups—the rich, socialite children and the townies. All through the time they were in school together, the two groups melded into a happy democratic melange. But all of them were aware of the eventual sifting that would occur when boarding school age arrived. The estate dwellers went away to school and the town students muddled on through Greenvale to graduation. The boarding school prospect left each student in no doubt which group he or she was a part of.

Augusta and B.K. were not so easily categorized. They clearly had less money than some of the local children and were less able to devastate their classmates by reporting a grand-slam family expenditure—a new car, a sailboat, a swimming pool. But because of their large house and their parents' socializing with the snob group, the Tollover girls were granted provisional inclusion in the charmed half of the student body.

Augusta and B.K. were popular with their schoolmates— B.K. for her cheery gregariousness and her prettiness, Augusta for her cool intelligence and unflappable reserve. B.K. inspired a warm friendliness in everyone; Augusta, on the other hand, brought out a respect that kept people at a slight distance. She managed to impart a sense of specialness without allowing that stance to slip into a smug superiority. She had grown adept at timing small jibes at herself just when the distance between herself and other fourteen year olds was growing dangerously wide. She was often elected to class offices, indicating that her classmates didn't begrudge her assets.

The sisters' closeness all but precluded close friendships with the other girls. An exception, Sandra MacNeil, did not please Tom Tollover. Sandra was not a townie, but the daughter of the most casebook pair of nouveau riche social climbers. Sandra's father had made himself an enormous fortune through a cosmetics empire he founded; her mother, Gwen MacNeil, who had had a brief film career, mostly in a bathing suit, seemed to live in dread that one of her husband's dollars would go unspent, or if spent, unnoticed. She had hired a publicist to make sure her dinner dances, her yacht parties and her weakness for couturier clothes were recorded by the press.

To Tom Tollover, the publicist capped an extravaganza of vulgarity that, because of its money-backed potency, posed a bigger threat to real society than the middle-class townies. Tollover did not forbid the friendship, however. With the MacNeil swimming pool, stables, boats, and tennis courts at his daughters' disposal, he decided Sandra was a nice girl and not to blame for her mother's excesses. This verdict was, Kate told him, a triumph for democratic fair play.

At nine A.M. the Saturday morning following the Tollovers' Memorial Day dinner, the MacNeil chauffeur pulled a sleek gray Bentley up to Mapleton to take Augusta and B.K. to the MacNeil estate for the day. B.K. grew giggly and embarrassed by the chauffeur's formal attentiveness, but Augusta relished it. She settled into the soft gray plush that looked and smelled as though it had never before encountered a human.

At the entrance to the MacNeil grounds, a guard sat in a gatehouse and, as the Bentley approached, electrically opened the gates. The car moved slowly up the white-gravel drive through a wooded area that was just coming to life with infant green leaves and lacy dogwood. They emerged into a courtyard that ran the length of the main wing of the enormous house that had been built only a few years before the war on the site of a Victorian monstrosity that had burned down. The style was a cream-plaster formality that owed much to French provincial but had become so commonplace among the rich of Palm Beach, Beverly Hills and elsewhere that it had evolved into a nouveau provincial style of its own.

A butler admitted them to a spacious entrance hall whose white marble floor was set with small black squares. Sandra MacNeil came running down a flying circular staircase, her dark hair flouncing around a handsome, almost too long face that looked more mature than her fourteen years. In jeans and a western shirt, she showed a more womanly figure than either B.K. or Augusta.

"Hi, gang," she greeted them breathlessly. "Isn't it a gorgeous day? Let's go right away for a ride. I think mother has something for us to do later. We might go out on the *Gwendolyn II!*"

They set down their bags that had the tennis clothes, bathing suits and dresses for later—four changes for a one-day visit—then followed Sandra into the parking court where they boarded a golf cart. With Sandra driving and B.K. hanging her legs off the rear, they drove past the garages into the woods. Presently they came to the stables—huge, eaved buildings built in the Victorian Gothic style of the earlier house.

Two grooms awaited them with saddled horses. They mounted and rode off along a wooded trail, trotting first, then breaking into an exhilarating canter. The path descended gradually through the trees, coming out onto a narrow beach and an open expanse of Long Island Sound, now dotted with white sails.

They walked their horses along the beach until the woods opened up to the vast sweep of lawn that rose to the house. A hard dirt trail separated the quarter mile of open lawn from the strip of sand beach. The girls instinctively broke into a canter, then pushed their horses into a race.

At the end of the lawn, laughing, out of breath, the girls pulled up their horses. "Don't you jerks get too excited," Sandra said. "You've got two fabulous surprises in store!"

"What? Tell us," B.K. implored.

"Come on, Sandra," Augusta said, "don't be a tease."

"I can tell you one. Errol Flynn is coming to lunch! I think my mother may be having an affair with him. Isn't that exciting?"

B.K. whistled.

"What's the other surprise?" Augusta asked.

"The other one you'll both like even better. You'll hear about it later, but not from me."

Later, when they were riding back to the house from the stables in the golf cart, Augusta said, "Doesn't it upset you, Sandra, that your mother might be having an affair?"

"Only because she got Errol Flynn and I didn't." When Augusta didn't say anything, Sandra added, "Do you mean because of my father? Don't worry about him. He's having his fun too, I'm sure."

Tom Tollover would have been gratified at the distance his daughter felt from the MacNeils of the world at that moment, even though his view of matrimony was far closer to theirs than to his daughter's.

"If we hurry," Sandra said, "we can get in a swim before lunch."

"Won't the water be too cold?" B.K. asked.

"It's heated, stupid. Don't you know anything?"

When they entered the front door, they were met by the butler, who said, "Mrs. MacNeil would like to see Miss Augusta in her boudoir."

"Surprise number two," Sandra smiled. "Come on, B.K., let's go down to the pool and await developments."

The butler led Augusta up the sweeping staircase, down a long hall that ended at tall, double doors. They opened into a vestibule from which Augusta could look into a large, sunny bedroom decorated entirely in pale blue. Instead of entering this room, the butler knocked at a small door, opened it and said, "Miss Tollover, Madam." He closed the door behind Augusta and left.

Gwen MacNeil was reclining on a tan-satin chaise. She was wearing a voluminous peignoir of transparent white fabric through which a more solid fabric of pale pink was visible. There were fussy ruffs at her throat and sleeves. Augusta had seen her often before and never thought much about her looks, which her father dismissed as cheap. But now Augusta saw that she was a very good-looking woman somewhere in her thirties with soft blonde hair in a loose pageboy. Abundant makeup did not obscure excellent features. Her chaise was placed at an angle in a large bay window through which Augusta could look down across the lawn to the water of Long Island Sound. Gwen MacNeil was writing in a small notebook of red suede. She looked up at Augusta, snapped shut the notebook's gold clasp and held out her hand.

"Augusta darling," she said with theatrical melancholy. "So nice to see you. Come sit by me." She gestured toward a small armchair at her side. "How are your beautiful parents?"

"Fine, thank you." Augusta was at a loss.

"The finest," Gwen said, as though correcting Augusta. "As any member of the North Shore social set knows too well." Augusta suspected that the sarcasm meant Gwen knew the Tollover opinion of her. "And your poor, overworked mother? Is she having any fun? Your father is such a charming tyrant."

"Mother is fine," Augusta answered, with enough firmness to serve notice she would not sit for long and have her parents ridiculed and patronized.

Annoyed at being cut off, Gwen shot her skirt noisily over her legs. "You haven't much humor, have you, darling? Let me tell you what I wanted to speak with you about. Sandra is so fond of you and darling B.K. You really are her only true friends at Greenvale. She was so looking forward to you both being on the trip to Wyoming this summer. Now I understand some family complications have arisen and you were thinking of not going . . ." Her tone had switched to benevolent affection.

She paused, then smiled broadly at Augusta. "I want you both to go to Eaton's ranch as my guests—the plane tickets, everything . . ."

Augusta was stunned. A picture flashed into her mind of a poor schoolmate bedridden with spinal meningitis whose family had been disgraced in the eyes of everyone that knew them by accepting a gift of a phonograph from a classmate's wealthy mother, then later a check for a thousand dollars.

Augusta fought back her anger and humiliation. That a

woman like this would brush aside her brilliantly plausible story about studying French, would say in effect, "We all know, dearest, your snobbish family has not got two nickels . . ." She felt a rare flash of anger toward her father for allowing her to be put in such a position. As always, however, the anger got short-circuited and diverted elsewhere.

"That is extremely kind and generous of you, Mrs. MacNeil," Augusta struggled to keep the anger from her voice, "but Sandra must have misunderstood. Our plans are made. We must take the French course."

"But we thought that you might do both, that you might . . ." As Augusta's response sank in and Gwen realized she was receiving yet another snub, this one from a fourteen year old, her jaw tightened in fury. "I'm so sorry. You've both been so kind and done so much for Sandra. I thought it a way Mr. MacNeil and I could show our appreciation . . ."

Both wanted desperately for the conversation to end, but neither knew how to bring this about. Augusta was frantic to be away from this woman's overdecorated sitting room, out of this flashy house. Why had Mrs. MacNeil not put the invitation to Augusta's parents? Did everyone at school talk about the Tollovers' poverty? Did they all sneer, as Mrs. MacNeil clearly did, at her father's pretensions to position?

Of all the painful thoughts racing through Augusta's mind as she descended the movie-set staircase, one thought firmed to a fixed resolve: she would never forgive Sandra.

The summer was a particularly drab one for Augusta and B.K. The worst of it, of course, was knowing their classmates were pack-tripping and galloping through the cool mountains of Wyoming. This was made worse by the hottest Long Island summer in years. Those of their friends who didn't join the Wyoming trip were one by one whisked away to cooler settings, bringing home to the Tollover girls not only how much less privileged they were, but how much they relied on their friends for swimming and tennis at their clubs or private playgrounds.

Tom Tollover was absent most of the summer, claiming business trips. Letters to his daughters from their friends, however, placed him in such unbusinesslike watering spots as Bar Harbor and Newport. The two girls would pass on these reports, sometimes innocently, sometimes, in Augusta's case, with a vague, troublemaking maliciousness, to their mother.

In some ways, Tollover's absence made life easier on all of them. Aside from the respite from battles, the daily routine was substantially relaxed; meals were served in the breakfast room, and Kate would use the time saved to enliven her daughters' summer with excursions to Jones Beach or, once, a picnic at Montauk Point.

Augusta's desperation for diversion overcame her aversion to anything so plebeian as a state-run beach. She did, however, make a few adjustments to differentiate their outings from those of the thousands of families whose cars jammed the parking lots. She spent hours making particularly elegant tomato sandwiches (skinned tomatoes sliced very thin and drained, some mayonnaise and about a quarter inch of butter), iced tea with fresh orange juice and pound cake. When they arrived at the beach, she insisted they carry their blankets and hampers great distances up the beach, far from the crowds who herded near the parking lots and refreshment stands. When B.K. and Kate would refuse to lug their burdens any farther in the loose sand, Augusta would decide if the spot was deserted enough, then permit them to establish their camp. Once settled, Augusta would survey the stretch of empty sand, the clean, rolling surf that sparkled in the morning sun, and say something self-justifying like, "There. Isn't this nice? Just like East Hampton."

Both girls were addicted to root beer. Somewhere Kate got hold of a bottle capper, a hundred bottles and a recipe for homemade root beer. Hard as Kate tried to make an amusing project of the enterprise, Augusta was convinced the true motive was to save the nickel a bottle their beloved Hires cost. Kate's brew wasn't too bad, both girls agreed, but with the first July heat spell, the bottles, which were stored behind the kitchen in the laundry, began exploding at the rate of about one a day. The noise had all three Tollover women unnerved, and finally Kate got rid of all the root beer.

One soggily hot day in August, their mother had gone into

Manhattan to have lunch with her brother. The girls had exhausted every stratagem for amusing themselves and they had just received a letter from Sandra that raved, not only about the ranch, the horses, the scenic Rockies, but also about the darling boys they were all meeting at the ranch.

In black moods, they wandered down to their fountain. They had undertaken to repair it earlier in the summer, but had given up when it had turned out to be too difficult. Lying on their backs on the cooling stone benches they stared at the sky, which buzzed softly with small flying creatures.

B.K. broke the silence. "You were a moron, Augusta, to tell Mrs. MacNeil no."

"Come on, B.K. You know Daddy would never have let us accept a present that big from people like the MacNeils." Augusta's voice had a warning edge of testiness.

B.K. was bored and sour enough to ignore the signs and provoke her sister into a diatribe. A good fight would at least stir the torpid air. "Just think," B.K. teased, "we could be riding into the Wyoming mountains right now . . ."

To B.K.'s surprise Augusta didn't blow up. Instead she replied thoughtfully, "I know. I should have thought of something."

5 The long, low-ceilinged dining room of Charles à la Pommes Soufflé was a gaggle of animated lunch parties and black-suited waiters agilely avoiding each other. Kate Tollover had chosen the restaurant for her meeting with her brother despite his dislike of high-priced enclaves of chi-chi and pretension. Of the many French restaurants opening in the basements of Manhattan brownstones, drawing the carriage trade away from the large hotel dining rooms, Charles was one of the most popular. Kate's North Shore friends mentioned it often. She loved French food and felt she deserved a treat. She was always hoping, too, that her gruff brother would be won over to one aspect, at least, of gracious living. What was there to

dislike about a stylish, intimate atmosphere, nattily dressed fellow diners and superb food? Harry was doing well in his scrap-metal business. He should learn to appreciate these luxuries he could now afford.

Knight was in his mid-forties, eight years older than Kate. He was below average height, powerfully built, with strong, dark features under thinning hair. He looked uncomfortable in a double-breasted brown worsted suit that constricted his shoulders. He took a drink from his old-fashioned and threw down the menu.

"You order me something. I can't make anything of this."

"Would you like some fish?" Kate asked.

"Fish is O.K. if they give you enough. I'm hungry."

Harry was letting his sister's announcement sink in. For several years, he had worked on Kate to leave Tollover, but had yielded to her determination not to disrupt her daughters' lives. Kate's obstinacy was fortified by her own self-sacrifice in remaining in a marriage that clearly offered her nothing but pain. Harry Knight had not liked Tollover from the start. He thought him a snob and a four-flusher. Knight had little use for the posturing, the conceit and the superficiality of self-styled society; to affect that sort of life without the necessary money was, to him, beneath contempt.

Each time Kate, in her exasperation, would tell her brother about one of Tom's derelictions, Knight would increase his campaign for separation. Usually in these exchanges, Kate had merely wanted sympathy, not calls to action, and she would temper the complaint and her brother's ire by pointing to positive aspects of marriage to Tollover. "It isn't so bad," she would say. "Tom is really wonderful with the girls. They adore him. And his connections bring them many advantages."

The snob implications of the last item would invariably launch Harry Knight into a diatribe against the phoniness of the rich and the wrongheadedness of Kate's thinking wealth and social position were steps toward the Good Life. Kate, who would have sold her soul for a full-time maid, had given up trying to persuade her brother of the desirability of "living comfortably" or of the girls' growing up among the privileged.

She justified her resolve to stay with Tollover on the grounds of maintaining a stable family for Augusta and B.K.

Today, however, during their cocktail at Charles à la Pommes Soufflé, Kate said something quite different: she wanted to leave her husband but couldn't because of his inability to support a separate household for her and the two girls. Something had collapsed in her, she confessed to her brother, when the day before she had received word of cancellation of their charge account at a local grocery store, then, within minutes, had seen a newspaper photo of her husband at a Newport party.

She had picked up the phone and arranged this meeting with her brother. She still felt the problem insoluble, but she wanted her brother's advice on her legal resources. She was launching a major change in her running dialogue with her brother on the subject of her marriage. From his saying "Leave him," and her replying "I won't," it was now "Leave him"; "I can't."

"You've got to make the break, Kate," Harry said, putting as much sympathy as possible into his voice without losing his authority. "It's no good arguing you'll stay with him for the girls' sake when he's away half the time, the other half trotting his lady friends under their noses."

"I know I should leave him, Harry, but how? Squeezing support from Tom would be impossible. He doesn't make enough—even if he were sufficiently honòrable to do the right thing, which he isn't. I can't get a job. I've no experience—I've even forgotten how to do secretarial work. Besides, the girls are still too young to be left alone. At least B.K. is."

"What about Tollover's fancy relatives? Wouldn't they help you out?"

"I doubt it very much. At least not in any way I could count on. Uncle Jack helps us out now only when he feels like it or isn't furious with Tom. He might stop altogether if I left Tom. The others don't have any money to spare." She looked forlornly at the shad roe the waiter was placing in front of her. "I'm stuck with him, Harry, and the bastard knows it."

Knight's jaw tightened. "Leave him, Kate. I'll look after you and the girls."

Kate was stunned. "But, Harry . . . that's terribly sweet, but it takes a lot of money. You know, two teenaged girls—schools, doctors, clothes—it's endless."

"How much would it take? Eight thousand dollars a year . . . ten thousand?" he said, certain the Tollover family had been inching along on less.

"Could you afford that much?" She knew her brother's business had burgeoned with the war, but she had thought little about how much. Real wealth was something that happened to other people, not to her family.

"Good grief, Harry. That could be our salvation." Kate began quick calculation. "I could take a simple apartment in Manhattan, something small but in a good neighborhood—the East Eighties would be ideal. I might even find a job—in a museum or bookstore, something suitable. The girls could go to Chapin or Brearley . . ."

"Hold on. I said I would see that you didn't starve and keep a roof over your heads. I didn't say I would bring up Gus and B.K. like heiresses."

"But, Harry, they've been brought up a certain way. You can't just throw them into public high school now, force them to make brutal adjustments. It's not fair. It's asking too much of them. They have certain types of friends . . ."

"I know about those private schools, and I know about boarding schools. They're goddamned expensive. And all they do is convert nice kids into snobs with rotten values."

"We've never agreed about this, Harry. Bastard that Tom is, he at least will see that the girls go to decent schools. If you won't, then I'm not leaving him."

Kate correctly judged her brother's determination to liberate his sister from Tollover.

"All right. All right," he said. "I'll spring for private schools on one condition. The girls get summer jobs. . . ."

"Oh, Harry, be reasonable. That's not . . ."

"That's my offer, Kate. Take it or leave it. You can get your apartment in Manhattan and send them to any school you choose. But in the summer they are to learn a little about the way people live. Real people, not those stuff-shirt phonies that Tollover prizes—and you seem to as well. Another thing. I'm not paying for a lot of extras like fancy clothes and parties. The girls must learn they are not rich, that a lot of decent people are not rich either."

In a rush Kate saw how enormously her life had improved since the start of lunch. Why haggle over terms that might anger her brother into withdrawing his offer? "All right, Harry," she said. "I'll yield to your stand for democracy. Summer jobs it is." She sipped her coffee. "Don't think I'm not grateful. You've saved your sister's life. You must understand if I seem demanding. I've got to protect Augusta and B.K. above everything else."

"Protect them from what? Reality? Look, Kate. They're nice girls, good looking, too. They don't have anything to worry about. In another few years they'll both catch men who will spend their lives supporting them. But why the pedestal? Why the security net? They've been made to feel they're special for too long now."

"They are special, Harry." Kate said this without a hint of maternal pride, or even joy, but as a simple fact that she, and now her brother, had to confront.

The remainder of lunch was taken up discussing whether or not Kate should divorce Tollover. Harry was all for the complete break and said he would pay the legal costs. They agreed Kate should see a lawyer to advise her how to proceed.

As Harry Knight handed the waiter the check and a fifty-dollar bill, he said to Kate, "I've got to hand you one thing. Since you've been married to that s.o.b., you've picked up a lot of polish, a lot of style. It's not as though you and I grew up in the gutter—you know what I mean—but you're a real lady now."

She beamed broadly, as little Kate Knight used to smile years ago, he thought. Then a woman he barely knew reached a white-gloved hand across the table and, as Kate Tollover of Mapleton, Old Westbury, squeezed her brother's hand.

6 Manhattan apartments were scarce in those wartime years. Through some Old Westbury friends who owned a building at Eighty-third and Madison, Kate was able to get the apartment she'd envisioned, a pleasant but inelegant two bedrooms and living room for $135 a month. Similar string-pulling got both Augusta and B.K. into Chapin, which was as fancy a school as Kate could wish. In addition to its social cachet, it had the great advantage of being within walking distance of the apartment.

With Kate congratulating herself on how well things were working out, the girls were in an altogether different mood. Nothing about the separation gave them any pleasure, but the apartment was a particularly bitter blow. Up till the move, their only knowledge of New York apartments was their great-uncle Jack's sixteen rooms at Sixty-seventh and Park or similar luxurious spreads of their wealthy Greenvale classmates whose parents kept in-town digs. For Augusta and B.K. the Eighty-third Street apartment their mother had found was a descent into squalor. They made little effort to hide their disdain—even the good-natured B.K. grumbled about having to share a bedroom with her sister, and a dark bedroom at that.

Kate accepted her daughters' sour bitchiness as the inevitable reaction—with luck a temporary one—to being wrenched from the father they adored. This was the central agony around which swirled countless minor ones. They missed the spaciousness of Mapleton, their wide lawns, their wooded fountain, their friends at Greenvale, the swimming, riding, boating and tennis of country life. Such losses, however, were nothing compared to the loss of their father.

B.K. was still young enough to be confused and hurt by such a calamity. Augusta, on the other hand, had feared an upheaval was coming. She knew her father was much at fault, but still nurtured an aching resentment that her mother had not, by being more understanding of her father's weaknesses, held them together. Augusta saw her mother's unexpected takeover of all their destinies as a shattering of their lives for selfish motives. Exactly what these motives were, Augusta was not certain. But they certainly did not take into account the wants of herself, B.K. and their father. She would always hate her mother for ripping apart all of their existences. It was a bitterness that would remain long after she ceased thinking about its cause. A scar from a forgotten accident. But one part of Augusta held her mother in new respect for having successfully defied a god like her father.

At the less analytical age of thirteen, B.K. was far too concerned with her own unhappiness over the events to brood about the people and forces that caused them. She worried constantly about her father and called him daily at his office and sometimes at home at night.

If Augusta was impressed with her mother's unsuspected assertiveness in moving them all out, Tom Tollover was dumbfounded. He couldn't believe that his passive, former-secretary wife had found both the strength and the financing to leave him. (Harry Knight, of all people!) He was even more surprised to learn how much his daughters meant to him. He had always considered them joys and consolations—but immutable joys and consolations like his good looks and self-assurance. In the rare moments when he took seriously Kate's threats to leave, he had cold-bloodedly decided that the love he felt for Augusta and B.K. and the satisfaction he took from them did not require physical proximity—especially now that they were jelling into the poised and burnished young women he had worked on for so long.

No sooner had Kate informed Tom she was leaving than he realized how false this rationalization was. He was aghast at losing his daughters, at not having them there when *he* wanted them to be—to observe, to correct, to advise. In his dismay and confusion, he poured attentions onto the two girls. In part this was a clumsy attempt to change Kate's mind with a display of good fatherhood. When he saw the futility of this, he continued the program to toughen up the father-daughter bonds, to make them strong enough to survive the shock of separation. He also hoped to repair whatever damage might be done to his heroic image by the entire untidy business.

Even after his family had moved into Manhattan, Tollover was assiduous in his attentions. He sent them gifts, phoned them often and invited them on frequent outings, more often than the agreed-on Sundays. Using every contact he had, Tollover stirred up as much advance excitement as he could in his daughters' paths. He had once met a teacher at Chapin, whom he called with the request that the startled woman "look after my girls."

Tollover was also frantically curious about their life apart from him. Sitting in the Central Park Zoo's outdoor terrace cafe one bright Sunday in October, Tollover vented his spiteful curiosity. "How do you like that tenement your mother's found for you?"

"It's awful, Daddy. It's small and Augusta and I have to share a room."

"There's not much sunlight," Augusta added. "And the cars on Madison Avenue make a lot of noise."

Assured they were unhappy with the new arrangements, Tollover had a pang of guilt and turned conciliatory. "You'll find it exciting living here in town. There's a great deal to do. You're not far from the museum. You should go every chance you get. It's terribly important for young women to have a thorough knowledge and appreciation of art. And you'll meet some nice girls at Chapin. It won't hurt a bit for you to get to know the city crowd as well as the Long Island bunch."

"But where will you be, Daddy?" B.K. whined, feeling the list of advantages had gone on long enough.

"Oh, you know me. If I'm not off climbing an alp or shooting a rapid or dancing on a riverboat, I'll be right here exploring Manhattan with you two."

The decision about school had been that both girls would go to Chapin for the first year in town to avoid separating them from each other as well as from their father. After one year, however, Augusta was to transfer to Ethel Walker's in Simsbury, Connecticut, for her final two years.

The girls fitted in quickly at Chapin. They were not the only offspring of split marriages. And some of the girls' fathers were in the service overseas. Augusta and B.K. were readily accepted by the other students, some of whose parents knew their father. To this species of teenager, a parent's saying, "Oh, yes, the Tollover girls; I know their father, he's charming," carried great weight. They were treated as "somebodies."

The two girls came to love their walks to and from school which soon included detours. The most interesting streets were Madison and Lexington avenues. Augusta particularly liked the posh shops along Madison, the antique stores and art galleries with exquisite merchandise lighted and displayed with great skill and art. She got a feeling of living among throngs of clever and adept people whose talents were aimed at enticing her to acquire their goods. She liked the feeling.

The girls became friendly with one or two doormen along their route with whom they would exchange greetings and chat about the weather. One day Augusta recognized Wendell Willkie coming from a building where they knew the doorman. Augusta got terribly excited.

"B.K., look! That's Willkie!"

"So what?"

"He was almost president. He might have beat Roosevelt."

"But he didn't."

"Don't be so unimaginative. He is one of the most famous men in the world. If he comes out of that building, just think who might be in there now—or in one of the other ones."

Finally, B.K. picked up Augusta's mood. "What do you mean, someone really famous like Clark Gable?"

"Why not?"

Augusta went right to her doorman friend and asked him point-blank if any other famous people lived in his building. Her curiosity produced a well-known stage actress, a radio newscaster and a film director Augusta had never heard of. Thrilled with this harvest, the two girls made similar inventories with their other doormen and cultivated new informants at the most impressive-looking buildings. B.K. was now as enthusiastic about the game as Augusta.

Within a week they were on their way to having enough information for a celebrity map of the Upper East Side. Tom Tollover found out about the activity and put a stop to it. "I'm surprised at you, Augusta, and you too, B.K. I thought you had a better sense of who you are. Those film people and politicians who have you so fascinated, they should be interested to know where *my* daughters live, not the other way around. Next you'll be running around with autograph books like those runny-nosed bobby-soxers at the Roxy."

Augusta made light of their lapse, insisting it was just a game to enliven the walk from school. Her father's point struck home, however; she was embarrassed at her breach of Tollover dignity.

Harry Knight had given his sister a Macy's charge to furnish her apartment (she had pleaded for Altman's) and Kate was surprised at how many of her Long Island friends came to her assistance with loans or gifts of household items. When envisioning the separation, Kate had resigned herself to losing most of her North Shore friends. She knew that they were "their" friends in name only, that as soon as she left, she would see that they had been "his" friends all along. She was gratified to find she had been wrong and that a good number of them issued signs that they intended remaining friendly with Kate. In part this was reaction to Tom's unfeeling treatment of her, but in part it sprang from affection Kate herself had won.

A fundamental aspect of the style she had acquired as Tollover's pupil-wife was an unassertive reticence in the company of her socialite friends. She had opinions, she didn't always go along with what was being said or done, but she made a point of being uncompetitive, of never trying to out-talk, outshine, out-barb her North Shore friends. For this, she was deemed a good listener, an appreciative audience, never a wet blanket, and, in general, to the outsized egos of New York society, a welcome presence.

After the separation, Kate was surprised to discover how many of her socialite cronies considered her not just an appendage of Tom Tollover, but a person in her own right, one they were reluctant to lose. Once settled in Manhattan, she received a few invitations to dinners, for which she sneaked two dresses on the Macy's charge account. She helped fan whichever friendships might be burning out with a campaign of note-writing. On the slightest pretext she would fire off a note to her former friends and acquaintances, all by way of making sure they had her new address and phone number.

Before very long, Kate was enjoying a regular social life with people Tollover would have had difficulty dismissing. At one of these dinners she met the owner of an art gallery in her neighborhood who offered her a job. She promptly took it. Kate felt altogether pleased with developments. She had sent up a signal for assistance—bright, cheerful and dignified—but still a plea, and the world had responded well. Deliverance from her old life and success in the new one had an enormous effect on Kate, some of it visible.

At first the girls were too taken up with their own adjustments to notice the change in their mother. But finally even they couldn't overlook that the drudge who on Long Island had cleaned their clothes, driven them to school and cooked their meals had turned into a smartly-dressed, vivacious career woman. She had more color, her hair was more frequently "done" and she seemed to have an exuberance and energy not there before.

Kate was not so caught up in her own new life as to neglect her daughters. She went to considerable effort to woo them to their new life and to divert them from missing their father. Augusta was aware of this—at times she played on it—but she had the disquieting impression that her mother's happiness was no longer tied up with her own and B.K.'s. For the first time, Augusta was seeing her mother as something more than a functionary in the spectacle of Tom Tollover and his admirable daughters.

Augusta was sensing the same independence of spirit that had taken her father by surprise, and there was still enough of the child in her to find this unsettling. For the first time in her life she felt herself to be the center of no one's world, certainly no adult's. The ties between Augusta and her mother had never been strong, and this new independence of Kate's did nothing to increase Augusta's feeling for her, but it did increase her respect. She began observing her mother with greater interest.

During the first year in Manhattan, with both girls in Chapin, they would spend Sundays with their father. In good weather this meant taking the train to Old Westbury where they would spend the day at Mapleton. The house, which had been shabby and underused when they lived there, was now like a house that had been closed up and unoccupied. Their father's ability to ignore the most flagrant deterioration in the place was noticed even by his uncritical daughters.

In the winter, he would come into town and take them someplace exciting. Occasionally this would be an educational event like a show at the Hayden Planetarium; more often it was a pleasure-ground of the city's wealthy: an armory polo match, the antique show, a slow tour of the Frick Museum (where Tollover made as many remarks about the vulgarities of the Pittsburgh millionaires and their debt to Duveen as he did about the art itself). These excursions were often capped by tea at the Palm Court of the Plaza where Augusta adored the powdered old women in broad-brimmed hats and crystal beads, the portly, impeccably tailored men and the general atmosphere of decadent European gentility.

On more than one of these outings, Tollover complained of a racking hangover. With him silent and out of sorts, Sundays became grim exercises in parent-child togetherness, and Augusta found herself wishing she could be home reading. It was painful for her to see the effort her father was making on these off days. One night about eleven, when Kate was at a dinner and B.K. was asleep, Augusta answered the phone to hear her father's slurred voice. After a few moments' conversation, Augusta realized he had nothing to say, but simply wanted to make contact with them. She worried that he was losing command of himself, and the contempt this inspired in her came from Tollover's teaching her to despise any such personal weaknesses. The sympathy and vicarious pain she also felt came from somewhere else.

[41]

One day on an impulse, Augusta defied her mother's injunction against riding the subways without an adult and took the I.R.T. to Wall Street to pay a surprise visit to her father's office. Her motives had been a confused tangle of her own needs and, to a greater degree, those she ascribed to him.

Tollover was delighted to see his daughter and introduced her around his office with pride. It was just the cheery surprise, he told her, to brighten a bad day: he had just learned that a large stock transaction he had been working on for months had fallen through. Other aspects of his life seemed to be going badly. He made some reference to his lady friends' proving as unreliable as his business friends. He also seemed irritated by reports of Kate's busy social calendar.

"I understand," he said, "your mother is becoming quite the gay divorcée, pending a final decree, of course. Dancing on table tops, is she?"

"She gets invited out a good bit."

"Buyers from Ohrbach's, no doubt . . . or hosiery manufacturers. I understand they're having a convention in town."

"A lot of it is connected with the gallery she works for, but some are friends from Long Island. She was at a dinner the Van Platts gave at the River Club last Saturday." Augusta knew the name would rankle her father, and so would the club.

"Thank God I taught her what fork to use."

That night Kate was particularly animated. As she served her daughters dinner, she chatted happily about things she had done in the past few days, people she had met. As she placed a dish of ice cream before each girl, she enthused about having met the playwright John Van Druten at a party.

"That's the marvelous thing about living in town. Our friends on Long Island are all very nice, but here in town you meet so many different *types* of people. It's so much more stimulating . . ."

Augusta had adopted a policy of live-and-let-live toward her mother. She tried to be cooperative and pleasant, and would make an effort not to reveal her bitterness over the separation. But tonight her mother's ebullience contrasted too cruelly with her father's depression. Her mother's self-congratulatory vein made Augusta want to hurt her.

"I went to see Daddy today in his office," she said flatly.

Her mother's startled look pleased Augusta. Kate took a sip of her coffee and paused before speaking.

"Did you?" she said evenly. "But that means you rode the subway alone."

"For heaven's sake, Mother. I'm fifteen."

"Please, Augusta. We've been through this. It's not safe at any age for a pretty woman alone. I would never have a tranquil moment if I thought you were riding around by yourself on those horrid trains. Your father doesn't want it either. Didn't he say anything?"

"No."

"You promised me once. Now promise me again."

"All right," Augusta conceded, completely deflated by her mother's focusing on the breach of rules rather than the larger implications of her visit.

"How was your father?" Kate asked brightly.

"All right, I suppose." Augusta felt conciliatory after her childish attempt to sow discord. Her mother was being so *nice*. In her guilt, Augusta ventured a momentary relaxation of the solid front she and B.K. had raised against Kate when she opposed their father. "I think he's lonely."

Augusta instantly regretted her lapse. With a cheerful, malice-free voice that ripped through Augusta and signaled total victory over Tom Tollover, Kate said, "Don't worry about your father. He'll always come out on top."

7 The kinetic euphoria that animated America in those first autumn months at the close of World War II penetrated as deeply into society and reached the newly arriving tenth grade of the Ethel Walker School in Simsbury, Connecticut. The usual ebullience of teenagers reuniting or meeting each other for the first time was heightened by talk of fathers coming

home from overseas, of an end to rationing, and the prospects of hitherto impossible treats like European travel.

As she registered and found her room, Augusta was preoccupied by the drabness of her clothing compared to the stylish outfits and show-offy luggage of the other girls, some of whom swept up to Walker's in fur capes and newly minted suitcases of red-and-green leather. To Augusta's relief, the school required all new arrivals to change promptly into the school's dowdy uniform. Perhaps her poor wardrobe would go unnoticed in the confusion of the first hours.

Walking with her bag toward her assigned building, she heard someone calling her name. She turned to see running up to her Sandra MacNeil, looking absurdly grown-up in a mink jacket and matching fur hat. She gave Augusta a hug and said, "Isn't it thrilling our both being here? Have you met your roommates yet? I checked and they didn't put us together. But we both made it, that's the main thing."

Augusta had seen little of Sandra in the year she was at Chapin. She had not forgiven her for her high-handed betrayal in the Eaton's Ranch business and she considered it rotten luck that Sandra, as aware as any outsider of the Tollover's fiscal problems, would also be at Walker's where she could brief the others. As she watched Sandra dash off, she thought perhaps she wouldn't be that gossipy, but being nice to her would probably help.

Augusta was assigned to a room with four other girls, three of whom had arrived. As she introduced herself to each, she decided that none posed any great threat. The previous year's uprooting from Greenvale had helped considerably toward overcoming her fears of new people and situations. She had developed a serviceable aplomb with which she confronted the famous boarding school. She knew she could compete with these girls on all grounds except one, the financial. And Augusta knew that Walker's was known as a rich girls' school, more so than most other boarding schools, so the matter was far from inconsequential to her.

The faculty at Chapin had been impressed with Augusta academically. They had questioned her about her future plans in a way that could only be considered highly flattering. She had told them she had only thought as far as a liberal arts degree from a good college; she would decide later on a career. This answer was to accommodate. Inwardly, she assumed she would go to college, but she felt no drive to prove herself in a man's profession.

Even at the age of sixteen, with the adult world looming nearer, Augusta could see no great glamour in commercial fields like merchandising or advertising. She didn't see how her success, or any other woman's, in an occupation traditionally a male preserve, would alter the occupation's ultimate banality. The struggle itself, which she knew she could win, seemed beneath her—unless perhaps it might be in an occupation of true prestige like the arts or publishing.

In the first winter after her parents' separation, Augusta had thrown herself into a reading program, triggered by school assignments. Eventless winter nights and easy schoolwork gave her ample time to escape through some of the lengthier landmarks of Western literature. She had a particular affinity for the nineteenth-century novelists of manners: Thackeray, Jane Austen, Trollope, Stendhal. She quickly perceived these writers' twin obsessions, matrimony and finance, yet she marveled at the intricate and diverse embroideries they could fashion from the two basic threads.

Colette was a revelation. Augusta had considered herself an oddly adult sixteen year old until she discovered the complicated schemings of Claudine. She began a diary of her own, the pretentious kind that focused on reactions to important events rather than a cataloguing of routine ones.

Several members of the Chapin faculty had encouraged Augusta about her writing style. When she told her English teacher about the diary, he had responded with an enthusiasm that surprised Augusta. It was an excellent way, he told her, of developing the ability to translate thoughts, impressions and emotions into sentences. When she arrived at Walker's Augusta was toying with the idea of becoming a writer. She was therefore thrilled that one of her roommates was Martie Dean whose father, Pritchard Dean, was a *New Yorker* writer and a particular hero of Augusta's. Martie, a shy, somewhat unattractive girl, was equally thrilled by Augusta's interest in her.

Tom Tollover had warned his daughters against becoming too friendly with the first people you meet in a new situation. "The ones who are the easiest, who make themselves most available to you, they're usually not worth knowing. The worthwhile ones will hold themselves aloof, and you should do the same. Hold back, look them over, then decide whom you'd like to know."

To Augusta, Martie's father more than offset this hard-line advice. And she liked Martie's quiet intelligence and was amused by her automatic reaction of despair at all situations confronting her.

The other girl who would be one of Augusta's two closest friends at Walker's was the roommate not yet arrived, Minnie Blanchard, who made a dazzling, two-day-late entrance one evening after dinner when the five roommates were chatting in their room. Minnie had missed the first two days of school for the glamorous reason that she was on her grandmother's yacht, which ran into impassable weather returning from the Galapagos Islands. Whatever impression this advance notice may have made on the other girls was quickly topped by Minnie herself. Just as a settled-in calm descended on the room, she swept in, her ruddy, tomboyish face incongruous in a beaver coat. She threw a Vuitton handbag down on a bookcase.

"So you're my new cellmates," she said with a raspy, almost tough voice. "Got the best beds, I'm sure. But don't worry. I probably won't be around long enough to crowd you."

She took off her coat and tossed it on a chair. It slid to the floor. "This is just one more school to get kicked out of. I'm sure you jerks are all academic virgins—not to mention the other kind. But at our age, who isn't? No hands raised, I see. Well, don't feel bad. I can't pull rank on you with *that*. But I can on getting expelled. Five schools in three-and-a-half years. Not bad. Poor Granny's going to run out of trustees. But I just can't seem to find the school that will let me stay in bed all day. Got to keep trying."

She looked around at the agape faces. "You'll get used to me. I'm not all that bad. Let's learn some names."

She went around the room introducing herself and shaking hands. When she got to Augusta, she said, "Oh, yeh, my mother told me you'd be here. She knows about your father. Says he's kind of wild. A great guy. Are you wild?"

"No," Augusta replied, smiling. "But I'm a great guy."

"Well, that's something, God knows. What do you think of that? They put us in the same room. Ain't it a small upper class?"

At first Augusta was put off by Minnie's brashness and her freckled commonness. Midway through her opening spiel, however, Augusta was won over. She decided to make a friend of this odd throwback to some pioneer roughneck. The Blanchards, Augusta knew, were very grand. They had hit big wealth about 1880, long after Philadelphia's other leading families. Their tardiness was held against them so they had to spend their way into acceptance—a huge estate on the Main Line, an oceangoing yacht, lavish parties. Now, three generations later, they were accepted by Philadelphia society, but were still surrounded by the outlandish trappings of newcomers.

Later, when the two girls talked alone, Augusta came to like Minnie even more. Her dismissals from other schools, it turned out, were not academic failures, but the results of wild escapades. Once she slipped out of Dana Hall in the middle of the week and hitchhiked to New York because she "was desperate to hear some good Dixieland." At a small school in Vermont she became a legend when she was caught peeking through the bedroom window of the headmaster and his wife; the operation had involved climbing a painter's ladder up the outside of his Victorian Gothic house ("I couldn't believe they actually did it," she explained to her Walker's roommates).

Augusta felt sorry for Minnie. She was in no way stupid, but she hated studying and had a strong pull toward terminal exploits. Augusta resolved to help Minnie remain in Walker's and gave her lectures on the pointlessness of getting into trouble. Minnie responded well to Augusta's campaign—perhaps from exasperation with her own cycle, or perhaps from admiration for Augusta and her need for a friend.

Minnie was not, however, a totally passive penitent. She would lecture Augusta in turn on the folly of being a goody-goody saint when they had so many advantages to fall back on. "What's the good of having a filthy rich grandmother and a guilty mother if you have to go around like little Miss Prim all the time? We might as well come from some poor, happy family. *Quel* bore!"

Augusta saw her point, but took a pragmatic line. Schools like Walker's, she argued, while the biggest snob institutions in the world, made a great show of their democracy, particularly in matters of discipline. The richer and more important a student's family, the harder the school was on that student if he or she flouted the rules. She cited examples from North Shore lore.

"And as for me," Augusta said, "I don't have a rich grandmother."

"So what?" said Minnie. "You're smart and good looking. And you've got all the social connections. Why should you have to weasel around like some frightened kitchenmaid?"

"The school thinks they're building our characters, turning us from spoiled brats into model citizens," Augusta replied. "All you have to do is play their game for two years, then you can give them your favorite expression . . ."

"Go fuck yourselves," Minnie said, savoring the words like an endearment.

Augusta got on well with her roommates and soon came to be quite popular with other classmates. A provisional hierarchy formed with remarkable speed among the new students, based mainly on considerations of status—family's social importance, wealth, professional glamour—but Augusta, known to be deficient in at least two of these departments, came to be admired for her cool intelligence and her adult reserve that was tempered with flashes of sly humor.

The roommates had just begun to feel relaxed with Minnie when she shook them one evening with the pronouncement that they were all at Walker's because somebody, probably their parents, wanted them out of the way. None of the girls was sufficiently intimidated by Minnie to accept this. They pounced on her.

"My family has gone here for three generations." "The finest education . . ." "Make us ladies . . ." "Meet others like ourselves . . ." "Lifelong friendships . . ."

At the door on her way down the hall to the bathroom, Minnie paused majestically and waited for the outcry to subside. When all were silent, she said firmly, *"Out of the way,"* and left the room.

Several nights after Minnie's hand grenade, Augusta could not sleep. She got up and went into the bathroom to read. Unable to concentrate on her book, she turned off the light and sat staring out the window at the field of fresh snow that spread off into the bright night.

Her mother was pursuing her own life in New York, a life that had nothing to do with her two daughters. She would naturally prefer having at least one daughter out of the way. And her father—he could have done a lot more to keep them all together. And sweet, lovable B.K.—even she seemed to be moving away from Augusta. Her last letter read as though written at her mother's insistence and was full of people and activities Augusta knew nothing about. Minnie's pronouncement on the function of boarding schools had come at the wrong time. Augusta looked out at the moonlit snowscape, vast and empty, and cried as she couldn't remember crying since she was an infant.

There were stables at Walker's. Some of the girls, Sandra MacNeil among them, had shipped in their own horses. Horses were also available through the school, but for a charge, and Uncle Harry's budget did not allow for such extras. Augusta covered by announcing that she was bored with horses. The lie came easily, although she yearned to canter off into the Connecticut hills. But it wasn't safe to lie too much.

Having Sandra with her at Walker's made it impossible for Augusta to distort her family's affluence, but the impulse for this sort of pretense was often stronger than practical reasons for honesty. For all her intelligence, she had a capacity for blocking out the chinks in her wall of pretense. If anyone were so unobservant as to think her an heiress, or just another Walker's rich girl, Sandra could correct their mistake—and would probably be happy to do so.

Any hope she had of fooling anyone was shattered on the Simsbury train platform when the girls assembled to leave for Thanksgiving holidays. It was the first time since getting acquainted they had seen each other, not in school uniform, but in their own clothes. The impact was startling. In a strange sense, it was like seeing people you knew naked for the first time—strange marks, folds, clumps of hair permanently connected to familiar hands and faces.

The girls were unabashed in their appraisal of each other's sudden display—outlandish furs, ostentatiously matched luggage, others in conservative but expensive wool coats of perfect taste, a few like Augusta in shabby cloth coats of no taste, good or bad. Augusta was particularly ashamed of her suitcase, a bedraggled affair of imitation leather with frayed corners. As she stood chatting with a few friends waiting for the train to New Haven she edged slowly away from the bag, leaving it alone and disowned in the middle of the platform.

After the Thanksgiving recess, Ethel Walker's began humming with talk of glamorous winter vacations for the Christmas holidays only a month away. Several girls were flying to family homes in Palm Beach. Winter resorts such as Acapulco, Barbados and Cuba were mentioned. Some were going with their families to ski resorts like Sun Valley and Aspen. Minnie Blanchard was flying to Nassau, where her grandmother's yacht was moored and where, among other delights, there would be a large dinner on board for the former viceroy and his wife, the Duke and Duchess of Windsor.

At first Augusta simply envied these jaunts, but as the time approached she felt increasingly the stigma of having nothing more to announce than a three-week confinement in the four-room apartment of a working mother. She began listening for a winter resort that was not being mentioned by any of the other girls.

One day at lunch, the talk turned again to the Christmas vacation. Augusta blurted out, "I've just had the most exciting news! My father's taken a house at Montego Bay and my sister and I are to spend the entire vacation with him there. Isn't that great? I've never been to Jamaica before. I'm just going to lie in the sun for the entire time. Nothing else!" Her friends were genuinely pleased for her.

A bit later, coming out of English class, Augusta was stopped by a snobbish girl she didn't much like, Buffie French. "Augusta! I just heard the news that you're going to Jamaica. That's wonderful because I'll be there too. We're going—my whole family—to stay with my uncle in Port Antonio."

"That's a long way from Montego Bay, isn't it?" Augusta was stunned back to reality. How stupid to put herself into the power of a jackass like Buffie. One lie.

"It's not so far. And we have to go into Montego Bay all the time for shopping, to meet people at the airport. Why don't you give me the phone number where you'll be staying and we can get together."

"I have no idea what the number is. I suppose I could get it from my father." Then she added quickly, "But you wouldn't believe how possessive he is. When he takes us on a trip, he wants us all to himself."

"How incestuous," Buffie added slyly. Something about her switch in tone told Augusta that the horrid girl wouldn't accept she was being snubbed but suspected instead Augusta was lying about going to Jamaica. How dare she see through the fiction so quickly?

In the following days, Buffie kept after Augusta unmercifully. There was no longer any hope in Augusta's mind that Buffie believed she was being cold-shouldered. No one with any self-respect at all would have persisted after so many stalls and discouragements. Buffie was playing a sadistic game and it had Augusta in a panic. She could keep stalling about the phone number and hope that Buffie would give up or get bored with her sport. Or she could make up a fake name of the house's owner, then say later he must not have been listed. Or she could simply tell Buffie she didn't want to get together with her in Jamaica.

She decided on a modified version of the last course. She'd do better to make one enemy than risk being the butt of the entire school.

"You see," she explained at their next encounter, "we don't get to see our father very often and he has every minute planned. He would be furious if we went off and did something on our own. I hope you understand."

Buffie smirked. "Still sounds incestuous to me." She laughed maliciously, then, turning abruptly, walked away.

8 In the lugubrious luxury of a Beekman Place apartment lobby, Kate waited for the elevator. A man and a woman, also in evening dress, came through the door from the street. Since they appeared to be on their way to the same party, Kate brought to the ready her most ladylike nod-with-tight-half-smile, the greeting she reserved for unavoidable confrontations with well-dressed strangers. She relaxed to a full smile when she saw the woman was Sarah Rusk, an acquaintance from North Shore horse events.

"Kate darling. I haven't seen you in ages. You're going to the Pomeroys' too? What fun."

Sarah was a tall, good-looking woman in her late thirties whose lock-jawed, upper-class accent promised little fun. She appraised Kate's plain black dinner dress and gray tweed coat coldly. Like Kate, Sarah had left an irresponsible husband, but unlike Kate, Sarah had no children and enjoyed a comfortable inheritance. Further fueling a formidable assurance was her reputation as a sculptress. Kate, with her recent knowledge of the New York art world, knew that Sarah's success reached beyond the society art market and touched, to some extent, the serious art market as well.

"You know Bryce Hartshorne, don't you, darling? Bryce, this is Kate Tollover."

Kate had been at the point of recognizing the well-known statesman and F.D.R. insider. He was a man in his mid to late fifties, as tall as Sarah, with a full head of graying hair, sympathetic eyes and a handsome, refined face. Hartshorne, Kate also knew, was the heir to a railroad fortune. Like Roosevelt himself, he had been born to money and position yet had worked hard all of his life carving out a place for himself at the center of national affairs.

As the ambassador shook her hand and smiled, Kate felt he knew who she was. Kate took some pleasure in knowing that Tom Tollover's fame in society's inner sanctums gave her a certain celebrity as well. *Everyone* knew that the dashing Tom Tollover was recently divorced from his wife; anyone meeting an attractive woman of early middle age named Tollover en route to a smart dinner would assume that that was she.

The elevator arrived and the elderly uniformed attendant, embarrassed at keeping three such distinguished passengers waiting, outdid himself with obsequiousness as he ushered them aboard. They sped upward in silence, giving Kate a chance to compose herself as she so often had when about to enter for the first time the home of one of her rich friends.

These elevator rides always gave Kate a few seconds to make the psychological shift from a working woman who cooked her daughters' dinner in the kitchen of a four-room apartment to a valued member of the Long Island estate set. This forced immobility as she soared upwards invariably brought the usual trepidation she felt before entering a party. Who would be there? Would she meet amusing people? Would she shine? Would she make new friends? Lose old ones? These routine anxieties were usually forced aside by the more complicated mixture of envy and ambition that marked Kate's feelings towards her wealthy friends.

The elevator opened directly into the white-tiled apartment foyer. A maid in black uniform with a white apron took their coats and motioned them toward a walnut-paneled library where Thea and Ralph Pomeroy were receiving their guests.

Thea was the daughter of the founder of Darby and Fentor, one of the most prestigious Wall Street investment houses, which was now prospering, under her husband's direction, as never before. The Pomeroys were avid horsemen and spent every weekend at their manicured farm in Westbury not far from the Tollover house.

Their New York apartment, now animated with about twenty men and women in evening clothes, was decorated like an estate in horse country. Illuminated paintings of thoroughbreds punctuated the dark wood walls; a bronze statue of a horse stood on the mantel over a roaring fire, harness brasses framed the fireplace and two engraved silver riding crops were affixed to one wall below some hunting prints. The entire setting suggested that stables full of live horses could not be more than one hundred yards away.

Immediately after receiving warm greetings from both Pomeroys, Kate was asked what she would like to drink by a black butler holding a silver tray. She made her order and looked around the room to see that most of the other faces were familiar. Most were acquaintances of many years from Long Island—pleasant enough, but people with whom nothing had happened and nothing would ever happen. Seeing no other choice, Kate was about to join a friendly married couple when she heard a voice at her elbow.

"I see by the chart that we are to sit together at dinner."

Kate turned and smiled at Ambassador Hartshorne.

"Our hostess will never let me talk to you now," he said conspiratorially, "but tell me quickly one or two of your interests so I might have time to prepare a brilliant conversational line."

Without thinking Kate replied, "Art and my daughters. And yours?"

"For the time being, art and your daughters . . ." He turned and rejoined Sarah, who was laughing noisily with a woman she had just kissed. Kate had long ago mastered the art of negotiating a social gathering alone. For years Tom had dinned into her never to look frightened and ill at ease; it sends off repelling shock waves "as surely as if you had rolled in horse manure before dressing." Failing everything else, he said, stand in the middle of a party alone but bristling with confidence; someone will approach you in a matter of seconds. She had tried it and he was right.

Tonight, she had no need for such experiments in human magnetism. She greeted several friends (Tom had also told her how to perch lightly enough with a group to permit a hasty and inoffensive escape), then settled into a conversation with Betty Satterthwaite, who could talk intelligently about the New York gallery business.

As they chatted, Kate's ear was caught by a woman's voice behind her saying, ". . . The war may be over, but *nothing* will be as it was. We're running our place with only four in the house and two outside. Who can afford more? After what they all made in the defense plants, they won't work for servants' wages anymore."

"Perhaps," a man's voice put in, "but so many new products are about to be introduced on a broad level, products that will reduce the need for labor. All sorts of electrical appliances like dishwashers . . ."

"I can't have thirty to dinner with a dishwasher . . ."

"Surely they have an electrical butler in the works."

"Laugh if you want, but I say out our entire way of life is finished."

The butler announced dinner in a voice that only a few heard.

The first half of the meal, Kate discussed art with the man on her left, a visitor from Boston who was a director of the Fogg Museum. Their discussion of how long the abstract movement was likely to survive interested Kate so much that she thought little about her impending conversation with the famous statesman.

When, at the hostess's signal, the guests, like well trained pointers, turned their heads to their other partners, Hartshorne said to Kate, "I've been thinking about art and, to some degree, your daughters, and I have a number of questions."

"I have decided, Ambassador," Kate said solemnly, "that it is not cricket to have preparation time for these dinner-table bouts. We must choose other subjects."

"But I have such astute observations, all ready to go . . ."

"I would like to hear them another time. But if we are to match wits we must both start from the same point. It's only fair."

"You probably are right. What will it be, then?"

"You are involved in government dealings all of us are interested in. If you expose yourself at a gathering like this, shouldn't you be forced to deal with the uninformed curiosity of people like me?"

"But that keeps you at a disadvantage. We would be talking about my field."

"Are you saying that in polite conversation ignorance is a disadvantage? Like Jinx Falkenburg, I'll wield it like a club and have you down in no time. What I'd like to know is, why are we working so hard to keep Germany powerless when they could in time be our staunchest allies against the Communists?"

"If you think that question is easy, you're wrong, but I'll try. The feeling of our government is that sentiment runs too high against the Germans right now. In addition, too many people recall how quickly German belligerence returned after World War I. But we are in sympathy with your point. At the moment, however, we must continue treating the Germans as treacherous and dangerous enemies."

"You mean, our government treats them as enemies now but doesn't really think of them that way?"

"You talk about governments as though they were immutable." His tone had none of the amused condescension that Kate usually received in similar conversations with experts or insiders and which, in this instance, she had invited. "They change constantly just as the situations they confront—other governments, for example—change constantly. For the time being, the Germans are officially enemies, and enemies to be watched carefully. That policy will surely change with time."

Kate nodded, satisfied with the answer.

"Have I now won the right to ask you about art and your daughters?"

She smiled sheepishly. "Of course."

"I know about one of your daughters, Augusta. A niece of mine used to compete against her in horse shows. My niece said she was unbeatable."

"Augusta rides very well. She is also a competitor."

"And both girls are good looking too, I understand, which is natural, I suppose—but atomic mutations pop up everywhere."

Kate stiffened slightly at the compliment and he switched abruptly. ". . . And they live with you here in Manhattan, I understand."

"Augusta is at Ethel Walker's . . ."

"Yes, yes, but I mean you are managing your family alone now. That is so admirable."

"I work. And my brother has been most helpful."

"I wasn't actually referring to money," Hartshorne said. "I am sure it is difficult singlehandedly taking on the burden and responsibility of raising two girls. How many women here tonight could do it? Even those with fortunes?"

Having instigated the split with her husband, Kate had never asked for a minute's sympathy from anyone. Things had gone smoothly for her, even with tight money and censuring coldness from Augusta and B.K. But still—Kate had felt moments of worry and loneliness when she had wished herself back in the ramshackle Tollover mansion waiting for Tom to return from an escapade. She had grown so accustomed to having the presence, even occasionally, of an ultimate authority, even titular, her elation at being free of the marital travesty was often interspersed with despairing moments when she felt overwhelmed by what she had undertaken. While others had hinted their admiration for Kate's enterprise in setting off on her own, no one had so gracefully sympathized with the burden of raising two children. Commiseration was rare for her and she was not good at handling it. She felt her poise collapsing, but caught herself. She laughed.

"Courageous Woman Faces Perils of Upper East Side

Alone . . ." Kate saw her hostess rise. "We certainly have swung from the largest to the smallest issues."

"We still have to cover art."

"That will take some time."

"I'm glad to hear it."

Kate smiled and turned to follow the ladies into the main living room.

As the women were arranging themselves in the commodious beige room bristling with eighteenth-century English furniture, Thea Pomeroy steered Kate away from the others. "You've made a hit, I see, with Bryce Hartshorne, but be careful darling, Sarah considers him her property."

"Are they having an affair?" Kate asked.

"I haven't the foggiest. But they are always together when he's in New York, and I know she often visits his place in Maryland."

They were joined by some other women and they sat chatting as the butler served demitasses.

"Did you hear about Polly Kipness? She hit Drake for two million."

"Well, he asked for it. He didn't lift a finger to hide his affair with that entertainer."

"Entertainer?" said another. "I don't find checking hats very entertaining."

"Whatever she is, sweetie, she will soon be a full participant in Drake's millions."

"Oh, God, one more nail in Palm Beach's coffin."

"I'm glad Polly came out of it all right. Is she seeing anyone?"

Kate lost the thread of the conversation as she worried about Thea's warning. When a conversational opportunity presented itself with Sarah Rusk, Kate decided to try those waters and found them icy. Shortly thereafter, when the men joined them, Sarah pounced on Hartshorne and led him to a sofa at the far end of the room. It had been a long time since Kate had played such games, and in one way it delighted her—she felt young and mean—but it also made her uneasy.

Kate was joined by Drew Witten, a bachelor in his fifties who like herself was not rich but was valued in this society as an extra man, and in Drew's case, an amusing one. Kate and Drew liked each other but, with a tacit acknowledgement of their special position in these precincts, tended to avoid each other during the social action.

"You know, Kate," Drew said, lighting a cigarette, "I've always thought of you and me as attendants at these frolics, not as major players. I based that on neither of us having a great fortune. Also I have no intention of marrying so I'm eliminated from those sweepstakes. But I see tonight I was wrong about you."

"You make it sound as though the only purpose of social activity is matchmaking."

"Not the only purpose, luv, but certainly a dominant one. Most people, when they dress and come to a dinner, are seeking to make a marriage or to destroy one. At the least they hope to pass judgment on other marriages, weaken some, perhaps devastate others, but of all these pastimes, making a marriage is the most entertaining. Above all matrimony is the principal business."

"And good conversation, good companionship, making new friends?"

"All peripheral to the main event—like you and me." He swirled amber brandy in a melon-sized snifter. "But tonight I realized with a start how wrong I was to relegate you to my supernumerary status. You are in a position to make a brilliant second marriage."

"Good grief," Kate smiled. "You'd think Ambassador Hartshorne and I had fallen into each other's arms during the meat course."

"There was a perceptible spark."

"In your keenness for main events, you are exaggerating terribly." Kate was turned towards Witten on the sofa and did not notice Bryce Hartshorne's approach. Seeing the ambassador standing above them, Witten rose and said slyly, "I probably am, Kate. Excuse me. I must speak to Thea about the library benefit."

"Then I've come just in time to save you from abandonment."
Hartshorne sat down.

"But now we *are* breaking a rule," Kate said, with no hint of
coyness. She knew her niche with these people was precarious
enough to demand total adherence to form. Over the years her
strict observance of the rules had become a reflex. It was, like
her erect posture, a part of her. If people had noticed
Hartshorne's interest before, this present breach would cap the
scandal. She also knew that when blame was assigned, she, and
not Hartshorne, would be the culprit. She was pleased that
Hartshorne liked her—she liked him—but she did not want to
sacrifice her good standing with the few friends salvaged from
her former marriage to this man's one-evening flirtation.

"I know of no such rule. I thought you only switched partners
after dinner if you had exhausted all conversation at the table.
And we still have art to discuss. You are working in a gallery?"

On several occasions since her separation, Kate had been the
target of dinner-party campaigns, a few of them honorable.
Most of these men had been agreeable but lackluster prospects,
middle-aged bachelors with small incomes who feared the
approaching cold of old age. Others were recently divorced and
terrified at the prospect of running their own households. The
dishonorable suitors were more interesting, but such sport had
long held a minor post in Kate's consciousness. With so many
survival concerns, erotic fantasies were the furthest thing from
her mind.

The prospect of a haven suggested by the more serious
suitors—perhaps two she had met could have been maneuvered
into that category—was tempting to Kate, but only momentarily. She would catch herself up, going over in her mind how
fortunate she was, how generous her brother was being, how
much better off she and the girls were now compared to their
life with Tom. But still, what if Harry should get mad at her?
What if he suddenly had money problems? The arrangement
was not secure. And wouldn't it be nice to live on a budget not
calculated to the last penny? She had time, that was the
advantage she should make the most of.

She was adept at turning aside the advances of the handful

who had shown interest. She could play the game without spoiling dinner-table fun and without offending the more sincere. The time had come with Hartshorne, she knew, where she would have begun, with any of the others, pouring cold water. But then something else entered Kate's mind—if she didn't want to spend the rest of her days as some sort of craven society hanger-on, she had to take a few chances, be audacious when the right moment occurred. And looking at this handsome man, an international celebrity, an anchor of the eastern political and social establishment, a man who could immeasureably transform the lives of Kate and her daughters, she decided the moment had occurred.

Kate felt a rush of anxiety. She was being a fool. Her position with these people was not so secure that she could cause trouble. She resented the way others of these women could behave outrageously—get drunk, vamp friends' husbands, insult bores. Such rule-breaking was invariably in direct proportion to the firmness of the woman's position. The fearlessness was not so much a reflection of confidence in their actions as it was a certainty that the others in their group would accept such behavior *from them*. Kate had no such assurance.

How could she gracefully extricate herself from Hartshorne? It was almost the hour when she could leave the party. But that would do violence to yet another stricture of her marginal status; she could not be the first to leave. She would excuse herself from him by saying she must discuss a school matter with one of the other women.

It was too late. Sarah Rusk was standing over them.

"Harold has had too much to drink and is being a boor," she said angrily. "We should be going before too much longer, Bryce."

Hartshorne leaped to his feet. "Sit with us for a minute while I finish this brandy, my dear. We were talking about your field, contemporary art."

"How fascinating," Sarah said dully as she sat on the sofa close by Hartshorne. Looking hard at Kate, Sarah crossed her long legs and said, "Tell me, sweetie, what are you up to?"

There was a skipped beat while Kate wondered if Sarah could

really be throwing down the gauntlet so crudely. Sarah seemed to relish the confusion she caused, but continued, "I understand you're working in a shop."

"An art gallery," Kate corrected.

"Of course, I remember now. Well . . ." Sarah's voice dripped solicitude. "We all think it's fabulous the way you've pulled everything together and are taking care of those adorable girls. Bryce is dazzled by that kind of resourcefulness in a woman. I'm simply in awe of it. Simply in awe."

Kate chatted politely and got away as quickly as she could. Others were saying good night to the Pomeroys, so Kate exited with them. She declined the offer of a lift and had the doorman get her a cab.

As the taxi left the sheltered elegance of Beekman Place and turned northward into the tawdriness of First Avenue, Kate felt furious with herself. For all her fantasies of abandoning the squalid life of a working mother to become the chatelaine of a Maryland plantation, she knew she had done nothing more than make a powerful enemy in Sarah. And for what? To provide a few hours' exercise for the ego of a vain old man.

9

B.K. Tollover was too caught up in her own social life to pay great attention to her mother's. She was popular both with her classmates and with boys she had met at the Browning School and Dalton, several of whom tried but failed to fix her as their regular girl friend. More important to B.K. than any one boy was a dance series all her friends were talking about, the Chums. This series of four winter dances was a New York social institution; for girls who hoped to make a bona fide debut in New York society, admission to the Chums was an important first step. Then there was the Mets, a slightly older group, and finally the debutante big time, the New York Assemblies.

Girls could jump on this society conveyor belt at various stages, but their path was easier, they won pioneer status, if as thirteen and fourteen year olds they had belonged to the

Chums. B.K. did not think in terms of such calculated steps to social advancement. To her, the Chums were just a series of parties that her friends all were excited about, all aspired to, and most important, "All the most sensational boys go to it."

To B.K. and her schoolmates, sensationalness in a boy meant looks, polish, self-assurance—but it also meant money. They may not, at that age, have thought of their boyfriends' money as something they might profit from—although none of these adolescents were indifferent to a pre-dance dinner at a chic grown-up nightclub like La Rue or the Stork Club—but it meant having the wherewithal to attend a prestigious college like Harvard or Yale. Perhaps it meant that when the girls traveled to Europe the boys could too. It meant many such vague eventualities, but for the moment money meant the boys belonged to their group. The many uses of money were still vague to these girls, but its importance to a boy's allure was not.

Having none of her own, B.K. probably made less of this financial stipulation than her wealthier friends. She rather leaned toward dark eyelashes. As for the Chums, B.K., like most teenaged girls, needed little more motivation to want the parties than that all her friends wanted them. And like most teenagers, the more discouraging her mother was about her going, the more desperately she wanted to go.

Kate was chilled by the cost: two hundred dollars for four dances. A lot, Kate thought, for a party with no liquor and no dinner. Also, she was not certain B.K. could be accepted, although a friend later relieved this worry, saying, "Darling, the Tollover name is a lot better than many of the names of those who waltz into the damn thing."

Kate had been managing on the income her brother Harry provided, but she did it by budgeting to the penny. There was no two hundred dollars extra for four parties. Finally, when she could no longer stand B.K.'s pleadings, she agreed to ask her brother for the money the next time he was in New York.

"In a pig's eye!" was Harry's angry reply when Kate brought it up. "Now you listen to me, Kate. We're going to stop this right here. You got me to subsidize these damn snob schools on the grounds they were good education. Now you're twisting my arm for four dances because 'all her friends are going.' Well, I can see it coming. *All her friends* are going to have coming-out parties. *All her friends* are going to Europe, ride to the hounds, wear diamond tiaras, give to the poor . . . I'm not going to let it start. I told you when we began I had no use for that society bullshit. Even if I would pay for it, which I won't, it would ruin them, turn them into grabby little snots, looking down their noses at the rest of the world. You won't get one nickel from me for this program."

B.K. was working on her homework in her bedroom, which was separated from this diatribe by two walls, yet she heard every word. She could also hear her mother's quick collapse.

"All right, Harry, all right. It seems to mean so much to the girl, I just thought I'd ask. I won't mention it again." And then B.K. heard the familiar wind-up to all of their arguments about money, ". . . You mustn't think I don't appreciate all you're doing, Harry . . ."

B.K. told her best friend, Cissie Glover, that she couldn't go to the dances, admitting that her mother couldn't afford them. Cissie offered as much sympathy as anyone could wish from a friend, but still, B.K. noticed a look in Cissie's eyes, an almost invisible clicking shut, like a shutter faintly seen through the lens of a camera. The look stung B.K. and she wished she had a shield against this kind of superiority.

The night after Kate's argument with Harry, he had agreed to stay with B.K. while Kate went to a dinner party, a service Harry had often performed when he was in town, although B.K. preferred being sent to her father for the evening. Her uncle generally took her down the street to Schrafft's for an early dinner, then right back to the apartment for homework.

On this night, Harry announced with avuncular expansiveness that he was going to take B.K. for a treat. Where would she like to have dinner? Anyplace she liked. B.K. was nimblefooted enough not to blurt out the places she would really like, La Rue or the Stork Club, as she knew these chic choices would make her uncle uncomfortable. She asked if they might go to the restaurant in Rockefeller Center, the one with windows onto the skating rink.

"Why, sure, if you like. But if we're going to Rockefeller Center, why not the Rainbow Room?" For a minute B.K. was tempted, but remembering a magazine advertisement of the Rainbow Room that pictured an elongated couple in evening clothes sitting at a table with a champagne bucket by its side, decided the skating rink restaurant was a better choice for Uncle Harry.

Dinner was pleasant. Harry made an effort to jolly up B.K., tossing out questions about school, her friends, her activities. While she spooned into a chocolate parfait, she told her uncle a joke she had heard at school that sent him into spasms of laughter. The mood was so relaxed and warm that B.K. decided to try where her mother had failed.

"Uncle Harry," B.K. began in a tentative voice, "do you mind if I ask you something."

"Sure, go ahead," he said, still chuckling.

"I know mother already spoke to you about it, but would you let me explain why the Chums dances are so important to me?"

His expression shifted quickly to one of tight-jawed anger. "Go ahead," he said in a flat, low voice. "I'd be interested to hear."

"Well," B.K. started up enthusiastically, not sensing a trap. "All of my friends will be going. Everybody knows they are just the best parties of the year. It is a wonderful way to meet people from other schools, the boys down from boarding school for the holidays . . ."

"Do you really mean that *all* your friends will be there?"

"Well, not all of my friends, of course." She wondered how he knew that only a handful of her Chapin class would be going. She groped for some clarifying adjective. "But certainly all of the . . . nicest girls." B.K. heard how weakly the word fell on the table. For a terrible moment she thought her uncle was going to ask her definition of niceness, but he let it pass.

"You're rather caught up in all that social stuff, aren't you, B.K.?" Harry Knight was in control. He unwrapped a cigar and lit it with boss-man calm.

"I know it sounds frivolous to you, Uncle Harry, but it's not just the party and the fun and everything. It will let me get to know the nicest . . ." That word again. Oh, God. ". . . boys and girls, so that when I go to college, I'll know more kids than just those at my college, whatever that is; but suppose I end up at some dumpy place in Ohio or something, I'll still be friends with the boys and girls from the best families in New York."

Feeling herself on the ropes, B.K. was relieved to have come up with some justification other than all-purpose niceness.

"The best families. I see. Well, B.K., you're turning out just the way your mother wanted. And your father will be tickled pink. But you listen to me. In this world there are some very *nice* . . ." he spat out the word, ". . . people who have never been to your Chum dances. And if I have anything to say about it, you're going to be one of them."

"That's not fair, Uncle Harry. They're just parties, they're just fun, that's all. When you're my age, these things are very important . . ."

Her uncle handed the waiter the check with a fifty-dollar bill. "I see a difference. I'm sorry, B.K. I don't like the idea of those dances and I won't underwrite something I don't like."

B.K. now realized the trap she had been pushed into and it made her angry. She was a little ashamed that her uncle considered her such a snob, but he just didn't understand young people. With this rationale firm in her head, B.K.'s determination to get to the dances returned with full force. "Your father will be tickled pink . . ." Of course. Why hadn't she thought of it before? Her father would surely help her.

10

On his way into the shower, Tom Tollover stopped to admire his new chamois shirt from Dunhill's. How well it would look, he thought, with a green paisley scarf and his dark brown Harris tweed jacket. His schedule didn't include as many country events requiring this sort of outfit now that he had sold Mapleton and moved into town. But there were still house parties in Connecticut and Long Island; the shirt would also be ideal for after-ski sessions at Stowe.

It had been a relief to unload that enormous house; almost as great as the relief at no longer having to play the upright family man and provider. He could shrug off losing the house as an inevitability of the marital break-up, but it would have been more to the point, he sometimes admitted, to put it the other way around: his marriage broke up because he couldn't maintain the bloody house.

Who would have thought the Depression would drag on until Pearl Harbor? It had been *after* the goddamn crash that he'd made the traction windfall that enabled him to buy Mapleton. What reason was there to think it would be his only big deal in ten years? With the war, business had picked up for him, but not enough to pay off his debts and keep up with the skyrocketing costs.

Why did the big money always elude him? He couldn't stay up all night reading financial reports like some of the others—too boring. Besides, that was not the route to real money. You could hire the best securities analyst on the Street for ten thousand dollars a year. The guys making money were the ones with contacts, and God knew he had the contacts.

Why hadn't the business flowed his way, then? What was stopping his rich friends? Jealousy, maybe. Too popular with the wives, less so with the husbands? That wasn't it. The men liked him too, Tom knew. Too devil-may-care? That was more likely. Would you trust your family fortune to man who wore gardenias and danced down staircases?

So what? Life was too short. Most people were too boring, too afraid of violating convention, of living beyond their means, of living, period. Tom knew he was not boring and that was why he was sought after by the money-grubbing men and their cautious wives. Why should he have to grub? The Tollovers had always had money. Well, not always, but long enough for the habit to become fixed. If money had to be made, it should be made in a leisurely, gentlemanly way—not by staying up all night reading financial reports.

Tollover stripped off his silk dressing gown to step into the shower, stopping to appraise himself in the mirror. The face was holding up well, but he'd better be careful about a certain loosening of the skin of his torso. No fat, thank God, but still not as firm as it used to be. He took a pinch of flesh from the underside of his upper arm. Far too loose. More tennis, perhaps some squash at the Racket Club.

As the water assaulted his chest, he felt a surge of satisfaction about the turn his life had taken. The apartment he had found was ideal, small but in a chic building on Fifty-first Street not far from Beekman Place. For the first time since his marriage, he did not have brutal financial worries. The apartment cost a fraction of what Mapleton had cost. He had salvaged enough good furniture from the house to give his two-bedroom flat a look of urbanity, almost connoisseurship, that befit an aristocratic sensualist.

What a break Kate was not pressing him for support. Her request that he undertake the girls' medical and dental bills was most reasonable. For the first time since he could remember, he had a few dollars to spare. Maybe he would take Harriet to Nantucket for a few days. Or Prout's Neck. They could eat lobster and screw away the weekend. What a relief not to have to sneak his ladies off to the Traymore in Atlantic City where the corridors smelled of institutional deodorant and where there was never a fear of seeing "anyone" unless they were up to hijinks as reprehensible as his own.

Surely that was the biggest benefit from his changed life—the freedom to pursue his love affairs. He could go after whomever he wanted, wherever he wanted—in his clubs, at parties, on the tennis court, at the Stork Club, on Fifth Avenue. God, how he loved the chase! During the first years of his marriage to Kate, he had even relished the need for secrecy for the added challenge it presented. But that had quickly grown tiresome and interfered with the true pleasure: winning their attention, breaking down their resistance, refuting their objections, making them discard all considerations except wanting what he wanted as much as he wanted it—and then deftly extricating himself when they came to want it more.

The only drawback to the broken marriage, of course, was the separation from his daughters. No longer controlling his access to them, he found himself missing them more and more—particularly Augusta, who was reaching an age that interested him. She was becoming the kind of woman he most admired—striking, intelligent, reserved and with a cool style of her own. Now that all his training, advice and example were producing an exemplary young woman, he was not to be allowed to witness his triumph.

He would not take Harriet to Nantucket. He would spend the money instead on the girls. Perhaps he should take them to Bermuda over the Christmas holidays. No, he wasn't *that* far ahead. At least get them expensive presents for Christmas. Yes, that was it. What must they think of their Uncle Harry's supporting them? They thought *nothing* about it, if they were his daughters. Bills got paid somehow. Aristocrats gave the matter no more thought, and neither did kids.

Perhaps a fur coat for Augusta. She was looking shabby the last time he saw her. Not good for Walker's, where the little dears do everything but check each other's labels. How could Kate have let her go off to school that way? What did she and her junk-dealer brother know about boarding schools? Yes, nice presents. Also, he should take them on a special outing over the holidays. Perhaps a hit Broadway show. *Carousel* would be ideal. Terese could set that one up.

Harriet Deuprie, a slinky divorcée in her thirties, appeared in the bathroom door. "Hurry up, darling," she said in a throaty voice, "B.K. said she'd be here at six. You know you need at least twenty minutes in front of the mirror—even for your daughters."

"Especially for my daughters. I've taught them to abhor slovenliness. I can't appear before them looking like Jeeter Lester—green teeth, stubble beard. Would undermine the entire program. Be a sweetheart and get out some ice. And see if there's any ginger ale."

Tom dressed with his usual narcissistic care. He debated wearing the chamois shirt, but dismissed the notion as entirely inappropriate for a meeting with his younger daughter. Besides, he and Harriet were dining out that evening and he would have to change again. Tawdry of him to think of parading the new shirt. Nice people kept new clothes for weeks, even months, before wearing them. Let the drawers and closets get used to the garments, let them lose their smell of the stockroom, before delivering them from their dear little cellophane covers.

What could B.K. want to talk with him about? For once he wasn't terrified of a financial request. Had *he* ever wanted to talk with his parents about anything else since he was ten?

What suit to wear? They were dining with Cole Porter and Jean Howard at the Colony. A black pin-stripe and white shirt, because it was the Colony, and an outrageous necktie because it was Cole. He patted a handkerchief into his vest pocket, then splashed some cologne onto his cheeks. The dark hair fell into place with a few swipes of the silver military brushes, just as it always did. He checked the brushes for hairs. Almost none.

When he went out to the living room, B.K. was already there talking with Harriet. Good God, the girl was growing pretty. And a figure, too. Augusta was his favorite, and he'd always felt more ambition for his older daughter. It was not that she was smarter—she *was* smarter—but B.K. was smart enough. Rather it was a certain wary alertness that gave Augusta such a formidable potential. In addition, Tollover sensed a core of glistening brass inside Augusta that contrasted sharply with B.K.'s marshmallow goodfellowship.

But these looks of B.K.'s . . . They changed the proposition. He personally preferred the more exotic beauty of Augusta, whose features were clearly Tollover, clearly himself. But he knew that B.K.'s more conventional prettiness was highly marketable. And her personality was losing some of its gee-whiz sweetness. She seemed to be taking to New York social life with an impressive relish. She was proving adaptable and—this pleased Tollover most of all—appreciative of her opportunities.

B.K. rose from the sofa and greeted her father warmly. As he poured her ginger ale, she assured him that everything was going well for herself, her mother and Augusta. Tom handed B.K. her soda and Harriet a rye and soda.

Falteringly at first, but quickly picking up momentum, B.K. conveyed her keenness to subscribe to the Chums dance series and was encouraged by her father's familiarity with the parties. She said that her mother could not afford the two-hundred-dollar cost of the series and her Uncle Harry had turned her down flat.

"Don't say another word, darling," Tom cut in smoothly. "Of course I'll give you the two hundred dollars for the Chums. I just can't understand why your mother didn't come to me sooner about anything so important."

Yes, Tollover thought to himself, B.K. was going to be just fine.

11 Kate sat on her living-room sofa glancing through a copy of *The New York Times* she had brought home from the gallery. She noticed with mild interest that Bryce Hartshorne was being sent on a mission to Germany by President Truman. She had enjoyed their dinner together when Hartshorne had been in New York several weeks earlier. She had only been to Pavillon once before in her life, with Tom, for their tenth anniversary, as the guest of Uncle Jack.

Hartshorne had been amusing, relaxed and relaxing, in that he skillfully cut through his elder-statesman aura and talked easily about everyday matters. At the same time, he seemed happy to talk seriously with Kate about his State Department work and the swift and opposing currents swirling over Europe.

In one regard, he behaved quite differently from the night that they had met. He was no longer flirtatious; instead he treated Kate as a friend, perhaps a colleague. Lacking the safety of party playacting, he abandoned the ardent-suitor role, and kept the talk free of the innuendo and flattery that had dominated their first meeting. He also sent out a number of signals that he was not a prospect for matrimony. ("I've been married twice and made a hash of it both times. And I'm an even worse father than husband. My son considers me a reactionary stuffed shirt. His only pleasure is humiliating me. I was never cut out for family entanglements.")

All right, all right, Kate had thought, I won't plan the

redecoration of your plantation, but may I please finish my turbot in peace? She had considered ribbing him about his matrimony-phobia but felt that he might be even more alarmed at her bringing the subject into the open, even in a joking way. Also she liked him too much to risk offending him. He was excellent company. More than that, his fame and wealth gave Kate a rare bath in a kind of security she had never known, a security which, even on brief loan, gave respite to millions of strained, nervous ganglia.

She heard the bed groan in B.K.'s bedroom.

She could do with a little of the Hartshorne stability right now. B.K., who had always been a rock of equanimity, had fallen apart. Since receiving the monstrous letter of rejection from the Chums three days ago, B.K. had insisted Kate phone Chapin she was ill and refused to come out of her room except to poke at special meals Kate had labored over to revive her daughter's spirits. When B.K. ate only half a piece of her favorite Boston cream pie, Kate knew the trouble was serious. She tried talking to B.K. about the disaster, but got only "It doesn't matter," or "I don't really care for that kind of thing anyway."

Kate found the rejection had smashed the fragile structure of B.K.'s optimism and well-being. While the girl had never suffered from her family's poverty as much as Augusta, she was not, Kate knew, immune to the constant sting of having less than everyone around her. B.K.'s instincts, however, were optimistic; Kate could see that she had always taken solace in the things she *did* have: her looks, her ability to win friends and, to some extent, the pride her father had drilled into her in being a Tollover.

But what was acceptance to a dance series but affirmation of your popularity and your family's social standing? And the stiff white letter had said these two qualities, in her case, were insufficient. Only too aware of how insufficient the money was, this now left B.K. with nothing.

In desperation, Kate had phoned Tom Tollover, who was appalled at the development. He cross-examined Kate on her approach to the Chums. Satisfied with the recommendations used, he announced a mistake had clearly been made, and he would set things right. Just as he always had, Kate thought bitterly.

She considered phoning Augusta and asking her to come down from Walker's. The sisters were far closer than Kate had ever been with either. Perhaps Augusta could bring B.K. out of her despondency. Among other reasons Kate decided against this plan was the thought of making B.K.'s defeat the gossip of Ethel Walker's, as it soon would be of Chapin.

Kate's confusion and frustration jelled into anger. She decided that she would confront the woman who administered the series and ask her why her daughter had been refused. Kate knew quite well that such things were not done, and the knowledge of this social law—that one must accept kicks in the teeth like a lady—increased her determination to confront the bitch who had had her daughter weeping in her room for three days.

When Kate told B.K. her intention, B.K., in the first glimmer of life in days, said that she wanted to accompany her mother. Kate refused. It would be too brutal for the girl, and if Kate lost her temper, B.K.'s humiliation would be increased by the spectacle of her mother yelling like a Neapolitan streetwalker.

B.K. insisted. Kate mulled it over. Tactically, bringing along her pretty, almost beautiful daughter, with her fine cheekbones, her soft brown hair and her refined, gentle manner—such an unimpeachable exhibit A would demolish whatever trumped-up reasons the woman gave for the rejection. Kate knew Tom Tollover would be aghast at this tactic, so she didn't tell him. The next day she put on her smartest suit and hat, and with brave, pathetic white gloves for herself and her daughter, set out to see Miss Wyndham-Burn at her headquarters on East Eighty-first Street.

The office, in the living room of a dilapidated brownstone apartment, was a confused litter of paper-stuffed boxes, piles of magazines, card files, several flowered hats and an angry-looking cat. Miss Wyndham-Burn was a homely woman in her sixties whose upsweep hairdo was escaping in a number of gray wisps and whose pince-nez had cut two red furrows in her nose. She was clearly a woman who felt that a formidable aristocratic *savoir faire* could overcome the most disorderly office or unruly gray wisps. She received Kate with the icy civility of a duchess whose cook has come to ask for Christmas off.

"As I said in my letter, Mrs. Tollover, the membership was already full. There were no more openings."

"I assure you, Miss Wyndham-Burn, I would not have troubled to come here if I thought there was the slightest chance of that being the real reason. I happen to know that two girls were accepted on the day my daughter was refused. And one I know of received her acceptance the following day."

The older woman's eyes flashed as though grateful for this green light to let blood. "I was hoping, Mrs. Tollover, that you would recognize and accept tact. The committee who decided on the list felt that the financial resources at your disposal would put Belinda at a decided disadvantage with the other girls . . ."

"My daughter has a grandfather and an uncle both of substantial means. I can name three girls in your group who have neither."

"Money is not the prime consideration, although we have found that mixing girls of too widely disparate economic levels creates unhappiness."

Kate simply stared at Miss Wyndham-Burn, refusing to allow this red herring to conclude the matter. She would wait for the "prime consideration" if she had to sit there two hours. Her adversary, Kate saw, read her resolve.

"All right, Mrs. Tollover. You are forcing me to be brutal. The matter was decided on the basis of family. Your daughter was simply not distinguished enough. That was the decision of the committee."

Kate did not dare look at B.K. She cursed herself for having subjected her to this. "That is absurd. The Tollovers are a highly respected and old family . . ."

"The Tollovers, my dear lady, are marginal at best. But I am afraid, Mrs. Tollover, it was *your* family that tipped the scales away from acceptance. Now if you will excuse me . . ."

"My family!" Kate knew that her family, while in no way distinguished, was free of any of the notoriety or religious and ethnic taint that were usually cited in these siftings of the worthy from the unworthy. She could see by the hostile triumph of the dragon's face that Miss Wyndham-Burn believed that Kate's deficient bloodlines were the blackballing obstacle— as well as the justice of the reason.

Kate was certain that even this brutal excuse was not the true reason. Family was never an element if there were other claims—money, popularity, and, in Kate's case, a socially prominent husband—provided the family was, like Kate's, no worse than a Protestant nonentity. When the sting of the woman's insult subsided, Kate was convinced of her suspicion: some other force was at work, something vindictive.

"Miss Wyndham-Burn," she said, "I insist on knowing the names of the people on your selection committee."

"I am not at liberty to divulge them. Besides, there would be no point. I'd have thought this meeting would have convinced you of that."

"On the contrary, it has convinced me that a stupid blunder has been made. It would be laughable, if it were not so destructive to a thirteen-year-old girl."

Walking with her daughter up Madison Avenue, Kate attemped to disentangle the tentacles of her rage. She was no longer angry at the Chums' admissions apparatus and at snobbery in general; she was angry at herself for having let B.K. witness the degrading scene. They walked in silence for several blocks. Then, waiting for a green light, B.K. turned to her and said, "Why did Daddy always make us think the Tollover family was something so red hot?"

Kate, who had grown sick of the same boast, was surprised to hear herself reply, "It is, darling. Something else is behind this."

Kate got on the phone with her friend Thea Pomeroy, who was always an excellent source of information. She was able to give Kate the name of one member of the Chums' admission committee and would call her back with the others. When Thea phoned twenty minutes later she sounded contrite.

"I think I've found the problem and I feel I am to blame."

"Whatever do you mean, Thea?"

"Well, there are only two other members of the selection committee and one is Sarah Rusk."

At first Kate was dumbfounded, then perversely delighted. She laughed out loud. "Don't worry, Thea. If I insist on vamping other women's beaus at your house, it is not your fault." Kate felt relief that the problem was so petty and personal. As she talked with Thea, she was wondering how to deal with it. Surely it was far easier to combat than the invisible wall of mindless snobbery. Still, Sarah was powerful and not one, as this astounding revenge proved, to cross lightly.

Kate took heart as she realized that Sarah had made a bad mistake and left herself vulnerable. But how to rectify things without inflating the feud and increasing the scandal? In her anger she thought of phoning Hartshorne in Germany. Then she pictured him being pulled from the highest councils of government to deal with a teenager's party invitation, and she ruled out that approach. It was incongruous, and in addition, Kate thought of his horror at anyone, even the jealous Sarah, putting such a loaded reading on their friendship.

Kate thought of writing the other members of the committee, accusing Sarah of misusing her power over thirteen-year-old girls to settle personal scores with their mothers. This was a definite possibility, but as a last resort, not an opening salvo. It was better to avoid putting such squalid things in writing. The same applied to writing an angry letter to Sarah. Could she confront Sarah directly? Would Sarah let her? Perhaps a less sententious note with no hostility and no specifics, just a vague statement that Kate was aware of Sarah's "action" and planned "to pursue the matter" unless Sarah rectified "things" immediately. Yes. That was it.

"But Kate darling," Sarah said two days later when Kate phoned her, "your cryptic note made no sense to me whatever. I don't even know your daughter, do I?"

"Listen to me. You have done a frightful thing. You are using your pathetic power to hurt me through a thirteen-year-old girl. I will make a nasty scandal of this unless you call Miss Wyndham-Burn right away. I have done nothing to you. It is in your head. But even if I had, show enough character to retaliate against me, not a child."

"But, darling, you are mad. You can't prove one bit of what you are ranting on about."

"I don't have to. The few people who know what has happened—that B.K. was turned down and you sit on the acceptance committee—none of them have the slightest doubt that you are to blame. It is an unavoidable conclusion. And frankly, it makes you look ridiculous."

"Now Kate, calm down, for God's sake. A row with you is the last thing that I want. I can understand your being upset that your daughter was turned down. Perhaps I can help. I will talk to the others."

Kate told Tom what had happened. He laughed. "Is that all it is? That's what you get for stealing other women's septuagenarians. Rich old bachelors are prime catches, you know. No one gives them up lightly."

"Bryce is not old. He does not belong to Sarah. And I don't want him. Stick to the point. Do you think she'll come around?"

"She would have anyhow. I've called about ten people, all of whom will be contacting members of the committee. Three I know of plan to phone Sarah. She will have no choice."

The phone call finally came from Miss Wyndham-Burn saying that several cancellations had made it possible to accept Belinda. If Mrs. Tollover would send in the check for two hundred dollars . . .

The battle was over. Kate marveled at the forces marshaled to keep a thirteen year old from going to a party. B.K. resumed her old cheerful insouciance and quickly reignited her excitement about the dance series and about Augusta's imminent return for the Christmas holidays. Sympathetic friends had seen that B.K. was invited to three dinner parties before the first dance. But now, not far beneath B.K.'s pretty, sunny surface, Kate noticed, was a thin crust of cynicism that had not been there before.

12

Augusta told her friend Martie about the Jamaica lie. Just telling someone, even someone sworn to secrecy, made Augusta feel less dishonest. It turned a fraud into a prank. Martie was sympathetic, but surprised that Augusta would care enough about such things to lie. Martie responded by inviting Augusta to spend the last three days of their holidays with her and her parents at their farm in Vermont.

Augusta's elaborate deception wiped out what little fun she might have had in New York during the holidays. She had been invited to two parties—one was a glamorous supper dance at the Cosmopolitan Club—but she had refused, saying she would be in Jamaica. She had trapped herself in this ridiculous sham; the lie was already punishing her and she might, in the bargain, suffer the humiliation of disclosure. Never again.

Augusta was excited about seeing her father and B.K., but the holidays would be soured by the fear of running into a classmate. The invitation to stay at Martie's home in Vermont not only brightened the vacation prospect, but allowed her to shift her focus away from the world of monied society, for which she felt woefully ill-equipped and in which she felt she was failing ludicrously.

In that period between Thanksgiving and Christmas, Augusta's life at Walker's brightened considerably. Perhaps she was more relaxed and less defensive. Maybe the Jamaica lie had made her see what a close brush she had had, was having, with a humiliation far worse than not being able to afford a winter vacation. Perhaps fear of exposure made her make more of an effort with her classmates. Whatever it was, her popularity burgeoned and she found herself enjoying school far more.

Sandra MacNeil came to Augusta in despair over her schoolwork. She would flunk out, she knew it. Her mother would never forgive her. She would never get into a decent college. Her life would be ruined. When Augusta offered to help, Sandra accepted so fast Augusta could tell that was just what the other girl had been hoping for. Several evenings a week Augusta would spend two to three hours guiding Sandra through the thickets of trigonometry, European history and the French irregular verbs.

There was a tea dance with a busload of Choate boys, for

which Augusta's class donned their dress uniforms and lined up along one side of the room and glowered at the enemy tittering and playing buffoons along the opposite wall. Augusta could see how grotesque and silly the ritual was but that awareness didn't prevent her from sliding into a pit of embarrassment and self-consciousness that all but immobilized her.

Augusta was saved by a glimpse of Martie Dean, who was visibly trembling. And why wouldn't she? Martie was shy even with a close friend like Augusta, someone she knew wished her well. Where would she find the confidence to deal with these homicidal savages? And poor Martie brought so little to the opposite sex—stringy hair, a bad complexion, and a limp figure whose meager assets were wiped out by a slouch that bordered on a cringe.

Another glimpse, this one of Minnie Blanchard, dauntless with her chunky body and round, red face, propelled Augusta's confidence to the heights. In a second Augusta threw off her anxiety and proclaimed herself better looking than most of the girls and smarter than most of the boys. And then, too, came the awareness that here at last she was on her own—she succeeded or failed on her own merits, not her family's money or position.

Later she would discover that these oversexed, underpoised schoolboys were as concerned with such snob considerations as they were with the size of a girl's breasts, that they knew, if not in advance, within the initial fifteen minutes, which girls had fortunes, which would have big debuts and which had fathers who could help their careers. But at this first dance, Augusta warmed to the fantasy that she had found a milieu where it was herself alone who would determine her success or failure. She loved the feeling. She also loved the enforced superficiality of it all. There could be no probing conversations, none of the heart-to-hearts which both boys and girls of her age seemed to cherish and which she loathed. She would not be judged by how much sympathy she could dredge up for one boy's hatred of his stepmother, another's fear of flunking out. She was not good at feigning such feelings. She would be judged by the way she could banter and by the way she walked across a room. She knew she bantered with more spirit than most and that she walked across a room very well.

Once in New York, Augusta got so caught up in the excitement of pre-Christmas Manhattan, she forgot about the glamorous vacation spots she would not be visiting. She was dazzled by the window displays, the Christmas decorations in the stores and the beautifully-dressed women on upper Madison Avenue. She and B.K. would walk the few blocks to Yorkville, where Eighty-sixth Street was arched with lights and where the German stores behaved as though Christmas were a German folk festival.

By planning carefully, Augusta could afford the presents she had picked out for her father, mother and B.K.—then have enough left for a sun lamp. If she could return to Walker's with a tan, that would settle the annoying Jamaica business. But what if someone forgot she was in the Caribbean and phoned her New York apartment? Was Buffie horrible enough to get someone to phone? Probably. Augusta shrugged off these fears; if she were found out, she would simply say her father's business commitments forced them to abandon the trip. She told herself to stop worrying.

August commiserated with B.K. about a dress for the first Chums. "All the others are going to Bergdorf's and de Pinna for their dresses," B.K. moaned, "and I have to wear that thing mother made."

Augusta promised to look at the dress to see if there was a way to improve it.

On her second day home, they were in Abercrombie's looking for presents when Augusta was chilled to hear a girl's voice call out, "Augusta, why aren't you in Jamaica?" It was Sandra MacNeil, who had come in from Long Island to shop for presents. The day after Christmas, she told them breathlessly, she was flying with her parents to St. Moritz for a week.

"We didn't go," Augusta said. "I'll phone you and explain everything."

"Why don't we have lunch? I have to come in again on Friday to buy some clothes for Switzerland. Let's have a chic lunch someplace terribly grand."

[80]

"I don't know, Sandra . . ."

"I'll treat. Then we can go shopping together."

"That will be nice. But don't tell anyone I'm in town. I'll explain everything Friday."

"I love intrigue. I can't wait."

They met in the Edwardian Room of the Plaza. Augusta had never been there before; it immediately became her favorite room in New York. She loved its vastness, its high ceilings and most of all the huge windows overlooking Central Park. So many of the fancy restaurants Augusta had seen in Manhattan were totally closed in. If there was a window to the street, it was curtained in heavy velvet to create permanent, seasonless night. Here she could look out at the bundled-up Christmas shoppers passing by, see patches of snow at the edge of the park and the steamy breath of the carriage horses. In front of her was a large expanse of white-linen tablecloth, an array of heavy hotel plated silver, and a vase of pink carnations.

"I like restaurants with more chic," Sandra said. "You never see any fabulous people here. But I can charge our lunch and that makes everything much simpler."

Augusta thought how, on the other occasions she had been taken to lunch by contemporaries, it had been at private clubs where paying the check had been simple to the point of invisibility. The two girls discussed ordering a cocktail, then decided they probably wouldn't get away with it.

"Let's have the eggs Benedict. They're terrific. Have you ever had them?"

Augusta said she couldn't remember if she had, but would like to try them. Sandra ordered the eggs and then said, "So tell me, what happened about Jamaica? I was so thrilled for you and B.K., getting a wonderful trip like that—and with your father, too."

"Well, that's just it," Augusta said, "he couldn't get away from his office. Some important stock deal I don't understand. But from the start that ghastly Buffie French hinted she didn't think I was really going. I hate giving her the satisfaction of being right, so do you mind not letting on we saw each other in New York?"

"Oh, sure. I can't stand Buffie either. I'll tell her I got a postcard from you covered with the most beautiful foreign stamps."

"That would be terrific of you, Sandra." For some reason Augusta noticed that she no longer resented Sandra's sympathy and began thinking how nice it was to have a friend who could charge lunch at the Plaza and lie for you. Perhaps the difference was that now she felt Sandra in her debt over the tutoring.

Sandra started talking about Walker's. "I like it well enough, I suppose. There are some neat girls there, don't you think? But God! It's a lot tougher than I thought it would be! If it hadn't been for your helping me, Augusta, I don't think I would have made it this far."

After lunch they went first to Bergdorf's, where Augusta watched Sandra buy a fur-trimmed ski parka, five pairs of hand-knit knee socks and a pair of red leather mittens.

"Let's go to de Pinna's," Sandra gushed, her acquisitive juices coursing through her. "They have the best sweaters. Surely you must need a sweater."

Maybe it was the suggestion, but at de Pinna Augusta saw a sweater she fell in love with. It was a cashmere cardigan, a deep burgundy that looked wonderful, she felt, against her dark hair. She knew Sandra noticed her trying it on, then removing it and folding it slowly. Sandra came over to her. "Why don't you get it, Augusta? It looked sensational on you."

"I can't afford it. I've bought my Christmas presents and . . ."

"Oh, that's right," Sandra said matter-of-factly. "You never have any money. I'll get it for you."

Augusta knew she was at a dangerous juncture but felt a strange excitement. "Oh, Sandra, I couldn't let you do that," she said with no determination.

"Of course I can. I'll just charge it. It will be my Christmas present to you."

Augusta looked at her for a moment, then smiled. "That would be terrific of you, Sandra."

Later, burdened with packages, they went to Schrafft's for milkshakes, which Augusta had suggested and intended paying for. Sitting at the counter stirring a straw in her mocha shake,

Sandra said, "Look, Gus, you've always been very nice to me and now you are really saving my life at Walker's. I know you don't have much money and I really should do something in return for what you do for me. I mean, why shouldn't you get something out of it? Well, I have a terrific idea. I have charge accounts at a bunch of clothing stores. I can charge whatever I want—within reason, of course. I mean, I couldn't charge a mink coat. They would notice. But routine stuff. Well, I have enough clothes to outfit five Walker's girls. I can cool it for myself and charge things for you! Whatever you need. In return you see to it I don't flunk out of Walker's. How's that for a deal?"

Augusta turned and looked directly at her. "Are you sure your parents wouldn't notice?"

"They never see the bills. They're paid by Mr. Wexler down on Wall Street. If we try the mink coat, he'd be sure to phone my father, but anything else, he just sends off the old check. I noticed that coat you had on coming down on the train. It was positively morbid. Let's go out right now and get you a better one."

Augusta's mind raced. How could she explain a new coat to her mother? Hide it? No, she would want to use it here in New York more than anyplace. She could tell her mother she was earning money at Walker's. But how? Of course, she was tutoring other girls. But she should plant the idea in her mother's mind, let it germinate, before showing up with a new overcoat.

For Augusta and B.K. Christmas itself was a fragmented occasion marked with forced gaiety. They spent Christmas Eve with their mother and Uncle Harry. Kate had trimmed a tree and presented a roast beef to celebrate the end of rationing as much as the holiday. Each girl received a fifty-dollar savings bond from their uncle. Augusta got a green lambs' wool cardigan sweater from her mother, B.K. a badly needed raincoat.

They were to have eaten Christmas dinner with their father at their great-uncle Jack's apartment, but Tom Tollover had a falling-out with his uncle and took them instead to the Knickerbocker Club, where he made a show of his two daughters to the friends who stopped at their table. He would embarrass them with remarks like "That son of yours better get his bid in before these beauties get snatched up." Or, to another, "I've trained them to be duchesses. Consuelo Vanderbilt was only seventeen, wasn't she, when her mother married her off to the Duke of Marlborough?"

Augusta no longer thrilled to her father's grandiose visions. The Jamaica story and her new arrangement with Sandra had made her feel sharply the difference between leading the good life and *appearing* to lead it when you had no money. She felt increasing disgust for this sort of pretense and, to the extent which she had attempted it, disgust with herself. In a few days she would be going off to visit Martie Dean in Vermont. Until then she would steep herself in reading good authors—she had just discovered E.M. Forster—and struggle with some writing of her own.

Her other side, however, took satisfaction in knowing she would be leaving home this time with two new sweaters, a navy-blue wool coat from Bergdorf's and a tan she might have gotten under the Caribbean sun.

13

So far it had been the most thrilling night of B.K.'s life and it was only ten-thirty. Her mother had said she could stay out until one. That was two-and-a-half hours more of paradise, three hours if she pushed her mother's patience. She had never seen a party like the dinner one of her classmates gave in her parents' East Sixties brownstone. The house was not large but, B.K. thought, the most elegant she had ever seen. The living and dining rooms were up a curved flight of stairs from the street and had been filled with small round tables accommodating four or six dinner guests. Black butlers in dinner clothes had served her classmates and their boy friends a shrimp bisque and then filet mignon with a yellow sauce with specks in it that had been the most delicious food B.K. had ever tasted.

While they were eating a fabulous chocolate dessert, a woman named Martha Wright, who B.K.'s dinner companion told her was a big Broadway star, sang for them all. She had been so close and looked beautiful as she strolled among the tables in the flickering candlelight.

Because it was a freezing night, after dinner they all took taxis the few blocks to the Ritz Hotel for the Chums. At the ballroom entrance, Miss Wyndham-Burn sat at a table checking names. She wore a blue velvet evening dress but otherwise looked as disheveled as before.

The ballroom was incredibly beautiful and, to keep from exploding with pleasure, B.K. had to remind herself of how close she had come to missing all this. The thought of the rejection letter stunned her for a moment. Her mother had tried to hide the real reason she had been turned down, but B.K. had overheard enough to gather an inkling of what had happened. Then at Chapin one day, Cissie Glover had rushed to her before the first bell with the Sarah Rusk story. B.K. had been dumbfounded that a grown-up woman—and from a good family—could be horrible enough, cruel enough, to try to keep *her*, B.K. Tollover, from her natural place at the Chums.

Another aspect of the business intrigued B.K.—that her mother was capable of alluring a man and rousing the jealousy of another woman. B.K. was aware of men phoning her mother and occasionally calling for her in the evening, but she had viewed these attentions as adult companionship, a social, not sexual, business. So impressed was she by this new view of her mother, B.K. sat down and wrote Augusta a detailed account of the entire affair, starting with the letter of rejection.

Suddenly, en route to the Ritz ballroom, B.K. tripped. To her horror she saw that the hem of her skirt was opening and trailing on the floor. She could have killed her mother for not sewing with steel thread. God did not want her to dance and have fun with the snappiest group of young people in America. B.K. looked around desperately for Cissie. She spotted her about to settle at a nearby table and gestured frantically for her to come.

Cissie was sympathetic. She was sure someone they knew would have a safety pin in her evening bag. She parked B.K. on an upholstered bench in front of an enormous mirror and went off looking for a pin.

Inside the ballroom the orchestra was playing its most insistent good-times rhythm song, "The Lady Is a Tramp." Latecomers hurried through the foyer, eager to get onto the dance floor. Most of the boys were rather odd-looking young men from Andover and St. Paul's, so awash in arrogant self-confidence that they were oblivious to such flaws in themselves as plain faces, pimples or glasses. They raced toward the dance floor with their partners, their elbows flapping in time with the beat, spinning onto the floor with an air of belonging even Fred Astaire would have found impressive.

B.K. noticed a very handsome young man enter by himself. His dark hair was longer than the close, military trims of the other boys, and B.K. would have taken him for an Italian waiter except for his elegant, erect bearing and the calm assurance with which he passed in front of her. He noticed B.K., paused, then walked toward her. Oh, God. Wallflower, abandoned, disabled, in need of repairs—his being the best-looking boy she had ever seen made it worse.

"You look troubled," he said with a slight accent. "May I be of assistance?"

"I'm fine, just fine, thank you. I am waiting for a friend." I would do anything for those eyelashes, she thought.

"Ah, good. Then I will see you inside." He bowed slightly and, without smiling, turned and went into the ballroom.

Cissie came running out. "No one has a pin, but Gerrie told me that maybe the ladies' room attendant will have one. Let's go."

The attendant did better than hoped. She sewed the hem, in return for which B.K. rated the emaciated old lady on a par with Molly Pitcher, Amelia Earhart and Mary Cassatt as a truly great American woman. B.K. gave her a precious dollar and headed back into the ballroom arm in arm with Cissie, to whom she swore revenge on an unjust world.

"Getting to this damn party has been harder than taking Guadalcanal. I'm going to vamp the richest, most social snot at this party. I'm going to snare him, then break his heart. Lead him to his ruin. Point him out to me, Cissie. You know all the big wheels."

B.K. knew most of the crowd at Cissie's table and a boy she knew immediately asked her to dance. Once on the floor, B.K. began to relax. When she returned to the table, Cissie leaned over and whispered, "I've picked out your prey. The perfect boy for you to destroy."

"Oh, good. Which one?"

"That guy at the next table talking to Aggie."

B.K. looked over her shoulder and saw the dark-haired boy from the foyer. He smiled and nodded at B.K., who thought she smiled back but couldn't be sure if her face was responding to her brain.

"I can't ruin that boy's life."

"Why ever not?"

"Besides you and the ladies' room attendant, he's the only person here who's been nice to me."

"I'm sorry, B.K. You swore to destroy the richest, most social guy here, and hands down, that's him. He's Paulo Colonna. His mother is a Venezuelan oil heiress and his father is from one of the oldest families in Italy. He goes to St. Paul's and—I haven't told you the clincher—he's a prince."

"I know, Cissie," B.K. said with exaggerated boredom. "They all are."

"No, I mean a *titled* prince. The Colonnas are the real stuff, like the Borgias and the, well, you know. They have a gigantic palazzo in Rome, a house in New York and God knows what else. And Paolo has been around. He had a date with Princess Margaret Rose and he knows everybody in Europe."

"Charles de Gaulle?"

"Probably."

"Well, okay, I'll vamp him. It won't be hard. But I don't know about destroying his life. We'll see."

Cissie had already forgotten Paolo Colonna. "Oh, B.K., see that girl over there—with the wavy blonde hair? That's Peggy Bedford. Try to get to know her. Standard Oil. She's sure to have one of the best coming-out parties ever."

B.K. felt a pang of anxiety as she always did when the subject of debuts came up, but the party spirit of the Chums soon swept her up. She danced with all the boys she knew and one or two new boys who cut in. When Paolo finally cut in, she was at peak form.

"I've been watching you," he said. "Someone cuts in on you every three-and-a-half minutes on an average. That is not enough time for me to get to know you, so I must act quickly. May we sit down?"

"I'd like that," B.K. replied. "I'm out of breath."

She felt nervous. He seemed so refined, self-assured, intelligent. B.K. felt awkward, ignorant, unsophisticated, a girl with a torn hem. Maybe Augusta could handle this prince or whatever he was, but he was clearly too much for old B.K. As he pulled out her chair, B.K. noticed beautiful studs of dark red stones on his chest.

They exchanged names and schools. "You live in the city then?" he said. "So do I."

"How come you have an accent?"

"It's dreadful, isn't it?" he said in exquisite English. "I was born in Italy, but my father was against the Fascists. So during the war we lived in New York. We Italians are in disgrace with Americans right now, isn't it so?"

"I don't understand all that," B.K. said, happy to have a chance to be charitable. "It got so confusing after Mussolini was killed. But you weren't there, anyhow. You were here. It's not your fault your country fought on the wrong side."

"It was not easy for my father. All of his friends were Fascists. We will go back now, but we have no idea how it will be for us."

B.K. looked into his soft, dark eyes and hoped fervently that it would be all right. "Those beautiful studs. Are they rubies?"

"Yes. They were a gift to my grandfather, who was the Italian ambassador to Siam. For rubies, they are unusually dark."

"Your family sounds horrendously distinguished."

"Very old, certainly, but don't make me sound like one of those Puccis who are always boasting how much older their family is than the Medici."

"What makes the Colonna family so important?"

"Back in the Middle Ages, they fought, bullied and plundered better than any other family except possibly the Gaetanis, who were equally rapacious. It is amusing to me how ancient families look down on the newer families for having made their mark in commerce—the Medici, for example, were bankers. But the really old families achieved their prominence, or rather their wealth, with a club or a long bow—not very admirable, really, and certainly not very refined."

B.K. was dazzled. "But I'm sure they did something more than rob and wound people."

"I suppose. In our family, there have been four popes. Whatever sanctity that lends our name is wiped out by another ancestor who tried to murder Pope Boniface the Eighth with his bare hands."

B.K. looked at Paolo's delicately veined hand, so dark on the white tablecloth. In those veins, she thought, rushes the blood of popes, and murderers of popes. How insignificant such a history made the silly boasts of people like Tom Tollover, Sarah Rusk, even Miss Wyndham-Burn.

"You must find our snobbish families over here a joke," she said.

"I don't like snobbism anywhere. But I disagree with you about your country's families. America is a great country. The families who created it have every reason to be proud—more so, I think, than families like mine who have done very little the last five hundred years."

B.K. smiled graciously, knowing full well that, to the snobs around her, what a family accomplished was far less important than how far back it went. How fabulous it would be, she thought, to have five hundred years' worth of protection against the Wyndham-Burns and anyone else who tried to make her feel cheap and not good enough. Then one of the boys B.K. knew came over and asked her to dance.

"You see. Even hiding with you, I am not safe."

Later on, when Paolo had cut in on her for the third time, he asked if she would go with him to La Rue after the party. She lied and told him she had already made plans with someone else.

How could she tell an Italian prince that her mother would kill
her if she wasn't home by one?

Kate Tollover was up reading when B.K. came in, still
floating on a wave of Lester Lanin rhythms.

"You had a good time then?" Kate asked, pleased to see her
daughter so happy.

"Unbelievable, Mummie! There will be a man calling in the
morning with one glass slipper. Please don't send him away."

"How was your dress?"

"My dress? Oh, fabulous. Well, I mean, it started coming
apart at the beginning . . ."

"Coming apart! Oh, B.K., I'm so sorry. What did you do?"

"It was nothing. The ladies' room lady fixed it. No problem.
But let me tell you the incredible thing that happened! I met a
prince. A real one. From Italy. And he is the most beautiful
boy, person, I have ever seen. And he's not a boorish yo-yo like
most of those Andover boys. He's refined and gentle and so
handsome!"

B.K. gushed on for a while until Kate sent her to bed. B.K.
was so wide awake she thought of phoning Augusta but
remembered that Augusta was visiting the Deans and would not
arrive at Walker's for another three days. She fell off to sleep
thinking of swarthy men with thick, dark eyelashes strangling
popes. She was completely in love.

14

"Don't be fooled by all this marble and gilt,"
Minnie called over her shoulder as she carried Augusta's suitcase
up the enormous staircase. "My mother and I are strictly poor
relatives in this place. Sweep out the stables, polish the silver—
that's how we pay our rent."

Augusta had never seen a house like it, except maybe the
Phipps' estate in Old Westbury, or mansions in one or two
European films. As they entered the driveway, they could see
the house, on a distant hill like a Loire château with formal

gardens spread out before it. When the chauffeur dropped them at the front door, they were greeted by a butler but Minnie sent him away, saying she would take Miss Tollover to her room.

Passing through the broad entrance hall, Augusta received a quick impression of antique tapestries, classic statuary and huge vases full of fresh flowers. There had also been enticing glimpses into exquisite rooms—one light, delicate and French-looking, another dark-paneled and masculine. On the landing there was a magnificent portrait of an eighteenth-century aristocrat— Catherine the Great? Marie Theresa?

Still chattering, Minnie led Augusta into a bright corner room. The large bed was canopied in white organza, and two pink velvet armchairs flanked a pink marble fireplace. From the window a view of vast lawns and the rolling terrain of Radnor, Pennsylvania, could have been the English midlands. As Minnie chattered on, Augusta's eye was caught by a solitary gardener, carrying a basket through the rose gardens, picking up random twigs and dead leaves.

"You have arrived in the nick of time, Gus. Things have not been too great on the parental front. I seem to have screwed up again. My mother is *très* pissed at me. You won't believe what happened. Some ring-tailed bitch friend of my mother's spotted me smoking on the streets of Haverford and felt it her ring-tailed-bitch duty to call Mother and report me. Can you imagine such a prick? One tiny Camel! Was it hurting her? If you want my opinion she was hoping to worm her way in with Mother so she'd snag an invitation to one of Granny's do-do's. You see, the Blanchards are considered pretty hot stuff in these parts—well, you saw for yourself all the white gravel. I'm an innocent victim of their jerk-off social climbing. Can you beat it? I'm a member of the goddamn family and they finger *me* to get in good with my old lady. God, do I hate that bitch!"

"What did your mother do?" Augusta said as the gardener disappeared behind some bushes. She turned back to the room and started to open her suitcase to unpack.

"Oh, don't touch that. The maids will think you're trash like me if you don't let them nose through your things on the pretext of hanging them up. And whenever you're finished with a blouse or something, just drop it on the floor. You're barely out of the room, and one of the creeps swoops in, picks it up and washes and irons it before you get back. Granny runs a tight ship."

"What was your punishment?" Augusta persisted.

"Oh, yeh. Mom confined me to quarters. It happened four days ago and since then I haven't been allowed out of the house. Four days of a ten-day spring vacation! She said I had to stay in till you got here. If you'd called up and canceled I would have staged a break. Getting out wouldn't have been so hard. Christ, I've done it a hundred times! It's just all the extra aggravation when I get caught. I suppose it might have been worse. They might have canceled my trip to Europe this summer."

"Trip to Europe? You didn't mention that."

"Didn't I? Yeh. They're sending me with a friend of theirs whom you'll meet later, a Mrs. Fort. They want me to get some polish and a little culture. I plan to cheer up the G.I.'s that haven't made it home yet."

Augusta took the burgundy cashmere sweater from her bag and smoothed it, still folded, against her body as they planned Minnie's first day of freedom. If the weather was good they would go for a picnic on horseback. Minnie said she could get the cook to pack them a hamper that evening so they could take off in the morning. "My grandfather sometimes likes to go for an early ride—or he did—so he insists on a groom getting to the stables every morning by seven."

There was a knock on the door and a butler appeared. "Excuse me, Miss Blanchard, Mrs. Blanchard would like you and your guest to join her in the Hepplewhite Room at seven o'clock."

"Thank you, Jasper." He vanished. "I hope you brought a dressy dress, Gus, it gets pretty formal around here."

"I did. What about your grandmother? Will I meet her?"

"Whenever one of these stiffs says 'Mrs. Blanchard' they're referring to Granny. Mother hated my fortune-hunting father so much she went back to her maiden name—and took me with her. She calls herself Mrs. Blanchard, but to the servants she is 'Miss Agnes.' I'm 'Miss Blanchard.' If I screw up anymore around here, she might change me back to my father's name. You get cleaned up and dressed while I go talk to the cook about tomorrow. I'll pick you up at two minutes to seven. As I was saying, Granny runs a tight ship."

The elder Blanchards were haughtily formal with Augusta at first, but warmed slightly to her impeccable manners and to her many other attributes at variance with their granddaughter's. Minnie's mother, on the other hand, was from the start friendly to Augusta. She was a large woman, not particularly attractive but with a country-gentlewoman style that was familiar to Augusta. Mrs. Blanchard also seemed to have a cautious reticence that Augusta rarely saw among rich adults; the poor woman had probably developed it, Augusta thought, living under her parents' stately roof with the boisterous Minnie.

Another woman present, about the same age as Mrs. Blanchard, was introduced as Mrs. Fort. She said little during cocktails and sat quietly working on a needlepoint cushion cover as if she were part of the family. When she finished her whiskey and soda, Mr. Blanchard made her a fresh drink without speaking.

The gathering was clearly Minnie's first return from banishment; Augusta sensed that everyone present was trying not to let their anger with Minnie carry over to her innocent house guest. The talk was about the house and gardens, how beautiful the dogwood would soon be and how Minnie must take her guest the next day to see the spring garden.

A butler announced dinner and Augusta and Minnie followed the older people through a vast, dimly lit dining room into a smaller dining room beyond: a pavilion with French doors on three sides opening onto a terraced lawn, with a gracefully arched ceiling and a floor of green-and-white marble of an intricate design. The round table was set sumptuously for five—long-stemmed crystal, green service plates with gold borders and in the center a large gold bowl filled with cream-colored roses.

Augusta was seated to the right of old Mrs. Blanchard, who asked her polite questions about school and her family. Augusta felt that she should inaugurate some conversation. She remembered her father's saying that, no matter how rich people are, they never mind talking about their possessions.

"Mrs. Blanchard," Augusta said, "that beautiful portrait on the stair landing, is that Marie Antoinette?"

"No, my dear, it is the Duchess de la Moilles, a contemporary of Louis the Fifteenth. It is a handsome work, isn't it?"

"It's a Boucher," Mr. Blanchard said, coming to life for the first time. "Would you believe we found it in a small shop in Vichy before the war. A Boucher! Should have been in the Louvre, and there it was. We had Fiske Kimball authenticate it for us, of course, and it's the real McCoy. They weren't giving it away, not by a long shot, but still not asking anything like what it was worth . . ."

Mrs. Fort spoke. "Many think it is as fine as his portrait of Madame de Pompadour, isn't that so, Elsie?" she said, turning to old Mrs. Blanchard.

"What did you say? Now that I'm losing my hearing, you've taken to mumbling. I didn't understand a word."

"I was just saying it's as fine in many people's eyes as . . ."

"Of course we had a devil of a time getting it out of France," Mr. Blanchard interrupted as though Mrs. Fort weren't there.

For the rest of the meal, Augusta was included in all conversation. She had established herself as a person in their eyes by the simple ploy of appreciating one of their possessions.

After dinner, the two girls excused themselves and Minnie took Augusta on a tour of the house. Even tomboy Minnie was enthusiastic over the room fitted out with European plunder—furniture from a Loire château, wood paneling from an English manor house, paintings from French and Italian castles. Stopping in front of a painting over the fireplace in the main drawing room, Minnie said, "Now this little number is supposed to be the most valuable item in the whole goddamn house . . ."

Augusta recognized a pastoral scene by Watteau.

"I'm not sure how much it's worth, but I think a hundred thousand easily. Can you imagine the time we could have on a hundred thousand? We could slip it off the wall after lights out—there's a guard but he's deaf and sleeps most of the time. Then we could take it off in the station wagon and make it across the Canadian border by tomorrow afternoon."

"Good God, Minnie. I just got my license and you've got me driving the getaway car for a major art theft."

"Don't rule it out too quickly."

Augusta sometimes thought maybe Minnie wasn't joking with her lunatic suggestions. She asked Minnie about Mrs. Fort. Was she a relative? Did she live with the Blanchards?

"She's nobody. And she's not my grandfather's mistress, if that's what you think. Nothing so glamorous. She went to school with mother. She never had much money; then when her husband was killed in the war and left her with only a pension, she moved in with my grandparents. She helps Granny run the house. And she does dirty chores, like taking me to Europe. She's not so bad, but she doesn't really figure. It's like she's not there most of the time. I sometimes think if you stepped on her foot she'd look at Granny for permission to say 'ouch.'"

Augusta asked where Mrs. Fort's room was.

"On the third floor. Right over mine. Probably so she'll be the first to smell smoke if I light a cigarette or set fire to the place."

"She has no other place to live?"

"She used to have an apartment in Washington, but she let it go. This is her home now."

Augusta didn't know quite why, but she had a strong desire to see Mrs. Fort's room. She knew she could never take such a risk for so hazy a whim. But she could picture it. Immaculately neat with a minimum of personal touches: a framed photograph of her dead husband and probably a framed snapshot of herself with the Blanchards in some exotic setting—by the pyramids or on the deck of the Blanchard yacht.

Even Minnie, who was frequently contemptuous of wealth and its trappings, even she wrote Mrs. Fort off as a nonentity, a minor attendant to the lives of *real* people. Mrs. Fort seemed attractive, stylish, educated, intelligent—could Augusta hope for more assets than these?—yet this admirable woman was little more than a servant to the people closest to her in the world. The spectacle filled Augusta with dread.

The next day was beautiful and bright, a mild spring day aching to be warm. The sun splintered through the still leafless branches of the trees, whose buds gave a chartreuse haze to the landscape. Augusta had heard that the arch superiority of Philadelphia's Old Guard was based on the city's historical importance, but seeing this ethereal spring she thought it might stem instead from the beauty of the city's surrounding countryside.

Minnie had been driven into Ardmore to get her shots for the European trip, so the two girls didn't get started on their picnic ride until about eleven o'clock. A stable boy was awaiting them with saddled horses and they were soon off cantering along trails of the Blanchard estate, their picnic lunch distributed between two knapsacks.

Minnie turned them off a main trail and they walked their horses along a path for a few hundred feet and finally came out into a shady clearing through which a broad brook passed. They followed the brook a ways, sometimes taking their horses into the shallow water, and eventually arrived at a stretch of stream bordered on both sides by great expanses of daffodils and narcissus.

The got off their horses and sat for a while to drink in the momentary splendor of the spot. Augusta wondered if any of the Blanchard adults ever came here. Or did they remain in their treasure-filled rooms, remembering the beauty of the spring garden from years past and taking satisfaction from having created it?

Minnie took them down a back road that led off the Blanchard property. They walked their horses alongside a paved road, then turned off into a riding trail that soon followed beside a broad stream. Occasionally they passed other riders and one elderly bird-watching couple. When they stopped, with the horses' hooves and their own voices still, Augusta could feel the suppressed roar of erupting spring.

It was almost two o'clock when they stopped to eat their lunch. Minnie wanted to find a spot of high ground with a view; they only achieved this by tying their horses and continuing on foot. Settled on a rock, Augusta began unwrapping chicken sandwiches and deviled eggs.

"Have I got a surprise for you, my girl," Minnie said, yanking open her knapsack. She pulled out a bottle of red wine, then rummaging some more, produced a corkscrew. "Lafitte Rothschild 1941! A bottle that Goering didn't get his fat hands on."

"Good heavens, Minnie, you've just finished one punishment. What if they miss it?"

"Are you kidding? Grandpa's got cases of the stuff. Since at least three of the staff are lushes, I'd be way down on the suspect list—for once."

Minnie opened it and poured them both a paper cup full. "Not bad," she said, savoring it professionally. "Better than Coke but not as good as Scotch."

Augusta drank a glass with her lunch but refused a second. Minnie propped herself against a tree and, talking with mounting expansiveness, proceeded to drink the entire bottle.

"Now this is what I call the life. No school, no parents, no grandparents . . ."

"If it weren't for your grandparents, Minnie, there'd be no horses, no countryside and no bottle of vintage wine."

"Don't be a spoilsport. You don't have to remind me how dependent I am on everyone else. But it won't always be this way. One day, not too far from now, I'll be able to get what I want and get it on my own. I won't have to kiss one of their asses."

"Do you really have to do so much for them now?"

"Are you kidding? Trained seals do a lot less for their fish: an hour's performance every day or so. I've got to be up on top of that stool clapping my flippers in time to the music every goddamn hour of the day. But sometimes I get a moment of freedom—and this is one of them. Isn't it great? When I think of being kept inside my room for three days—for nothing—it burns my hump. I want to kill somebody . . ."

She downed the last bit of wine.

"But you have to fight for your few little moments of freedom. Even now some ringed-tailed bitch is probably watching me polish off this wine—hanging by her tail from one of the trees—so she can go and phone in to headquarters and get me locked up again. Why are there so many goddamn bastards in the world? Why can't people leave you alone?"

When they returned to their horses, Minnie mounted unsteadily and set off at a gallop. She took them back along a trail that was cut along the tree-covered top of a steep hill. Slowing down, they came to a spot where, looking down through the tree trunks, they could see the manicured lawn of a country house where a garden party was in progress. The girls stopped to take in the pretty scene of ladies in pastel dresses, broad hats and white gloves and men in linen jackets strolling amongst white-clothed bars and umbrellaed tables set up at the far end of a broad lawn.

"I don't believe my luck," Minnie whispered. "I knew there was some reason why God sent us along this route. Do you know whose house that is? The bitch who reported me for smoking! Gimme your handkerchief—quick!"

Augusta couldn't understand why Minnie had become so excited. Handing Minnie the bandana, Augusta had the sinking feeling she was collaborating in some terrible business. In horror she watched Minnie tie the bandana around her face, outlaw fashion, kick her horse hard and charge down the steep slope of the hill.

A female guest was first to spot the bizarre apparition galloping across the lawn towards the party. She screamed. Before the others knew what was happening, Minnie had galloped through their midst, upsetting a waiter's tray full of cocktails and sending the dumbfounded guests clambering for cover. Through the screams and commotion Augusta could hear Minnie yelling "Scatter, you bitches!"

She would pull up her horse, then turn, spot another clump of frozen guests, and charge her horse toward them. The mayhem only went on for a few minutes. When a few butlers and other men had recovered themselves enough to try to grab Minnie's reins, she turned her horse and headed back up the hill to Augusta.

Breathing hard, but aglow with triumph, she said to Augusta, "Well, that probably finishes off Europe, but just to see the expression on that broad's face, Christ, was it worth it!"

Minnie's disguise had been an absurdity. Within an hour everyone on the Main Line knew what she'd done. The

Blanchard family was up half the night deliberating. By morning, the conclusion was that her behavior went far beyond mere hell-raising and should be treated rather than punished. The first thing the following morning, Minnie's mother drove her to a psychiatric clinic in West Philadelphia where she would remain for several days of observation. Before leaving, Minnie had stopped by Augusta's room.

"Well, so long, chum, they'll see that you get back to New York O.K. If I'm still in this nut house in two years, will you come and testify that I'm not crazy—just freedom-loving and bitch-hating?"

"Oh, Minnie," Augusta said, "I'm so sorry. I tried to stop you . . ."

"Don't worry about it. Between you and me, I think I'm going to get off easy. I should have thought of the loose-screw bit long ago. They treat you a lot better. They haven't even canceled Europe. I'll see you back at school."

Minnie's mother returned in the late morning and came looking for Augusta. She found her reading in the library.

"I'm sorry Minnie spoiled your visit with this escapade, Augusta. We've decided to let her remain at the clinic for a few days for some examination and testing. Under the circumstances, I imagine you'd as soon return to your family. We've booked a chair for you on the three-thirty to New York. Henry will drive you in. He has the ticket."

Augusta thanked her and said it was better for her to return home. "I can't tell you how sorry I am, Mrs. Blanchard. If I'd had any idea of what Minnie was planning to do, I would have tried to stop her . . ."

"I know you would have, Augusta. Do you mind taking a little walk with me? There's something I'd like to speak with you about."

They went out through a French door onto the grass terrace, then down marble steps to a long walk flanked with just-sprouting tulips.

"We are all very pleased about your friendship with Minnie. Some of the people she has taken up with in the past are more horrifying than you can imagine. We know what a good influence you are. She speaks of you often and we can see many improvements in her since you became friends."

Augusta was impressed to be walking in this magnificent estate, the woman who lived here speaking to her as another adult. She felt Mrs. Blanchard was going to make some sort of appeal and the thought filled her with a sense of opportunity.

"I just wanted to say to you, Augusta, how it pleases us you don't share Minnie's impulses for trouble. We want to ask you to keep trying to calm her, to restrain her from some of her more appalling notions. She admires you and I'm sure will listen."

"I'm very fond of Minnie, Mrs. Blanchard. She does have these impulses, as you say, but very often they can be squelched—and the moment passes. I'm happy to do whatever I can to keep Minnie from getting into trouble."

"It is extremely important for us that she get through the last year at Walker's. We never thought she would make it this far. We feel it is in large measure due to you."

"I hope I've been helpful."

"You have and we're very grateful."

Mrs. Blanchard's voice had a concluding ring to it. Was that all there was to be to this discussion?

"But then of course," Augusta continued, "Minnie goes many places I am unable to go . . ."

"What do you mean?" the older woman said, alert.

"This summer, for example," Augusta said coolly, "Minnie will be in Europe for several months. I would be happy to keep an eye on her, but can't afford such a trip."

Mrs. Blanchard looked at her for a moment. "I'm not sure I follow you exactly. However it may appear to you, Augusta, I am not a woman of unlimited resources. I simply was asking for your good judgment when you and Minnie are together."

Her manner became stiff and correct. "Jasper has some lunch for you in the sun room and I have some things I must do. Goodbye." She extended her hand. "We've enjoyed having you, and we're sorry your visit had to be cut short by Minnie's escapade." She turned and, leaving Augusta among the flower beds, started back up the marble steps to the house.

15 Harry Knight reminded his sister of the promise that Augusta would get a summer job; B.K. was let off because of her youth. Kate appealed to Tom Tollover for job ideas. He was appalled at the idea of his seventeen-year-old daughter working, but knew how much he was to blame for the necessity of it. To salvage his pride he forbade her taking the routine, pleasure-tinged summer resort jobs of students. Too menial. Besides, what if she should end up serving dinner to some of their friends? As the potential horrors unfurled themselves, Tollover put his mind to finding a solution that would minimize his own loss of face.

He sent Augusta to a crony who was a vice president of the Hanover Bank; she came away with a job photographing checks in a machine called a Recordat. The pay would be sixty dollars a week, the hours eight to four-thirty. The work was hypnotically monotonous, the other women she worked with an alien species.

At first, Augusta feared antagonizing these women by some inadvertent put-down, but later, as she felt more at ease, she observed them with interest. As she got to know them better, she discovered that the biggest difference between them and her friends was not intelligence—she found the same approximate incidence of smarts and dumbs at Walker's—or even of sensibility; the difference was in the smallness of their ambitions.

They seemed to want nothing more from life than a call from so-and-so for a date, a five-dollar raise or getting off a half hour early on Friday. Not one of these women seemed to be saving to go to Europe, to take a night course in banking, or even to have her teeth straightened. Not one of them seemed to envision more to life than eight hours a day in this large, noisy room on Wall Street.

One of the few pleasant aspects of the summer was being able to have lunch with her father, but he was out of town a good bit of the warmest months. Even when they did lunch, Augusta grew irritated by his incessant questions about herself, B.K. and their mother.

The summer was also improved by friends like Sandra asking her to Connecticut or Long Island for weekends but these sources of relief evaporated as most of her friends retreated to cooler locations like Maine and Nantucket.

In the middle of that summer, a sizzling day in August with all the windows in the accounting department wide open and two large electric fans whirring at top speed, Augusta saw herself clearly for what felt like the first time. With the sweat running down her back as she pumped checks into the narrow slot, incessantly recording other people's expenditures, she felt the dream of specialness that Tom Tollover had worked so long to instill in her dissolve.

She wasn't self-pitying enough to relegate herself to the status of the women around her—she felt immune from that fate—but she was hit by the absurdity of thinking herself another privileged rich girl like Sandra or Minnie with only a piece or two missing from the ideal picture. She was not one of them. She was something else, but she wasn't quite sure what.

B.K. probably had an even worse summer. With her mother and sister both working, she was left alone in the airless apartment most of each day with no entertainment. She had a few invitations from classmates with summer places but what most brightened her vacation was her correspondence with Paolo, who was spending the summer at his family's villa at Porto Santo Stefano on the Tyrrhenian coast north of Rome.

B.K. and Paolo had seen each other often the few times he had been in New York after Christmas; he was particularly keen on art galleries and had made B.K. familiar with all of them. She grew discouraged at times with the rarefied social world he moved in—a letter from the Netherlands reported how he had escorted one of Queen Juliana's daughters to a party—but on reflection B.K. knew she had nothing to fear. On the last day they had spent together before his departure in June, they had been sitting in Kate's living room when he grabbed B.K. and kissed her, then told her she was beautiful and was not to have other boyfriends while he was away. His lips had been soft and knowledgeable, his breath neutral and his manner authoritative. The kiss was all that was needed to assure B.K.'s fidelity, even if he remained away a lifetime.

Kate's gallery closed down for a month in August. She used the time to take a three-week course in Renaissance painting at the Metropolitan Museum, then joined a house party at Bryce Hartshorne's summer place in Nantucket for the remaining week.

While their mother was away, the girls stayed with their father on Fifty-first street. Ordinarily such a reunion would have been a treat for all three, but Tollover, while struggling to be hospitable and upbeat, seemed out of form. Perhaps it was the late August heat or perhaps the spectacle of his archduchess daughter taking the subway to the accounting department of a bank each morning. Perhaps he was between love affairs. One evening he flared up at Augusta for looking so disheveled when she arrived home from work. On two of the nights they were with him, he went to bed noticeably drunk.

Augusta was relieved when the summer ended and she could return to Walker's. This year B.K. would be joining her and she was grateful for the company. She no longer identified with the charmed girls around her. All her thoughts were turned toward getting into a good college and hoping that, somehow, the money would be produced to pay for it. After that, well, there had to be some middle ground being a pampered heiress or an aging hag in the accounting department of the Hanover Bank.

Minnie Blanchard returned from Europe a reformed woman. She'd had enough fun, she said, to last her the rest of the school year. Mrs. Fort had proved to be either a good sport or deaf, dumb and blind, Minnie wasn't sure which, but she'd romped through Europe with few restraints. "Wait till you get there, Gus, it's incredible! Full of young American kids like us, most on their own. Two hours a day of seeing the sights—and even that isn't always so bad—then fifteen hours of solid fun! It's unbelievable. And old Forty was so glad to be out from under Granny's roof she let me do what I wanted."

Martie Dean had returned from Vermont in a fast friendship

with a younger student—even less prepossessing and attractive than Martie—who lived in equal loneliness in a town not far from the Deans' farm.

Martie was just as affectionate to Augusta, but her new friend took up most of her time and gave her a new confidence. Augusta figured she could apply the hours she had formerly put to bolstering Martie to winning a scholarship to Smith, her first choice of colleges. Her second choice was Sarah Lawrence.

Kate Tollover grew concerned over Augusta's college prospects. Her brother Harry was either in financial trouble or had grown sick of supporting them all; he was lobbying for Augusta to stop school with Walker's and start a career. If she had to go to college, Harry saw no reason why she couldn't attend any of a number of good schools in New York City and live at home.

Kate had grown weary of trying to justify her standards to her philistine brother. At the same time she had grown exasperated at the permanently fixed low pay of her genteel gallery job. At the suggestion of a friend, she was exploring a real estate course with the idea of qualifying for a job with a prestigious firm like Douglas Elliman where there might be the hope of making more substantial money.

At Walker's, B.K. fell in quickly with a lively group made up in part of friends from Chapin and Greenvale. Occasionally she and Augusta would meet for a long talk, but their daily lives were as separate as they'd been when one lived in New York and the other in Simsbury.

Shortly after the midterms, a communication from Smith made it clear that the college did not consider Miss Tollover eligible for financial assistance; her family's financial resources did not warrant such aid. Thunderstruck, Kate wondered briefly if Sarah Rusk might still be having revenge, but she saw no point in combating this judgment. She appealed to Tollover to obtain assistance from his rich relations, but this produced nothing, his stock being low with them all.

Strings were pulled to get some reading on the Sarah Lawrence prospects and the answer was far more encouraging. Through a connection with Walker's faculty word came back that Augusta Tollover was all but assured a scholarship.

When Tom Tollover heard this, he flew into a frenzy. "No daughter of mine is going to be a scholarship student and serve dinner to all those radical Jews," he ranted to Kate over the phone three times a day.

"Would you rather she didn't go to college, Tom?"

"What's so terrible about that? Plenty of women I know never went to college, yourself among them."

Kate, who had thought she knew every strand of Tollover's skein of vanity, was astounded by this new selfishness. Although thoroughly exasperated, she was far from checked by her former husband's obstructiveness. She didn't consider that Tom Tollover had any rights in this matter. Strangely enough, Augusta thought he did. She didn't want to go to any college, she said, that would make her father miserable and ashamed. She would choose another school, one where she could work off her scholarship unobserved by the offspring of Tom's friends. Obviously, Vassar and Wellesley were out. But when she thought of attending a "safe" school, she could not face the prospect. She might as well apply to the University of Colorado, disappear forever, and say she died in a skiing accident. Besides, it was now too late, she discovered, to pursue *any* scholarship alternative. It was Sarah Lawrence or secretarial school.

A phone call from her mother one morning in March brought this worry—and many more—to an end. Kate said she would be marrying Ambassador Hartshorne at the end of April and that they would all be moving to his plantation in Maryland. Ambassador Hartshorne insisted that his new stepdaughter go to Smith and he wanted to give Augusta a large coming-out dinner dance.

"You're happy for me, aren't you, darling?" Kate's voice sounded exhilarated, higher-pitched and, was it Augusta's imagination, or did the voice have a more aristocratic accent?

"Oh, yes, Mother. Of course." Augusta's voice was wooden. She was trying to take it in.

"This will change all our lives enormously. You do understand?"

"I think so, Mother."

"You will tell B.K.?"

B.K. was dumbfounded and hit Augusta with a flood of questions, only a few of which she could answer. "He's terribly rich, isn't he? Do you suppose the plantation has horses? A swimming pool? Will we be able to invite our friends? Won't Paolo be impressed?"

These material aspects did not engulf Augusta. Was she growing up? Or had she worn out her covetous impulses? Within seconds of hearing the news, she had adjusted to no more worn-out skirts, no more standing away from shabby suitcases on train platforms, no more lying excuses about why she would not be joining some expedition or other. All of these embarrassments, once so painful to her, now seemed petty compared to other changes she could envision.

She knew that as the stepdaughter of the famous Ambassador Hartshorne, she took on a new celebrity and prestige. She knew enough of his high-level world to visualize the opportunities, the friendships, the social activities that would open up for herself and B.K.

But even more than this, she saw that her mother had, with a single stroke, all but immunized them from a certain kind of hurt, the hurt that is nurtured by shabbiness and squalor. They had been lifted above a pain-inflicting, tormenting plain and placed beyond the jurisdiction of unsympathetic boors like Uncle Harry, beyond the reach of enemies's cuts and digs, and maybe beyond the betrayals of careless adults who put their own vanities and ambitions before the happiness of their children.

A fierce exhilaration surged through Augusta. Fates could be altered. You didn't have to accept whatever was laid down for you. There were courses of action. Choices. Augusta was overwhelmed with what her mother had accomplished. And it had been so simple. So laughably, mysteriously simple.

16

"Forget the fancy French menu." B.K. fished for a cigarette in her Nantucket whaler's bag. "It's all frozen Styrofoam. But for some reason this pretentious dump serves a first-rate martini and an epic chicken sandwich." She leaned forward to accept Brandon's light.

"Should we have invited your man to join us?"

"Gus's man. I told him we had family business to discuss. It's a bitch sometimes, trying to figure out where servants stop and associates begin."

"Or where associates stop and friends begin," Brandon added. "Although generally I've found—they don't. If they carry your martinis around after you, I think they're still servants." Brandon placed their order. "After your morning rummaging through your past, how do you feel?"

"Like after four hours of analysis, except no analyst could dredge up as much childhood as that damn trunk did. It's hard to explain how just one object can evoke so much. Like that sweater, the hand-embroidered one. My great-aunt Mable brought me that from a trip to France in the late thirties. It was excellent wool and the needlework was superb. But when I was six, all I cared about was that it was *new*. Augusta had not worn it, no one had. It was expensive and it had been bought for *me*. I used to have nightmares that I would lose it or that it would get torn."

"I used to hate the expensive presents dumped on me," Brandon said, "but that is a different agony, I see that."

"Very different. But, God! Why are we all so determined to find reasons to feel sorry for ourselves? Anyhow, it wasn't just the reminders of painful things, it was the wrenching up of your entire childhood—report cards, Halloween costumes, hand-made ashtrays your parents didn't want. The pathos of it all! But I was good about crying, wasn't I?"

"I would hesitate to use the word 'good' about three break-downs in two hours."

"Still the bastard. Even ringside at my middle-age crisis."

"Not ringside, corner," Brandon said emphatically. "Learning so much about your pre-Maryland years made me feel even worse about my behavior toward you and Gus at first."

"Your welcome to Tidewater Farm was not warm."

"Part of my reaction was territorial, of course. You two hotshot sisters were invading my terrain. But it went beyond that. The war with my father had reached the showdown point just as you arrived. I was about to bail out. I considered all the luxury of that plantation as tainted and corrupt. The spectacle of you and Gus splashing around in it, your new tub of whipped cream—that made me contemptuous of you as well. I saw that estate as a mother lode of bigotry, reaction and injustice. You saw it the way the young Marie Antoinette saw Versailles—a vast factory for her comfort and pleasure."

"We came from four rooms with hamburgers in the kitchen to your father's thirty-three rooms with butlers serving sweetbreads from silver salvers. You can't imagine the effect on us."

"Yes, I can, particularly after this morning's odyssey into genteel squalor. But in my boyhood radicalism, I abhorred such money-worship. Like other rich kids, I knew that the money doesn't help. Gus never learned that. Maybe the money arrived too late. Her hunger was locked in."

"Easy, brother dear. She is still my sister, you know."

"Get off it. I'm not saying anything that isn't said by every gossip columnist in the world."

"They don't say it to my face."

"And they don't spend hours going through your old dresses and report cards either."

"Point. Say your worst."

"I'd rather talk about *me* some more. When you two foxtrotted in, I was going through the roughest period of my life. I was brimming with political venom. Like every radical, my outrage at any institution with even a hint of authority— Congress, the F.B.I., the State Department—was really inspired by my father. Daddy was devious and treacherous, therefore all entrenched authority was. I arrived at that all by myself. No help from marijuana paranoia. At fifteen, I saw my hatred as the direct result of my political purity. And anyone who stood up to my political vision was corrupt."

"You can't accuse me and Gus of resisting your politics. We had none of our own to fight with."

"I saw everything politically. My shiny little stepsisters were vain self-seekers without a shred of altruism, for whom the rest of humanity was a pool for recruiting your servants and your suitors."

"How foresightful of you, Bran! That's the way the rest of the world views us now."

"I never said *you* had changed, only that my ferocious idealism has. Back then, if I met someone who wasn't working to help the blacks or to bring the giant corporations to their knees, I dismissed them. Thank God you were intelligent. If you'd been dumb, I think I would have poisoned your orange juice."

"*Gus* was intelligent. I didn't get smart till later."

"You weren't as dimwitted as you keep saying."

"Next to you and Gus, I was retarded."

"I admit, it was Gus's brain that first softened me to the Tollover sisters. Also, your odd detachment. I envied that. Your relations with your mother were cool but correct. My father was nothing to you but a courtly old gentleman who rained gifts on you. I began to view you both as laboratory creatures, free from psychic alignments and snarled parental histories. I didn't know, then, about your own Oedipal tangle, of course. In the controlled hothouse of Tidewater Farm, you were free agents."

"It was like being air-lifted into a well-staffed Garden of Eden."

"With me as the snake."

"I wonder," smiled B.K., "why Adam and Eve never thought of our ploy? Befriending the snake."

"Neither was as resourceful as your sister Augusta."

Part Two

17 For Augusta and B.K. Tollover, the spring of 1948 was an exciting blur of events. There had been Augusta's graduation from Walker's, where a polite Kate and Bryce Hartshorne had confronted a politely sober Tom Tollover. A few days later, Kate and Hartshorne were married at a small ceremony in a friend's Sutton Place apartment and left immediately for a week in Paris, where Hartshorne had to attend a conference.

The girls stayed with their father, who celebrated his former wife's marital coup with several drinking sessions of unfocused bitterness.

If Hartshorne had been *nouveau riche*, Tollover could have laughed him off. Had he been a penniless aristocrat, he could have enjoyed torturing him indefinitely. If an unaccomplished loafer, devastation would have come instantly. Hartshorne, however, was maddeningly free of any of Tollover's pet imperfections. So he had to content himself with attacks on Hartshorne's age, his stuffiness and his liberal politics. The unspoken argument was that Kate's new husband could never rival Tollover for charm or fun.

For the girls, the stay with their father was more time than they had spent together in years. Both were so caught up with their own social activities—particularly Augusta, who spent three nights on Long Island at friends' debuts—they paid little attention to his anti-Hartshorne campaign.

During Augusta's final months at Walker's, the mounting excitement over classmates' coming-out parties had been a final reminder of the discrepancy between her own prospects and those of the girls around her. Now she could sip their champagne and dance to their orchestras serene in the knowledge that she could do similar things, and when her opportunity occurred, do them better.

When Augusta returned to the East Fifty-first Street apartment, she regaled B.K. for hours with accounts of the parties. B.K. was ravenous to hear who had been there, what everyone wore, how the party was decorated and whom Augusta had danced with. Stimulated by these spectacular offerings of wealthy parents, the two girls fell to speculating what their lives would be like at Tidewater Farm. They were already living in a world that excluded their father, and he sensed it.

When Ambassador Hartshorne brought his bride back from Europe, he left her in New York and went directly to Washington to report on his conference. The next day, his car and driver arrived from Maryland to collect the girls and their mother and bring them to Tidewater Farm. Augusta and B.K.'s clothes had gone ahead in trunks, so they made the trip with a small overnight bag, as though off for a weekend.

Tollover discreetly made certain to be out of his apartment when the limousine arrived. The drive to Maryland passed quickly, with Kate enthusing about her stay in Europe, deftly inserting tidbits that underlined Hartshorne's international importance.

Shortly after crossing the Delaware River, the car turned off the main north–south highway and headed down the Chesapeake Bay's eastern shore. At first the road was out of sight of water, the scenery was farm country, flat and green; as they got farther south, glimpses of water—streams and inlets—occurred with increasing frequency. Finally the car arrived at a large iron gate, incongruously majestic after the simple farms and fishing shacks they had just passed. As the sleek car crunched into the gravel drive, the three women fell silent.

Everything about their arrival suggested a brief visit. To the girls, impressive homes such as this were places to be entertained for two or three days, to ogle and envy before returning to reality. Now they had trouble absorbing a new reality: after a few days they would not be returning to upper Madison Avenue; this magnificent plantation was their new home.

Both of them were stunned by its beauty—the long alley of trees leading to the house, the red-brick and white-trimmed portico, the black butler standing at the door to receive them, their adjoining bedrooms—bright and airy—filled with softly gleaming eighteenth-century American furniture.

From one of her windows, Augusta looked down over a broad oak-shaded lawn to a wide expanse of Chesapeake Bay where two sailboats moved idly across the tableau. It was somewhat similar to views of Long Island Sound, but the greenery was far more abundant and there were no traces of other inhabitants. She had never seen anything so unspoiled or peaceful.

"Gus, Gus!" She heard B.K.'s voice from the next room. "Come look! All my clothes are hung in the closets and my sweaters laid out in drawers. Can you believe it? My bed has a canopy. Does yours?"

Augusta was trying to remain calm. She was resisting feeling jubilant over a triumph she still considered her mother's, not hers. But the incredible loveliness of everything! Her eye hit the small gift-wrapped package on the dressing table.

"Gus! My God, will you look at this?" B.K. came running into the room with a note, and showed Augusta a check for 500 dollars. The note read: "To help you fill the closets. Love from Uncle Bryce."

Augusta unwrapped her package. Inside were a set of car keys in a red-leather case. Augusta read her note aloud: "So you won't feel a prisoner at Tidewater Farm, there's a welcoming graduation present in front of the garage. Love from Uncle Bryce."

The girls raced down to the garage to see a svelte, dark-green sports car, a Triumph-3—its top down, its chrome gleaming.

"Oh, my God, Gus," B.K. said reverentially, "are we dreaming?"

Augusta looked at the car coolly. "It's awfully flashy."

"Flashy! You pompous phony! It's deee-vine! Let's take it out. Do you know how to drive it?"

"Of course. Minnie has the same shift in her MG. Let's go."

B.K. suggested they pass by the front of the house and honk for their mother to look out at them, maybe come along.

"Too exuberant," Augusta said solemnly. "Dignity, B.K. Let's not forget the Tollover dignity."

B.K. knew the mocking tone was serious.

"The Tollover dignity never got us a car."

"Maybe not. But a car is no reason to chuck it either."

They took off down a shady drive that brought them to the public road. Arriving at a straight stretch, Augusta floored the gas, pushing the car into a rapid acceleration. Over the motor's roar, B.K. let out a whoop. Both girls' hair whipped behind them and pulled over their faces. They were close to exploding with a sense of how it was going to be.

Kate Hartshorne had announced the beginning of her reign in the traditional method of second wives: the ritualistic redecoration of her husband's home. Some of the downstairs sitting rooms were badly in need of reupholstery, so her gesture was not as wantonly symbolic as it might have been.

Months before the wedding, well before anyone else knew of the planned marriage, Kate had quietly gone from New York to Maryland with a decorator friend who provided access to the fabric houses and other suppliers. As for the design, Kate proved as knowledgeable about eighteenth-century furniture as her professional friend, and as imaginative about suitable wallcoverings, curtains and carpets. Weeks before the wedding, the main house was alive with carpenters, paperers and painters. Many were still there, but the intensive work would go on in July and August when the family would be at Hartshorne's summer home on Nantucket.

Late afternoon of their first day at Tidewater Farm, Augusta and B.K. took a swim, then went to their rooms to change for dinner. Ambassador Hartshorne, determined to be present for his new family's first dinner, flew up from Washington in a small chartered plane. When the girls emerged onto the terrace, he was already seated with Kate having a drink. They hugged him and thanked him warmly for their gifts. If they needed anything, he told them, they should ask Harry, the genial black man who had first greeted them.

Hartshorne, usually so calm and unflappable, seemed edgy in his keenness to have everything go smoothly, for all to be at their ease. Augusta noticed him glance at his watch twice and turn toward the door from the house. Augusta was asking her stepfather about the boats when one of the French doors opened and a young man emerged. He was strikingly pretty—alert dark eyes and curly black hair set off by a white-linen jacket over a pink button-down shirt. Like Hartshorne, he wore a regimental tie.

With aggressive aplomb, he walked to Augusta, held out his hand and said, "Greetings, Augusta, I am the dreaded Brandon, your new baby brother. And you, B.K., greetings. Sorry I wasn't here to welcome you but I was off in Annapolis seeing my parole officer."

"My son, you will find, has a black sense of humor." Hartshorne's agitation was palpable.

Without looking at his father, Brandon said, *"Prends garde, Papa, Henry te sentira."* Having kissed Kate's cheek, he then faced his father and said, "I trust you and Mama had an enjoyable honeymoon in Paris while making the world safe for General Motors' unsafe cars."

Making a show of confiding to Augusta, he said, "Perhaps 'parole officer' was overstating it. Having committed various hallowed and traditional crimes against nature, I got my honorable discharge from St. Paul's only on condition that I have myself sanitized by an analyst before proceeding to Yale. Father's had me committed there for this fall."

"Surely, Brandon," Hartshorne cut in, "it's not necessary to tell all of your failings in the first ten minutes."

"With so many, I need a good start," he replied cheerily.

They moved to the far end of the terrace, where a glass-top table had been elegantly set for five. After a delicious crab bisque, Henry served a silver platter laden with slabs of pink veal lightly rubbed with garlic. He was followed by a maid serving fried eggplant, then asparagus hollandaise. Henry poured them all glasses of a chilled rosé that was dry and delicate.

The honeymoon trip was discussed in detail, with Augusta essaying astute questions about the Paris conference. Through most of this, Brandon sat quietly eating his dinner, but Augusta could sense the turmoil churning inside him. Several times she caught him looking at her; he would quickly look away and take a sip from his wine.

"Brandon," Hartshorne said with a bonhomie whose falsity was already established, "why don't you take the girls for a sail tomorrow? Show them the ropes so they can sail on their own?"

"You don't sail?" Brandon said with mild amusement.

"We've been on and around boats all our lives," Augusta said evenly, "but we've never had our own. Always passengers, never captains."

"It's very different," Brandon said pointedly. Then, with arch joviality, he said, "Isn't this cozy? A complete family, yet total strangers to each other. After we have all become thick as a gang of Sicilian bandits, we will look back with amazement at this meal when we were all so stiff with each other."

"I for one would look back with pleasure to any evening when you were polite," Hartshorne said. "You can count on my son to voice the obvious if it will make anyone uncomfortable."

"You wrong me, Father. I was simply trying to point out the oddity of the occasion. This awkwardness can't last." Brandon Hartshorne smiled. "We shall all quickly become either friends or enemies."

Augusta and B.K.'s first days at Tidewater Farm passed in a dream of pleasant discoveries. The Chesapeake water, even in June, was too warm to make daytime swimming invigorating, but the pool was spring-fed and bracingly cool. The bay was ideal for nighttime dips. Augusta and B.K. played tennis, drove into the nearby village of Chestertown to inventory the few shops, and took horses out from the Hartshorne stables for long, exploratory rides around the farm's vast acreage. Hartshorne had said they could pick horses for their own—and B.K. could, if she wanted, have hers shipped to Walker's in the fall.

Curiosity about Ambassador Hartshorne's good-looking new step-daughters brought forth a rash of invitations from neighboring farms and estates. The impact of their augmented status reached even greater distances; the number of invitations from friends in other cities increased dramatically from the year before—when they would have appreciated them so much more, Augusta thought bitterly.

All of these changes caused Augusta to see herself and her future in a different light. The mental energy that had gone into appearing "one of them" could now be redirected. But toward what? Marvelous times? They would arrive inevitably—no effort necessary. An important career? She would be entering Smith in the fall; with her stepfather's influence, she could have her pick of fields after graduating. But that was a long way off. A brilliant social life? That seemed a certainty.

For the moment, her energy could best be put to use fighting off her stepbrother, who had decided to amuse himself by baiting his new stepsisters. The ugly fights that erupted at dinner between Brandon and his father were a respite for Augusta and B.K. from the barrage of slurs and hinted insults that the boy usually directed at them.

She forced her thoughts away from this anxiety to the most pleasant of many pleasant aspects of her immediate future. Ambassador Hartshorne had announced he was giving Augusta a large debut party at Tidewater Farm.

"It will double as our wedding reception," he proclaimed expansively at a Sunday lunch by the pool. "Of course, it is too late for the spring season. We'll have to wait till September, just before you go off to college. It should still be warm, ideal for a large dinner dance here at the farm. We haven't had a proper party here in years."

Her own father could not give her a dinner dance, nor could her mother. The stables, boats, tennis courts and antiques belonged to her mother's husband. She was here because there was nowhere else to put her. All right. But what a glorious base from which to launch one's own life! Thank you, Ambassador Hartshorne, for your kindness, for the use of your props and your lovely settings, your lessons in taste, in how to spend money. I won't waste the opportunity. You will be glad you put these resources at my disposal. Tom Tollover will be glad I had them.

All of this was going through Augusta's mind as she sat trying to read one of her stepfather's books, his prognosis for postwar Europe. She had been looking up from the book at the genteel beauty all around her as she lay on a chaise at the far end of the terrace. She reached for the glass of iced tea that Henry, unasked, had brought her. The book slid from her lap to the flagstones. As she reached to pick it up, she heard a voice.

"Don't bother about that. Henry will get it. That's what servants are for."

She looked up to see Brandon walking toward her across the lawn from the swimming pool. He was barefoot, with a blue button-down shirt open over his boxer trunks. A few chest hairs protruded bravely from his sallow skin. His striking looks were undermined by his staccato speaking delivery and prissy manner.

Augusta laughed as she thought of Amy Bishop, a Walker's classmate whose mother, like Augusta's, had married a widower with a teenaged son. Amy and her stepbrother had launched an all-out affair that lacked the usual logistical problems of illicit young love. At the end of the evening, they would simply say good night to their parents and retire upstairs to the same room.

She expected no such alliance with Brandon; in fact, she would settle for a pact to avoid war. But she knew, as England now did, that appeasement only incited bullies.

"You'll have to forgive my sister and me," she said sweetly. "We aren't used to your level of luxury. At the end of dinner, it's all we can do to restrain ourselves from jumping up and doing the dishes."

Brandon eyed her warily. *He* was accustomed to being the perpetrator of sarcasm. He threw himself on an adjoining chaise and addressed the trees above him. "You love it all, don't you?"

"Love all what?"

"All this early-American opulence."

"I prefer it to contemporary poverty, yes. Is there something wrong in that?"

"There are more important things. Being productive and useful, for example. Doing something for your fellow man."

Augusta was not ready to be conciliatory, not until she had extracted from him some token of respect. "It's a matter," she said, "of whether you want to wash your own dishes or have someone wash them for you. The time saved can be put to any number of things—even humanitarianism."

"I'm afraid," Brandon said with cool superiority, "I find that a rather simplistic and self-serving bit of economic theory."

Augusta had encountered few boys her age she considered her mental equals. One that was patently her superior—certainly in terms of articulateness and erudition—was a novel experience, and not an altogether disagreeable one.

"Does our enjoyment of beauty and comfort make us corrupt?" she asked.

He frowned, then grimaced. "In this house it does."

An opening at last! They were away from sweeping universals and on to the specifics of his unhappiness. She wanted to ask him why he hated his father so, but knew she was still a long way from such intimacy. She approached from the flank.

"What did your mother die of?"

"Boredom with my father, I think. She was from a very old, very accomplished French family. She never adjusted to the quaint pretensions of the American upper class. She could have used some of your adaptability."

Augusta closed her book firmly. "Look, Brandon, through no fault of my sister's or mine, we have intruded into your life. We can be friends or enemies, either way, but it seems to me you don't need another enemy in this house. Why don't you wait until you have reason to hate us, before wasting that kind of emotion?"

He looked at her with haughty disdain. "It's a relief, I suppose, that you are not stupid."

"It's a relief to me," she said fixing him with her eyes, "that you are not trying to grab my ass."

For the first time, Brandon appeared thrown off balance. Augusta was taking a major risk by striking so close to the private vulnerabilities of this hypersensitive boy, and she knew

[119]

that their relationship would be decided in the next thirty seconds.

For a moment Brandon looked as if he had been slapped—then his face dissolved into a sheepish grin. She had seen him smile before, but not like this. It was the look of a person disarmed, and relieved to be disarmed. "It seems," he said in his old, insolent tone, "aberration has some advantages." He moved to leave. "Tomorrow I will take you and your sister—*our* sister, isn't it glorious?—for a sail. We'll leave at eight to have a good run before it gets too hot."

He turned abruptly and started into the house. He paused at the door and turned to her. "I was getting bored tormenting you anyhow."

18

Even at nine in the morning, the June day promised midsummer heat. Augusta had worn Bermuda shorts but realized a bathing suit would have made more sense. Brandon barked orders to his stepsisters as they prepared the cat boat to leave the cove and sail into the bay. Both girls were familiar with the tasks and satisfied Brandon that they knew boats and boat terminology.

Once on the open water, they watched the Georgian manor house grow smaller in an ever-widening stretch of trees. Soon they were out far enough for Brandon to indicate the limits of the farm's frontage on the bay. On the open water they found a breeze just sufficient for a relaxing sail. B.K. took the tiller and Augusta and Brandon sat facing each other on the combing.

B.K. had been relieved to hear of Augusta's conversation with Brandon; she was frightened of her stepbrother and had avoided him as much as possible. Now he was an altogether different person—relaxed, friendly, helpful.

"Are you aware," he said to Augusta, "the socializing around here gets heady at times? You never know who will show up at dinner—cabinet members, senators, journalists. We even had the President once for lunch—Roosevelt, not Truman—although my father would have been thrilled by either. His eagerness to play with the Big Boys makes him indiscriminate about his friends."

"You don't like Truman?" B.K. asked.

"Actually, I'm starting to like him quite a bit. It's my father's taste I'm talking about. I know that Truman is a type of man he detests—common, uncultivated, small-town politician—but Ambassador Hartshorne would wear Hawaiian shirts to the State Department if he thought it would please old Harry."

"Everyone tries to ingratiate themselves with their superiors," Augusta said.

"Clerks and functionaries, yes. Not ambassadors and statesmen. I can see you think I'm being hard on father. I admit to a personal reason for my dislike. I resent his disapproval of my interest in theater and the arts. He poses as a man of cultivation and liberal humanitarianism, but he feels gentlemen *attend* the theater, they don't *participate* in it. So my loathing of his hypocrisy is not totally abstract."

"You would like to go into the theater?" B.K. asked.

"Oh, yes," Brandon said wistfully, "but it would be over his dead body. Sometimes I wonder if his dread of the Bohemian world is old-school snobbery or if he fears it in my case in particular. I think he sees me as teetering on the brink of depravity; an involvement in show business would unleash the monster and bring scandal to the Hartshorne name. Or maybe he doubts my talent and fears the embarrassment my failure would cause the family. The upper classes will condone such pursuits as writing, painting and acting only if you are acknowledged to be very, very good. It's fine to be a mediocre lawyer or stockbroker, but God help you if you are a mediocre actor."

"Do you and your father argue mostly about politics?" Augusta asked.

"You've heard us. Politics is our arena, But the unspoken theme is that we basically disapprove of each other. We are both political. I like to think I am political in the European sense of the word and he in the American."

"What's the difference?" B.K. asked.

"To Europeans," Brandon replied, "a political man is one concerned about his fellow man, who cares about the greatest good for the greatest number. In America a political man is one concerned with obtaining power."

Augusta did not see the two interpretations as incompatible. "Don't the two go together in our system of government?"

"I can see, Augusta, you are not going to be a pushover. Of course, you must obtain power in order to improve the lives of others, but too often the scramble for it becomes the end in itself. This is my father's case. If, through some miracle, Lucky Luciano were to sweep the American primaries, Ambassador Hartshorne would be the first to throw a dinner for him at the F Street Club. But let's not belabor that pompous fraud, let's figure out how the Tollover sisters can best take advantage of him."

"Oh, please, Brandon, don't drag us into your fight," Augusta said. "He has been terribly kind and generous to us."

"Look at the dinner dance he's throwing for Augusta's coming out," B.K. put in.

"When he does it, he really does it. I'm sure everyone from Audie Murphy to Madame Chiang Kaishek will be there. The party could make you famous, Augusta. Don't get fat and develop pimples over the summer. The Associated Press is basically hostile to rich debutantes; they will show you no mercy."

In the days that followed, Augusta became increasingly aware of the way the father–son discord soured the atmosphere at Tidewater Farm. She saw it also as a reason she and B.K. were so fussed over—by Hartshorne and the servants. The two new members of the family, in addition to being attractive and well mannered, were *neutral*. Whatever problems they might bring into the house at least were not of the house. They were treated like visiting movie stars.

Rather than rankling Brandon, as it had at first, it now amused him. He began to project brilliant futures for his two good-looking stepsisters. In a way that made Augusta smile, he assigned himself Tom Tollover's role as head coach and trainer.

Augusta grew fond of her stepbrother and was even more impressed by his intellect. At times she ached for the hopelessness of his relations with his father; at other times she feared the tension was building—several dinner-table scenes had come close to violence. A part of her, however, weighed the advantages to herself and her sister of this father–son war.

The Hartshorne routine was to move on the first of July to the ambassador's house on Nantucket. B.K. was thrilled at this prospect, as Paolo told her he might visit a schoolmate there before returning to Italy. Augusta had grown to love Tidewater Farm and felt little enthusiasm about moving again so soon. She loved the understated luxury of the plantation—the unobtrusive servants catering to every need, the beauty of the house and its furnishings, the leafy informality of the grounds and the soothing expanse of open water.

The June weather was already hot and, she was told, would grow hotter, but something about the indolent southern mood of the eastern shore in the summer seemed to match a mood of Augusta's. Her impulse was to rest up after one struggle and gather strength for a new one.

One day Augusta was lying on a poolside chaise reading *Sons and Lovers*. B.K. and her mother had driven into Annapolis for a day of shopping and sightseeing. The midmorning sun was hot and Tidewater Farm was completely still except for the occasional flick of a dragonfly and the ever-present hum of minute, hot-weather life.

Putting down her new book, she began rubbing oil into her tan legs. She loved her legs, long and well formed, the only part of her appearance she would not change in any way. She took off her sunglasses and lay back on the mattress and closed her eyes.

Feeling her sun disappear, she opened her eyes to see a figure silhouetted over her. She screened her eyes with her hand and made out a young man in khaki shorts and a University of Maryland T-shirt.

"Well, well," he said. "Things are looking up here at old Tidewater Farm."

"Hello," Augusta said tentatively, wondering if she was prepared for another stepbrother, stepcousin or house guest.

"Yes, indeed," said the boy, who was coming into focus as clean-cut and handsome. "I'd heard there were to be some new arrivals from New York, but with my luck lately, I figured you'd be dogs. Boy, was I wrong!"

"When you finish appraising me, would you mind telling me who you are?"

"Oh, sorry. I'm Jeff." He pronounced his name as though it clarified vast areas of confusion, and broke into a big smile.

"Jeff?"

"Yes, Jeff Blain. Didn't they tell you about me?"

"No."

"I take care of the pool."

"You mean you work for Ambassador Hartshorne?"

"In the summers. The rest of the year I go to college."

"But *now* you work here?"

"You don't have to harp on the economic basis of the whole thing," he said. "One of my jobs is to see that the guests are comfortable and enjoying themselves. Let's go for a swim!" He pulled off his T-shirt, revealing a spectacular torso—smooth brown skin with well-defined yet supple muscles.

"No, thank you," Augusta said coldly, not sure how to deal with this brashness. She had adopted a cheerful civility with the household servants that seemed to work well, but they were docile and polite and never took advantage of her friendliness. She resented this boy's familiarity. Would he talk to Brandon this way? Or to one of her stepfather's guests? It made her angry to think that he had made certain decisions about the ambiguity of her status at Tidewater Farm.

"It was nice meeting you," she said. "If you don't mind, I want to get back to my book. And you can get on with your—chores."

"You mustn't snub me," he said cheerfully. "I'm quite nice and sensitive to snubs. And the ambassador is very up on me and wouldn't like your snubbing me. Wouldn't like it at all."

Jeff hunched down besides her chair and grinned. "You really shouldn't pass me up as a friend. There isn't that much going on way out here in the Maryland boonies. And who cares if we get off on the wrong foot, as long as we get off?"

He jumped up and dove into the water. He was so beautiful, she thought, that his physical presence seemed to give weight to his predictable banter. She marveled that such a magnificent specimen could talk at all.

At times over the past year, Augusta had worried that she might be a little askew in the realm of eroticism. Sex and boys did not interest her nearly as much as they did her friends at Walker's, most of whom thought of nothing else. She had seen how this preoccupation could land even the most invulnerable colleagues in trouble. One girl from a prominent Chicago family had been expelled for being caught half dressed in a darkened school room with a Deerfield boy during one of the school dances.

The only one of Augusta's acquaintances whom she knew had actually gone all the way was a deeply neurotic and trouble-prone girl. Most significantly, it was not her other transgressions but the girl's sex life that earned her the disdain of the Walker's girls.

But even though her contemporaries were inhibited about delving too deeply into sex and were scornful of those who did, they were all obsessed with it. Augusta found the preoccupation degrading and boring. Since the upheaval of leaving New York, however, she had noticed that her thoughts on sex were changing. Now that her obsession with keeping up a front had been alleviated by her mother's marriage, she had noticed in herself a relaxing of certain inner muscles. Perhaps the summer indolence of Tidewater Farm abetted this change, or perhaps she was that many months nearer adulthood.

Whatever the reason, since coming to Maryland she had found within herself a restlessness whose sensual component she couldn't deny. She would sometimes present this to herself as loneliness, a desire for a special friend, but she knew that B.K. was as close and devoted as any friend could be, and Brandon was fast becoming so. No, the gap, the feeling of emptiness, was different. She had grown aware of it, but the physical challenge of Jeff's presence now focused her awareness. Part of her was repelled and frightened at the idea. There had already been too many elements in her life beyond her control—her father, her status, her home life, her mother's remarriage. She saw the process of maturing, of moving up, of success, as the struggle to transcend the variables, to eliminate the surprises. Now came this new pull. She was dismayed and more than a little fascinated—less by Jeff Blain than by this new phenomenon in herself.

19

Tom Tollover threw down the copy of *Time* in disgust. The photo of the Paris conference delegation had given more prominence to that ass Hartshorne than it had to Dean Acheson and General Marshall. Tollover hated those well-born liberals who were handing the world to the Communists on a silver platter, an *inherited* silver platter. They were playing at statesmanship, every last one of them; pitting them against the Russians was like putting the Groton soccer team up against the Stern gang.

Tollover despised rich liberals as a group, but Hartshorne he particularly disliked. He didn't care about Kate—Hartshorne was welcome to her—but Augusta and B.K., that was something else. He had heard about the man's disastrous relations with his faggot son, and he saw too clearly how Hartshorne intended to co-opt his daughters, parade them as his progeny, as evidence that his flop as a parent was his son's fault, not his.

Tollover would not stand for it. He was confident of his daughters' loyalty. He knew their adoration of him was unshakable, but they were at an impressionable age, easily diverted. Tollover knew he must not lose touch, he must see as much of them as possible. He mustn't let that dullard sway them with blatant bribery.

He looked at his watch. B.K. should be waking up any time now, he thought. She is prettier than ever. But why hadn't Augusta come too? She was the one he really wanted to see. B.K. was in urgent need of a dentist, but Augusta could have used a check-up. Kate and her ambassador probably thought him unreasonable to insist on Manhattan doctors, but what would they find on the eastern shore? An ex-crab fisherman with a hand-cranked drill. Not in *his* daughters' mouths, thank you.

When B.K. emerged from the guest room, Tollover handed her a glass of orange juice. "I'm cook this morning," he said breezily. "How would you like your eggs?"

"You can't cook, Daddy. I'll do it."

"I've had to learn. You will be impressed. Scrambled or soft-boiled?"

"Soft-boiled, but not with any jelly in the whites."

"No jelly. Right."

B.K. thumbed through the copy of *Time*. "Oh, look at this!" she said excitedly as Tollover poured coffee. He groaned inwardly at her spotting the photo of her stepfather. "Here is a picture of Paolo!"

Relieved, Tom leaned over his daughter's shoulder to see a photo of Henry Ford II, his wife Anne, a Ford daughter and the handsome, dark-haired boy whose picture B.K. carried everywhere.

"Like all Italians," Tom said, "he seems to fancy rich Americans."

"He doesn't care about those people. He's told me. He has to socialize with the Fords because his family's in the automobile business too. Isn't he divine?"

"He is attractive, no denying it. But is he treating my daughter with suitable adulation?"

"Paolo's wonderful. We're going to see each other when I get to Nantucket in July."

"Ah, yes, Nantucket. How like your stepfather to choose that cemetery for his summer frolics. Nothing but a few musty Philadelphians and old New Yorkers too dim-witted to realize the action moved to Long Island decades ago."

"Don't be mean, Daddy, I'm looking forward to it. I've heard it's very nice."

"It's nice. You'll enjoy it." Tollover was contrite. "There are many worse places—with worse people."

He brought in their eggs and bacon, then said, "Now tell me all about Tidewater Farm. I must know how my daughters have landed after being cruelly wrenched from the bosom of their father's home."

All B.K.'s instincts warned her to tread cautiously in extolling their new situation.

"It's a very pretty setting, right on the bay." She glanced at her father to see if the information was upsetting him. "It's way out in the country, and not very exciting, of course. It takes almost an hour to get to Annapolis."

"Horses?" Tollover said glumly.

"Uh-huh."

"Boats?"

"Mm-mm."

"How many?"

"Three sailboats and a canoe."

"Private army?"

She looked at him and they both laughed. "It sounds very nice," he said expansively, "and you know I am very happy for you both. You deserve a nice home, the kind you are used to. And Augusta, she must be reveling in all that luxury."

"She loves it. She asked Mummie if she might be allowed to stay there over the summer."

"By herself!?" Tollover sounded shocked.

"Well, she wouldn't be alone. . . ." Despite her father's tone of sweet reason, B.K. was afraid to bring up the servants.

"You mean *staff* will remain. But no adult member of the family?"

"Mummie and Uncle Bryce haven't said yes."

"But they're thinking about it?"

She nodded.

"I don't think I'll approve."

B.K. said nothing, but he could see she was wondering if his approval was necessary.

20

The idea first came to Augusta when she saw the upstairs of the boathouse at Tidewater Farm. It was an enchanting apartment—one large bedroom, a living room and a small kitchen. The living room was furnished with heavy furniture upholstered in a dark flowered fabric. The walls were stained oak and the fireplace was rough fieldstone. The darkness of the room was alleviated by one large picture window that looked out over the glistening brightness of the Chesapeake. At one end double doors led onto a screened porch. If there was a breeze to be felt anywhere at Tidewater Farm, it would be on this porch, with its white wicker furniture and table for dining.

Augusta adored the boathouse. It was rarely used except for an occasional guest; V.I.P.'s were lodged in the main house where servants were on twenty-four-hour call. That this cast-off residence was furnished better than her mother's former New York apartment only made Augusta marvel more that it could be hers for the asking. Despite her fondness for withdrawal, for respites from human company, she realized this charming cottage was no place to live alone. It was, in fact, an ideal place for a prolonged affair.

She quite liked Jeff. She had never met anybody like him. All the other young men she had known were prep-school, pre-Ivy League apprentices to the upper class, either born to it or with enough of a toe-hold—scholarship-winning brain, family connections, growing up in a prime suburb—to entertain thoughts of entering the moneyed classes when they began earning the money their families had neglected to provide.

Jeff, on the other hand, came from a simple family; his father was a house painter in a nearby town. His mother worked part time for a local dry cleaner. Jeff had grown up aware of how little his family had in relation to the idealized American middle class of the movies, but he wasn't overly concerned about it. His ambition extended no further than moving up to secure middle-class status—modest house, one car, money to send his children to college. Nothing more, that was plenty.

Nothing more. Augusta found it hard to take in. Working at Tidewater Farm, Jeff was aware of how exquisite the world could be. Hadn't he seen the films about people with mansions on Fifth Avenue, who traveled to Europe, who entertained sumptuously? But none of that particular vision was in him. Driving home from town one night after a film, Augusta tried to goad him into justifying the smallness of his dream. But Jeff was unshakable.

"Why yearn for things you might end up not getting? Especially when you don't know for sure that you really want them? There are too many things I *know* I want, that I know I can get."

"Such as?"

"A comfortable home—nothing to knock other people's eyes out, just comfortable to live in. I'd like my own business, but not one that will make me a slave and have me burned out by forty. And of course I want kids and a sexy wife who likes to laugh and have fun."

"In other words, the most elementary gratifications. But you could have all that plus so much more. That wouldn't be nearly enough for me."

"You're different. You've always been around money. That's your world. It figures, I guess, that you would want to keep all those things."

Augusta thought bitterly to herself that she had had them for less than a month. She could see how profoundly different she was from Jeff, and she worried at times that she was too preoccupied with the material aspects of her future. The embarrassments of her childhood were, after all, behind her. But it was only with Jeff that she allowed herself such self-doubt. Knowing that he would not be part of her future permitted her a candor she would never have risked with anyone who was a part of the world she aspired to.

During the day when he was tending the pool, he would pass time with Augusta—often together with B.K., who thought Jeff was dreamy looking but dull. The evenings when Jeff took

Augusta out, he would go home to clean up and change, then return to Tidewater Farm in the 1937 Plymouth business coupe he had bought for fifty-six dollars. Leaving his car at the garage, they would speed off in Augusta's Triumph.

Most of their time together was free of philosophical debate. Each night when he brought her back to Tidewater Farm, he would pull the car into a darkened remote area—there was one on a back drive that had an idyllic view of the open bay—and proceed to make innocent love to her. She liked it when he kissed her, if he didn't get too sloppy about it; his pawings and grabbings excited her in a way. But she disliked the indignity of necking and petting, especially in the cramped front seat of a Triumph. It seemed so furtive and dumb, with a vague underpinning of dishonesty.

One particularly lovely night, mild and still, Augusta suggested they get out and walk. They found a path along the water's edge that was eerily dappled in the dim light. The moon was behind the trees overhead; a little of its light filtered through the leafy branches, but the bay beside them was bright and silvery—a setting for the swan princess.

They stopped and kissed. Augusta, always with suitabilities in mind, considered his six-foot-one the ideal height for a full-body embrace. Maybe any height would have seemed ideal after the contortions in the sports car. She loved the feel of his firm, vital body against her own. For once she had no impulse to pull away in a cool-headed move to keep matters in bounds.

Finally, Jeff ended their kiss and cupped the back of her head with his large hand. "For a snob, you're one terrific girl, Augusta."

She smiled and lightly kissed his cheek.

"I think I could like you a lot," he said darkly. His mood was not playful.

"Don't forget our agreement."

"Strictly summer romance. And not much of a summer if you go to Nantucket."

"Shall I stay?"

"You know I want you to."

She put her hand lightly against the green cotton of his polo shirt. She loved the soft resilience of his chest; the thought of the faint brush of golden hairs beneath the fabric gave her the urge to cool her cheek against his skin.

She was aroused, but more curious than passionate. She didn't know what the autumn would bring, but she knew that physical passion would not be a dominant element of the life that awaited her. This was her free period, a gift hiatus, before she began—began *what* she still did not know, but before she began . . .

"Jeff, would you like to make love to me?"

"What do you mean? Of course . . ."

"I mean really make love?"

"Oh, Jesus, Augusta, you know I would, but I didn't think that you . . ."

"I am a snob, but I am not one of your high-school teasers. Follow me."

She led him farther along the path and they quickly came to the small cove where the sailboats were moored. They circled around the water, crossing a small bridge over a stream that entered the bay there. Arriving at the boathouse, they climbed the open wooden stairs from the dock, the moonlit water sparkling up through the boards and making dull, slapping sounds against the pilings.

In the darkened living room Augusta stopped and turned to him. "Do you have anything? For precaution?

"No, I didn't think . . . I mean . . ."

"Never mind. I'll worry about it afterward." She realized she was being too businesslike and too assertive, but it was in part her rebellion against their teenaged fumbling, in part her way of handling her own nervousness.

"Let's both take off our clothes and get into bed like an old married couple." She spoke softly, with no trace of humor.

She went into the bedroom and stepped out of her skirt and draped it gently over the back of a chair. When she was completely naked she lay on the bed and watched as Jeff, sitting on a chair directly in a slice of moonlight, fumbled with a knot in his shoelace. In seconds he was naked too and stretched out on the bed beside her, their flanks touching. She was ready but still disliked the prospect of his grabbing her in a spasm of passion. When he leaned over and gracefully kissed her on the breast, she was relieved and impressed.

"You know this is the first time for me," Augusta said. "And for you, too, isn't it?"

Jeff didn't respond for a moment, then nodded yes.

"I know I've been bossy about this," she said, "but let me ask one more thing, then I'll do whatever you want."

"What is it?"

"Could we just lie here for a moment?"

"Augusta, you're driving me crazy. It isn't . . ."

"Please. Just for a minute. Without even talking."

She watched the reflections from the water dance on the ceiling and listened to an owl hoot softly and the slap, slap of the water against the boathouse. She had no fears that her bold experiment would unleash uncheckable passions and appetites in herself. For sheer physical pleasure she could not imagine a better partner than Jeff, but she hoped she could enjoy it enough to make up for the loss of dignity.

She forced her thoughts to Jeff. His naked body was familiar to her from horseplay in the swimming pool, his mouth and hands from sessions in the car, so little distance to closing the gap . . .

She saw that he had propped himself on one elbow and was looking down at her. She turned and smiled, then pulled his mouth down onto hers.

21 Augusta was impressed with her mother's performance as chatelaine of Tidewater Farm. Kate, careful not to antagonize any of the servants, took charge in a soft-spoken yet forceful manner. She supervised the redecorating with a resolute competence that left no doubt who was in charge. Her sure authority pleased Hartshorne. Everything she did pleased him, and the unreserved approbation fueled her confidence and enhanced her style.

Her facade took on greater dignity—a more erect carriage, a more matronly coiffure and, naturally, a more striking wardrobe. Hartshorne extolled Kate's taste, to the point that Augusta wondered if it had been the basis of his attraction.

Even in the small amount of entertaining they had done—some random guests and one informal dinner for twelve—Kate had been a relaxed and poised hostess acutely aware that most of the guests, old friends of Hartshorne's, were watching her performance like Olympic figure-skating judges.

Augusta had to admit that her mother had taken over the management of an important estate as though she had done nothing else most of her life. In a world where birth was important, Kate managed to persuade the most discerning and skeptical critics that she was reared to run a house like Tidewater Farm and to be the wife of an important man.

Bryce and Kate Hartshorne agreed to let Augusta remain alone in Maryland over the summer. Augusta's announced reason for wanting to be left behind was her love of horses; she could ride at Tidewater Farm but not on Nantucket. Her mother knew, as did everyone, that she was seeing the young pool attendant, but she occasionally went with other boys to parties in the area so Jeff was not considered a dominant force.

In addition, Augusta's entire manner precluded parental concern. It had been a long time since Kate had worried about Augusta's behaving foolishly in any situation. Whatever apprehensions Kate had about leaving Augusta alone were dispelled by the presence of three of the servants, who were to be left behind, and by Hartshorne's promise to look in from time to time during flying trips to Washington. Kate also made Augusta promise to visit Nantucket.

Brandon dropped hints to Augusta that he knew she was up to something—including several insinuations about Jeff's striking physical attributes—but Augusta remained noncommittal. B.K. suspected nothing, so Augusta decided that, for the first time in their lives, she would keep a secret from her sister. B.K. was still infatuated with Prince Paolo and was more caught up than ever in notions of good family and society. Augusta saw her affair as a controlled experiment that had a predetermined, pre-announced end; she knew, however, that no one else would see it as dispassionately as she did, even B.K., who knew her as well as anyone.

Brandon, having for once pleased his father by agreeing to spend the summer with them in Nantucket, had then infuriated him by getting a job in a summer theater in Siasconset on the far side of the island. ("My son has an unfailing instinct for depraved company and can ferret it out even in the bracing, healthy air of Nantucket.") To everyone's relief, Brandon subsequently got a better job at a theater on Cape Cod, so would be conducting his "apprenticeship to Bohemia," as his father called it, out of sight.

Finally they were all gone and Augusta found herself alone on a 150-acre Maryland plantation with her own car, servants to look after her, horses to ride, boats to sail and a nineteen-year-old Adonis for a lover. She was amazed at the way things had fallen in place and proud that she herself had effected the finishing touches to her luck.

She loved being alone at Tidewater Farm. For the first time in her life she didn't have to put up with the moods of roommates, the battles of parents, the curiosity of B.K.—nor did she have to suppress her own flashes of hostility toward her mother. For once she had nothing to think about but her own immediate pleasure and her own auspicious future. Her mind would make rapid scans of her present life and, amazingly, could trip on nothing that caused pain or anxiety. Except, perhaps, her father . . . No, even he was doing all right in New York. She would see him from time to time, he had his girl friends to keep him from growing lonely, and he couldn't help but be pleased his daughters were being so well taken care of in Maryland. There was no escaping it: her life was as idyllic as any she could imagine.

She and Jeff spent more and more time in the boathouse, often sleeping there. Having established to the servants that she liked the place, Augusta eventually told them she was moving there and would take care of it herself. When it needed more cleaning than just routine tidying, she would call down one of the maids to give it a thorough going over. In this way she made sure there were no surprise visits.

At first she would have lunch and dinner at the main house, often inviting Jeff, but eventually she undertook cooking for them both in the little boathouse kitchen. Within a few weeks she found herself going to the main house rarely and moved her everyday clothes to the boathouse. The frenzied redecorating at the house gave greater logic to this shift.

She felt sure the servants knew what was going on, but she didn't care. If they alerted her mother and stepfather, the worst that could happen would be incarceration on Nantucket. She doubted such a dramatic reaction. They would have to acknowledge that as far as her chastity was concerned, the damage was done. In addition, she had suspected from the start of discussions about her staying in Maryland, that her mother and stepfather, in the first months of their marriage, relished the prospect of less family togetherness. It was unlikely they would let a little servants' gossip wreck an arrangement that worked out so well for everyone.

The days fell into paradisical pattern. Augusta would go for a long ride in the early mornings while Jeff did his chores. After this she would swim, then lie by the pool reading until lunch. She had given up D.H. Lawrence; his breathless eroticism seemed incongruous to her own cool detachment with Jeff. She backed off to the arid refinement of Henry James and Edith Wharton, particularly relishing the latter's *House of Mirth*.

When Jeff stopped work at noon, they would swim together and have a sandwich either by the pool or in the boathouse. He could finish his tasks by four o'clock and they would go for a sail, sometimes stripping off all their clothes, which was in small part lasciviousness, in large part the heat. On particularly warm days, they would stay out on the cooler water till just before dark, bringing with them food and cold beer.

Occasionally Jeff proclaimed himself in love with Augusta. When he did, she would deliver him her lecture: she liked him enormously, but it was far too soon in her life to think of a long-term involvement. She had many things she wanted to do before considering settling down with one person. If this much negativism didn't squelch Jeff, she hit out directly. Even if she were to consider marriage, Jeff would not be her choice; they wanted such different things from life.

The first time she confronted him with this stark fact, they were lying in adjacent chaises by the swimming pool. Suddenly he swung his legs around and sat up facing her.

"Prince Baby Lamberghini!" he said.

"Who is that?"

"That's who you should marry! Prince Baby Lamberghini. He owns most of the car companies in Italy and all of the parking lots."

"There is no such person."

"Of course there is. Don't you know anything about international high society? His friends call him Prince Baby. He hunts in India and skis the polar cap. His mother was a Lucretia and his father was a Borgia. One brother is president of Italy, his sister is married to Andrei Gromyko. All the paintings in the Vatican Gallery are on loan from his collection. He has houses in Rome, Paris, London and New York."

Augusta had settled back on her chaise and put on her dark glasses. "But is he powerful?"

"Of course. Last year he was the single largest contributor to the Democratic party, anonymously, of course. He has Truman in his hip pocket. Dean Acheson doesn't sneeze without first calling Prince Baby."

"Is he handsome?"

"Tyrone Power."

"Amusing?"

"Noel Coward."

"Kind?"

"Mother Cabrini . . ."

Her eyes still closed to the sun, Augusta said, "I'm glad to see you're getting the idea. You understand now why a liaison with you is impossible. I am already spoken for."

Jeff leaned across her confidentially. "But there's one thing I forgot to tell you about Prince Baby . . ." He paused dramatically. "He never changes his socks. It's a thing with him.

Absolutely refuses. And wears them to bed. Also . . . he has a tiny thing."

"No problem. Part of the agreement, which was drawn up when I was four years old, is that we have separate bedrooms, if not separate palaces. It's the art collection that interests me . . ."

"But he only likes guys. He has the men servants lined up . . ."

"Live and let live is my motto. He must have his amusements and I will have mine. You may come for a visit at our summer estate at Ischia."

"I will not have dealings with a married woman."

"Pity."

Augusta could sense that Jeff was irked by the ease with which she got the upper hand in his game; still, Prince Baby remained as the code word between them for Augusta's Jeff-less future.

One night in mid-July, Jeff once again brought up the forbidden subject. They had been for a swim in the black, cool water of the small cove below the boathouse. Jeff decided to swim out into the bay for exercise. Augusta had left the water, dried herself with a beach towel and gone up to the living room.

A few minutes later, Jeff had come bounding up the stairs and into the room. Water was not dripping off him but rolling off in sheets.

"Gus! You should have swum out with me. It was the most beautiful fucking sight I've ever seen, the stars from in the water, the lights across—"

"For God's sake, Jeff! You're soaking everything. Do you have to be such a boor?"

He was dashed by the vehemence of her outburst and stood staring at her for a moment.

"Sorry," he said, and went out onto the landing and dried himself with one of the towels hanging over the railing. Then, from outside, his high spirits restored, "But you should have come with me! I've never seen so many stars. And there were a few lights along the shore, just enough to make the bay sparkle."

"It sounds lovely," she said as he came back inside. She knew her flare-up had been out of proportion and she wanted to be pleasant, but still she carped. "Get a mop and get that water up. And hang the rug over the stair railing."

She wondered why his routine carelessness angered her so. Maybe it triggered guilt she felt at making such thorough and unauthorized use of her stepfather's facilities. But she knew, too, that Jeff's oafishness pointed up the gulf between them. Jeff cared nothing for his surroundings or for the rare luxury they were enjoying. She had always been aware of Jeff's limitations, but sometimes a welling-up of aggression made her want to take him on, to shake his smug values with their insinuation that she was, in opposing them, superficial and materialistic.

She knew he would be just as happy acting out their affair in an eight-dollar-a-night motel room; he had implied he would be *happier*, since it would have been he who paid for it. He had suggested it once, but only at the beginning when he felt uncomfortable about making such free use of his employer's premises. On nights like the present one, with a starlit dip or sail, followed by supper in the boathouse and lovemaking, he forgot his uneasiness. It was still in him, however, and this only furthered her exasperation.

If he was merely a fool, why should that make her angry and unpleasant to him? After a supper of lamb chops and fresh corn on the cob, Augusta tried to assuage her confusion and guilt by more purposeful lovemaking. Her intention was to make peace, but instead she brought about an unwelcome surge of emotionalism from Jeff.

Lying in the darkened bedroom, they listened to the sound of the water below them, both startled into quiet by the intensity of their energetic passion. Jeff spoke first.

"If you think I'm going to let you go in September, you're dead wrong."

"No threats, please, I'm still recovering." She lay her head on his chest and brought his arm around her waist.

"We fit too well together, Gus, you think this sort of thing will happen over and over?"

"Jeff . . ." Her tone was warning.

"Come on, Gus, you can't be as cold-blooded as you pretend. I know you must feel as strongly about me as I do about you or you couldn't make love like that."

"You aren't very good at keeping bargains, are you?"

"Fuck bargains! It's not human, saying you're going to love me desperately for two months and eleven days. Then goodbye, I never want to see you again."

Angrily, Augusta got up from the bed and yanked on a seersucker bathrobe. She snapped on a table lamp and turned toward his naked body, brown and gold against the white sheets. "The reason I told you I don't want to talk about this is that I don't want to keep saying things that must hurt you."

"Why hurt me? I'm all right. The only thing that could hurt me is if you said you didn't feel anything for me, and even that couldn't hurt since I wouldn't believe you."

She sat on the edge of the bed. "You'd be right. Of course I have feeling for you. A lot. But our outlooks are so completely different. What's the point of analyzing all the reasons we would be miserable together after a time?"

He thought for a minute. "Maybe we should consider compromising, meeting each other halfway. Maybe I could try to work up a little more of your kind of ambition and maybe you could lower your sights." He looked at her hopefully.

"You don't understand, Jeff. Compromise, making do, adapting is all I've ever done. I don't want to compromise again."

"Not for me?" He was half coquettish, half desperate.

"Not for anyone." Her thoughts sank into areas so private even Augusta couldn't verbalize them, only feel their existence.

22

B.K. adored Nantucket even though Paolo was unable to get there. The island's spread of open spaces had a crisp clarity; exhilarating winds seemed to sweep it clean of mainland grit and tawdriness. The town of Nantucket, a charming jumble of eighteenth-century white frame houses, looked frozen in time. Every vista, whether in town or on the moors, was indiluted, unsullied history or nature.

For all of Nantucket's beauty, B.K. doubted if Augusta would like it. The summer houses, despite their historical authenticity and venerable grace, were too simple for Augusta, whose taste leaned more toward the sumptuous cottages of Newport and Bar Harbor. Nantucket's glory was more subtle. The handsome old houses, expensively maintained and tended by skilled servants, gave off a feeling of perpetual affluence. The strong aura of history, with many of the houses still occupied by descendants of the original builders, appealed strongly to B.K.'s fascination with old families, but would mean less to Augusta's here-and-now pragmatism.

Ambassador Hartshorne's house was one of the town's most impressive. It sat in patrician grandeur on the tree-shaded cobblestones of upper Main Street. From the front, it had the appearance of a large town house; the gardens behind it were so commodious they reminded B.K. of the grounds around the Maryland house.

Hartshorne had strong Nantucket connections. His family tree reached back to two of the island's settling families, the Macys and the Coffins. His house had been built by a Coffin, a whaling captain who eventually expanded his fortune by giving up whale hunting for purveying whaling apparatus. The house was an antiquarian's dream—polished oak floors, spacious antique-filled rooms, each with a handsomely manteled fire-place, family portraits and, throughout, a museum's worth of old silver and Chinese porcelain.

B.K. had thought it odd to leave the country in the summer and move to a town; she soon saw the logic of this move. Apart from the vastly improved summer weather, the town of Nantucket was little more than a quaint set for resort activities. From her stepfather's house, she could stroll through the town's center, an intriguing jumble of shops and restaurants, and arrive quickly at the picturesque dock area where the steamer arrived from New Bedford and where many residents kept their pleasure boats. A short additional walk brought her to the Yacht

Club, the most desirable center of action for the summer young people, whose favorite action was sailing, followed by tennis. Hartshorne had already arranged for B.K. to have membership privileges.

She quickly got to know a number of people her age, mostly through a young man named Ben Brockton, whose family invited B.K. to dinner shortly after she arrived. The Brocktons were probably the leading clan of summer dwellers, a fact in which they took more pride than in their national prominence. A Brockton had sat on Lincoln's cabinet and each successive generation had wielded comparable political power, often in invisible, king-making roles.

Occasionally the family took time out from guiding the nation's course to replenish its fortune, which was now of mammoth proportions. In recent years, with politics once again becoming a field for gentlemen, several Brocktons had run for office and won handily. Ben's uncle, Blake Brockton, was the most glamorous and promising of the Senate's younger members. The Brocktons all seemed to possess the knack of holding the public eye, as useful an asset for a politician as a family fortune. Todd Brockton, Blake's brother and Ben's father, was regularly written up in the press for his sailing victories, his business coups and friendships with film stars.

Ben was a year older than B.K. and not attractive. He had a tall, ungainly body and a bland bespectacled face that lacked a distinct chin line. Even with these drawbacks, he was a ringleader among his friends because of a driving, wily intelligence and a fingersnapping restlessness that kept those around him off-balance yet amused. In addition, his quick mind and nervous aggressiveness made him an important contender with girls.

B.K. had heard these things about Brockton, advance billing from school friends who frequented Nantucket, so was surprised to find him subdued throughout the dinner. While he did not seem the least intimidated by either B.K. or his mother, he confined himself to an occasional polite question while a butler served bluefish from a large Imari platter. Mrs. Brockton, on the other hand, was animated, asking many questions about Kate's refurbishings of Tidewater Farm.

After dinner, Ben suggested he show B.K. the Lobster Pot, the island spot for young people. B.K. accepted, thinking peevishly that the evening was shaping up to be a date and she was too old to have dates arranged by parents.

They got into Ben's jeep. Once they were alone, his manner changed abruptly. He turned to her and said, "You know, you're a terrific-looking girl. Good build, too. How would you like to be my girl for the summer?"

B.K. rarely became as angry as this made her, but she couldn't marshal her outrage into anything more than an icy, "I already have a boy friend."

"Don't get pissed about it, kid. Waste of energy. Is he here?"

"No."

"Well, then. What's the problem?"

She wanted to say "You are, you conceited jackass," but, remembering Ben's position as a kingpin of this new territory, said only, "We're serious about each other."

Ben shot the car out of the driveway. "You're sixteen, right? That's too young to throw yourself away on someone who's not even here."

His obliviousness to B.K.'s irritation tended to eradicate it. "I'm too young to get involved with boys at all," she said. "A long-distance romance is my way of easing into the whole thing."

"That's bull. In the Middle Ages a woman would have been married two years at your age." He chatted, then pulled the car into the parking lot of a dimly lit roadhouse. He snapped off the lights, pulled the ignition key out and turned toward B.K. "Well, how about it?"

She was still angry at his brashness; at the same time, she was flattered and pleased to have her likes and dislikes persist as the center of anyone's thinking.

"No deal," she said pleasantly, "so if you like, we can go Dutch in here."

Ben roared. "Pretty sharp, Miss Tollover."

They entered the dark club, which was jammed with young people. A harried headwaiter, little older than the teenaged crowd, was telling standing couples there were no tables. He spotted Ben and said, "Hi, Ben. We haven't got a thing tonight."

"Oh, you can find something, Charlie," Ben said airily as he grabbed B.K.'s arm and steered her past the agape couples. Charlie responded and led them into the packed room, frantically scouting two empty chairs. Several people from a corner table shouted and waved at Ben. He dismissed Charlie and led B.K. to his friends, a sun-tanned group of teenaged boys and girls who were clearly Ben's sailing, tennis-playing cronies.

"This is B.K. Tollover, everyone, a major new acquisition of Nantucket's elite. She's pretty, rich and—involved. So you girls can relax. I'm still all yours."

From that moment on, B.K.'s summer became a charmed one of sailing, biking, tennis and picnics with this entrenched crowd, and, in the evening, parties at one or another of their houses. They were a lively group who had grown up together in the summers, scattering in the winters along the upper East Coast. Most of them were now in boarding school, one or two already in college. They were attractive, bright and their families rich. Because of this and because they had come to Nantucket every summer since any of them could remember, the island was theirs. Some of the town boys didn't agree and there were a few fracases—shoving matches and car chases—but all harmless enough to add spice rather than anxiety to the summer pleasures.

B.K. was thrilled that the young crowd befriended her so unquestioningly; she was sure a major reason was Ben's sponsorship. In spite of the family wealth and social position of the group's members, they all deferred to Ben. He was quicker and more assertive than the others, to be sure, but his family was also richer and more powerful, a fact not lost on one of these sixteen and seventeen year olds.

In addition, Ben himself could top each of them for glamour. His senator uncle had arranged for Ben to spend a month the previous summer in Kenya working at a Friends Service hospital, during which time Ben had kept a diary. There was talk that the diary might be published. None of his friends had any doubt that it would. At times B.K. was bothered by Ben's overbearing manner with salespeople, waiters or anyone outside his well-born tribe. But part of her was dazzled by his unflappable self-assurance, and she was glad to be under his protection.

One member of their immediate group was a pretty girl named Betty Ann McDevitt. Betty Ann was the only one of them who was not from a summer-colony family. Her father had a grocery store on the outskirts of town and Betty Ann herself worked in a Main Street clothing store during the summer. She was tolerated in Ben's inner circle only because she was the girl friend of Seth Jones, Ben's best friend and Andover roommate.

Betty Ann's less than plush circumstances reminded B.K. of her own recent past, and she was impressed with the self-assured way the girl dealt with it. Betty Ann had a cheerful nature and a total openness and lack of embarrassment about her family situation. Recalling her own childhood of pretense and sham, B.K. admired greatly such unapologetic candor. Another thing that made Betty Ann a heroine in B.K.'s eyes was her being the only one in the group who could stand up to Ben. When he was being at his most overbearing and dictatorial, she would blithely tell him to go to hell.

Ben was less than taken with such *lèse majesté*, but swallowed it out of friendship for Seth. He was aware that the others relished Betty Ann's fearless defiance but knew they wouldn't dare emulate it.

Ben planned to follow his uncle in Democratic politics and was aggressively liberal on all the timely causes; Europe's d.p.'s, the necessity of a strong United Nations, the new Israeli state, and the injustices to America's blacks. B.K. was stunned to learn he belonged to the National Association for the Advancement of Colored People; she had thought only black people could belong.

Ben would lecture them for hours on his pet causes, deftly

demolishing his friends' limp arguments, usually watered-down droppings from their parents' watered-down Republicanism. He succeeded in making them all, B.K. included, more aware of the current issues. Another thing made B.K. a contented subject in Ben Brockton's kingdom: his acceptance of her not wanting a boy friend. He made sure she was included in all activities with or without a specific date, he himself paying for her if they were at a restaurant or sandwich shop.

At the Yacht Club she could sign, but at other places this might have been awkward. Ben always had plenty of cash and didn't mind spending it on B.K., even when he was rushing another girl in the party.

B.K.'s summer was so filled with fun and stimulating new experiences, she couldn't imagine why Augusta would want to isolate herself at Tidewater Farm. How hot it must be. She wrote her sister a number of gushy letters extolling the glories of Nantucket and urging her to come up. Augusta would write back about the reading she was accomplishing and how she loved the peace and tranquility. B.K. thought her sister was getting old.

Despite Ben's finger-wagging sermons on human miseries, Nantucket was for B.K. an enchanted island completely immune, not only from the world's problems, but from its ugliness as well. There was almost nothing to offend the eye, very little, in fact, that didn't delight it. She loved the vast empty beaches of the south shore with their strong surf and endless white sand. And she particularly liked the open moors in the middle of the island with low pine and bayberry bushes covering the gently contoured landscape with its glimpses of blue sea in the distance. It was ironic that it would be in the midst of this pristine landscape that B.K.'s halcyon summer was brought to an abrupt end.

One evening in early August, a picnic supper was arranged by Ben and some others at Tom Nevers' beach where the group would surf cast and fry whatever fish they caught. They brought hot dogs in case the fish weren't biting. Ben and Seth and another couple were in the jeep when they picked up B.K. Then they swung by the shop on Main Street to collect Betty

Ann, who got off at six o'clock. As they sped along the Polpis Road to pick up another group who were staying at Sankaty Head, spirits were high—so high, B.K. suspected that Ben and Seth had been drinking. The other group would follow them to Tom Nevers' in their own car.

"Do you all have enough room back there?" Ben yelled to the four crowded into the jeep's rear. "If you don't, B.K. can come up here and sit on my lap."

As the road twisted and circled through the dense shrubbery, passing an occasional house, their jeep got stuck behind a slow-moving pickup truck, old and dilapidated, whose back was loaded with cut brush. Several times Ben tried to pass the truck but was discouraged by a blind curve ahead. He honked. He yelled, "Either park that thing or drive it!"

Suddenly he said, "I've got it. There's a cut-off up here. I can overtake it that way. Hang on everybody."

At a small opening in the scrub pines to the right, Ben bounced the jeep onto a dirt road and pressed down on the gas, sending up clouds of dust behind them. The road ran parallel to the paved road for about a hundred yards, passed a trash dump, then made a rather sharp left and rejoined the main road about a hundred yards ahead.

"Look at him," Ben yelled, motioning through the trees to their left. "That son-of-a-bitch is speeding up." B.K. could not see that he was. She was frightened when Ben gave the jeep more gas as they approached the turn back onto the highway. She felt sure, however, they were far enough ahead of the truck to make the intersection safely. They hit the sharp turn in the dirt road and B.K. remembered experiencing an avalanche of terror as the jeep tipped to the right, then didn't right itself but continued over.

B.K. awoke in a hospital a few hours later. There was a bandage on her forehead and one on her arm, but she was all right. Ben was sitting by her bed along with Seth, whose wrist was bandaged.

"You ought to learn to roll with the jeeps better, B.K. my girl," Ben said with his usual breeziness, "you missed all the fun." He had not a scratch, the other couple was O.K. as well, Seth had merely sprained his wrist when he tried to break his fall. "The only one hurt at all was Betty Ann," Ben said. "The rest of us were thrown clear. She almost was, but the jeep caught her below the knee. Bruised her pretty badly. She'll be all right."

Betty Ann was not all right, B.K. learned a few days later. Her kneecap was crushed and she would never regain the use of one leg. She was crippled for life. The incident was fully covered in the local papers and became the talk of Nantucket. Because the only serious casualty was a permanent resident, the incident activated the usually quiescent antagonism between the resort people and the natives.

This feeling was exacerbated by a hostility to the mighty Brockton family who, like Ben himself, were not hesitant about wielding their influence around Nantucket just as they did around Wall Street or the corridors of the United States government. Ben warned the others there might be repercussions and that he would expect them to stand by him. An inquest was scheduled and a police lieutenant was assigned to question each of the people in the jeep.

The Brocktons' lawyer, the son of a well-liked summer-colony family, spoke with Ambassador Hartshorne, with whom he often played bridge. Shortly thereafter Hartshorne asked B.K. if he might speak with her. They went into the garden and sat on sunlight-dappled chairs in a cool, hydrangea-banked corner of the lawn. B.K. felt they looked like two heads of state you see in photos chatting informally on the palace grounds.

"You know, B.K., this could be quite serious for Ben," the ambassador began. "He is a young man with a splendid career ahead of him. I've talked with him and he really has a head on his shoulders and the right slant on many things. Given his dynamic personality, there's no limit to what Ben might achieve. You must be extremely careful when you talk to the lieutenant."

"But surely, Uncle Bryce, you want me to tell what happened? I mean, the truth."

"Of course I do, B.K." He almost snapped this, underlining

that they were discussing Ben's future, not the ambassador's integrity. "It's only that there may be a slight effort at twisting Ben's role in the accident."

"But Ben was driving . . ."

"I *know* he was." B.K. hated to exasperate her kind and generous stepfather. "But the other car could not see what happened. This puts the burden on you and the other passengers to reconstruct the incident. You know how there has always been a certain antagonism between local people and summer people? It is not unreasonable to assume that the authorities will make it as tough on Ben as they possibly can. They will push the law to its limit, but the only ammunition they can use is what you and the others tell them. I am not asking you to lie. I am simply asking you to be extremely cautious in what ammunition you give the town authorities, whose motives may well go beyond simply uncovering the truth of the situation."

B.K. thought quite hard about this for the next few hours and decided it was strange that her stepfather, who showed such an intense interest in the accident, never once asked her what actually happened. Reviewing the conversation in her mind it seemed he had vigorously *avoided* hearing B.K.'s version. Did he want her to lie yet not be a party to the lie? It began to look that way.

She asked her mother if they could discuss it. Kate said it was a very serious matter but she could not add anything to what her Uncle Bryce had said—he understood both Nantucket and legal matters far better than she did. B.K. had never felt so isolated.

Ben was less subtle. "They're trying to hang me for reckless driving, but they can't lay a finger on me unless someone in my jeep says I was driving too fast. The only one who might try anything so shitty is Betty Ann, and we've taken care of that."

B.K. was baffled and later asked Seth what Ben had meant about Betty Ann. "Paid off her parents, dum-dum. Brockton lawyers had a little talk with Betty Ann's parents and they had a little talk with Betty Ann. You might as well start learning that cash is good for more things than cashmere sweaters."

Even the Brocktons' smug assurance was shaken a few days

later when the news shot around the island that Betty Ann had suddenly died. An embolism had developed in the middle of the night and reached her heart before anyone knew she was in trouble.

When the lieutenant finally came to question B.K., her head was a tangle of conflicting truths which had been force-fed her by everyone close to the situation and a few who were not. "Won't bring her back . . ." "Why ruin another young life?" "Who can remember exactly what happened anyhow?"

She thought with terror of being tricked into saying she suspected Ben had been drinking. How wrong that would be, when she didn't know for certain. And how dangerous for Ben. Surely this was what Uncle Bryce had been talking about.

B.K.'s apprehensions were only increased by Lieutenant Hussey's calm and friendly manner. He was a short barrel-chested man who looked more like a laborer than an investigative officer, but B.K. quickly came to respect his intelligence and his awareness of the forces opposing him.

He asked many questions, some seemingly unrelated to the accident itself. He never challenged her answers and she kept to the prearranged story: they had turned onto the dirt road thinking it was a short cut to Sankaty Head. When they learned their mistake, they had headed back onto the main road. Ben was unprepared for both the sharp turn and the loose dirt. The jeep had turned over. No, he wasn't going too fast. Jeeps turn over all the time.

"We have reason to think he was driving recklessly," the lieutenant said. "The driver of the pickup truck said Brockton had been trying to pass him. We think he was trying to pass on the dirt road. But this is just conjecture. Unless someone who could actually see what was happening testifies to this, we have no case."

"As far as I could tell," B.K. said evenly, "he was not trying to pass anybody. Why would he turn off the main road to pass?"

The lieutenant left, but he returned a number of times in the following days to go over B.K.'s account. At first she assumed he did the same with all of the jeep's passengers, but she was unnerved to learn he was focusing on her. Did he think she was the weak link in a chain of false testimony? Did something in her manner suggest she might waver?

The last time he saw B.K., the policeman said nothing about the particulars of the accident. Instead he spoke only about the need for traffic laws, for safety and the need for enforcement of them. This need was particularly pronounced when someone gets hurt, he said, or, as in this case, killed. The need is also great if the suspected law-breaker is a person from an important family. Thwarting justice in such an instance was demoralizing for everyday citizens, it hit out at the entire democratic system of government.

As the hearing date approached, B.K. thought about little else besides her role in Ben's drama. He had been very nice to her; he would be nice to her in the future. So would his friends, who would probably end up at college with her or nearby. And how could Lieutenant Hussey talk about damaging the government? The Brocktons *were* the government. So was Uncle Bryce. Behind it all she saw the overriding question. Why make trouble for a friend? Kids snitched for each other all the time. Why make them hate you?

Two days before the hearing, something happened that diverted B.K.'s attention from the general, almost abstract issues involved in the affair and refocused it on her own situation which, in the excitement, she had forgotten. Since her mother's remarriage, B.K. felt that the painful circumstances of her childhood were behind her. No more arguments with her Uncle Harry about nice people and the right parties. She was one of them now. Her house was bigger, her clothes nicer, her family more important.

She was walking across the porch at the Yacht Club. Two older women, whom she had seen many times but didn't know, were sitting in wicker armchairs close to the porch railing. They turned their necks stiffly as she passed by and bestowed on her frigid smiles. They watched her pass by, then resumed their conversation. Remembering she had left her tennis racket in the dining room, B.K. returned to the porch in time to hear one woman say to the other, "Who knows *what* she'll say or do. She's not a Hartshorne, you know. She's a Tollover. They're not people of substance. They're nothing but *café* society."

23

As the summer progressed, communications between Tidewater Farm and Nantucket intensified as plans progressed for Augusta's debut. Kate badgered Augusta for a list of the friends to be invited. With all her acquaintances from Greenvale, Chapin and Walker's that she liked at all, her list was no more than a quarter of the total list; most were close friends of Hartshorne's or colleagues too august to ignore—plus the college-aged children of both groups.

Augusta, irritated when pressed for decisions, could still see the humor in the rarefied nature of this sole disruption to her idyllic summer. Judgments were being coaxed from her on such thorny matters as the fabric for her dress, the location of the outdoor dance floor, the menu for dinner, the floral decorations. Eventually Augusta was caught up in the plans. Hartshorne was surprised that his stepdaughter took such a keen interest in the smallest details; he expected her to leave them to the professional party organizer, a Mrs. Hughes from Philadelphia, or to the various purveyors and caterers. Kate, on the other hand, was not at all surprised at Augusta's close involvement and was careful about deciding anything without first checking with her older daughter.

Towards the end of July, Kate came down from Nantucket to push ahead the arrangements. She didn't come out to Tidewater Farm but stayed at a small apartment Hartshorne kept on Connecticut Avenue, a few minutes from the State Department. Augusta drove into the capital for a day of fittings, meetings with suppliers and a long lunch with Mrs. Hughes, who had flown down from Philadelphia wearing a large hat and carrying a notebook full of questions for Augusta.

Augusta was delighted that Meyer Davis would be conducting the orchestra himself; she knew this was a crucial status designator on the deb-party circuit ("He played for mother's debut, so wouldn't *dream* of letting me come out without him," was a frequent gush at Walker's.)

That evening over dinner with Hartshorne at the Metropolitan Club, an awkwardness arose. Hartshorne had been to a party the previous summer in Upperville, Virginia, that had had portable fountains set up around the lawns with lights playing on them. They had struck him as just the thing for Augusta's party. Augusta had never seen fountains of this sort, but thought they sounded jerry-built and cheap. Having never crossed her stepfather on anything, she was reluctant to do it on an aspect of his most magnificent act of generosity toward her. On the other hand, she was horrified at the thought of having any feature of her party look flashy or gimmicky.

"It sounds so expensive," she said tentatively.

"Nonsense," said Hartshorne. "It's surprisingly reasonable and the effect is stunning. And compared to what Meyer asks now, it's nothing."

"Aren't the wires and pipes visible?"

"They are concealed beautifully. When it's dark, you don't see them at all."

Augusta thought of the beauty of estates with real fountains like the Blanchards'; she hated the idea of guests arriving at Tidewater Farm in daylight and seeing wires and rubber tubes running over the lawns like at a traveling carnival. Her stepfather seemed unshakable in his enthusiasm for his budget Versailles.

She thought of a plan. She asked if she could deal directly with the fountain company. She wanted to learn the various choices and see what they might be able to improvise. She made contact and asked if they could set their fountains up in the bay. The fountain people consulted for a while: they could give her several large jets straight up from shallow water, but they would have to be illuminated from on land.

Augusta had been considering placing the dance-floor marquee on the water's edge across the lawn to the left of the main house, by the path toward the swimming pool. She ordered the company to install two large jets in the shallow water of the bay about thirty feet offshore behind the dance floor. The jets would provide a festive backdrop to the pink-and-white striped tent; they would clearly be part of the temporary party arrangements.

As the summer progressed, the mounting excitement drove Jeff deeper into a sullen depression. Augusta chided him for his indifference to such a big event in her life.

"Why should I get overjoyed at our farewell party?" he said. "I understand Prince Baby Lamb is flying in on his own DC-6 from which he will parachute gracefully onto the lawn at the stroke of midnight . . ."

"Don't worry, Jeff," Augusta consoled, "if you aren't sick of me by then, you will be when you see what a ruthless, calculating snob I am, playing up to the important guests and ignoring the nobodies."

He said nothing, leaving her attempt at humor to fester and pollute the atmosphere between them.

Late one morning Augusta was sitting alone by the pool reading. Jeff had gone into town to buy chemicals for the pool. He told Augusta to eat lunch without him. She had grown so accustomed to seeing no one around the extensive grounds, except Jeff and an occasional black gardener, that when she saw her father walking through the path out into the bright sun of the pool flagstones, she thought she might be hallucinating.

"You wouldn't come to see me," Tom Tollover said cheerily, "so I thought I'd better come to you."

He looked wonderful, tanned and lean as he used to be all year and immaculately dressed in an off-white gabardine suit and orange tie. Her first reaction when she realized he was not an apparition was delight, so great a delight that he became the reality and, for a moment, Tidewater Farm and her recent life the apparition. She felt the same sparks of excitement she had felt as a child when he would return to Mapleton from one of his expeditions—the feeling that her period of getting by, of passing the days as best she could was over and another period of fun and excitement was about to begin.

After Augusta had risen to kiss him, and they had settled in chairs by the pool, the reality of her new life reasserted itself and an uneasiness spread within her at his presence here, the scene of her new life, a life that was dominated at the moment by the affair with Jeff, a development she knew her father would deplore.

Or would he? She didn't know for certain, but suspected he would despise Jeff, for reasons of class if not of morality. But Augusta didn't care. She had no intention of announcing to him her initiation into womanhood, of laying this major step into adulthood at her father's feet the way she had all the other forward steps: her first horse-show win, her class presidency at Greenvale and later at Walker's, her acceptance into Smith. After this succession of girlhood triumphs, the coupling with a pool attendant might be something of a let-down to an ambitious, form-obsessed parent.

As with her mother and stepfather, Augusta felt secrecy and deception was justified, since she knew beyond any doubt that Jeff was transitory in her life. Parents' primary concerns, Augusta knew, were always about what their children were "getting into." Adults were most concerned about their offsprings' directions, life trends, slides into profligacy and the like. Augusta knew that, with Jeff, she was not "getting into" anything. She also knew she lacked the energy and persuasive power to overcome the programmed reactions of adults.

As she looked at her father in the sun-drenched terrace, she thought that at least he wouldn't come down as hard on the moral issue as most parents would, including her own Maryland set.

It would only be a few years later that Augusta would be amused to see, with the advent of the contraceptive pill, how handily American parenthood dropped its moral preoccupation with unmarried sex. It had never been *wrong*, it turned out, only risky and potentially messy. Pragmatism masquerading as decency. To Augusta this so-called revolution was an overdue sane attitude toward something not all that important.

Augusta's uneasiness at her father's surprise visit had little to do, she decided, with fear of his uncovering her summer affair. He was unpredictable, subtle and, she knew from overheard battles with her mother when his vanity was in jeopardy, capable of cruelty.

Also, there was something inappropriate, unsuitable—words he frequently wielded—about his coming uninvited to his rival's house. The audacity of it was enough to agitate Augusta.

"This is very pleasant," he said, looking around, "but I wish your stepfather would decide if he is a venerable elder statesman or a Hollywood matinee idol. All this," he gestured around the pool, ". . . smacks more of Beverly Hills than of George-town . . ."

Augusta considered her father's sleek good looks and thought how many times she had heard people accuse him of looking more Hollywood than Wall Street. Surely he had heard similar remarks, if only in a flattering way.

The more Augusta got used to his presence, the more menaced she felt by it. She had everything worked out so neatly, everything so beautifully under control, with her mother in Massachusetts and her father in New York—all of them terribly loving and devoted and concerned about each other's well-being but all many miles apart. Now there was this major figure in her life, the wrong time and the wrong place . . .

"I just thought it was odd with me alone in Manhattan and you all alone down here. I'm here to suggest you come back and stay with me for a week or two."

Only six months ago, such an offer would have been the answer to many prayers. Now her mind raced to figure a graceful way out. Was such a change caused by her romance? No, the compelling excitement of that had already worn off, and Jeff would still be here when she returned. Was it the swimming pool and the horses? Maybe. She was reluctant to give them up for a hot, cramped East Side apartment. But they too would be here a few weeks hence.

Dimly she saw that it was a combination of things, with Jeff the principal one, that made her view her father differently. Her life was not really centered on that green college boy, but he was the instrument of her realization, both obvious and surprising, that henceforth her life would center on men *other* than her father.

She resolved to be calm and "handle" his visit. Once assured it would end as she wanted it to, she could even enjoy it.

"That's very sweet, Daddy, but I can't. Mummie is coming down from Nantucket in a few days to work with me on plans for the party in September. Suppose I come for a few days in September on my way up to Smith?"

"That would be splendid," he said, his voice full of annoyance at the quick dismissal of his whirlwind plan. "And by that time you will be a celebrated debutante. I saw Harry Luce the other night and told him if his magazines don't make you debutante of the year, there will be strong suspicion throughout the land that he was paid off to honor one of the also-rans." His momentary ebullience disappeared. "But no New York this summer, then?"

"I don't see how, Daddy. There is so much to do to get ready for the party and I have a reading list to finish for Smith. I'm way behind . . . You'll stay to lunch, won't you?"

From the sudden change in her father's eyes Augusta could see that he was as aware as she of the major shift in the political balance between them signaled by this casual, gracious invitation. This was *her* turf, *she* made the decisions, offered the gestures, the consolations. Far more than if he had caught her in bed with Jeff, the last few words altered forever the way both viewed the other. Nothing would be the same.

"Yes. That would be nice, thank you."

Augusta picked up the phone at her side and buzzed three times for the kitchen. "Oh, Millie, there will be a guest for lunch, that's right, two . . . on the terrace . . . the fish will be fine. Can you do it by one?"

She hung up the phone and smiled at her father. "This Chesapeake seafood is fantastic! Wait till you have Millie's fried fish."

Suddenly the bayside quiet was shattered by an ear-breaking yell. Through the bushes shot Jeff, propelling his Cellini body across the flagstones and cannonballing eight feet into the air and crashing into the still water of the pool.

"Good God!" Tollover said, "what was that?"

Augusta had just enough panicky sense of the humor in the scene to reply, "What was what?" but decided that sarcasm was not the best vehicle for the next few exchanges. "That's Jeff Blain, he . . ."

Jeff's head emerged from the water in front of them. "I finished my chores early," he gurgled, "so rushed back knowing how forlorn Tidewater Farm must be without me."

"Jeff," Augusta said primly, "I'd like you to meet my father." Jeff sprang from the pool, instantly sobered, and gave Tollover a dripping hand. "Very nice to meet you, sir."

"Daddy and I are going up to the house for lunch. Millie didn't know you'd be here. Go up and ask her, I'm sure she'll fix you something in the kitchen." With her last three words, Augusta's voice trailed off to near-inaudibility in an attempt to soften the directive's implications.

Jeff looked at her for a moment. "Right," he said, his face recovering its cheerfulness. "I'll just put the new chlorine in." He picked up a towel and headed into the pool house.

Tollover had been watching his daughter intently during her exchange with Jeff. "It's just as I always foresaw," he said slowly, "you're going to be the more beautiful. And you're developing a kindness in the eyes, a suggestion of sympathy which is not altogether bad—provided it doesn't bespeak the real thing, of course. All this luxury hasn't turned you soft, has it?"

"Tougher than ever. The eyes lie."

"That's a relief. I prefer my women to have a haughty, imperious look. But the compassionate look is not bad on you; will make you an even more formidable heartbreaker."

She jumped up. "Come on. Let me show you around the farm before lunch."

They strolled around the grounds, Tom Tollover slipping his hand through the arm of his daughter's white terry-cloth robe. She showed him the rose gardens, then the bay-front expanse of trimmed grass, pointing out where the dance floor would be for her party.

"Mummie and Uncle Bryce and I will receive on the terrace right there; then the guests will walk across the lawn to the marquee, here. Behind it, there will be those two ghastly fountains that Uncle Bryce is so keen on."

"Who's playing?"

"Meyer Davis," Augusta replied almost sheepishly.

"Will he be here?" Tollover asked, fighting to keep from his voice any hint he was impressed.

Augusta nodded yes, then said quickly, "We're serving a wonderful crab dish that I had at a restaurant in Washington. The caterers have learned the recipe. Uncle Bryce has gotten Hildegarde to perform and there's a chance Ezio Pinza will come to sing also."

"Sounds spectacular. Do you think you could wangle me an invitation?"

Augusta laughed, never thinking that her father wouldn't be there. "God, Daddy, I don't know. Is there some sort of rule about divorced husbands? I couldn't bear it if you weren't here."

Tollover laughed and put his arm around his daughter. "Don't worry, Augusta. It won't matter. If I'm banned from the Maryland festivities, I'll just have to throw my own debut for you in New York. Perhaps I could get the Ballet Russe, and it might be amusing to get Toscanini and the NBC Symphony to play dance music . . ."

"If you can't get Fred Astaire, I'm not interested."

Augusta left her father on the terrace while she went to change. When she came down, lunch was on the table but her father was not around. She sat at the head and told Henry to serve the cold crab soup. Tollover emerged from the living-room French doors.

"Well, except for the Pissarro, the pictures aren't much," Tollover gloated, as he snapped his napkin across his lap, "but I've got to admit, the old boy has some damn fine furniture."

"Didn't you see the Delacroix in the library? I was planning to show you around after lunch."

During the meal, Augusta played down the lady-of-the-manor aspects of her role, but knew her father would dislike even more a gee-whiz, isn't-this-silly pose.

They discussed B.K. and her Paolo infatuation, Tollover conceding that he sounded like an altogether suitable young man "for B.K. to pal around with." Augusta wondered if her father, knowing the extent of her involvement with Jeff, would refer to the relationship in the same way. She was surprised that he had not mentioned the boy, but eventually he did.

"That young man down by the pool, nice-looking young fellow. Is he anything special to you?"

"Jeff? Oh, heavens no. He just works here."

"He seemed quite familiar with you. Then less so when he learned I was your father."

"Parents are always intimidating, anybody's parents."

"He didn't change toward *me*, but toward *you* . . . You're not doing anything dumb, are you?" Tollover asked.

"No, Daddy. Everything is under control."

The fried flounder was delicious—crisp on the outside, fluffy and moist inside. Augusta had introduced Henry to her father and Henry entered the drama by producing unbidden a bottle of the ambassador's best Pouilly Fumé. Tollover asked Augusta many questions about her mother and stepfather's life, so many she began to deglamorize her answers, downgrade the information to cause him less pain.

Over dessert he waxed expansive and sought to take charge. "But surely, Gus, you must get lonely here all by yourself, just you and these servants—and that pool attendant . . ."

"I know some young people nearby," she put in hastily, dreading what was coming.

"Why don't I stay here a few days to keep you company? There seems to be room. I can't see that Kate and the elder statesman would mind. We would, of course, check it out with them, but . . ."

"You put me in an awkward position, Daddy. I don't think it would be right to ask. They would probably say yes, but . . ." She hated the thorny emotions his proposal brought forth in her—pity, love, tenderness on one side, but all fighting with annoyance, disdain and, more than anything, embarrassment. She knew Tollover's presence at Tidewater Farm would infuriate her mother and stepfather, but that it would also be a minor and stupid scandal among Tollover's gossip-starved circles. How could he ask anything that would leave him so vulnerable? And he of all people, who always made such a religion of what was and was not done.

All of this must have flashed through Tollover's mind as quickly as through Augusta's; before she finished her discouraging considerations, he broke in. "Bad idea, I guess." He finished his demitasse and pushed his chair back from the table, the metal leg making a ratcheting sound against the flagstones.

"I should go," he said cheerfully. "It's over three hours back to New York and I made an alternative plan in case you barred the door to your father."

"You mustn't think . . . I mean, you understand . . ."

"You've got to allow me a few bad moves. It makes me more human."

"Please stay for a while."

Tollover kissed his daughter on the cheek. "I'll save the Delacroix for another time. Thank you, Augusta. You throw a good lunch." He turned and was prepared to exit leaving her sitting at the table. She jumped to her feet. "If you don't let me walk you to your car, I'll know you're angry with me." She grabbed his arm and walked him through the house. "But you mustn't be. It's not for me to . . ."

"I know. I know. Please don't let's mention it. I'm not mad. I've had a good time. But I'm dining in Princeton tonight and I must press on."

They kissed again over the door of his Buick and Augusta watched him shoot his car along the gravel drive and disappear into the trees. She wanted to cry, and she wanted to cry out in victory. Where was Jeff? She needed him now, God, she needed him. But not for comfort or commiseration. She would never expose her father's defeat and unhappiness to someone like that. But Jeff's firm body against hers, his ready desire, would reinforce the idea of herself she was struggling to maintain: a woman who was needed by people, but didn't need them.

24

Augusta surveyed herself in the full-length bedroom mirror. The dress was designed by Ceil Chapman, who was a friend of her mother's from New York days. The fabric was white bengaline, the skirt held very full with a stiff petticoat. She knew the effect with her dark hair and tan was stunning, but she thought the dress too girlishly dramatic; she longed for the day when she could wear more subtle evening clothes. She was contemptuous of the society women who now clung to these debutante styles well into their thirties.

Even without the reassurance of what she saw in the mirror, she was strangely calm about the evening. Mrs. Hughes had lectured her on not assuming she would automatically be the center of the party merely because it honored her. Augusta must work, the older woman told her, to hold the center of the stage. There were always many around only too willing to snatch it from her; in this crowd tonight, there would be many accomplished scene stealers.

To lose the spotlight, even at her own debut, held no special dread for Augusta, but she felt no need of Mrs. Hughes's wise coaching. Getting people to notice her had never been a problem, even when she was awkward and far less striking. Once again she realized her insecurity was in dealing on a personal level with people she didn't know well.

There was little about the evening stretching before her that frightened her and much that excited her. The casual contacts with 350 people, many of whom she did not know, loomed less of a chore than dining with two or three strangers. Tonight, she knew, would be a happy blur of handshakes, kisses on perfumed cheeks, smiles, endless, nameless dance partners and an occasional breather at a table of close friends. In her mother-hen way, Mrs. Hughes had brought Augusta a glass of champagne to sip while dressing. Alone again, Augusta gave a last look at herself, front and back, then held her champagne glass up to the mirror and said to herself, "Here's to absent fathers." She turned and went downstairs.

No guests had arrived, but the terrace was abuzz with waiters carrying trays of glasses, florists making last-minute adjustments to large pots of white roses, gardenias and lavender chrysanthemums, caterers with lists and mysterious white boxes. She saw her stepfather at one corner of the terrace in thoughtful conversation with Mrs. Hughes. Spotting Augusta, he took the woman's arm to turn her toward the evening's star. The ambassador bowed from the waist and Mrs. Hughes curtseyed. "There's my girl," she said in her raspy voice. "I know royalty when I see it."

Augusta walked to them and was kissed on the cheek by Hartshorne. "Well, how do you like it, my dear?" He turned and gestured across the lawn. Concealed floodlights illuminated the trees. Flowers were massed everywhere. Near the house they had been placed to look as though they were growing in beds. The eye was quickly pulled across the lawn to the festive pink-and-white-striped tent on the water's edge, glowing softly from the lights inside like some gigantic Christmas-tree ornament. Behind the tent, jets of water shot high in the air. A strong whiff of gardenia hit Augusta.

"It is all breathtaking, Uncle Bryce."

Augusta's awe at what she surveyed did not translate into egocentric delight that so much had been done for her alone. She saw herself as the centerpiece for an elaborate ritual which celebrated many things besides herself. Not just the marriage of her mother and stepfather (the pretext for not inviting Tom Tollover), but familyhood, loving parenthood, coming-of-age-hood. Above all, the party celebrated the fact that the American upper classes were safe and flourishing after the recent disruptions in Europe and the South Pacific.

Kate joined them, kissed Augusta regally, saying how beautiful she looked. Kate's beige crepe de chine dress was by Balenciaga, a present from Hartshorne in Paris. It was extremely becoming, Augusta admitted, even though she considered her mother too short to do justice to couturier clothes.

Mrs. Hughes arranged the family where she thought they should stand—at the most flowered corner of the terrace but easily viewed from the hall doors through which the guests would be emerging. B.K. entered with Paolo, who had come back from Italy early to visit various friends, but, as much as anything, to attend Augusta's debut. He was staying at Tidewater Farm and, in the few days he had been there, had won every heart from Ambassador Hartshorne's to Big Millie's. Even Brandon found him polite and "not unintelligent." With his swarthy looks radiant from the sun, and in a white dinner jacket, Paolo was an apt complement to B.K., whose exceptional beauty was set off by a tan and a pale orange organza dress.

"You look lovely, B.K.," Kate said, "but aren't you showing a touch too much bosom?" For a minute B.K.'s hint of cleavage was contemplated by all of the group except Paolo, who looked at the flagstones. "Oh, mother, to show any less, I'd have to wear a turtleneck. And the dress is no lower than Augusta's strapless."

"I hope no one makes a joke about 'coming out' parties," Hartshorne said. "Both of the girls look fine, Kate darling, and I'm a lot older and stuffier than you are."

Guests emerged from the house and soon the terrace was full of animated people—an admixture of middle-aged and teenaged with few in between. As was so often the case with these people there was no awkwardness between the generations. They played tennis together, sailed together, dined together and kept undesirables out of their enclaves together. Gathering for cocktails on the terrace of a splendiferous Maryland plantation was not an ordeal for either age group; it was a pleasurable perquisite of being born into *the club*. Conversations were animated, the Bar Harborites, Nantucketites, Easthamptonites noisily identifying themselves, while others from large eastern cities reunioned after a summer apart in resorts differing only in their locations and outward appearances.

As a particularly distinguished guest approached Augusta in the receiving line, Mrs. Hughes would come up behind and whisper the name, and perhaps the rank, into Augusta's ear. There were many stars from Washington: columnist Drew Pearson, Senator Vandenberg and several other senators whose names meant nothing to Augusta, Averell Harriman and his tough-talking wife, Marie; there were a number of State Department luminaries, including Joseph Davies and his famous wife, Marjorie. (His best-selling book on their years at the United States embassy in Moscow, *Mission to Moscow*, had caused a stir.) There was the *Washington Post* publisher, Philip Graham, and his plain, shy wife, whose father had owned the paper, and *The New York Times* Washington bureau chief, Arthur Krock, and columnist Walter Lippmann.

Perhaps even more interesting to Augusta than these power wielders, power brokers and power referees were the two Washington social stars, Alice Roosevelt Longworth and Perle Mesta; the latter was just beginning to attract press attention with her lavish, howdy-bob parties; she would shortly be inviting Augusta to some spectacular ones.

The excitement Augusta felt at meeting for the first time so many nationally-known figures was interspersed with the more relaxing excitement at greeting her own friends. Sandra Mac-Neil came down from Long Island along with several other of Augusta's schoolmates from Greenvale. Minnie Blanchard appeared with a more fully developed bosom which heaved merrily above a low-cut blue-taffeta dress. Augusta smiled as she remembered how Minnie had said she always wanted to get up the courage to go through a receiving line sweetly smiling and saying "Kiss my ass, Mrs. Throckmorton; Up yours, Mr. Throckmorton," and see how far she could get.

Augusta spotted Martie Dean approaching in the line, looking forlorn and miserable with a boy Martie knew had agreed to escort her only because of the party's allure. The arrivals seemed endless—her old life and her future all in a happy montage of handshakes and kisses and constant compliments about how beautiful she looked. Then suddenly standing before her was Jeff, looking awkward in a too-tight white dinner jacket and a clownish plaid bow tie.

"So I'm finally going to meet Prince Baby Lamberghini. Is he here yet?"

Augusta saw he was slightly drunk. How tiresome. She had worried that he might create some sort of unpleasantness but dismissed it as behavior too loutish and trite even for Jeff's bitterness. The preliminary drinking, however, did not bode well.

"He couldn't get here," Augusta said brightly. "His plane developed motor trouble over the Azores."

"I don't believe you," Jeff replied sourly. "I think he's here and I intend meeting him."

Augusta took the hand of the woman behind Jeff, a neighbor from Long Island, and Jeff moved on.

When dinner was announced, the guests strolled across the

[165]

lawn to the marquee where Meyer Davis's orchestra was already playing its one raucous, gloom-defying beat to every song, whether a sentimental ballad like "My Funny Valentine" or a peppy tune like "You're the Top." The beat would continue without let-up to an inexhaustible supply of Rodgers and Hart, Cole Porter and Irving Berlin until four in the morning.

The ages were segregated at the dinner tables, Augusta, B.K. and Brandon each seated at a different table for twelve. A number of the tables had been placed around the dance floor, a good many more outside the tent on the water's edge. Seated at Augusta's table were her closest friends and the most eligible young men: a brainy senator's son, a young Whitney who was astoundingly handsome in a dark way, and several other young men who, because of their family and wealth, were already accustomed to being given places of honor at grandiose entertainments.

Augusta had been to enough debuts in the spring to know how quickly spoiled these young people become, entertained almost every night for a month at opulent parties in magnificent settings where they, and not the older people, were the parties' centers. It was a champagne shock-initiation into the upper class, sufficient to last the novitiates the rest of their lives as a reminder of their specialness—even if those lives were devoid of booster shots of distinction.

B.K. couldn't imagine being happier. Paolo was here, had flown the Atlantic to be with her. For once she didn't feel she was forcing this blueblood to descend from his noble existence. She was thrilled to lay before him this lavish party, a party *her family* was giving. God, it was beautiful—and so was Augusta. B.K. was thrilled to see her sister pulling it all off so smoothly. B.K. knew she could never shine with equal luster when her turn came, but what did that matter? Paolo was here with her and he had never been warmer toward her. Adding to her ecstasy was his constant denunciation of the dreadful, boring European girls his family foisted on him, all of whom could "say nothing in four languages."

On a nighttime sail the night before, Paolo had kissed B.K. and they had necked for over an hour. For once she could feel him growing as excited as she was, even within the decorous bounds of kissing and nuzzling. She loved him desperately. Even with him responding now as she had hoped, life for B.K. had become a terrifying high-wire act. While she was up there, the center of his attention, everything was overpoweringly wonderful. Anything less would plunge her into unspeakable misery.

Somehow she had gotten through her Paolo-less summer. Nantucket was beautiful, and the friends she had made there had been fun. Except for the accident, the summer had been crisp, lovely days spent seeking fun with attractive new people. Even the accident, for all its horror, had permanently linked B.K., if in a tragic way, with one of America's most important and powerful families.

She was glad she had decided to keep silent. While still on Nantucket she had sensed she had done the right thing. Once the inquest was completed and Ben was cleared, older people she barely knew had smiled warmly and said hello at the Yacht Club, or greeted her by name on Main Street. The upper ranks had looked upon her kindly, and here on her stepfather's plantation, surrounded by music, flowers, good food and the pick of the East Coast establishment, B.K. felt very much one of them.

As the soup course was being cleared, Paolo asked her to dance. He told her it was one of the loveliest parties he had ever seen.

"Come on, Paolo," B.K. replied. "I'm always reading in magazines about the fantastic parties you Europeans have in Venetian palazzos and French *châteaux*.

"There *have* been a few since the war," he said pensively, "but none lovelier than this. Your mother is a superb hostess."

B.K. had never thought of Kate as a hostess. "Mother is very thorough about everything she does."

"I can see that, but it is no good unless the hostess is also relaxed and appearing, at least, to be enjoying herself. Your mother does that."

"She's a much better actress than I am. I'd be petrified—and show it."

"Nonsense. You could do anything she does, and do it better.

You have the poise and the knowledge, but you have more warmth, a greater naturalness. And you are a lot prettier . . ."

"Don't forget younger."

"I'm serious, B.K."

She looked him in the eyes, something she did whenever he was anywhere nearby. Paolo had been maneuvering her adroitly around the floor as they talked, but now he slowed them to a near halt. "You know how much I like you, B.K., but we Europeans don't always marry the women we like best. We have affairs with them and marry women who meet other requirements. I do not plan ever to marry, but if I did, it would be to you. You meet the other requirements, and—I like you best."

B.K. was reeling with happiness. That this announcement should be made on the dance floor, on *this* occasion, with *this* music, *this* clatter, *this* motion—imbedded his declaration, when she mulled it over years later, in a half-dreamed, half-fantasized tableau.

She could feel Paolo release her as someone cut in. His words were still swirling in her head as the new partner took Paolo's place and began chatting merrily. *It would be you.* She still couldn't believe it. The threat never to marry seemed the merest ripple on her vast ocean of happiness.

Brandon didn't know which he hated more, the party or his own role in it. He had heard his father tell Kate it would cost over forty thousand dollars. Incredible! You could buy an attractive house for forty thousand dollars—a nicer house than most Americans would ever enter, let alone own. With all the postwar misery in the world—all the homeless, foodless, nationless people—to spend so much money to celebrate one teenaged girl's coming of age was wanton profligacy. Brandon felt ashamed for his family.

He surveyed the people around him wolfing down their crabs, swilling down the Chablis. How smug and complacent and indifferent to others they all were! To each one of these selfish snobs, it was a matter of sublime indifference if one of their fellow humans starved or contracted typhoid—unless, of course, they belonged to the same club or went to school together. They dismissed the hunger of others as resulting from their indolence; disease, from their untidiness.

And here he was, parading and preening among these jackals, passing himself off as a prime catch of the moneyed classes. Dinner jacket, pearl studs, hair trimmed, Floris sandalwood cologne splashed under his forthright chin—paying court, playing the swain to a succession of moronic cows pushed upon him by conniving mothers. And how quickly the dim-witted girls adapted to the game—gussied, coquettish, cocksure of their budding sexiness, all perfectly unaware that he didn't want to play. Cocksure indeed.

Two nights ago at the Stoddards' dance, Monica Stoddard had assaulted his chest the entire evening with her outsized, cast-iron knockers. Then later she walked him to his car, saying, "Aren't you going to kiss me goodnight?" How close he had been to saying, "I would if you were a boy."

How had he let his father bully him into all these absurd postures? He was not the son his father wanted. He was sorry. Daddy wanted a blonde and got a brunette. Daddy wanted a boy and got a girl. Tough titty. For how many more years was he required to dress up and cavort like the man-child Daddy wanted? "Do you think Yankees will win the pennant again?" "Sorry, darling, I haven't the foggiest, and care *ever* so little."

And these people considered themselves aristocratic. How his mother had scorned their bourgeois attitudes. And how he loved the joke she had once told about the French aristocrat at a dinner party in London, bored by his titled host's monologue on the antiquity of his family. "My dear fellow," the Frenchman said, when he could tolerate it no longer, "when your ancestors were living in caves and painting themselves blue, my family was *already* homosexual."

Of all the major issues that he and his father could fight about, and frequently did, how absurd it was, Brandon thought, that their sharpest confrontation should be over something as inconsequential as whether or not he went to Yale. Totally inconsequential for his father and partially inconsequential for himself; at Yale he could acquire knowledge that would be useful later, most likely, but it was four years of his life spent in a finishing school for stockbrokers, four years he might spend moving toward some goal he cared about—and that he could realistically aspire to.

Brandon could see that his not fitting the Yale mold was the very reason his father was forcing him into it. The experience would remold him (reform him?) into, if not a smooth fit, at least an inconspicuous misfit. Or perhaps his father hoped youth's instinct for acceptance by peers would impede, perhaps halt, the misshapening process now so virulent in Brandon.

The thinking made Brandon's blood boil—whatever he was was not *that* dreadful; neither was it alterable with one coat of Ivy League varnish, and whatever he was was not so inferior to the vacant Yale ideal. Were such attributes as intelligence, literacy, erudition, political awareness, humanity really so worthless in the absence of Rotarian values and sexual normalcy?

He glanced two tables away and watched his father explaining the world to Walter Lippmann and Arthur Krock. Along with the usual loathing, he felt an uncharacteristic pang of envy at his father's niche of influence and power. The Hartshorne political vision, cliched and outmoded as it was, was being felt. Perhaps the two journalists, with their large and significant readerships, respected the experience and wisdom of Ambassador Hartshorne; more likely they listened and nodded their heads to his inanities because of the splendid dinner and opulent setting the ambassador provided. How many times had Brandon seen the truth of Scott Fitzgerald's simple observation: when a rich man talks, everyone listens.

Brandon knew he too could be a rich man and that he was flirting with giving up this easy route to audibility. And with it, throwing away a number of seductive benefits, like owning Tidewater Farm and enough money to buy the New York Yankees, have his way with each of them, then disband them on the grounds of moral turpitude.

No. To play the role of glad-handing Yalie was too great a price to pay for acquiring the Hartshorne millions. Brandon was confident enough to be certain he could find his own path to wealth and prominence. If left to his resources, he could triumph, he felt sure, and not make his life a bad performance of a miscast role. Nor would he make his life a craven apology for what he was. Didn't the liberal ambassador see that was what he was demanding of his only son?

Brandon's dinner partner, who had been babbling away about the thrilling vistas opened by her acceptance to Bryn Mawr, was asked to dance. Brandon got to his feet, felt the wine-soaked nerves scramble for equilibrium, then found Augusta on the dance floor and cut in.

"Let me be the last to tell you, sister dear, how lovely you look. Positively *virginal* . . ."

She glanced at him sharply. "That sounded like a specific allusion. May I ask to what?"

"The boathouse."

"Have you been listening at screen doors?"

"A midnight swim brought me directly under the nuptial chamber."

"Are you shocked?"

"Jealous. Jeff's quite beautiful."

First announcement, Brandon thought, as Harry Whitney cut in. His disappointment at her lack of surprise was nothing to the exhilaration at finally being honest about something so natural and, he felt sure, self-evident. "At last I can tell you all straight out; I have two heads. Such a relief to speak openly, so kind of you not to have noticed."

Kind, hell. He surveyed the dance floor as he made his way back to his table. A bunch of mindless turds all conspiring to make him feel like a freak, their precious sexualities suitably draped in pink tulle and black serge, their elbows pumping frantically to the beat and the joy of their own emptiness. Selfishness and heartlessness rewarded. *I never bother with people I hate . . . That's why the lady is a tramp.*

Kate Hartshorne was thrilled at the way the party was going. The dinner had been delicious, particularly the crab, the setting was lovely and the orchestra not as loud as she had feared. She was proud of the way both B.K. and Augusta were handling themselves. She was confident that Bryce was proud of all three of them.

The logistics of the elaborate party had been worked out by Mrs. Hughes, but the style and taste of it all had been hers. Well, to a large degree Augusta's; but the execution had been Kate's. It had been a revelation to her how almost any anxiety about things running smoothly could be solved by money. Where will they park the cars? You hire a car-parking service. How do you keep the dinners hot so far from the kitchen? You rent portable warming ovens.

As Kate listened to Arthur Krock expound on the prospects for a United Nations organization, she looked over his shoulder at the exhilarated young couples in black, white and pastels whirling giddily around the floor. She thought how she disliked large parties and was triumphant she had managed this one so well. Ten years earlier, for Augusta's eighth birthday party, she had worked feverishly for two days baking cookies, making punch and cutting out favors—and even then felt heartsick about the theft of the few dollars from the agonized family budget.

The only blemish on this dreamlike evening was Brandon. In fact the constant friction between him and his father was the only blemish on Kate's charmed new life. She began to wish the inevitable blowup would materialize; the unrelenting baiting and taunting were growing intolerable.

25

As the Baked Alaska plates were being cleared and the clatter of coffee cups subsided throughout the tent, Ambassador Hartshorne went to the bandstand and took the microphone. With Meyer Davis smiling broadly behind him he said to the attentive audience, "The function of debuts, as I understand it, is to announce the marriageability of a teenaged daughter. From the eager behavior of the young bachelors I have seen here tonight, I would not imagine it will take one of you long to snatch up our beautiful Augusta. But I ask you young men to be as forbearing as you can. The debut tradition is merely a formality and suggests no urgency or special need for marriage."

Polite laughter, then: "You see, Augusta has only recently come into my family and I would hate to lose her too soon. Few men at my time of life are fortunate enough to be blessed as I have been by my wonderful wife, Kate, and her two remarkable daughters, Augusta and B.K."

"But, Augusta," he now turned and spoke directly across the dance floor to her, "if you should decide to accept one of these eager beavers, I will be bereft, of course, but I am not so old and stubborn as to think I can fight nature. I only ask you leave your wonderful mother with me. This is your night, Augusta, so I ask you all to join me . . ." he raised his glass as hundreds of chairs scraped against the floor and the entire party rose to its feet, "in drinking to your beauty, your wisdom, and to a long, happy and eventful life."

Meyer Davis hit a downbeat of "The Most Beautiful Girl in the World" as the ambassador stepped down from the dance floor and walked toward Augusta. Smiling, clear-eyed and erect, she rose to intercept him. She hugged and kissed the handsome older man warmly on the cheek, then, as planned, they danced around the floor alone for a few bars. Other couples joined them and the floor was soon filled.

When dinner was finished, the ambassador again took the microphone and introduced Ezio Pinza, who serenaded the audience with "Di Provenza il Mar" from *Traviata* and Rodgers and Hart's "With a Song in My Heart." They were politely appreciative of the great singer, but were clearly more interested in each other than in an attention-demanding outsider, however distinguished.

Augusta later was amused to see the legendary Don Giovanni dancing with Kate, who looked as though she danced regularly with world-famous artists. When cut in on by Pinza, Augusta, for once during the evening, almost lost her even aplomb. He had criminal charm and warmth, and the voice, even when speaking, was mellifluous gold. She noticed that the young men were allowing her to dance with Pinza longer than the eighteen seconds they allotted each other. When she was finally cut in on, she was irritated to see it was Jeff. Jeff had cut in on her too many times, always with the same sour line about her having arrived with her precious swells, that she was now on the big-time map and that she was right to discard the people who didn't fit into her new life.

"Jeff," she said, "listen to me. I know you are angry and you may always be angry with me. I'm sorry about that, but it can't be helped. What you are doing now *can* be helped. I want you to leave the party. I want you to leave *now*."

He looked as though she had struck him. Then a snide smile crossed his face.

"Not that easy, I'm not leaving till we've had at least four more dances. I may not ever see you again. I'm waiting for a more tender goodbye."

Someone cut in, a boy from Long Island. As Jeff released his grip and the other boy started to slide his hand across Augusta's back, she stopped him and faced Jeff.

"I'm serious, Jeff. There are more security guards here. I can have you thrown out."

From his welter of boozy emotions, Jeff marshaled real anger. "Go ahead, bitch. You won't get rid of me any other way. And how appropriate, summoning the palace guards."

He turned and left the dance floor. There was a flash of pity in Augusta's eyes as she watched him stumble on the floor's edge. But as he brushed roughly by some startled guests, Augusta's eyes narrowed to a flinty anger.

A few minutes later Jeff was sitting at the water's edge on the lawn about a hundred feet from the animated dance pavilion. He tossed pebbles into the bay and watched the circles spread. A man's voice said, "Is this the guy, Miss?"

Two security guards in dark uniforms stood over him and pulled Jeff to his feet. They released him and he turned to face Augusta.

"My God," he said in amazement, "you really did it."

"You were determined to make trouble, Jeff. I couldn't let you."

He looked at the guards, then, incredulously, at her. "We're only eighteen, for God's sake! What are you doing?"

They stared at each other for a moment.

One of the guards said, "O.K., fella, time to go now." They took hold of Jeff again.

Jeff broke away from the two larger men and ran hard across the lawn toward the parking lot.

"Shall we go after him, Miss?"

"He'll be all right. Thank you for your help."

"If he gives you any more trouble, let us know."

As Augusta returned to the party she was intercepted by a good-looking young man she had noticed earlier. She didn't know him and had no recollection of his going through the receiving line either.

"Excuse me, Augusta, I couldn't help seeing you were having some trouble. Can I be of help?"

"Thank you. There's no trouble now."

"Will you dance with me, then?"

She changed gears abruptly. "Of course. Thank you."

They went to the middle of the crowded floor. Meyer Davis had switched to a waltz, which the boy led her into with masterful assurance. "I am Ken Fesenden . . ."

"I don't know you. Did you crash?" Her gears hadn't changed completely.

He laughed. "No. I'm a house guest of the Patricks. But I got them to invite me so I could come to your party."

"You don't get to many parties?"

"I'm from Greenwich. That's a party town." Both of them understood he was not talking about gatherings around the outdoor barbeque. "I wangled my way to this because I wanted to meet you."

Augusta was curious, and would have asked him more, but then they were cut in on. Soon she was back into the evening's heady rhythm, bestowing on her succession of partners eighteen seconds worth of blue-ribbon charm. When Brandon cut in and asked to talk with her she suggested they sit down. She wanted a glass of champagne.

"I saw you with Jeff. Trouble?"

"A little. It's all right now."

"I feared he was bent on making a scene. If there's any scene to be made here tonight, you can tell him, it's going to be mine."

"The stage is all yours. Jeff is gone."

Brandon looked surprised for a minute, then said, "It's my father, of course. Seeing him among his big-shot cronies in the midst of this criminal extravagance triggers all my hostility . . ."

She could see Brandon was drunk. He took a healthy draw on his champagne. "And for him to see me here in the midst of this celebration of wholesome young love probably triggers all his hatred of *me*. I have the strongest urge to fulfill his worst fantasies and make some scandalous scene. If it wasn't for you, I would."

"I thank you for that. But I hate to see you so unhappy. Why don't you just leave the party? Drive into Annapolis and get drunk or something?"

"I'm shocked. That's like asking Medea to leave her play at the beginning of the second act. It may be your party, Augusta, but it's my tragedy. I have some more scenes to play."

Two Walker's girls leaned over Augusta's chair and gushed that the party was sensational. Someone else asked her to dance and she was soon back on the floor, looking anxiously at Brandon sitting alone at the table, playing with a gold matchbook.

Kate returned to her table after a game waltz with Averell Harriman. She picked up a white rose that had fallen from the centerpiece and landed in an ashtray. She brushed the ashes from it and returned it to the arrangement. With other couples from their table on the dance floor there were empty chairs, but Bryce Hartshorne was in conversation with Alice Roosevelt Longworth. They were joined by Drew Pearson, who pulled his chair up to Hartshorne's.

"Listen here, Bryce," Pearson said, "I've just learned something I have to use but you're not going to like."

"What is it, Drew?"

"Your son just told me this party cost over forty thousand dollars . . ."

"Christ, Drew," Mrs. Longworth groaned biliously, "what a bore you are!"

"Please, Alice," Hartshorne said evenly. "Now surely, Drew, you do not find that sort of thing newsworthy."

"Not by itself. But he said your contribution to the American Cancer Society, whose board you are on, was only five hundred dollars. I've got to use the item. There is too much of this lavish spending going on right now, and it looks particularly bad with someone like yourself, who is supposed to be aware of the problems in the world. To spend so much on your personal pleasure and so little on a cause you champion—I've got to comment."

Mrs. Longworth turned to Hartshorne. "Your son is a chatty little bastard, isn't he?"

"Look here, Drew," Hartshorne said with heat, "there are extenuating circumstances with both amounts. I'll be in town Tuesday and we can talk then. I think I can make you see . . ."

"What's there to see?"

"We've been friends for too many years for you to toss a hatchet like that without giving me a chance at rebuttal."

"O.K., Bryce, I'll wait till Tuesday. We'll be starting back to Washington now."

Kate's graciousness in accepting farewell thanks from the man who had just announced he was going to attack her husband established her as an accomplished Washington wife. When he had gone, Hartshorne pushed his chair back from the table. Looking at Kate, he said, "That does it, I'm afraid. I can no longer tolerate such an enemy in my own house."

Steady and purposeful, Hartshorne weaved through the party looking for his son. Eventually he spotted him at a far table talking to the Boylstons, an attractive couple in their thirties who had become fixtures of Washington society.

"Brandon," Hartshorne said between clenched teeth, "I must speak with you right away."

"Go ahead, Father, I'm sure the Boylstons won't be shocked."

"It is a private matter. I would like you to come with me to . . ."

The Boylstons jumped up, saying they wanted a final dance.

"You little swine!" Hartshorne hissed when they were alone. "How dare you say such dreadful things about me to the press?"

Brandon started to rise shakily. "You're right, Father. It is late. It does seem to be time to run along."

"How can you accept my support, then betray me in such a vicious manner?"

With a slight grin, he looked directly at Hartshorne and said, "I never realized your support was buying my silence."

Hartshorne's fury had been controlled but still his tone was commanding enough to attract the attention of several nearby tables, who saw the distinguished, gray-haired man slap his son resoundingly across the face.

"You despicable pansy! Get out of my house. I never want to see or hear from you again."

"Does that mean I don't have to go to Yale?" Brandon said, rubbing his cheek. "Well, it's for the best. I might have enjoyed my classmates, but in a way that might have offended you, dear Father." He turned and pushed his way through the chairs, knocking over a few while a number of guests gaped at his shaky exit.

The thinned-out party continued even though everyone remaining quickly heard of the fight between Hartshornes father and son. Rather than dampening the mood, the drama infused a fresh exhilaration to those left on the dance floor. Blood had been spilled, but it was not theirs. Life to the living. In addition, the development was auspicious for the party's honored guest. If nothing else, these people were lightning quick to calculate the economic implications of any shift in relationships. Usually this involved a new romance or a marital breakup. But a rich father's break with an only child could be highly significant.

Both Augusta and B.K. were sad for Brandon, but in a sense shared their mother's relief that the agony was, at least for the moment, finished. The father–son deadlock, which was making them all miserable, had been broken at last.

At four-thirty in the morning Meyer Davis and his orchestra finally stopped playing. Most of the older people had already left, leaving about half the original number of guests. A breakfast of scrambled eggs, sausages and grilled tomatoes was served to those remaining. The still-animated young people, many unsober and disheveled, settled noisily at tables with their plates of food.

By prearrangement, Augusta, B.K. and Paolo took their breakfast plates and a pot of coffee the short distance through the shrubbery to the swimming pool where they planned to eat in royal isolation. Augusta had asked Minnie and Sandra and their dates to join them, Minnie coming later than the others; she had trouble spiriting away a full bottle of champagne without anyone noticing.

They decided to put the food in the pool-house oven and take a swim before eating. Enough bathing suits were found in the changing rooms and the group was soon splashing into the cool water as the dawn lightened the sky over the bay. Minnie complained stubbornly about having to wear a bathing suit, but Augusta insisted they were too near the party to abandon decorum.

The water was cool and purging of the evening's tensions and stiffness. They stayed in it for a while, then all dried themselves and settled down to breakfast, which Minnie and B.K. had laid out on a large glass-topped table. Augusta had found her white terry-cloth robe and was drying her hair when she spotted Brandon walking toward them from the far side of the pool. In the pale dawn she could see he was no longer in dinner clothes but had changed to chino pants, a blue blazer and loafers.

"I was on my way to the boathouse to leave a farewell note, Augusta, but I heard you here. Typically thoughtful of you to remove yourself so I can salute you without seeing the good ambassador. He and I both dislike prolonged goodbyes."

"I'm so sorry to hear what happened. What will you do?"

"The MG is in my name. I've got a few hundred dollars. That should be enough to get me established."

"But where?" B.K. asked.

"I'm not sure. New York, if I have the nerve. I'll send you tickets to my first opening night." There was a silence. "Well, sisters dear," Brandon said with forced cheer, gesturing with one arm, "I'm leaving you all this. Enjoy it. And as they say with most inheritances, make it work for you."

Augusta got up and hugged Brandon, holding him for a long moment. B.K. also rose and kissed him. He turned and walked away, ignoring the others.

26

Tom Tollover put down the issue of *Town and Country* and took a generous pull on his Scotch and soda. The photo of Augusta was good; she grew more beautiful all the time. That Kendall Fesenden she was seen with so often was a handsome adornment—good family, ample money, but, for Augusta, surprisingly dull. She could find all those qualities in a beau as well as brains, personality and some hint of individuality. Fesenden had no zip; he was so goddamn predictable—Greenwich, Choate, Yale, Racket Club. Tollover couldn't believe Augusta could be so quickly satisfied with such routine goods. Good God, she could have anyone she wanted. In the year since her debut and the picture spread in *Life* she had established herself as one of the most dazzling new ornaments in East Coast society.

The columns mentioned her frequently, she was a regular at the Stork Club when down from Smith, and was a prized guest at major parties in New York and Washington.

She's entitled to her success, Tollover thought; she's terrific. He'd never imagined, however, she would toss him off the way she had. All those qualities that made her such a cynosure came from him: her style, her wit, her poise, her taste—even her looks were ninety percent Tollover and ten-percent Knight. He couldn't believe she would pass him over, but there was no avoiding the ugly fact; he saw her only when she needed a place to stay in New York or when he pressured her into visiting him. He couldn't remember the last time she had come to him of her own free will. They had been so close, a very special father and daughter, and she was destroying that bond for a few horses on a Maryland fun farm.

He gulped more Scotch and looked at his watch. Wendy was late as usual. She would have the usual lament about not being able to sneak away from Ralph. It was boring letting an affair with a married woman go on more than a few weeks. You couldn't be seen anyplace. Half the fun of a good-looking lover was showing her off to your friends, taking her to nightclubs, parties, enjoying the envy of the others while scouting the next affair.

Often now when he thought of the coup Kate had pulled off in marrying Hartshorne, he wondered why he didn't take the same route to financial nirvana. His Wall Street fortunes had improved, but were far from supplying him with the money he required. He had been tempted when he was involved with Sabrina; she wanted to leave Boz for him. God, she had the dough. But Tom's father had always said that husbanding a rich woman was the hardest work in the world, and Sabrina, abloom with demands and complaints, was beginning to prove it. She wasn't above throwing matrimonial bribes in his path; the most enticing was the offer to build them a contemporary beach house in the dunes of East Hampton.

He would have liked that. But not enough to pay for it with his freedom. He earned enough money to live like a gentleman. All the sex he wanted was available for the asking; as for the other things—affection, warmth and love—he had his daughters.

He needed another drink, but better go slow. Wendy had bitched the last time when she detected a buzz. "I adore getting drunk together," she had told him, "but to find you smashed when I arrive is squalid and depressing." Sanctimonious bitch. Her lays are numbered.

He put fresh ice cubes in his glass, added Scotch and had his hand on the soda bottle when the doorbell rang. "Damn. The eager nympho is early." He put down the soda and drained his shot of Scotch.

When he opened the door to a distraught B.K., Tollover's

manner changed abruptly from smug lover to confused parent. "B.K., sweetheart, why aren't you at Walker's? How did you get to New York?"

"I hitch-hiked," she said in a quavering voice. "May I come in?"

"Of course, of course." Tollover stood back, then took her coat. "You're joking about hitch-hiking, aren't you?" He knew something was seriously wrong, but locked on the picture of his younger daughter standing on a dark highway with her thumb out. B.K. flopped on the sofa, hugged herself and shook her head. "Not joking, Daddy, not . . ."

She gave up to choked crying, then threw herself into the pillows and sobbed unrestrainedly.

Tollover sat on the sofa's edge beside her and smoothed her disheveled hair. "It's O.K., baby, whatever it is, it's all right now. You're here with Daddy. Nothing can get at you now." Then in a more typical tone, he said, "I'll get you a drink."

Tollover had never offered his daughters anything stronger than Dubonnet; he now mixed a strong Scotch and soda and brought it to B.K. "Drink this. You'll feel better."

B.K. looked up and took the glass. For a moment she was distracted by this notch up into adulthood.

"Oh, Daddy, I am so unhappy. I want to die."

"No you don't. Tell me what happened."

"Paolo's in town, so I decided to come down."

"You decided? Didn't he know?"

"He told me not to. He said he would be busy with his mother. She's here from Italy."

"So you just came?"

"I thought once I was here . . ."

"And?"

"He was furious, said it was crazy, not right. He said I was getting too involved."

"You made him feel cornered. That wasn't smart, B.K., darling, but no great harm done. He'll come 'round."

"No he won't. He said he doesn't want us to see each other anymore." Once again she burst into tears.

"Oh."

"He was so cold, so hard. I'd made a dumb mistake and I knew it, but he didn't show any . . . mercy. It was as though he was dismissing one of the servants. I could see he never thought of me as equal, he was just having an American fling before returning to his titled Europeans."

"That bunch of pretentious phonies! Why, your family's as good as . . ."

"Oh, stop it! *Stop it!* If I hadn't believed those lies, I wouldn't have let myself in for this."

"Lies?" Tollover was stung and unprepared for the sudden shift against himself. Was he consoler or culprit?

"You keep telling us how we are better than everyone else, how distinguished our family is . . . or *was*. Well, even if it was, Americans don't care about that sort of thing anymore. To Europeans, it's a joke."

"You're upset, B.K., and it's understandable, but . . . I think you may have picked up some bogus liberalism from your venerable stepfather."

"*He* doesn't constantly parade that old-family bull. He's accomplished things on his own."

"I see." The doorbell sounded and Tollover rose.

"I'm sorry, Daddy. I didn't mean . . ."

Over his shoulder he said, "At first I was pleased you would come to me in your distress, but if it means I am to be savaged by you, I'm not so sure."

He intercepted Wendy and pulled her into the apartment hall. "I'm dreadfully sorry, sweets, but there's a family emergency. My daughter has shown up with a broken heart and I've got to talk her out of suicide. I would have called you, but she just arrived this minute out of the blue . . ."

"Why, you lying bastard! I'll bet you have another woman in there. You couldn't get your matinee to leave so you pull a daughter out of the hat. Well, I'm not buying it."

"I don't give a good goddamn what you buy. I had hoped you'd be understanding about a father's duty."

"Father's duty? That's a laugh, coming from you. Let me take a look at this alleged daughter."

Still stung by B.K.'s slur, Tollover exploded at the absurd

irrelevance of this jealous fencing. "Why don't you and your sex obsessions get the hell out of here? On the way down, give the elevator man a try."

Tollover turned and opened his door, then winced from the pointed toe of Wendy's pump digging deep into his rear end. Without turning around, he went inside and slammed the door.

As he mixed himself another Scotch, he said, "It looks as though *your* romantic crisis is the first in a string of dominoes."

"I'm sorry, Daddy, I really am, I didn't . . ."

"No harm done. I was thinking of retiring her anyhow."

"I don't mean about that, I mean about Uncle Bryce. He's not nearly as charming and handsome and fun as you are . . ."

"That's more like it. I hate to think all those lollipops and piggyback rides had been for naught."

B.K. smiled, relieved to be forgiven. The famous Tom Tollover aplomb was snapping his ego back into form, but B.K.'s attack on good family rankled. If she dismissed this, it was serious. What else had he given her?

The one Scotch had made B.K. a little drunk. She talked about Paolo, breaking down sporadically. Tollover brought her a pill with a glass of water. "This will make you sleep," he said.

"Better hide the bottle," B.K. said sardonically.

He let her chat on a little about how angry she was at herself for trying to corner Paolo, how sobered she was by the slap he had given her, how she would be a very different person from now on . . .

Tollover led her into the girls' room and eased her onto the bed. He took off her shoes and covered her with a blanket. As he turned out the bedside lamp, he thought that he would phone Augusta first thing in the morning and tell her to come down for the weekend. He had just read in Cholly Knickerbocker that she was to be part of a weekend house party at the Nigel Saltonstalls at their estate outside of Boston; one of England's prime catches, Lord Ogilvy, was to be among the guests. Well, if she tried to wriggle out of coming to her sister's aid, she would get a tongue-lashing from her father she wouldn't shrug off.

B.K., already asleep, began moaning, then said loudly, clearly, as though wide awake, *"Betty Ann died!"* She moaned again, then repeated the three words over and over, more and more faintly. Tollover wondered at the lament, then decided it referred to a tragedy in a novel or film that B.K. related to her own.

As he walked out of the darkened bedroom, he tripped on a fold in the rug and hurled himself against the corner of the dresser, which caught him in the groin. Now he had a sharp pain both front and back. It had not been a good evening.

27

Augusta sat in the small armchair facing her sister, who lay flat on her back on one of the twin beds. Tollover had furnished the room with the few respectable pieces of furniture from the girls' two large bedrooms at Mapleton. Augusta had always liked this chair—it was one of the few pieces of furniture at Mapleton not in need of reupholstering. The rust-colored crushed velvet was still holding up.

Augusta watched her sister as she talked. How could anyone, she wondered, feel so strongly about one boy? She had no doubt that B.K.'s pain was real, but to have come through the childhood they shared without building the most elementary defenses seemed to Augusta an appalling waste of grim experience. Not only was B.K. permitting this boy's capricious rebuff to torture her, she was using it to throw over the entire world of comfort and refinement in which they had at last been voted tenure.

But why get too alarmed? B.K.'s histrionics were in all likelihood symptomatic of her youth, even if life-and-death love was not. She would get over it, quite quickly, Augusta suspected. And the denunciation of society would end with her first glimmer of interest in the next Yale or Princeton boy.

"You were really true blue to come," B.K. said, momentarily interrupting her catalogue of Paolo's irreplaceable virtues. "Daddy told me about the glamorous weekend party you had to cancel. Just think, you lost your chance to be Lady Ogilvy."

Augusta laughed. "I doubt I was in the running. I don't know him, but if he's anything like the other aristocrats wife-hunting around here, he has in mind a bigger fortune than I could bring to his stately home. My allowance from Uncle Bryce wouldn't go far toward repairing a leaking castle."

"He would have taken one look at those dark eyes of yours and that regal neck and forgotten all about his leaky roof."

"You are still the romantic. *He* might have forgotten about it, but *I* wouldn't have. Come on. Get dressed. Daddy made the reservation for eight o'clock."

Tollover had had to be his most persuasive with Henri Soulé to get a table phoning late on Saturday. The plea of family crisis had finally moved him to phone another party to ask if they would switch their reservation to ten. Even with this accommodation, Tollover, when they arrived, was not to be pleased by Pavillon's efforts. After two Scotches, he declared the wine corked and demanded another bottle, then consolidated the lifelong enmity of the waiter and the chef by pronouncing the vinaigrette too oily and asking for a fresh salad and bottles of oil and vinegar which he would mix himself.

Augusta too was drawing his disapproval. He criticized her for allowing herself to be photographed at the Stork Club holding hands with Kendall. "Just like some trashy starlet, Gus—and in the *Daily News* to boot!"

"I don't decide who will photograph me, Daddy."

"But you decide with whom you will have physical intimacies and where. And what is the point of announcing to the world that you are tied up with one young man? You aren't, are you?"

"No, but I could do a lot worse than Ken."

"I see no reason to put that claim to the test. B.K. has found out how foolish it is to get involved with one person at your tender ages. There's too much fun to be had."

"You can't always help it, Daddy," B.K. put in timorously.

"Of course you can. There's an enormous amount of subtle pressure on young people—from advertising, films, novels—making you feel you should fall in love. Then if you meet someone halfway palatable, you think it must be the real thing. Take it from me, there's no reason in the world for either of you to fall in love—not for years yet—and I'm not sure if then. It's very overrated, and laden to the breaking point with impossible expectations."

More than usual, Tollover was in a mood to straighten out his daughters. Augusta steeled herself for a critical progress report.

"Kendall is nice enough, I suppose—family's not bad and adequately fixed—but you should be having the time of your life now. Meeting all kinds of people. If you parade yourself as some sort of moony, going-steady teenager, no one will bother with you."

"Daddy," B.K. said, "everyone bothers about Augusta. She's invited everywhere—even to Elsa Maxwell's parties."

"I meant to talk to you about that," Tollover said, tasting the second bottle of Montrachet. "You must be careful of that old bird. She may be using you—the prestige of your name and your good looks are a big asset to her assemblage of broken-down celebrities. And I'm not sure her crowd isn't too old and jaded for you."

"You'll be pleased to hear that Elsa doesn't let me bring Kendall to her dinners," Augusta said good-humoredly.

"No?"

"She is adamant about selecting every person at her table. No house guests and, above all, no dates. She believes one dullard can kill a party."

"She must have a problem with most marriages—or does she just invite the lively one?"

"That's her one exception—but if the dullness problem is serious enough on one side, she does without the couple."

"Does she find Kendall so boring?"

"She doesn't know him. But that's just it—she won't take anyone else's word for it. She's the sole judge of who's fun and who isn't."

Tollover was not to be won over by Elsa's good taste in opting for Augusta. "I still think her crowd is too old for you—and probably too dissolute.

"And B.K.—what is this I read about you going to one of the parties of that vulgar Perle Mesta?"

"My God, Daddy, the President was there! And the most powerful men in government. Everyone in Washington tried to get invited to that party."

"I suppose if you find it amusing to be around a lot of cigar-chewing boors. Most of them are glad-handing used car salesmen who got lucky. That's the best of them, the rest are simply crooks."

Augusta started to bristle. "You are a terrible snob, you know."

"I should hope. You've got to be careful about getting too carried away by famous names. Those Washington political stars will all be forgotten tomorrow, unless they're indicted. And as for Elsa Maxwell and her Texas millionaires, film stars and ex-kings—they are all people who *require* publicity. Without it, they don't exist—to themselves as well as to others. You both are better than that. The group you belong to doesn't fade in and out with each good review or rigged election. That's what social position is all about—*permanence*. Those people need you far more than you need them . . ."

Augusta felt B.K. kick her under the table. "Don't worry, Daddy," Augusta said, trying to regain the bantering mood, "I'll be extra careful which senators I'm seen with. Since you saw the *Town and Country* article about Mrs. Mesta's party, did you approve of my dress?"

Tollover responded as though he was counseling her choice of college major. "It was becoming and in good taste, but if anything you could get away with a bit more drama—at your age, at any rate. You know, you can go too far the other way—good taste yourself right into invisibility."

Augusta spotted Wendy at a banquet not far from their table. She was surprised to see her father's girl friend lean forward to catch Tollover's eye, then in a gesture that about fifteen people could see, give him a raised middle finger. Tollover bowed his head in return, eyes closed and with a smile of all-suffering toleration.

"Oh, look, B.K.," Augusta said, to distract her sister's attention and to show the fifteen onlookers that the Tollover table was unmoved by such rudeness, "there's Bernard Baruch in the corner. How handsome he is!"

"A frequent guest at Tidewater Farm, no doubt."

"He *is* a friend of Uncle Bryce's," B.K. said, "but I don't think he's been to Maryland—not since we've been there, anyhow."

"Your liberal stepfather doesn't care for Jews?"

"Oh, really, Daddy! You can be so mean about Uncle Bryce," Augusta said. "Two of his law partners are Jewish; many of his closest political associates are too."

"Did he invite any of them to your debut?"

Augusta was furious to be unable to produce a name. When later she thought of some, she registered the exchange as one more instance of her father's growing unfairness toward Hartshorne and, in a sense, toward all of them.

The rest of the meal passed in discussion of B.K.'s debut, little more than a month off. The party would be a replica of Augusta's, only this time, since it would be in June rather than September, there would be spring flowers instead of chrysanthemums. B.K. had little enthusiasm for the event, groaning that it was a big deal over nothing; the boys she knew were all selfish opportunists, out only for the biggest party with the best champagne, then going after the fastest girls.

Tollover was not to spare B.K., even in her grief, from his censorious tact. "All right, Belinda Knight, that's about enough renunciation of the world. You've had one case of puppy love go awry, but it's no excuse to take the veil, to turn against your opportunities."

"It was *not* puppy love. I'm never going to love anybody again."

"Good," snapped Tollover, "you're too headstrong for the sport."

"You're making me cry again."

Tollover leaned across the table toward B.K. and said, as though explaining something extremely elementary to an obstinate child, "You don't cry at Pavillon. At Baroque maybe, but not at Pavillon."

Augusta was relieved to see B.K. smile in spite of the welling tears. Her father could still do it. More and more he was becoming the sole thorn in an otherwise enchanted existence. She was very fond of Kendall. He didn't excite her the way Jeff had, but on the other hand, he didn't threaten her either—no challenge to her values, no attempts to use his sex appeal to motivate her in other things, no adolescent displays of independence.

Kendall was a haven, and a useful one. He adulated her and would do whatever she wished, even to leaving her alone for a few weeks. He was a visibly suitable escort and had plenty of money to parade Augusta through the smartest restaurants and nightclubs. He was comfortable to be with—no great stimulation, but no surprises either; that was worth a lot.

His biggest advantage was the excuse their vague relationship provided Augusta to decline the attentions of other boys. It all suited her perfectly for the moment. Everything did. Even her college courses were interesting and challenging.

Perhaps the high point in her inventory of satisfactions was her new celebrity. She loved it—not just for the exciting people it made available to her in a seemingly endless supply, but also for the ill-concealed awe it seemed to produce in her Smith classmates and the boys she met on Yale and Harvard weekends.

At the age of twenty, she had already learned that celebrity was self-perpetuating: the greater her reputation, the less she had to do to earn it. Her most commonplace remarks were greeted as incisive wit, an occasional dishevelment was taken as majestic contempt for goody-goody tidiness, her moody unfriendliness as patrician reserve. The more she became known up and down the Eastern Seaboard as the fabulous Augusta Tollover, the less she had to do that was fabulous—provided she dressed well and was civil to all but the most blatant boors.

And she loved having plenty of money—at least enough to buy the clothes she wanted and travel where she wanted. She thought nothing of flying from Massachusetts to Washington for one party. Her stepfather encouraged her in this sort of thing to the point that Augusta began to suspect he coveted the publicity she earned him. Why not?—she could hear her father saying—there isn't a politician alive who wouldn't sell his soul for a mention in the press, and for a dry-bones old State Department type like that, it helps a lot to be mentioned in connection with a glamorous young beauty like yourself.

There was no doubt; her father's cynicism was now hers—as were so many of his attributes. But there he was hovering over the solo dance of the enchanting Augusta Tolliver like a grouchy archangel—hypercritical and impossible to please. Augusta would chide herself for letting his negativism, an attitude so readily explained, bother her to the extent it did. She saw all his worst aspects: the selfishness that had destroyed their home, the vanity, the elitism, but still she could not shrug off his opinions.

Instead, she still cared very much what he thought or if she were making him unhappy. But why? This was not the cold, self-contained Augusta Tollover she had worked to create. Caring was a weakness, an invitation for others to wound. She would steel herself into this flinty attitude, even towards her father, then he would manifest some remnant of the charm that had dissolved her as an infant—the tweak of B.K.'s nose, for example—and Augusta would become as desperately under his spell as she had always been.

The years had brought one important difference, however. Now her surge of love did not translate immediately into feelings of hopeless yearning, of worshiping an elusive god. Now these feelings brought on an instant pity and anxiety about how it would end. Her father had worked his way into a corner; there seemed to be no possibility of improving conditions. She could see only aging, more drinking, greater loneliness, more bitterness . . .

She looked at her watch. "I've got to go, chaps. I promised Kendall I'd meet him at El Morocco at ten-thirty."

"Ah, our allotted time has expired," Tollover said poisonously. "It's home for milk and cookies for us, B.K. We shall read about our glamorous Augusta in Walter Winchell tomorrow." He paid the check without looking at the waiter. "Isn't El Morocco a bit racy? I thought LaRue was the place for your age group."

"El Morocco is more fun. You see more interesting people. Besides, Ken's father is well known there so we always get a good table."

"The sins that are committed in pursuit of a good table!"

The zebra-striped booths in El Morocco's front room held a melange of café society—theatrical producers with their most promising ingenues, middle-aged millionaires with striking younger women, a sprinkling of bona fide celebrities: C.Z. Guest with two younger men, Ethel Merman with a raucous group of six, and for a dash of Hollywood, Joan Fontaine with three attractive men.

Augusta had not grown so accustomed to famous faces that she did not look, but she knew enough not to be caught at it. The headwaiter led her to the small table where Ken was already sitting with another couple, friends from Greenwich whom Augusta liked.

"At last," Ken said, jumping to his feet with a big smile, "the evening can begin. How was dinner with Papa?"

"It was fine. He took us to Pavillon."

"Is that his regular feeding place," the other boy asked, "or is he guilty about something?"

"Neither," Augusta smiled. "He was trying to cheer up my sister, whose heart has been broken by Paolo Colonna."

"I couldn't figure why she was so stuck on him," Ken said. "He always struck me as stiff—more like a sixty year old than a college guy."

"Who cares?" the other girl said. "He is beautiful. But so is B.K., Gus, she'll find someone else soon enough."

"Try telling *her* that," Augusta said. "I've been at it all afternoon."

She ordered a Grand Marnier. The couple got up to dance. "At least B.K.'s little drama proves one thing," Ken said when they were alone. "Your family is not totally heartless."

Augusta smiled. "B.K. has enough for the rest of us. Then if you consider my father's romantic drive, it's not surprising there was no passion left over for me."

"For *me*, you mean."

"I'm not your only chance. But pity me—I'm all I've got."

"You're not cold, Gus. I can tell. I just don't bring the warm side out in you."

"Of course you would if I let you, Ken. But, for me now, there are more important things."

Over the sound of the orchestra Augusta could hear a disturbance breaking out at the club's entrance. Others heard it and the clatter of conversations died down, allowing the voice of an irate Tom Tollover to pierce Augusta's equilibrium.

"What do you mean you have no table? Where's Perona? Let me speak to Perona!"

Augusta caught sight of him, red with anger and liquor, a terrified B.K. at his side. Augusta could feel her insides giving away. She immediately reconstructed their arrival. "Why should Augusta have all the fun?" she could hear him saying. "Why shouldn't we go to El Morocco too?" Now, for some reason, they were being barred at the door. She later learned, as her father was learning at this moment, that Tollover's girl friend, Wendy, had told *her* friend John Perona that Tollover had punched her; she knew that the club owner's abhorrence of violence on his premises, or against his friends, would be sufficient to get Tollover blackballed. Augusta at the moment saw only a hideous eruption of the family wound and she had a frenzied need to escape.

"Excuse me," she said to Ken, who didn't yet know the connection between the disturbance and his date. "I'm going to the ladies' room."

Unseeing, she pushed her way past startled couples already riveted by the loud voices at the entrance. Where was the damned ladies' room in this place? It didn't matter, she was headed toward the back, away from the horror. She heard a scream and the noise of a blow, and she knew her father had hit the maître d' and that now two oafs were throwing her father into the street.

Oh, poor B.K. But she could do nothing for her. She saw the kitchen door and headed into it, almost colliding with a tray-bearing waiter. She found a chair by a counter and sat there holding her head in her lap as cooks and waiters scurried by her, looking down at the nodding mass of dark hair but not disturbing it.

28

B.K.'s breakup with Paolo transformed her. B.K. walked through her debut dutifully, but with little enthusiasm, her disinterest communicating itself to the party. She would also attend the major social events of her friends— sometimes, as with the debuts of old Greenvale classmates, traveling considerable distances, but she felt increasingly removed from the silky social world of which her sister was such an adornment.

Augusta worried that, more and more, she had to coax B.K. to make these social efforts. It was as though B.K. had grown tired of her social career before it had started, as though she had seen enough to be bored by it all. But only Augusta noticed this disaffection; to her busy parents and her friends, none of whom were close since she'd gone to Wellesley, she seemed as active as Augusta. On the occasions when she did go to a party or a public place, she was often photographed, particularly if with Augusta. One *New York Journal-American* photo of B.K. at the Stork Club created the impression she was there frequently, just photographed rarely. She wasn't.

Paolo's defection caused a dangerous falling off in B.K.'s school work. In the last month at Walker's her work deteriorated to a degree that jeopardized her graduating. Augusta, learning of this before either parent, traveled from Smith to Walker's on weekends to prepare B.K. for her finals. The effort succeeded in getting her through. Based on her previous good record and on string-pulling by Ambassador Hartshorne, B.K. was admitted to Wellesley. She arrived in the fall of 1950 with a rich-girl wardrobe, a generous allowance and no enthusiasm whatever.

Augusta's life proceeded in the same Ivy League superstar vein, with energetic shipping of evening dresses from one city to another and smug, sybaritic weekends at the estates of friends on Long Island, Virginia or other horsy precincts. At Smith she pursued her courses with predictable diligence and did brilliantly. She took pains not to flaunt her high-flying social life. Such an effort would have been redundant. The occasional press mentions of her activities registered resoundingly with her impressionable classmates, middle-class girls for the most part, whose robust ambitions rarely reached further than landing a pre-med student from Harvard. They held Augusta in awe.

B.K.'s looks and prominence brought an onslaught of invitations to boys' colleges, most of which she turned down on the grounds she was too dumb to go away every weekend and still make it through Wellesley. On the few occasions that she would accept a football weekend to Harvard or Yale, she would sit around the parties in suites or clubs watching the determined joviality with a detached incredulity others took for boredom.

As Augusta was building her reputation as a thoroughbred catch, B.K. was becoming known as a beauty, but a cold and dull one. The only activity for which she had any enthusiasm was her sketching; she now spent long hours in her college room drawing and perusing art books from the college library.

The blue-chip acquaintances of her sister and their high-toned recreations did not escape B.K.'s mounting cynicism. As her disdain for their brutal snobberies increased, so did her contempt for their conceit, which she now saw as propped up by an array of rationales: their old families passed on secrets of style and refinement from generation to generation; their privileged upbringings honed them into superior beings; they had code words like "Piping Rock," "The Oval Room," "Hobe Sound" that meant nothing to the rabble and everything to them.

But the bedrock of their elitish self-esteem, B.K. knew, was that they had more money than other people. While others wondered if Bromley would have skiable snow, Augusta's *jeunesse dorée* would fly off to Sun Valley feeling disdain for those who couldn't achieve this simple means of circumventing such petty frustrations as inappropriate weather. They reserved the more complicated talismans such as family background and breeding for combating people with equal money who did not belong. To B.K., Augusta's rich friends were stupid, empty, arrogant people—and above all cruel. The only thing good she could see in them was that they prized her remarkable sister.

B.K. would accept an invitation from them only when she was bored and tired of her sketch pad. Even then, she noticed with a bit of self-contempt, she chose the most prestigious or glittering event; she rarely decided on the basis of her regard for the people involved. But how could she? She had so little regard for any of them.

For the Thanksgiving holidays of her freshman year, B.K. found herself at Tidewater Farm. Her mother and stepfather passed in and out in pursuit of a high-voltage Washington social life that seemed to B.K. to have the fun and spontaneity of a world demobilization conference. Augusta would not be in Maryland at all: she was spending part of the long weekend with Kendall and his family in Greenwich, and two nights with their father in New York to attend two parties. Kate Hartshorne feared B.K. would be bored, so with a thoroughness that increasingly marked her administration, had arranged for her daughter to go to a dinner party given in the vicinity of Tidewater Farm by some casual friends. The party was for the son of these friends, a student at the University of Maryland.

The night of the party B.K. drove herself in one of the ambassador's cars to the modest country house where she found about twenty young boys and girls, none of whom she had seen before. She surveyed the group with no interest and braced herself to parry the attentions of the three or four boys she saw eyeing her acquisitively.

The host had introduced her to a few people, then left B.K. alone at a makeshift bar in the dining room where she helped herself to a weak Scotch and soda.

"Well, well," she heard a male voice behind her say, "I didn't know the international jet set would be here tonight."

She turned to confront Jeff. A tweed sport coat and regimental tie enhanced his looks, which B.K. had always acknowledged but deemed ordinary. Previously, when B.K. had seen Jeff, she had been so much in love with Paolo that she had viewed Jeff as a fine specimen, but of a lower order. To compare him to Paolo was like comparing an alley cat to a cheetah. She never could understand how Augusta could be so bored as to even go to the movies with him.

Seeing him here, awash with male vitality and untainted by the world of refinement she now loathed, her reactions were more positive.

"How are you, Jeff? What have you been doing since you left Tidewater Farm?"

"After your sister gave me the old heave-ho, I considered the French Foreign Legion, but decided to finish Maryland U. instead." He poured himself a bourbon. "How is the old girl keeping herself? Has she snagged herself a baron or millionaire yet?"

B.K. looked at him for a moment. If anyone should feel sympathy for a broken heart, she should, but she could not acquiesce to slurs on her sister. "Aren't you overdoing the bitterness routine? You were infatuated with Gus and she thought you were nice, that's it."

"If she could screw like that for two months with someone she 'thought nice,' I'd sure like to see what she did with someone she cared for."

B.K. wanted to hit him, but was too thrown by his remark. "What do you mean?" was all she could manage.

"Don't tell me you didn't know about me and Gus? I thought you sisters told each other everything."

"Only things of some consequence," B.K. snapped, now outwardly recovered. She turned and walked away.

She couldn't believe it. Could Augusta actually have had an affair with Jeff? Could she have taken such a major step without telling her? B.K. was sure her sister had never withheld anything before. That was the strength of their bond—the two of them united against all others. The shock of this news, coming on top of the upheaval of all her other values, was almost more than she could bear. She wanted to leave the party. She was so numbed by the blow, however, that when another boy pulled her toward his group, she was unable to resist.

Later in the party, the boy who had co-opted her went to get them coffee, leaving her alone on a sofa. Jeff came over and took the place beside B.K. "Look," he said, "I'm sorry. I'm not a bastard. You really didn't know, did you?"

B.K. was silent for a minute. "It's true, then?"

"I'm afraid so. You see, I really cared a lot for her. And she did for me. She always leveled with me, told me it was just for the summer. Somehow, that didn't make it easier for me, when the time came. I didn't like getting the old pink slip."

Looking at this new Jeff—calm, level-headed, decent—B.K. felt with a sudden shock that she might have more in common with him than with her sister. How could Augusta like someone well enough to do *all that*—while telling him that their intimacy would end on such-and-such a date? It was so cold-blooded. So opposite from B.K., who had loved once—and that once would be the only time in her life. What had actually occurred between her and Paolo? Just some ineffectual necking in a boat, a few pats on the head and a swift kick in the ass.

Once again B.K. looked at Jeff, trying to see him through more worldly-wise, wanton eyes. What would it be like to have those large hands caress her breasts? To have that flat, muscle-etched belly she had seen so often by the pool contorting against her own flesh? The thought excited her, frightened her and repulsed her at the same time. B.K. wondered if the inhibition was a loyalty to Paolo's memory. Was she a prisoner of the conventional morality which seemed to give her paragon sister so little trouble? Or had she quickly replaced such predictable fears with a new one? Fear of encroaching on Augusta's private areas? She concluded that Jeff was off-limits for reasons that concerned Augusta, but precisely how they concerned her she wasn't sure.

29

In the packed bar of the darkened nightclub, Brandon maneuvered his Canadian Club and soda from waist level to his lips, careful not to allow the drink to be jostled by the dark-blue suit pressed against him. The act appearing at the

Bon Soir, two men named Tony and Eddie who did lampoon performances of various singers, synchronizing their lips to the actual recordings, had enthralled New York nightclub audiences; reservations were hard to get and the stand-up bar area, a favorite haunt of the better-dressed homosexuals, was more packed than usual. Most were affected men in their thirties and forties, all in dark suits, white shirts and conservative ties, some with cigarette holders, all highly animated. They were New York's display artists and housewares buyers, hoping to be taken for theatrical producers and theatrical agents.

The flame from a silver Ronson flashed perilously close to Brandon's ear. He looked around at his group and wondered if they were, indeed, his group. How he loathed those effeminate traits, whose existence he had puzzled over, and which he had not completely eliminated from his own developing style.

Did he have anything in common with these creeps? He adjusted his feeling of alienation around himself like a protective cloak. Most of his friends in the homosexual world were, like himself, new to that world. They were thrilled, as he had been, to find so many of like libido. They allowed themselves to be swept up socially, if not sexually, by older queens—jaded, embittered and dehumanized beyond redemption—the newcomers' character judgments submerged in the relief of finding a *group*, any group. Brandon thanked his Hartshorne snobbery for its useful reapplication in preventing such mindless assimilation.

For all their swagger and shrill bravado, these piss-elegant types, Brandon knew, were the most craven homosexual group and probably the largest. They asked nothing more from the world than livings sufficient for the white shirts and dark suits and the prices of drinks at fancy and ambivalent cafes like this— plus, of course, the forbearance of the law and society as they pursued their meager sexualities in the privacy of their over-decorated rent-controlled apartments.

Brandon would make no such compact. He was unwilling to settle for so little in return for a look-the-other-way toleration. That smacked too much of his sham existence as the heir apparent to His Eminence, Ambassador Hartshorne. Thanks to that over-ambitious sixty year old, Brandon had to salvage a commendable career from his sexual liberation. If he ended up a window decorator like the rest of them, he would have netted an existence as despicable as the closet. Even worse, he would have given his father the last laugh.

The ghost of Brandon's future—a grotesque phantom with dyed hair and pinkie rings—passed as quickly as he appeared. After all, he had not wasted his time in New York and was already making progress toward his goal. His job in the box office of the Cherry Lane Theater was familiarizing him with much of the underpinnings and many of the people of the burgeoning Off-Broadway movement. With the help of one thousand dollars borrowed against a trust fund from his grandmother, he was able to support a fifth-floor walk-up apartment on Thompson Street and enroll in Stella Adler's acting classes, where he had learned how to walk into a room and, in the second lesson, how to answer the telephone.

And now, his affair with Sean McDevitt had greatly expanded his acquaintance with Manhattan's simmering substrata of talent. Sean's screwball plays had made him the darling of the Off-Broadway movement; as Sean's lover, Brandon was accorded instant status in the snobbish avant-garde underworld; he consolidated his acceptance with his wit, brains and unusual background.

For a time he had tried to conceal this background, knowing that these inchoate "beats" with their disdain for comfort and hygiene held in contempt coddled upbringings like Brandon's. He came to realize two things: his accent gave him away—better to be taken as the real thing than as an affected phony—also, that these social mavericks were *impressed* by Brandon's aristocratic origins. To them, it showed far more character to have been born to decadent power and luxury and to have rejected it, than never to have known it, all the while fiercely proclaiming they *would* have rejected it given the chance.

Brandon was glad he had decided against moving in with Sean. They were totally absorbed with each other, but both had strong ambitions and needed the freedom to pursue them. With Sean this often meant days of concentrated writing. Except for these patches, they spent almost every night together, either at Brandon's or at Sean's Jane Street apartment. On hard-drinking nights, they opted for Sean's two flights rather than Brandon's four.

Part of Brandon missed the promiscuity of his first year in the Village. It had turned out to be so much more exciting than even his most feverish, loneliness-inspired fantasies at Tidewater Farm had suggested. For one thing he had been ignorant of the availability of desirable partners or his ability to attract them. Both worries had been wonderfully allayed—almost nightly.

The bars Brandon frequented in his pre-Sean days had far more attractive clienteles than the present one. Among the happiest surprises of his emergence were the bars full of attractive, unambiguous young men. He had known his preference was males who seemed, on the surface, at least, to be normal, but he had assumed that the epicene types were all that were available, and that congress with them was preferable to celibacy. He had been wrong on both counts.

With Sean, Brandon felt he had achieved a higher level in his odyssey. Their lovemaking was frequent and terrific. As a mental sparring partner, Sean was ideal for Brandon, he was brilliant but had a strong mistrust of intellectualism, particularly if it had an academic cast. Five years older than Brandon, Sean was a college graduate, but felt the four years had been of small value. He set out to prove it by undertaking the rounding-out of Brandon's education.

Their non-working hours were spent seeing plays and films or pushing ahead on a joint reading program. With Sean charting their course, they devoured not just books, but authors. Right now they were self-consciously immersed in works by and about Verlaine and his lover Rimbaud. Sean was given to black moods, to an extent which diverted Brandon from his own similar tendency. Brandon would stay away from him on these occasions and Sean would usually throw himself into his writing. He was in one of these periods at the moment, so Brandon had seized the opportunity to catch Tony and Eddie, an act Sean had denounced as "too faggy."

The comedians burst onto the stage and mimed their way through a blaring recording of the Andrews Sisters singing

"Don't Sit Under the Apple Tree." They were irresistibly funny in their send-up of the gum-snapping sisters and the pre-sold audience was screaming with delight.

Brandon looked out over the crowd seated at tables and saw nothing but straight couples from uptown who thought they had infiltrated the demi-monde by coming to the overpriced nightclub on Eighth Street that catered to people like themselves. They seemed to be vying with each other to laugh harder at the routines, which were satiric pretexts for female impersonation.

Brandon contemplated the explosive delight of the males at these tables, most of whom were lapping up the comedy more than their dates were, and recognized the same frenzied release he had felt on first encountering similar demolitions of the man–woman boundaries. Would they migrate in the coming year to Brandon's stand-up side of the bar? Probably. Laughing all the way.

At the song's end, the performers turned their backs on the clamoring audience, spinning back suddenly as Nelson Eddy and Jeannette MacDonald, the latter festooned with parasol, bonnet and sausage curls. The taller of the two was as convincing as the blandly male Eddy as he had been as Laverne. As their mouths caressed the words to "Sweethearts," the audience was sobbing with delight.

Brandon was thoroughly amused by the antics, but became increasingly fascinated by the abandon of the uptown audience. Didn't they realize that the two comedians were not just laughing at the treacly romanticism of 1920s operettas, but at all heterosexual mating rituals? They were skewering, not Jeanette MacDonald and Nelson Eddy, but the paying customers themselves—all those dating couples with their handholding, knee-grabbing, check-paying, flower-sending, breath-sweetening, hair-combing, body-deodorizing and on and on *ad coitus.*

Nothing is so absurd, Brandon saw the comedians saying, as the orthodox human as he moves slowly, resolutely, proudly, scurrilously, furtively, ruthlessly toward the grotesquely undignified sexual act. You are being mercilessly derided, you dolts, and you are loving it.

As he looked around the room of stage-lit faces contorted with laughter, his eyes hit something that in no way belonged in this bizarre straight–gay pageant. At a table just to the right of the stage he saw his two stepsisters. It couldn't be. They were off at colleges somewhere. He saw items about them in the newspapers. It was undeniably them.

Gus looked sensational in a plain black dress and single strand of white pearls that perfectly set off her dark hair. B.K.'s impact came more from the cameo face than the overall ensemble, but impact there definitely was. He recognized their dates instantly as the kind of boys he had grown up among but could not stand: uselessly handsome, expensively dressed in clothes designed to obscure the male figure, and, worst of all, totally at ease in this or any other world—too dumb to know that all they surveyed didn't belong to their fathers.

But Augusta and B.K.! How strange and unlikely to see them. The apparition was such a jarring mix of his two lives. Was he glad? In their brief overlapping at Tidewater Farm, he had grown fond of them. They had been sympathetic to his predicament, never seeking to profit from it as others might have. Instead they had offered him as much moral support as they could.

And he had come to value them because he considered them to have futures worth watching. This was already coming to pass with Augusta, who was moving, according to the columns, in extremely high-toned circles. This was remarkable for a girl as young as Augusta, if for no other reason, because the women who controlled the blue-chip guest lists were rarely enthusiastic about beauties twenty years younger than themselves. Such victories spoke volumes, he thought, about her admirable control of her aggressions and her astute tact.

He liked both girls. He applauded them. He wished them well. But did that mean he wanted contact with them again? Hadn't they both, he and they, taken leaps too large in opposite directions? What would these two white-gloved egrets think of the mirror over his and Sean's bed? Or of their Communist friends? Or of his job in a box office?

Oh, the hell with it. They were growing up—*all* of them, not just him. He wouldn't have to spill the details of his erotic life. He could let it go at "How have you been?" If the rest followed, well, let it.

Of course he would speak to them. Just as soon as the act ended and the house lights went up. What fun to catch up on the ambassador and his bride! And to see how the girls had developed. What he really craved, he knew, was their reaction to his new life. Part of him was still the Brandon who had given the finger to Tidewater Farm and all who felt at home there. But he had made the transition, he had not given up or cried for assistance. He felt secure enough to hope for approval from that quarter, or at least a withholding of condemnation.

Yes, he would go to their table. He rehearsed his opening line. Something like, "So you finally caught up with me." Standing at the bar anticipating their reunion, feeling better and better about it as he played it through his mind, he felt fingers slide, stealthily yet purposefully, across his groin. In the crush of hilarious queens, he received a full-fledged, direct-hit grope. Not now, you idiot, I'm joining the ladies.

30

As Brandon talked about his New York adventures, he relished the tableau of his two engrossed stepsisters. Transfixed on the sofa of their father's living room, B.K. had kicked off her loafers and pulled her legs up under her wool plaid skirt. Augusta was setting a dining table at one end of the room.

"So *this* is the setting for Tom Tollover's debauchings of New York's shelved debutantes. It doesn't look so sinister."

"That's part of Daddy's scheme," Augusta said, straightening a place mat on the polished wood of a Sheraton table. "The trappings of a proper gentleman. By the time they learn he's Jack the Ripper, it's too late."

"Tell us more about your life, Bran," B.K. said, with more enthusiasm than she had shown for anything lately. "Daddy's is too talked about as it is."

"Let's see, did I tell you about working as a stockboy at Macy's? I was writing a three-act play in the housewares stockroom. I had finished two acts when they found out and fired me. I tried finishing it but I couldn't get back into the mood. I worked on it in my kitchen. I'd set up in plain view all the appliances and utensils to put me in the housewares mood, but it didn't work."

B.K. laughed happily. What had Augusta meant over the phone, that Brandon would find B.K. changed—less light-hearted, more cynical? She seemed as merry as ever. If there was any change, she was less shy, and that was fine. Any fears about his sisters' being shocked by his free-form existence, he could dismiss. B.K. was clearly relishing it and Augusta seemed amused but with occasional reservations that showed in her facial expressions. Then too, he hadn't gotten too explicit. Not yet. He hadn't connived to conceal anything either. A great deal of talk about Sean, who Augusta had heard of as a playwright, and no talk about girl friends.

He had the feeling Augusta and B.K. were both anxious to get this part of his saga out into the open, but he couldn't be sure. He liked to think that his reticence was respect for the other people's sensibilities, but he suspected it was a mask for a lingering shame. What the hell. *Que será, será.*

Coming out of the kitchen, Augusta said, "Have you decided yet which route you'll take to fame and glory?"

"I'm studying acting, but I'm not sure that will be my métier. I fear I may be too beautiful for a nation that has taken Turhan Bey to its bosom. I am thinking more and more seriously about directing. I haven't signed up for courses in it, but the acting classes are relevant. In addition, I'm seeing every play I can get in to. The theory is that if you see enough bad stuff it will bring your talent surging angrily to the surface while teaching you what not to do. The only trouble with this educational strategy is that you hate paying good money for bad shows, especially if you are as poor as I am. Fortunately I can cadge seats to some through my box-office connections, Sean gets us free tickets occasionally, and then for Broadway plays, ANTA has a giveaway program for deserving beginners. One way or another, I've seen everything in town. Whenever two actors stand up in a church basement and start railing at each other, I'm there ready to scoff and figure how it *should* have been done."

"You must be meeting fascinating people," B.K. prompted.

"The people you meet in the Village are the real education. I see a play and am profoundly moved, I say as much to one of Sean's firebrand friends—then receive an hour's lecture on why the work's emotion-evoking qualities are so much flummery and lies. Sometimes I stand firm, but many times I am convinced, and, as a result, have had my taste and perceptions raised one notch. But the opinions! Greenwich Village is a sea of opinions, most of them negative, all of them absolute. But out of this vast chorus of nay-saying will emerge a few positive results; people who step forward and say, 'I will do it right'—these are next year's playwrights, artists and musicians. I plan to be one of them . . ."

Brandon paused. B.K. stared at him enthralled and said nothing. He laughed. "Am I getting too carried away by the sheer inevitability of it all? But surely you find my optimism contagious? You should both quit that vapid world of moneyed society and join me here where so much more exciting things are happening. You could both be Judy Garlands to my Mickey Rooney. Make it to the top . . . all that sort of thing . . ."

"It would be no use, Brandon," Augusta said, bringing a platter through the kitchen door and setting it on the table. "Once Ann Rutherford, always Ann Rutherford. Come get your lunch."

B.K. got to her feet and stretched. "Do I have to put on my shoes?"

"Not if you keep your feet off the table," Augusta said sweetly.

"You've picked up so much refinement from Elsa Maxwell and C.Z. Guest," Brandon chuckled. "What is this I see? *Salade Niçoise?* I haven't seen an anchovy since I left the ambassador's table."

Augusta re-emerged from the kitchen carrying a chilled bottle of Chablis. She handed it and a corkscrew to Brandon.

"Now this is the stuff! And to think I found you both eating raw turnips in the dust of a Maryland farm."

"You're making me feel like mother at her first Tidewater dinner party. Did I place the silver correctly?"

"Get off it, Gus. You taught Kate everything she knows."

B.K. beamed. "Isn't it wonderful seeing Bran again, Gus? He's the only honest person I've seen in months. I didn't realize till you left that you were Tidewater Farm's only vestige of life."

"That's because you had other things on your mind," Brandon said, then grimaced and said, "oops."

"Don't be silly," Augusta said, "there are no unmentionable subjects with us."

"Of course there are," Brandon almost snapped, then, smiling, "but I hope they become mentionable quite soon." He raised his glass. "I want to propose a toast. I never tried to contact you both because, for the moment, I had to put everything about Tidewater Farm behind me. I didn't know what would happen to me, and if my liberation turned out to be a fiasco or a disgrace, I didn't want word of it to get back to *him*."

"There has been no contact between you?" Augusta asked.

"None, *grâce à dieu*. But no questions yet, I'm not finished with my toast. Now that my life has settled into a pattern that causes *me* no shame, I hope we will remain in contact and resume our friendship."

"Of course . . ."

"How great!" B.K. added.

"But one condition—no, let's make it a request. Don't tell my father you've seen me or where I am. I doubt he would care much, but there's always the danger he might take it upon himself to rescue me. I'm still under age, alas."

"At least let us tell him we saw you and that you are O.K.," Augusta said.

"I'd rather not. He'd know I was in New York then and he'd be sure you knew how to find me. Then he'd bring out the nail-pulls and thumbscrews . . ."

[207]

B.K. laughed. "I wouldn't break."

"I would," Augusta said. "Brandon's right. If Uncle Bryce knows we have your address, he'll feel obliged to do something. Both he and my mother are worried about you. Let me do this. I'll tell them that a friend of mine ran into you in any city you want to name . . ."

"Let's make it Chicago. It's big enough and I have no designs on it."

". . . The friend knew you only slightly so had no idea what you were doing there or where you lived—only that you seemed fine."

"Perfect. With a knack like that for whipping up salient lies, you should be a lawyer." Brandon poured himself some more wine. "That's enough about me. I want to hear about you. First, your love lives. Those boys at the *Bon Soir* last night, are they the semi-finalists? They looked sanitary enough, but somewhat lacking in splendor. I hope you were just using them to get you to the *Bon Soir*."

"I'm sorry to tell you," Augusta said, "we aren't the scheming temptresses you'd hoped."

"There's time yet . . ." Brandon said encouragingly.

"Kendall is Augusta's boy friend. Mine was just a prop."

"Is your romance with Kendall serious?"

"I wouldn't even call it a romance. He's very nice and fiercely loyal. We enjoy doing things together—but decorating a home and making babies aren't among them."

"He's mad for Augusta, but Augusta's got him trained. She uses him to hold all the others at bay."

"The ones who aren't so easily trained," Brandon ventured.

"Right," B.K. said happily.

"Not right," Augusta snapped. "This is the thanks I get for spending the morning opening cans of tuna fish and boiling eggs. You should switch your attention to B.K. My life is the same old thing. She's the one who just entered college and is having new experiences."

"O.K., tell me how you like Wellesley, B.K."

"I loathe it."

"Sounds promising," Brandon said, delighted.

"What do you mean, B.K.?" Augusta said, stunned. "You never told me you felt that strongly."

"I knew it would upset you if I did. Brandon has brought honesty back into fashion."

"What's so loathsome about Wellesley?" Brandon asked, clearly relishing the frankness he had inspired.

"It's a bunch of soppy girls who think they are really hot stuff for getting into a name college. Some are bright enough, I suppose, but they all yearn for the day when they can settle down in suburbia keeping house for a general practitioner and lord it over the other housewives who didn't go to Wellesley."

"Does the school administration encourage this attitude?" Brandon asked.

"God, no. They tell us how we are to be the nuclear physicists and corporate executives of tomorrow. The little dears sit there in their cashmere cardigans thinking only of the breakfast nook colors and which silver pattern they'll have."

"Surely there are some girls with broader vision?" Brandon said.

"I suppose, but they're just the same snobs I've grown up with. I don't know which group is worse, the socialites or . . ."

"The Doctors' Wives of Tomorrow," Brandon concluded.

"Come on, B.K.," August said soothingly, "you're still upset about Paolo. You'll change your mind in a little while."

"Don't mollify her!" Brandon said sharply. "Insight like that should be encouraged, not neutralized like a skin irritation. Maybe B.K. was not cut out for the world you seem to thrive on."

Augusta was not ready to be bullied by Brandon's iconoclasm.

"B.K. can have any world she wants," Augusta said, with an edge appearing in her voice for the first time. "As for choice, I don't know *what* world I want. I'm just following along to see where it all leads."

"I can tell you for a certainty that Elsa Maxwell's dinners are *not* a way station on the road to missionary work, or internal medicine or . . ."

"You'd be surprised who I meet at some of those parties."

"Leon Trotsky? I'm not criticizing your life. But I think you are kidding yourself to think that you aren't headed in a very specific direction."

"But what's wrong with it? Gus at least is having fun. *I'm* the needy case. I'm desperate there in that nunnery."

"What are you interested in? What would you rather do?"

"I haven't a clue . . ."

"B.K. spends a lot of time sketching. She is getting very good."

"Do you want to paint?"

"I would love to, but Wellesley thinks that's an unrealistic ambition for a woman. Art teacher maybe."

"Then it's very simple. Quit Wellesley, come to New York and enroll in art school."

"She can't quit college like that, she, she's . . ."

"Why can't she? I never even started Yale and each day rejoice in that decision more and more. I'm not suggesting she go into burlesque. There are plenty of quite respectable art schools in town. The college compulsion is nothing but middle-class insecurity or lower-class ambition. It has very little to do with education, at least in the United States. If you switched to art school, I even think the ambassador might approve . . ."

"This is incredible! Leave Wellesley and come to New York? I never thought I had any choice!" B.K.'s excitement burgeoned. "Of course. There are *plenty* of things I can do without becoming a lost woman. Why did I feel I had to go through four years at one of those places? Probably because you're doing it, Gus."

Caught up as Brandon was in his role as B.K.'s emancipator, he thought briefly about the ramifications for himself. If B.K. came to New York, she would become familiar with the details of his life. That was O.K. Eventually she would have to tell her parents she was seeing him. That was less O.K.

But then, so what? His being under age probably gave his father some leverage. But hadn't his father ordered him from his house? This made him something other than the traditional runaway. There was no evidence—not from the girls or from anyone else—that Hartshorne had the slightest desire for a rapprochement with his son. What was he worrying about? Augusta and B.K. were discussing their parents' reaction to B.K.'s switch. Augusta didn't know how it would sit with Tom Tollover.

"Who knows?" B.K. said. "I don't know where art school stands in his litany of do's and don'ts."

"He might surprise you," Brandon offered.

"He wasn't that wild for Wellesley," B.K. said. "And I'm sure Uncle Bryce will help me out if I convince him this is what I want to do." She jumped to her feet and clapped her hands. "I'm so excited. To live in Manhattan! Will you show me all the seamiest parts, Bran?"

"With judicious editing."

Augusta had been resisting the others' enthusiasm. "At least I'm glad to see you no longer think your life is over, B.K."

"I never thought that. I was just through with the part of it I knew. I felt sure there was more."

Brandon got up to go. "Take it from one who's lived hard the past two years—there's a lot more."

31 Accepting Brandon's light, B.K. said, "I don't think this restaurant existed when we lived here thirty years ago—or if it did, we couldn't afford it. Daddy hated the cheap restaurants—Howard Johnson's were springing up; parents loved them because they were sanitary and kids loved them for the twenty-eight flavors, but Tom Tollover would feed us scraps from Joan Payson's garbage before he'd let us be seen in a Formica booth."

"What an odd way to be deprived," Brandon said with no irony. "Maybe the old boy wanted to make sure you developed the tastes that you did."

"It would have happened anyway. You can develop a taste for many things by simply knowing they are there."

"Your Sussex manor, for example?"

"Exactly. Fifty-seven exquisite rooms, twenty acres of formal gardens, three hundred acres of wooded hills, twenty servants to keep it all tidy. I could have taken to that without years of training."

"It must be glorious. I will get there for a visit one day."

"God, I wish you would. I rattle around in those rooms, each with fresh flowers and a crackling fire, and I think of that old question of the tree falling in the forest. If there's no one to hear it, does it make any noise? When I'm alone in that vast house—which is most of the time—I realize that the opulence of it all is not so much for the owners, but for others. And if there *are* no others . . . The beauty of the place is not lost on me, but it's almost canceled out by the inconveniences. The disturbances, for example, from one place to another. My maid and I spent an entire morning looking for my reading glasses."

"You have guests."

"Not many."

"The kids?"

"Harry's at school and Belinda is always in London. You saw, I'm sure, she's a front-runner in the Prince Charles sweepstakes."

"Good God, no! You'd be the queen's mother! Augusta would never stand for merely being the queen's aunt. In a way it's fitting that you sisters should marry into the British royal family. It's one of the few goals you haven't scored."

"Our goals were always very vague. Yours was specific—you wanted to be a serious filmmaker whose pictures made money—that's damn tough and you've done it."

"I've always kept in mind one rule: you must get the suckers into the tent before you can tell them how to live. Too many of the self-proclaimed artists forget that. They feel no obligation to entertain, they want to start preaching or edifying in the first frame with occasional digressions to parade their esthetic sensibilities. They don't allow their audiences any reactions except admiration and uplift. But let's get off my field. I have everything I want—and that's boring—certainly to relate. You're the one dropping hints of discontent. Let's get back to you wandering those vast rooms looking for your glasses."

"It's absurd for me to whine. My life is blissful. A smashing-looking husband who is kind and whose family dates back to the late Pleistocene period, two non-addicted children who say 'Thank you' occasionally—but it's funny. Everyone always thinks of Augusta and me as terrifically ambitious, as two women who are striving toward something. I see us as two women trying to *escape* something."

"Housework?" Brandon purred.

"Exposure to hurt, vulnerability. Like other frightened, bruised animals, we sought out height. We didn't so much crave dominance or preeminence, only safety. Great wealth and things it can buy, like Augusta's private guard and the double electrified fences, represents one kind of security, and protection from certain dangers and annoyances, but more important, it symbolizes another, that the pains and hurts of ordinary people can't reach us, not anymore."

"Very neat. Has it worked?"

"Strangely enough, it has. But what ticks me off is that Augusta's security is so much more fun than mine. I vegetate in that vast country house while she jets around from one unearthly residence to another, lunching with popes, skiing with Agas, dancing with Khans. The only time my life gets lively is when I travel with her. Maybe it's not just circumstances, maybe she's more fun than I am."

"Nonsense. Everyone always thought of her as the serious one, and you the . . ."

"Zany. Well, it hasn't evolved that way. Of course, to my neighbors in Sussex, I am Bianca Jagger, but next to Bianca Jagger I'm about as exciting as a steamed pudding."

"But as girls, you went a lot farther than Gus did . . ."

"Guido Trappetti is about as far as a girl can go . . ."

"It's odd, isn't it, how well he's done as an actor. I tried to get him for my next picture and Sue Mengers said she had him booked through 1983."

"Why odd? He's talented, sexy and ruthless."

"I mean only that if you'd married him, back then, you would have ended up in the Great World anyway."

B.K. fished in her handbag for a comb. "Sweet Augusta did not see him as the appropriate route."

32 B.K. told the driver the Greenwich Village address and settled back into the cab. She couldn't relax—she would prefer riding on the roof, her arms outstretched to the populace. Had it really happened? Her own apartment in Manhattan? Her own choice of work? Freedom to do whatever she wanted?

It was inconceivable that she could get into a taxi and tell an adult male to take her wherever she desired in the infinite city. New York was a sampler of the universe; anything humans could imagine was represented here, every possible aspect of life. All she had to do was learn of its existence, then ask a taxi to take her to it.

Of all the lucky aspects of her Wellesley deliverance, snagging the apartment was the luckiest. When she had first broached the plan to her mother and stepfather, they said it all sounded feasible, provided she live with her father on East Fifty-first Street. To escape four years at an all-girl college, B.K. would have accepted any condition; in fact she had suggested living with her father when she had presented the plan.

But her Maryland parents, having made that a condition, decided, on reflection and learning of Tollover's deterioration, that that was one of the plan's worst aspects. Having gotten themselves into that hole, they seemed at a loss how to get out of it; there was even a point when the entire proposal was about to be scuttled as a result of the embarrassing impasse.

B.K. only discovered this when she happened to overhear her mother phoning New York friends in search of a small apartment. Luckily one turned up. A divorcée friend of Kate's who lived in a converted brownstone on East Sixty-fifth Street said a studio had become available on the top floor. The neighborhood was excellent, the subway was only three blocks away, and the rent was $110 per month. Uncle Bryce paid her rent, her tuition at the Art Students' League and an allowance sufficient for taxis at night.

Some furniture that Kate had loaned to friends when she moved to Tidewater Farm was recalled; other items were bought or donated to outfit a charming studio for B.K.'s return to New York. A dining alcove off the one room had been converted to the sleeping area and given an amount of privacy with a folding Japanese screen. A sofa of Kate's made an adequate bed, which meant that Augusta could visit New York occasionally without activating her father into spasms of parental nagging.

The move from her mother's drab Madison Avenue apartment to the splendor of Tidewater Farm produced nothing like the excitement B.K. now felt at her studio on East Sixty-fifth Street. What made the first place of one's own a high point of anyone's life? Was it the fantasy of an unfettered sex life? No, you could achieve that without a place to yourself. Augusta had managed it rather neatly, hadn't she?

In her case, B.K. knew the bliss of solitary living was the control it gave to *every* aspect of your life. This was almost unimaginable for her. On those rare occasions in her youth when she was unpoliced by parents, servants, relatives, teachers, housemothers—even alone with other children or in the woods of Mapleton—there was always Augusta. She as much as the adults, perhaps more, oversaw, edited and corrected B.K.'s conduct.

Augusta was a wonderful sister—kind, wise, loving, even fun—she could never have gotten through the past years without her, but the decisions were always Augusta's. That they were invariably the right decisions didn't change their origin.

Until quite recently B.K. had been comfortable with the arrangement. She liked not having to think everything through, knowing that Augusta would do it for them both, and do it better than B.K. could have. But now she had an excellent reason for wanting to break this judgmental bond: she no longer wanted the same things.

She watched the lights of Park Avenue streak by—the Waldorf, where Sandra had had her party, the building where a friend's grandmother had had them to dinner. The city was not completely strange to her, but she knew there was much, much more. The cab entered the tunnel that would take them up and around Grand Central Station. It was all so massive, so powerful, so rich—and so full of people who wanted things. Not like the zombies of Maryland who hoped for little more than nice weather, nor like her social friends who waited passively for the right invitations. The city teemed with people who had concrete, clearly-visualized goals and were pushing away to get them.

The world of "ordinary" people—people not born to her two-car, private-school world—had little reality to B.K. Like most of her well-heeled friends, she made a great show of "loving" a servant, a teacher or some other "neat" walk-on in their lives. But she never thought of these people as . . . people. It was not that she admired the citizens of her world and put them on such a high plane; they were simply the ones whose good will and friendship she needed, whose disapproval upset her life—and to a certain degree, she understood.

If B.K.'s emancipation had an element of rebellion, it was her relief that these people need never again have any influence over her life, if she chose to avoid them. Now that she viewed most of the girls she knew as bitches and the boys as jerks, the possibility of trading them in for new friends was highly alluring. But trade them in for what?

In the two months she had been in the city, she had met a number of Brandon's friends. She was starting to lose the uneasiness she felt at the distance between herself and them. It wasn't from feelings of superiority, God knows, but that she had so little in common with them and that they were so much more worldly-wise than she.

Brandon had blasted her for this, saying her feelings were nothing more than poorly disguised snobbism. But at first she'd been at a loss what to talk about to these hard-bitten Villagers of nineteen and twenty. The Greenvale School and coming-out dresses were no longer subjects that gripped her, but at least they were familiar territory. These people talked about things she had never heard of, places she'd never been, emotions she'd never felt.

At first it had been overwhelming, but she was pleased at how quickly she had grown attuned to their subculture once she had become acquainted, even on the most rudimentary level, with their enthusiasms—psychiatry, for example, or existentialism.

And the more at home she grew with their vernacular, the more she realized how little they differed from the people she'd grown up with. Most pronounced was the rigid hierarchy these self-proclaimed creative people imposed on their group. Just like B.K.'s status-aware schoolmates, these Bohemians had their own leaders, people whose opinions were awaited before the others could condemn or applaud a new film or book.

The only difference was the basis of the status; before it had come from family wealth or position, now it might have been earned by a poem read in a coffee house, a fiery letter in the *Village Voice* or a new concept in ceramic jewelry. (B.K. was happy to learn that looks accorded status in both worlds.) The Villagers were just as brutal toward applicants to their circle as the most snobbish girls at Walker's or Greenvale, capable of the same meannesses, but to B.K. they were still far more interesting.

For the most part, Brandon's friends relaxed their exclusivities for his reformed-debutante sister. Her assimilation had been painless, almost cordial, making her eager for new groups, new types. Suddenly the rest of the world's population was coming into focus—tableau figures frozen in the backdrop of B.K.'s sheltered life were stirring to life, starting to move, to talk, to look at her . . .

She glanced at the cab driver. He was a ruddy man of about thirty-five, not bad looking according to his license photo, with soft curly brown hair. She looked at his neck—nothing special but thick and straight with a few curly wisps lolling over his plaid collar. Here was a human neck that someone had kissed, maybe bitten in passion, perhaps would do so tonight. She felt she had returned to the world of the living—or entered it for the first time.

Climbing the three flights of stairs to the party, B.K. trailed behind a couple drawn toward the clatter above. The girl, not more than a year or two older than B.K., wore drop earrings and a brown velvet cape and had black bangs across her broad forehead. Two months ago such a warning preview would have sent B.K. fleeting into the street. But then, two months ago, Brandon would not have asked her to meet him at the party; he would have picked her up and escorted her.

She entered the crowded apartment and saw no one she knew. A typical Village assortment hard at their conversations. Some glanced up at the newcomer, but no one greeted her. She followed the stairs couple into the bedroom, left her coat, then went to search out Brandon.

After only a few of these parties, she had learned how to dress in a way that would blend in without making her look like a Reader-Advisor. Tonight it was a plain navy skirt and a red turtleneck. She had no urge to go Bohemian; she doubted she could pull it off, but more than that, she still never put on a sweater, a scarf or a pin without considering Augusta's reaction and, to an extent, her father's.

As she looked around the group, thoughts of Tom Tollover again came to mind. How he would loathe them all. Not one man wore a necktie and several had no jackets. The women wore little or no makeup and most had hair longer and less groomed than the current fashion. Two that B.K. could see had affected the frizzed halo of Edith Piaf, whose raspy voice lamented behind the chatter. One man, a heavy, bearded fellow, greeted another man noisily with an affectionate bear hug, lifting him off the ground.

B.K. spotted Sean sitting on a sofa talking with two women on the far side of the living room. She had come to like Sean quite a lot. His reported wildness frightened her some at first; his world and background were as much a mystery to her as hers were to him. But he was quick to sense B.K.'s eagerness to find for herself a new system, and he went out of his way to make her emergence as easy for her as possible.

Sean had been against telling B.K., she learned later, of his relationship with her stepbrother. He felt it would require too radical an adjustment from her on top of all the others required of her. Brandon had argued for a clean breast right from the start; if she wanted no dealings with homosexual lovers, she could be spared the effort of becoming acquainted with their world, only to huff out shortly.

B.K. had no such impulse when the frank declaration finally came; still, it had been a shock. She had dimly perceived that Brandon was askew sexually, probably homosexual. It was a long jump from that possibility to the certainty of a homosexual love affair. Over a long dinner without Sean at Chumley's restaurant the night after B.K. moved into her apartment, Brandon had told B.K. everything.

With the air cleared and B.K. relaxed about the situation, he went on to regale her with tales about his first promiscuous year in the city. She laughed till tears came at the story of his first trick, of returning the following night on the assumption that they would go through life together and having the guy not remember him. ("The very next night, for Christ's sake! I don't care how drunk he said he'd been, he could have said my face looked familiar! You toughen up fast in this game.")

B.K. was delighted to have such openness between them, but she could not unrestrainedly endorse Brandon's rush into homosexuality. She still had an aversion to the specter of two people of the same sex making love. The promiscuity and the uncertainty of it all caused her to worry about Brandon's future. When she mentioned this to him, he kissed her on the cheek. "The day I can no longer land a partner," he'd said, "I will take a chastity vow and devote myself to good works."

Except for these qualms, which Brandon characterized as her foot-dragging in outmoded propriety, B.K. adored the frankness and honesty of their new relationship. She had never had such candid, intimate talk with anyone, not even Augusta, who had told her years earlier, when B.K. had asked about masturbation, "Do it if you have to. Everyone does. But I don't want to hear about it."

How exhilarating to have someone confide in her the way Brandon did! And he would be there when she had similar tales to unload. Nothing scattered goblins faster than listening to someone as witty and ebullient as Brandon regaling her with mishaps that, had they happened to her, would have terrorized her with fear someone would learn of them. How easily Brandon transformed such pitfalls of humiliation into material for amusing anecdotes. Her conversion was opening up and dispelling little pockets of anxiety she didn't even know she had been carrying around.

Sean spotted her and got up and approached. "Brandon didn't come with you?" he greeted her. "They should have closed the box office by now. He'll be along. I'll get you a drink. Do you know any of these weirdos? They're not as scary as they look."

He handed her a glass from a punch bowl; it tasted like rum and pineapple juice. "One nice thing about the Village," he said, "you can find any degree of depravity here—anything from groups long gone on hard drugs to N.Y.U. students giddy with debauchery because they're wearing no undershirts under their oxford button-downs. I'd say this group tonight is about medium-civilized."

"You mean they won't try to seduce me?"

"I can't promise that. I mean that if you make one of them a gift of your wristwatch, they might say 'Thank you.' They still possess some of the accepted responses."

Sean asked B.K. to join him on the sofa where they were discussing Camus, specifically *The Plague*. Brandon had warned B.K. about clinging—not that he minded, he assured her—but she would never meet new people that way. She told Sean to return to his conversation; she'd amble around for a while.

As soon as she saw he was going to take her up on the suggestion, she regretted making it. She remembered her father's conviction that an attractive person, alone but poised at a party, would soon draw the attention of someone more at home. Very nice, but this assumed a certain amount of manners and kindness in the other guests; manners and kindness were clearly out of vogue with this crowd.

She looked at the group standing talking near her. Several pairs of eyes met hers but looked away quickly, perhaps not wanting to add to her embarrassment, but not wanting to alleviate it either. The eyes of a woman in her thirties locked onto B.K.'s in a way she already understood. She would escape to the bedroom to pretend getting something from her coat; perhaps she would encounter someone there or en route.

She squeezed by some couples standing chatting in the narrow corridor; some smiled but no one tried to stop her. She would reach the bedroom immediately, then the return trip to the living room and that would be that. Well, if nothing happened she could give up and join Sean, waiting with him for Brandon to arrive.

At first she thought the bedroom was empty. But then she saw a dark-haired young man, scruffily dressed in a loose white T-shirt and jeans, leaning over a desk reading some papers.

"I'm sorry. I didn't mean to come barging into your bedroom, I thought . . ."

"It's not my bedroom," he said, turning and looking at B.K. appraisingly. "Not even my apartment."

"But you are going through the things on the desk . . ."

"Hank's a playwright. I'm an actor. I wanted to see how he wrote." Then with a sly smile he added, "Or if there's a part for me."

It was not B.K.'s nature to chastise anyone, no matter how wrong she thought they were, and least of all a stranger. But there was something about this boy's manner, an insolence, that angered her. She could see clearly now that he was sneaking a look—his standing rather than sitting, his not moving the papers from their pile by the typewriter.

"Don't you think you should have asked? Maybe the writer doesn't want anyone reading it yet."

As he turned toward her and straightened she could see that he was shoddily good looking. Strong neck and arms emerged from the loose T-shirt beneath which a classic torso insinuated itself. The face was unusual—high cheekbones and deep, dark eyes arrested the attention in a positive way—but there was something odd about the mouth. Its whole structure protruded slightly and the well-demarked upper lip was all of a piece; it lacked any cupid's-bow depression in the center. Both abnormalities combined to give his face the look of a not-to-be-trusted wild animal.

His physical assets—the well-formed body, the handsome

head, the large eyes—were more than enough to carry the strange mouth with it into the realm of arresting male looks. Her evaluation only added to her dislike. He clearly counted on his looks to excuse breaches like reading other people's desk matter—or anything else he cared to do.

"You're right. I should have asked permission. But most writers are happy to be read—under any circumstances." He walked to the bed, dropped onto it backwards and sat looking up at her, his body propped by his elbows.

"Now that you straightened out my morals, would you tell me who you are? I suspect a caseworker from uptown, infiltrating the Village in search of the one hundred neediest burned-out causes."

"I'm not a caseworker . . ."

"But definitely uptown."

"I haven't lived in New York long enough to be so rigidly typed."

"Uptown is not a neighborhood, it's a level of being." With one hand he fished a pack of Lucky Strikes from his jeans, offered her one, then got one into his mouth. Still with one hand, he found a Zippo and lit it, closing his eyes against the curling smoke.

"That's very interesting," B.K. said in her best Augusta voice. "I must be getting back to my friends."

"You don't have any friends here. Only your brother's lover. I saw you wandering around trying to catch hold of someone in there. That's why I came in here. Not to steal a playwright's material, but to wait for you. I knew you'd get here."

The flattery that he would go to this kind of trouble to meet her was outweighed by her dislike of being seen through and manipulated.

"My name's Guido Trappetti. I'm an extremely promising young actor. Extremely promising. Coffee houses today. Hollywood tomorrow. It's definitely in the cards. What's your name?"

"B.K. Tollover."

"Nice to meet you. You've got a drink and I've got a cigarette. Why don't you stay here for a minute and get acquainted. It will give you a new experience to take back uptown with you. Here, have a seat."

"The bed?"

"Too soon? I guess you're right. There's a chair."

As B.K. sat down she noticed a grimace of victory flash over his face that fortified her dislike. Better to let this conceited jerk practice his line on her than to wander around by herself—or to retreat to Sean so soon. In addition to his obnoxious manner, the man's effusive sexuality made B.K. nervous.

"What do you do in New York?" he said, his voice now losing its sardonic leer.

She wanted to ask why he didn't already know, if he'd learned so much from others about her, but decided the fencing had gone on long enough. "I study painting and drawing at the Art Students' League."

"Ah, now I've got you pegged. You're a society girl who wants to be an artist and have come down to the Village to absorb some of the creative vapors. Your instincts are right, but you won't absorb much wandering around parties like this. What you need is to have a full-fledged affair with a native son— you know, live together, stay up till four in coffee houses, go home and make love all night, get up and go out for breakfast, buy the *Voice* . . ."

"I'm too young for all that," B.K. smiled. "I'm limited to movie dates with milkshakes at Schrafft's afterwards. And if I moved in with anyone, there'd have to be room for my governess."

He looked at her for a moment. "Sharp, a lot of class . . . I like that. And you know, you're terrific looking? I think we should get serious about all this."

"All what?"

"You and me, of course. You just registered as sharp. It's too soon to try for dumb. Look. You could do a lot for me . . ."

"I could?"

"Sure. As an actor, I've got the looks and the brains. You could give me the class."

"That's very nice, but . . ."

"What could I do for you? I was getting to that. I'm the beat

Bohemian you need to round out your education. Also you don't look too experienced—how much can you learn at Schrafft's? I could change all that—in ways I think you would like."

"But you're an actor. I had more in mind a fellow painter."

"Too competitive. I'd broaden your range professionally as well as—the other thing." He leaped up from the bed and stood over her, then squatted by her chair holding up his arm. "Feel that muscle." B.K. felt she had been holding her own quite well; now she felt unnerved again. "Go ahead, feel it. I work out. I'm really built. All those muscles could be yours."

"Do you mind going back to the bed?"

He threw himself back down on the bed and addressed the ceiling. "I look at it this way. When I see a sensational-looking woman like yourself, I figure somebody's got to take her to bed. Why not me?"

Up to then B.K. had been titillated by the abstract, disconnected nature of their banter. No one could hear what they were saying; they knew no one in common. At any point she could get up, walk out of the bedroom and her life would move ahead as before. Nothing had changed. She had never had anyone speak so directly to her before and it was intriguing to learn where it would lead.

Now she concluded that it led nowhere. His first five words had established that he was brash and conceited; the talk since then hadn't expanded the outlines. Notions of sex and romance were linked in B.K.'s mind with an intense personal intermeshing, shared interests, feelings, responses—and probably background. She was moving to leave the bedroom when Brandon suddenly entered and pinned her to her chair with a kiss. "So here you are. What's going on?"

"Do you know Guido?" B.K. asked with a certain bona fide curiosity.

"Sure. How are you?"

"Your sister and I were just discussing the terms of our affair."

"For God's sake!" B.K. exploded, with annoyance that didn't convince Brandon.

[224]

"You could do worse, B.K.," Brandon said. "I've always suspected he's not the cad he pretends and God knows he's sexy."

"See there?" Guido said, resting his case.

"Brandon," B.K. said, trying to adopt the mock serious tone, "since you are the only representative of my family, I had hoped you'd take a more protective stand. Not avenging my honor maybe, but at least tossing a little cold water on Mr. Hot Pants here."

"You ought to give it a try, sister dear. What have you got to lose?"

B.K. couldn't believe his attitude, now unmistakably serious. "I think I'll jump out the window," she said. "It will clear my head."

Guido rose from the bed to an upright position, as though pulled by invisible cables.

"You're doing much better for my cause than I was. Keep at it. I'm going for a drink." He didn't offer B.K. one.

As soon as he was gone, B.K. blasted Brandon again for not rescuing her from a situation that was becoming disagreeable—in fact for adding to it.

"Don't make such a big deal about it—or I'll send you back to Wellesley. I'd go to bed with him if I had the chance—and if you say 'that's different,' I'll cry. If the idea repels you, all you have to do is say 'Not on your life.'"

"Not on your life."

"O.K., then. Let's go join Sean."

They pressed their way into the living room, now even more crowded, and got to the sofa, where Sean was still in conversation with two others. B.K. and Brandon squeezed in beside him. As she sat listening, she spotted Guido standing in the kitchen, which opened off the living room. He was talking to an attractive girl in a bright yellow sweater and dark slacks. He seemed unaware of B.K.'s whereabouts and never glanced around to spot her. What an ass!

Her mind kept turning to Paolo, but for the first time her ruminations were analytical and almost free of the harsh stabs his image usually brought with it. Paolo had been the opposite

[225]

of this creature. He had been sensitive, intelligent, educated, well bred, well mannered, tactful, subtle. He had a softness about him—a gentleness, a near asexuality that held none of the menace of Guido's overly masculine posturing. Yet Paolo had, in the end, kicked her in the face and caused her as much pain as she was capable of bearing.

She lost sight of Guido. She couldn't spot the girl in the yellow sweater either. Oh, there she was. B.K. marveled at her own train of thought. She saw the back of his head in another group, but when it turned, it was someone else. She suddenly panicked that he might be observing her from some part of the crowd and would see her looking around. With his ego he would only assume she was looking for him. He'd had enough victories over her. B.K. turned her attention back to Brandon and Sean's group, which was now discussing the new English playwrights.

After about twenty minutes, B.K. excused herself to go to the bathroom. Once again she edged her way through the groups talking in the corridor. She felt a wrist grip hers and hold it firmly. She turned to face Guido, who was leaning against the wall, now alone.

"I knew you'd come back."

"I was going to the bathroom."

"If that's what you want me to believe."

She glared at him, his hand still holding her wrist. His face was twisted in an insinuating smile. "You'll come with me?"

"No," she snapped, yanking her wrist forcefully from his hand.

"Look, I'm just appealing to you for tenderness, affection, mutual pleasure, love. If you're not interested, that's how it is. But what does anger have to do with it?"

She wanted to spit in his self-satisfied face. Why was she being persecuted by this person? Why repeatedly embarrassed? But a different sensation was coming over her. In his skimpy clothing, standing so close, she was more aware than she had ever been of the jumble of contours, veins, body hairs and smells that defined the male. Out of the welter of angry responses, he provoked one overriding conviction emerged; she

[226]

wanted to go to bed with him more than she had wanted anything in her life.

33 At the corner of Fifty-first and First Avenue Augusta hailed a cab with one hand, and with the other protected her hair from the stiff March breeze. The cab driver appearing safe—she had been scared once—she asked him if he would mind taking the F.D.R. Drive to East End Avenue. She loved the East River at night—lights shimmering in the ripples, an occasional barge or other boat slicing through the black water. Part of the highway was so low to the water that driving along it was like being on one of the boats.

She needed pleasant images to expunge the scene she had just had with her father. He was growing difficult. Augusta would have preferred staying at B.K.'s place. But her father had heard about the party and called her at Smith—for no other reason, she was sure, than to find out if she planned to come down for it. He hoped she was; there was something he wanted to talk to her about. She couldn't get out of staying with him, and the blowup that she had feared came to pass.

Up till now, all of his feelings of neglect since her mother's remarriage had come out in snide asides and antagonism toward Hartshorne. But this time he accused her directly of having abandoned him for the greater material allure of her stepfather. She no longer felt toward him as a daughter should feel toward her father. Ugly as the accusations were—unspeakable, she would have liked to believe—it was better, if such thoughts existed, to get them in the open.

But how do you convince someone as vulnerable and cynical as her father that she was unaffected by her stepfather's gifts of clothes, a car, airline credit cards? She had tried, but with little success, to make her father see that Ambassador Hartshorne had come into her life at the precise age when young people are shifting their attention from parents to friends and interests of their own. She may have seen less of her real father than before, but neither was she spending much time with her Maryland parents.

She could see that her father's preoccupation with wealth, status, social position had turned on him and was torturing him. Since these attributes were so important to him, and since Hartshorne bested him on every one, nothing could convince him they were not the underlying reason for his daughter's defection. For Augusta, it was agony to face his brutal accusations, and even greater agony to see him demean himself to such an extent.

Augusta thought bitterly of the irony in his pleading for more attention from her. There was a time when she lived for the few tidbits of attention he tossed her way. But then, damn it, he had changed since then more than she had. He was never altogether sober now—still charming, ebullient, witty—but never quite sober. And there were more engaging topics of conversation than the deplorable failings of her Uncle Bryce.

She wondered if there were some truth to the other accusation: that Hartshorne's generosity had turned her head. Her coming up with the logical explanation of the negligence, the natural shift of adolescent allegiances from parents to friends, had a meretricious ring. Augusta knew she had a facility for quickly producing impeccably logical explanations for things when she didn't want to face the real reasons. She already knew that human behavior was rarely logical and that motivational reconstructions along purely rational lines were probably off the mark.

Did the real reason matter in this case? Of course not. The obstinate fact was that her father was intent on being miserable because of her abandonment of him for richer fields. There was only one remedy: to spend more time with him. A heavy depression settled over her, a gloom that the lights of Queens dancing in the water of the East River couldn't lighten; she didn't *want* to spend more time with him. Regardless of how often she visited the East Fifty-first Street apartment, she knew it would not be often enough.

Strange that in all his diatribes, he said little about B.K. After all, B.K. was in New York now and Augusta in Northhampton. She knew B.K. was not paying that many duty calls. Brandon had told Augusta about her sister's new romance with the Italian actor. It sounded horrible. Perhaps it was something B.K. had to get out of her system—as Jeff had been with herself.

In a sense, Augusta was proud that her unassertive younger sister had found the backbone for her own sexual explorations. Augusta thought she had been alone in such a cold-blooded approach; at times, she feared worryingly alone. She smiled at the new view of B.K. They must have a long talk about it all when they had lunch. She wanted to hear everything about this Guido—everything—and she would relate the whole Jeff saga. She'd been meaning to for some time anyhow.

The taxi drew up to the building. She paid the driver and stepped out to a hat-tipping uniformed doorman holding her cab's door. She had not been to the apartment of Kendall's aunt before, even though he often stayed there when sleeping over in New York. She knew the category, however. The aunt was a successful dress designer; like most people with a social background who had scored a success in one of Manhattan's glamour industries, she aspired to a salon where "nice" people could meet "interesting" people. With a dull pang, Augusta placed herself in the former category; would she ever be in the latter?

Kendall affected a skepticism about his aunt's name-studded parties, holding to the socialite's condescension and suspicion toward people who "do" things, whose prominence is not a birthright but comes rather from accomplishment with its attendant odor of striving. Augusta thought one of the great advantages of social prominence was the access it gave you to distinguished artists, performers, intellectuals. Kendall saw this quite the other way around.

But with all his snobbery toward the successes of New York's success elite, he still got it across to Augusta that his aunt's party that evening for Dame Alicia Markova was a major one and that Augusta should feel honored to be invited.

A tiny maid opened the apartment door, the only door on the landing. Except for the trim black uniform with white collar, the maid could have been a housemother at Walker's. She took Augusta's coat and gestured toward a door. Augusta entered the already populated library with no nervousness. Her father had drilled into her the social suicide of betraying nervousness.

But now she rarely had any to conceal. She knew she would be the youngest and perhaps the most attractive person in the group; even the most distinguished careers and reputations did not diminish the value of youth and looks, provided a minimum of manners and intelligence went with them. Augusta had seen celebrated people visibly bored by other celebrated people, but she had never seen a celebrated man bored by an attractive young woman. She in no way considered it enough—for herself or anyone else—but she was comforted by the knowledge that it was a strong base from which to launch her gentle campaign of conquest.

Another reason the library door held no terror for Augusta was the certainty that the hostess would not let her flounder an instant before swooping on her and introducing her to other guests. If for some reason Kendall's aunt was out of the room, then one of the guests would greet Augusta and take her in hand. Thank God for manners.

"Augusta, darling," Millie Pape purred in a raspy baritone as she extricated herself from a just-arrived couple and swept to Augusta, the ample folds of her burgundy taffeta skirt whispering as she walked. She was a tall, striking woman whose tightly pulled-back dark hair accentuated a prominent nose. "It is marvelous that you came all the way down from college! Let me present you to my guests."

Augusta from the corner of her eye had already inventoried the room. She spotted Dame Alicia looking rigidly regal on a Louis Quinze sofa. Next to her was George Balanchine and someone Augusta did not recognize. Standing talking by the fireplace was Jock Whitney and Tex McCrary; to their left Augusta spotted Tex's stunning wife, Jinx Falkenberg.

As Mrs. Pape led Augusta around, the one-room *Who's Who* took on more names: fashion designer Charles James; an incredibly beautiful and expressionless fashion model named Orlofska; the *New Yorker* artist, Alajalov; and the woman who had choreographed *Oklahoma*, Agnes de Mille. There was a sprinking of faces Augusta recognized from purely social parties, emissaries from the "nice" camp. On first glance the group looked like many other smart dinner parties Augusta had seen in New York and Washington, but as the faces took on famous names, she acknowledged Millie Pape's claim of "major"—each guest was a catch either for their fame or for their social prominence.

Augusta realized that now she was contributing to such gatherings not just youth and looks, but a certain amount of fame as well. As one of the most prominent debutantes of recent years she was not only an ornamental, age-broadening addition to such parties, she was of her generation's Best Of Classification. These hostesses, who constructed their parties with a scrutiny of qualifications that would content a Yale secret society, welcomed people from any field—the more varied the better—as long as the fields were represented by their top practitioners.

The women viewed their tables with the same sense of importance with which Noah made up the Ark's passenger list; if the rest of the species should meet with a terminal calamity during dinner, there would be enough solid genetic material emerging from this dining room for their demitasses to give the human race an auspicious second start.

A beautiful black boy in a white jacket asked Augusta what she would like to drink. ("Isn't he divine, darling?" Millie gloated. "He's the son of the caretaker of my place in Barbados. I'm training him.") Her dry vermouth and ice arrived.

Augusta talked about horses with Jock Whitney, whom she had met once through C. Z. Guest. He was a pleasant man, but she was glad when Kendall came up and kissed her on the cheek. She loved the way Ken looked—so effortlessly and cleanly handsome, so at ease in dinner clothes, so relaxed with these weighty personages.

"Hi there, Gus old girl. Good evening, Mr. Whitney." They shook hands. "You beat me here. But then I have to work harder to make myself smashing."

Ken's aunt came over to them and said she wanted to take

Ken to meet the guest of honor. "You come too, Augusta."

Dame Alicia was amusing some others with her first experience on television. Her quiet humor and her total lack of self-importance captivated Augusta. There was nothing in her narrative to suggest she was one of the world's great artists, only a befuddled woman tripping over cables as she headed for the wrong set. Augusta reflected, as she listened, on how much of everything we do when with others is construed to explain who we are: what we tell about ourselves, what we inquire of others, what we admire, what we know, what we do, wear, laugh at. Constantly painting and retouching our self-portraits. How wonderful, she thought, to be world famous. Everyone *knows* who you are beforehand, thus freeing your energies for more meaningful purposes.

Augusta was basking in the warmth and assumed fellowship of this charming woman's story and glanced at a Georgian silver teapot on the polished walnut coffee table that held a free arrangement of white freesias and dark red roses. Augusta thought she had never seen anything so lovely. She envisioned the perfect dinner she knew was coming and the amusing conversations with her dinner partners—Ted McCrary on one side, who would talk of her stepfather's work in Germany and of his own encounters with Hartshorne, George Balanchine on the other, who told wonderful stories about Dame Alicia but asked Augusta a great deal about herself, capping the flattering attention with the insistence that she had a dancer's body, he had watched her walk—had he gotten hold of her seven years earlier, he could have made her a great ballerina. She was very glad to be here and among these people.

Ken had the cab drop them at Fifty-first and First so they could walk a bit. The night was fresh and cool. Ken suggested they go to the top of the Beekman Towers for a nightcap—it was a secret place of theirs when they wanted to be alone: a glorious view of midtown Manhattan, and despite the neighborhood, gloriously unchic. They could be confident of not seeing anyone they knew. Augusta said she didn't feel like a drink. The night was fresh and pleasant; why didn't they walk? Heading down First Avenue to look at the United Nations building, she asked Ken about his dinner partners.

"Jinx Falkenberg is sort of goofy. But nice—and what looks! We talked about tennis and she tried to sell me on Eisenhower. I assured her I'd vote for him even though he was way too liberal for me. But less so than Stevenson. Betsy Whitney and I talked about horses and about Greenwich versus Long Island. I said we had better hills and she threw the ocean beaches at me. She's quite nice, really. Did you enjoy yourself?"

"Terrifically. I've learned that the more prominent the company the easier they are to be with. Some of my father's social friends from Long Island and Wall Street are very stiff around new people, but not those of real accomplishment like your aunt's guests tonight. They seemed so relaxed. So unguarded. And so willing to show interest in *you*."

They walked on a way in silence, turning up Mitchell Place and onto Beekman. At a small overlook of the river they found a bench and sat down. Ken put his arm around her shoulders. "You look serious. What are you thinking?"

"That party tonight," she said slowly, "it was such a privilege to be there; the others were there because of their enormous success in their fields. I don't mean your aunt's dinner was the reward for their life works. But in a sense their being assembled in beautiful intimate surroundings is. What have we done to be there?"

"It's not like you to be so self-effacing, Gus. You know damn well you have as much to offer as anyone in that group. Plus, you were the best looking—in your age category."

Augusta laughed, "That means I'm better looking than you, and I don't think so. But another thing I worry about is that, if we go to parties like this now, when we are barely in our twenties, what will we do when we are forty . . . or fifty?"

"Go to more parties like that, eat more excellent food, enjoy more distinguished company."

Augusta thought for a moment. "No, I don't think we would. Not unless we make some sort of mark. We're included now *because* we're young. To be invited when we're fifty we would have to be Dame Alicia or Charles James . . ."

"The Fenwicks were there, and the Van Houtens—I haven't heard of them winning any Nobel prizes lately."

"They're good friends of your aunt's, They were invited the way you and I were invited—because we *know* the right people. That's different from *being* the right people."

"Come on, Gus. Let's not get into that argument again. I'm damn glad to be who I am. I don't want to be someone else. I might turn out black . . . or red-headed. And who cares what we'll be doing when we're forty or fifty. The very fact that we've been to parties like that when we're young means we can relax about them later. We don't have to be hungry for that kind of celebrity. We've had them and we know that, for all their interest, they're not going to change our lives."

"Mary Stanford tells about friends raving to her about a fantastically rich man on his way to Palm Beach, how Mary should be excited about meeting him. 'What do I care how rich he is?' she said. 'Is he planning to give me any of his money?' It's the same with those celebrities. Their fame is terrific for them, but what's in it for me?"

"It's not their fame for itself. It's because it usually means they are special people with special talents. They have wisdom and insights they can pass to others, experience, marvelous anecdotes. I want to learn as much as I can about the things that interest me. Ballet interests me. Isn't it natural I should relish the chance to sit down and talk with George Balanchine or Alicia Markova?"

"Of course it is," Ken said glumly. "I could keep struggling and point out that you could read their memoirs in the Greenwich Public Library, but I know when I'm licked. I'm just defensive because I don't plan to be famous. And if you want a celebrity next to you at dinner, there's a suspicion you might want one in the bridal chamber as well."

"That's different."

"Then you *will* marry me?"

"I seem to have missed the proposal."

"No you didn't. I've been saying for months I wanted to marry you when I finish college."

"You always made it sound so conditional."

"Only one condition . . ."

"Yes?"

"Your accepting me," he gently turned her face towards his. "Be reasonable, Gus. You know we are ideally suited to each other. When I graduate this spring, the family brokerage will take me on at ten thousand dollars the first year. That's damn good. I have some income from a trust fund. We could live comfortably on that in Greenwich. There will be lots more later, and you have some money . . ."

"Just my allowance from Uncle Bryce and that's sure to stop if I marry. Oh, then there's a trust fund from my Aunt Mable, but it's not a lot—fifteen or twenty thousand dollars, I think."

Oh, yes, marriage. The word sent images careening through her head. The fights of her mother and father, the smooth arrangement of her mother and stepfather, the split-level ranch house Jeff had held out to her, the nightly sexual gratification Jeff had given her, the relationship of Brandon and Sean, and then a parade of couples: Martie Dean's parents, Sandra MacNeil's, Minnie's grandparents. She thought of marriage in Greenwich—the kind of people Ken knew, the kind of people Ken *was*—and an unfamiliar feeling of security came over her.

The picture of marriage that came with Ken's proposal contained a comfortable, beautifully-decorated house, two servants, a husband who worshiped her, who would always be a gentleman, would never behave unpredictably—and she saw their world as a well-insulated one in which to raise children, where children would make the kind of friends she would want them to have, where they would be isolated from the danger-fraught hodgepodge of Manhattan, or the isolated solitude of rural Maryland.

She realized with an inward chuckle that she was not contemplating marrying a man, but a suburb. What if she was? Ken held out for her a specific kind of life in a specific place. He was not the sort of man who would suddenly run in a specific place. He was not the sort of man who would suddenly run for the Senate or get his brokerage to transfer him to its Paris office. Greenwich it would be and, to Augusta, it didn't look too bad.

On closer examination of her own reflections she realized

that, to the extent she had weighed Ken at all in her deliberations, it was in terms of what he was not, rather than what he was. She was considering him as a life-partner because he was *not* cruel, unpredictable, rude, improvident—not at all like her father.

Of all the men who appeared before her as possible husbands, and there were many in the past two years who either were contenders or could be maneuvered into that role, none of them elicited from her a more positive response than Ken did; in fact they quickly evoked more of the dreaded failings.

For all her apathy toward males in the specific, she never doubted she would marry one of them. That was what the people she knew did. After a certain age, if you were not married you were considered eccentric or—Brandon. You were the odd person out. Augusta had had enough of that distinction in her childhood: rather like, but not *exactly* like, the others.

The idea of normalizing the basic circumstances of her existence and letting those circumstances fade into the background of her image appealed to her enormously. In this way perhaps her own qualities would emerge more clearly, or people would make an effort to discover the more subtle ones. No one could quickly sum her up—and dismiss her—with some overriding anomaly like being poor among the rich or being single among the married.

Her mother had already shown her that the right marriage could provide a sanctuary, instant and, with luck, permanent, against the buffets and vicissitudes of a danger-fraught existence. She knew her present life held out far more glamorous prospects than Kendall Fesenden; but her father had held out glamour to her mother when he'd married her, Paolo had held out glamour to B.K.—Augusta was in a mood to trade considerable glamour for a guaranteed minimum of safety.

She kissed Ken lightly on the lips, and then again more lingeringly. "I would like to be married to you, Ken. But not now. I'm too young—and so are you. Why can't we go on like this? Is it so important to marry now?"

"I'm afraid if we wait, I'll lose you."

"I might lose you, too. But if our bond is so perishable, it's better to find out before we marry."

She was at it again. Impeccable logic—but not the real reason.

34 As Augusta closed the door of B.K.'s bathroom behind her, she heard her sister's voice call out from the living room, "I may as well tell you, since you'll find out anyway in there—Guido's living with me."

Curious way to tell her. At least it gave Augusta a few moments to digest the information. B.K. had been right; the bath was festooned with flat-out giveaways: the shaving mug and brush, the bottle of Mennen's Skin Bracer, the two toothbrushes, a pair of dirty sweatsocks tossed towards a full laundry hamper. And a male odor.

She came back to the living room where B.K. was lying on her mother's old sofa. Augusta wondered if her sister's outfit—beige turtleneck, green plaid slacks—or the announcement made her look older than her nineteen years. Whichever, in the year she had been in New York, B.K. had turned into a woman. It was the first time Augusta had thought of her that way. Still, the words came out:

"Aren't you awfully young for that?"

"I'm older than you were," she replied, in a cadence slowed for emphasis, "the summer you stayed alone at Tidewater Farm."

Augusta shot her a glance. "You know about that?"

"I ran into Jeff. He wasn't being a cad. He assumed you would have told me. Odd, isn't it?"

"Don't punish me for that, B.K., I intended to. As long as you bring up my affair with Jeff, I'll point out a difference. With him, I always was in complete control. You seem quite gone on Guido."

"What's so wonderful about control in a love affair?"

"It's essential, when the person is as wrong for you as Jeff was for me—and Guido is for you."

"Let's not go into all that. You don't like him, but that's not . . ."

"If it was simply my not liking him, don't you think I care enough for you to make the effort? I think he has no conscience, that he will harm you eventually."

"How can you know that? *I* don't know him that well."

"Call it a strong feeling. I also think he is blocking you from the fantastic life you could be having."

"Ah, *there* we have it." B.K. swung her legs off the sofa and faced her sister directly. "Look, Gus. I think it is fabulous the way you get around, meeting all those people, getting to all those exciting places. I just don't happen to want it. For the first time in my life I feel that I am not trying for things I don't really want. The friends I've met through Guido are every bit as stimulating and exciting, maybe more so . . ."

"*Are* they your friends? Don't they think of you as a society girl who is slumming? Won't there always be a wall between you and them?" Augusta could see this suggestion threw B.K. off balance. "And between you and Guido too. You like to forget the difference between you and the rest of them. That doesn't mean *they* forget it. I see something destructive about this passion of yours. Isn't it just a reaction to Paolo?"

"I've forgotten all that," B.K. said unconvincingly. "Guido is completely different, the opposite . . ."

"That's what I mean." Feeling she had won this down, Augusta shifted her field. "You don't have any idea of what you're turning your back on with this affair. We are in such a rare position—you and I—to have incredible experiences, meet such fantastic people, do impossible things. Whatever Guido may be, he's something *any* attractive woman could have—or you could have any time you wanted in the next twenty years. But what you're throwing away, very few people even know it's there, let alone have it at their disposal. We can have it now. We might not be able to in five years . . ."

"Over the hill?" B.K. put in sarcastically.

"Yes, that. Or married. Or . . ." She looked for a moment at her sister. ". . . too linked with scandal. The powerful of this world are skittish. Their rules are quite lax but they want to be sure you abide by them, that you'll stay within certain bounds. If you prove yourself to be rebellious and unhousebroken, they won't touch you . . . It is a very rare combination of circumstances that makes us desirable to the top people—we're young, attractive, single, well bred, well mannered, bright—we won't be *all* those things very long, we have to make the most of them while we have them."

"You sound like Daddy. What do I care about the top people? It's so snobbish."

"Don't be so stupid! Of course you care. You've been brought up to know the difference between a superb Bordeaux and Seven-Up, between Kirsten Flagstad and Kathryn Grayson, between a sparkling intellect and a dull toad, between people whose lives are shackled with economic realities plus their own petty ambitions and people who can do whatever they want, say whatever they think, buy whatever they wish. You can't now pretend there is no difference or that one is no more desirable than the other . . ."

"I want Guido."

"I promise you, B.K., after our trip to Europe this summer, you'll see how foolish you're being, you'll see what you're throwing away."

"That's what I wanted to talk to you about. I'm not going."

Augusta looked stunned. "What do you mean? The plans are all set."

B.K. looked away. "I'm sorry, Gus. My life is changed. It's with Guido. I can't go skipping off to Europe with white gloves and Temple Fielding like Cornelia Otis Skinner pretending I wasn't used to hopping into bed every night with that hard-muscled body and have it screw the bejesus out of me."

Augusta locked eyes with her sister's for a moment. She took a swallow from her Coke. "Are you talking that way for my benefit, to underline the changes? Or is that your new outlook?"

B.K. said nothing.

"Meet me at the fountain right away," Augusta said. "I'm calling a high-level meeting."

With an effort, B.K. smiled at her sister's attempt at nostalgia. "I'm sorry, Gus; the old ploys don't work anymore."

[239]

"B.K., listen," Augusta said, with a more earnest tone than she had ever used with anyone before. "Ever since we were little girls, we dreamed of going to Europe together. We couldn't because we didn't have the money, then the war. Since there's been the money, I've waited till you were old enough to enjoy it. I didn't want to go without you. You can have the rest of your life with Guido or whomever. But this is the last chance we'll both have to travel as girls, as single women out to have a good time. And now with Uncle Bryce's generosity and connections, and with the people I've met in the past two years—we could have a trip for the history books. I promise you we'll have a time that will make you spit on Guido, but that won't be the point. If you come back as in love with him as you are now, I'll be your fiercest ally. I'll do everything I can for you both . . ."

"Guido and I don't need anyone's help."

"You might. But I'm serious when I ask you to do this for me. Don't make me go alone. I've always dreamed about the two of us doing it together. But I never dreamed it would be the kind of trip we can now make it. It's two months out of your life. If Guido cares at all for you, he'll be more eager than ever when you get back. You've *got* to do it. You *can't* let me down on this."

B.K. looked confused. She hadn't expected her jet-setting sister to care so much whether she went or not. "If it means so much to you, Gus, I suppose I could go. You know I want to see Europe and I'd still love to do it with you. But you can't imagine how important Guido is in my life."

"You aren't choosing between the two things. You can have both and you know it. Oh, B.K. darling, if you will come with me, I will make this the greatest Grand Tour since Peter the Great's."

"You mean we'll visit the shipyards?"

Augusta raised her eyebrows. "Not bad for a college drop-out. No, we won't visit the shipyards. Only the ship owners. I will make our trip so plush and awash in champagne that you'll never want to see Greenwich Village again. You have to taste caviar before you can renounce it forever."

"Just remember, Gus. I'm doing this for you. If I can't stand being away from Guido, I take the next plane home."

"Oh, come on, be reasonable. If I have *that* threat dangling over my head, I won't have a chance."

"I'll try to be reasonable."

If Augusta felt relief it didn't show in her voice. "Let's see, I know I can get us invited to Lady Billingslee's house in Sussex, and I think we can wangle an introduction to Alice Toklas in Paris. We'll have to set something up for the Riviera and Venice, too. I don't know about Capri. It's supposed to be fabulously beautiful, but it is not strong on cultural importance. We ought to make this trip cover the most important sights. We'll have the rest of our lives for lolling about Capri."

"Better put Capri on our itinerary. *You* might plan to hop around the posh resorts for the next forty years, but not me. If I'm going to see it, I'd better see it now."

Both sisters now standing, Augusta gave B.K. a hug. "We'll see it now and you'll be hooked. You'll love it so much, you'll want it every year. Just wait . . ."

35
The white-jacketed majordomo descended the few steps to the lower terrace, passing a statue of a bacchante raising her cup joyously to the blazing blue sky of Tuscany. The servant was handsome and young, little older than Augusta and B.K.; he stood over their chairs and said with grave formality, "Signor Berenson is held by a telephone to America. He will be with you very shortly. He asks if you desire something?"

Augusta smiled and said they would wait for Mr. Berenson. She contemplated B.K., who chatted with some animation about the beauty of the villa and the view of the surrounding hills. Augusta had already impressed on her how lucky they were to be meeting the famous Bernard Berenson, who, in a sense, represented a culmination of their epic tour.

To be sure, they had met more famous people and visited

more splendid residences, but the high point of the summer for them both had been the magnificent art they had seen, some in homes, but most in the museums and churches swarming with young Americans. And here they were at the home of the man who had brought such a large portion of Europe's art master-pieces into the consciousness of the English-speaking world.

Berenson was a giant among that category of humans Augusta admired more than any other, the arbiters of taste. What an important form of power. To be able to say "This is beautiful because I say it is" and to have millions of people not just nod in acquiescence but be commanded into seeing and feeling the beauty that was always there. Augusta was so reverential about this power that she viewed it as a high order of healing, of making incapacitated, incomplete people complete.

The invitation to *I Tati* carried with it another thrill, of a kind Augusta had grown used to and was trying to accustom B.K. to as well. It was the exclusivity, entering confines from which ordinary people didn't realize they were excluded. The throngs of American college students pouring through the Uffizi and Pitti palaces below, guidebooks dutifully in hand, searching out the far corners of Botticellis and Fra Filippo Lippis for some magical key that would convert them into ladies and gentlemen of taste and sensibility, had little notion that what they were doing at considerable expense and effort resulted to a large degree from the life work of the distinguished elderly man who would soon come down the steps toward the Tollover sisters and grasp them warmly by the hand.

B.K. looked so beautiful in this setting. Augusta had taken delight in the way the young butler's eyes had lingered a fraction of a second too long on her lovely sister, dropping to her tanned and elegant legs. Then the vignette had reminded her of the menacing Guido; she hoped the Italian's appreciation was not noticed by B.K., sending her into the same reminiscences.

From that point of view, the trip had been reasonably successful. B.K. had not exactly thrown herself into their privileged episodes, but she had gone in good grace, showing appreciation for the effort Augusta and many others had made to provide their trip with a series of dizzying highlights.

God, the strings Augusta had teased, pulled and yanked! Anyone she knew in America who might have an entree of more than routine interest had been called on. Ken's aunt for an introduction to Jacques Fath, C.Z. Guest for her noble English relations, Elsa Maxwell, who fixed them up with a lunch at Jack Warner's villa at Cap d'Antibes with Ava Gardner a fellow guest.

The whole rarefied program was gilding on the basic delight of being a young American in Europe in the years following World War II. This year, 1951, was long enough after the war's end for the countries to be sufficiently recovered to provide comfort and prewar luxury, but close enough to the war to make the dollar a venerated unit of currency with a purchasing strength that embarrassed the most insatiable bargain hunters, and to make the bearers of those dollars not just targets of hunger and greed but glamorous and adored figures of charming goodness and innocence.

By all but the most embittered Europeans in the fifties, Americans were loved for their wealth and their extravagance in addition to their persona of heroic deliverer. The American tourists, who invaded in greater numbers than Patton's armies, loved being loved—and loved spending lavishly. It was a popularity machine that could only grow stronger.

But beyond all these special enhancements of the era, and beyond the delights of the particular day and the special treats of the Tollover sisters' Olympian connections—even beyond the abundant art treasures for culture-starved Americans—there were still the permanent everyday joys of Europe for the American first-time visitor: the throwing-open of hotel-room windows to a Paris roofscape, the one-handed service of vegetables from a silver tray by a fourteen-year-old white-jacketed waiter, the bakery and restaurant perfumes in the narrow streets of provincial French towns, the first summertime glimpse of a snow-capped alp or the awakening in the *wagon-lit* of Le Train Bleu to find the train coursing along the cobalt Mediterranean of the Côte d'Azure.

Augusta knew it was these pleasures available to all, as much as the house parties at Loire châteaux, that had distracted B.K.

from her passion for Guido. Even with such a massive onslaught of thrilling new sensations, however, the cure had not been total. When they dined alone, or when they were getting ready for bed, B.K. would often lapse into conversational keening for her absent lover. Sometimes these outbreaks would be cries of pain at the unnatural separation, one made all the more painful by B.K.'s own complicity. Other times the complaint was more earthy.

All of the many males who had presented themselves for B.K.'s approval—from hand-kissing Austrian barons with thin blonde moustaches, blue eyes and a ruddiness that could not have occurred in America, to muscular and self-assured Ivy League lotharios inviting the sisters to trout fishing in Spain, sailboating in the Greek islands, or canal-boating through Burgundy—all had as much effect on B.K. as magnets on aluminum. She was flattered and sometimes amused by their campaigns, but found them irrelevant to the point of daftness. She seemed unaware that even the most doggedly faithful lover was still capable of choice and, if not infidelity, at least a muscle-maintaining flirtation. She was never the slightest bit tempted by any of them.

Looking at her sister as she chatted on about Florence and how she would like to return here with Guido, Augusta marveled at the tenacity of the Guido obsession. Perhaps she should be grateful that B.K. took any pleasure at all in the trip, or indeed that she hadn't bolted to the nearest New York-bound plane, as she had threatened on two of the most virulent attacks of Guido-itis.

The summer was not over yet. They still had much of Italy to cover—a week hiking around Interlaken and then a reunion with Ambassador and Mrs. Hartshorne in Munich in September before flying back to New York. Many things could still happen in the weeks ahead. The constant injections of powerful diversions might eventually weaken Guido's power; privileged encounters with remarkable people like Berenson might make B.K. awaken to other forms of stimulation than the rudimentary one Guido provided.

And then there was always the chance that B.K. would meet

someone who might, if not break Guido's hold, at least remind B.K. that the world was not made up of men, women and Guido—that he was just one representative of a rather large category.

For the second time, Augusta told B.K. the title of Bernard Berenson's most famous book. Her sister's nervousness at meeting the great man gratified Augusta. If B.K. were completely alienated from Augusta's elite and accomplished world, B.K. wouldn't have cared if Berenson had written *Little Women* or *Gray's Anatomy*. Guido might possess most of her sister, but not all. The fight must continue.

As the small, trim figure of Berenson appeared at the top of the steps, smiling benignly at the two paragons of upper-class American girlhood, Augusta thought a prayer: "Please, Mr. Berenson, work the wizardry on us that you have on so many previous visitors. Enchant us with your wit, your erudition, your vision of what is worthy in this world. And, please, cajole, charm, inspire my sister away from a pair of bulging biceps and a hairy chest. Amen."

36 As Ken ordered cocktails from the middle-aged Italian waiter, Augusta surveyed the late-afternoon cocktail crowd on the terrace of the Villa d'Este. Almost entirely Americans. In the two days she and B.K. had been there waiting for Ken to arrive, Augusta had watched other young Americans stroll the monumental corridors, slouch in the palatial public rooms and gorge themselves at tables designed for German steel magnates and Bulgarian princes.

Now the world-famous hotel was reduced to a summer branch of Yale and Princeton clubs. Perhaps when Europe recovered more financial health, the Europeans would once again be able to afford the establishments which had long been models of luxury for the rest of the world.

"Isn't it strange that they placed this hotel right here," Ken said. "If they had moved it another mile or so up the lake they would have had a much more spectacular view. From here, you can see nary an alp."

"But it's still lovely," Augusta said, wondering how many thousands of people had made the observation Ken had just made, but not caring, rather taking comfort in his logical predictability. Augusta was very glad to see Ken. For one thing, he would relieve her in the B.K.-distraction project. Even though B.K. cared little for Ken, Augusta knew, she felt comfortable around him and he was yet another voice, another face, another presence to divert her attention.

Augusta was happy to see him for her own reasons. The summer's parade of exotic swains had impressed her more than it had B.K., but Augusta had begun to weary of the self-conscious posturing of the displaying European. She had grown accustomed to the woman-veneration and courtly manners of all but the youngest street urchins, but on the other hand she missed the unaffectedness of young Americans.

She had also grown bored with the threadbare pretense of even the choicest French and Italian young blades. She didn't know if her being American attracted only the most impoverished, or it was simply that they were all impoverished. It was a pleasant change to be sitting with a wholesome, attentive male who would pick up the check, whose pocket bulged with American Express travelers' checks and who could, if he wished, hire a car to drive them to Zermatt to watch the sunrise over the Matterhorn.

The summer had given her a disillusioning close-up of Europe's elite: vast homes, galleries of ancestral portraits, museum-quality furniture acquired six generations earlier, shown in pride by a generation that couldn't afford to have chair legs reglued. It was all so sad, so burned out, so hopeless.

"One thing you must say for your sister," Ken said cheerily as they took sips from Negronis. "She's more beautiful than ever. She must have turned heads as you traversed the Continent."

"You can't imagine," Augusta smiled. "Any American woman under the age of sixty sets them whimpering and howling, but one as lovely as B.K., who is said to be richer than most Americans, they turn to jelly. That may be the trouble.

With B.K., they're jelly, but with an average American girl they are damned effective."

"But you told me not to bring Hal Knudsen down from Paris with me. He's very attractive and good fun. I haven't met a girl yet who didn't go for him—or whom he wasn't happy to oblige with as much of his charm as they were prepared to take."

"It was thoughtful of you, Ken," Augusta said, "but baby sister can smell a set-up a mile away. It only makes her more negative, more faithful to Guido. But your coming now was a godsend. I made a terrible mistake in Rome. I arranged for us to have tea with the old Princess Doria in that incredible palazzo on the Corso. I forgot she was Paolo's great aunt. Frankly, I am so preoccupied with Guido, I forgot all about Paolo. Even if she hadn't been related, the thing was unmistakably an excursion into Paolo's world. And the old bitch was decidedly condescending to us. I'm not sure B.K. noticed that, but something about the visit sent her into one of her worst Guido-relapses to date. I had to lock her in our room at the Hassler to keep her from flying back to New York. One ploy was how embarrassing it would be for me if she wasn't here when you came, how disappointed you'd be—anything I could think of. But something about the Rome crisis suggested a connection between her obsession with that Italian actor and her old hurt over being snubbed by the Italian aristocracy. I should have stopped when I was winning in France and England."

"Look, Gus," Kendall said in a voice that announced The Long View, "what if B.K. wants to go to hell with some slob? Can you really stop her? She'll pull out of it when she gets tired of him—or vice versa."

"I won't give up that easily. If she goes on much longer with him, too many doors will be closed to her. She's wasting crucial years. As for B.K. growing tired of Guido, that is *not* her style. She has the most stubborn allegiances since Heloise. No, he'll grow tired of her, or get from her all that he wants, then leave, and it will kill her. I know B.K. She's too intense about these things—and she shuts everything else out, so that when the calamity comes, she has nothing to cushion her—no other interests, no friends, no social life. So you see I have two very strong motives for forcing her to see there is more to life than her Italian."

B.K. walked toward them across the terrace, the late afternoon sun reflected off Lake Como underlighting her delicate face like stage lighting. The shoulder straps of her yellow linen dress set off the luster of her tanned skin. The pang Augusta felt, as she did each time her sister looked particularly beautiful, only strengthened her resolve to rescue her from Guido. So did her disapproval of the way B.K. collapsed ungracefully into the chair Ken held out for her. Her movements were now Greenwich Village rather than Old Westbury.

"Well, what's it to be tonight, gang?" she said sourly. "Supper with the Toscaninis or dancing with the Agnellis? You're in for it, Ken. Gus doesn't fool around with the folk-song set."

"What will you drink?" Ken asked.

"Scotch. I don't know what came over me, but I wanted to look particularly virginal tonight. Did I pull it off?"

"You look lovely," Augusta said uneasily, feeling the truculent tone presaged some new twist in B.K.'s disaffection.

"Come on, B.K.," Ken said genially. "You know you've had a good time."

"Did Gus tell you about Frank Sinatra? I think he was the most plebeian person I've been permitted to meet this summer. Most of them are so aristocratic their blood doesn't bleed, it weeps."

Suddenly Augusta grew tired of this tug-of-war. "You haven't enjoyed any of it, then?" Her voice showed her exasperation.

B.K. turned toward Augusta with vehemence. "I'd trade it all—castles, duchesses and movie stars—for twelve minutes in bed with Guido!"

Augusta didn't flinch but stared at her sister for a moment, then, still fixing her with her eyes, said slowly, "My God, what have you become?"

Tears formed in B.K.'s eyes as she drank from her Scotch, then said with forced merriment, "A pregnant lady, for one thing."

Augusta sat speechless.

"Oh, boy!" Ken exhaled.

"Sorry to louse up the summer," B.K. said contritely, "but that seems to be it. The hotel doctor confirmed it. Emily Kimbrough will now switch to "Our Hearts Were Young and Knocked Up."

"You'll get rid of it, of course." Augusta was already thinking how.

"No, I've decided to have it."

Augusta turned to Ken. "I think you'd better leave us alone for a minute, Ken."

"All right, but it seems we are all pretty much in this together now."

"Ken's right," B.K. said morosely. "It looks like I could use another opinion."

Augusta had thought of a strategem. "I don't know what your reasons are for the lunacy of having this child, but I promise you, there would be no faster way of losing Guido." She could see she had B.K.'s attention. "His acting career is the most important thing in the world to him. What could be worse for an aspiring sex symbol than marriage and fatherhood?"

"I didn't say anything about marriage."

"I'm sure he wouldn't either," Augusta said, trying to keep contempt from her voice. "I was giving him the benefit of the doubt. Let's just say 'a roommate with a baby.' Do you think Mother and Uncle Bryce would support that household? I know your only concern is Guido. You know he would run so fast you couldn't catch him with a movie contract."

Ken jumped in on Augusta's side. "Nothing cools off the old ardor faster, B.K. It's pretty frightening for a young guy . . ."

"O.K., O.K.," said B.K., making a face. "Will you both please stop kicking the pregnant lady? I'll get rid of it. But how? Does American Express book abortions?"

"We could row up to Switzerland," Ken said cheerily, "as in *Farewell to Arms*."

"Maybe you could parlay it into an M.A. in English Lit," B.K. said snidely.

"I'm glad you both think this is so funny," Augusta said in her take-charge voice. "We've got to make a careful plan."

B.K. smiled brightly at Augusta. "We figured *you'd* do that."

"First I've got to send some telegrams canceling dates we have coming up. I hope we can get this over with by the time we're supposed to meet Mummie in Munich."

"It doesn't take long, does it?" B.K. asked.

"No," Ken said authoritatively. "Finding the right guy is the problem."

"I think we should go to a big city, not in Italy—a sanitary city. You're right about Switzerland, Ken. We're only a few hours from Geneva. That would be ideal. First thing in the morning, we'll rent a car, drive up to Geneva. B.K. and I will get a hotel and you go out and find us the right doctor . . ."

"How do I do that? The *Guide Michelin?*"

"Don't be so helpless. I thought you men could get that information in an instant. Even with *your* French."

"A classmate of mine lives there. He might know a name. You don't want this getting out. I don't have to tell him anything. I'll say I forgot to take precautions with a Swiss girl."

"Say French," B.K. said. "Swiss girls don't put out. He'd smell a rat right away."

"Good point."

It was almost dark. Ken signed for the drinks, then the three young Americans got up and reentered the old hotel. Dwarfed by the grandiose corridor to the main dining room, they looked childlike. If it hadn't been for their healthy suntans and grown-up clothes, they could have been the progeny of a prewar *haute bourgeoisie* European family, summering in one of the Continent's great hotels, coming from a walk along the lake to join their parents for dinner, only to lose the parents later to bridge and a stringed orchestra.

Instead they were three exceptionally endowed young Americans, the new rulers of the world. Their parents were represented only by the packs of travelers' checks and the letters of credit in their passport cases. They could enjoy the dinner they were about to have, food of a quality many people never experience in their entire lives, knowing that they had the money, brains and acumen to handle even the most adult problems.

37 A pink-and-gold Sèvres urn filled with plump white roses won Augusta's attention over all the other exquisite objects in the stately salon. The Louis Seize furniture, the Aubusson carpet that appeared to have been woven for the room and the beige damask hangings all gave Augusta the feeling that she had arrived at a safe harbor. B.K. was assured of the finest medical care. The only danger here was of being found out.

It had been a harrowing two days—the drive up from Como, getting a room in the Hotel Richmond and sending Ken out to find a doctor. The hour in the clinic, taking the ashen B.K. back to the hotel only to have her start hemorrhaging. The doctor's refusal to revisit his patient and their desperation call to the hotel doctor, who managed to stop the bleeding. It had all been terrifying and Augusta was relieved by her inspiration to call on the British ambassador to Switzerland and his wife.

Lord and Lady Shackleford had been in Washington during the war and become close friends of Bryce Hartshorne. When they visited America they invariably spent several days at Tidewater Farm; it was on one of these visits Augusta and B.K. had come to know them. Their embassy would not only have a doctor but a large staff, transportation if necessary, efficient communications and the habit of discretion.

A gilded white door opened and Lady Shackleford swept across the room toward Augusta. She was a stunning woman in her late fifties, tall, with gray hair worn in a soft bob and blue eyes that for all their brightness managed to look sad. Although she had rejoiced to Augusta that they would be alone at lunch, she was dressed to receive royalty. Augusta imagined that ambassadors' wives had to wear couturier clothes to rearrange the linen closets. The British woman came toward Augusta with her arms outstretched.

"My dear child," she said in a crisp Mayfair accent, "how happy I am that you came to me in your difficulty. Harold is very pleased as well and looks forward to seeing you at dinner this evening."

"I'm so sorry to impose on you this way. I thought it was just a routine case of the flu, but when B.K.'s fever returned and started to climb, I grew alarmed."

"Of course, of course. How right you were. The embassy doctor is with her now. There's no finer doctor in Switzerland—which is to say the world."

"I can't tell you how grateful we both are," Augusta said.

"Nonsense. I would have been livid if you'd tried to weather this in a hotel. And your parents would have been the same."

"I know . . ."

"There's just one thing, Augusta darling . . ."

"Yes?"

"You say it is flu . . ."

"That's what it appears to be. We've both had it before and B.K. says . . ."

"Augusta, let's be frank. I must insist you trust me."

They contemplated each other for a moment.

Augusta spoke first. "How did you know?"

"Let's just say I've been around a long time. I had a feeling the minute you phoned. So much insistence on the flu. But the doctor confirmed my suspicions after two minutes. You know it really is quite naughty of you, lying about something as serious as this. What if she grew worse and we didn't know what it was?"

Augusta felt genuine shame. "Lady Shackleford, please believe me when I tell you that if anything like that had happened I would have told you immediately."

"But why did you distrust me so?"

"My parents. I know how close you are with Mummie and Uncle Bryce and I was afraid you might feel you had to inform them."

"You were right, my dear, I do."

"Oh, Lady Shackleford, you mustn't!"

"But why ever not? These things happen."

Augusta told the story of Guido, of her belief that B.K.'s obsession with him was a reaction against the ambassador's world. If the Hartshornes came down hard on B.K. to end the affair with Guido, it would, Augusta was convinced, drive B.K. further from them all. Augusta was making progress, but the entrance of their parents into this crisis would devastate all chances of rescuing her sister.

"That's a rather dramatic analysis, don't you think?" Lady Shackleford said when August finished. "Mind you, I'm not saying it's specious. Let me think . . ."

"There's another reason I am frantic to keep this from them. If Mother finds out, she might feel obliged to tell my father. He's been behaving so erratically lately, he might do anything."

"Yes, I know a bit about your dashing father." At the appearance of a butler, Lady Shackleford rose to lead them into lunch. She paused at the dining-room door. "But Augusta, some responsible member of your family must know."

"Lady Shackleford. I am the responsible member of my family."

Dinner with the Shacklefords that evening progressed pleasantly. Because of the other guests, much of the conversation had been in French, which oddly diverted Augusta from her sister in pain above. Over coffee, Augusta sat alone with Lord Shackleford. She knew he had been informed of B.K.'s predicament, but he made no mention of it, sticking to questions about the Hartshornes and Augusta's plans for the future.

As soon as the ambassador was called to another group, Augusta asked Lady Shackleford if she might say good night and go to B.K. Lady Shackleford assured her that everyone would understand. She left the drawing room, climbed the grand staircase and walked the long hall to the room adjoining her own that B.K. had been assigned. It was a state bedroom with high, frescoed ceiling, French windows opening onto small balconies, and ornate eighteenth-century furniture that was dwarfed by the room's monumental proportions. B.K. was awake.

"How do you feel?" Augusta asked.

"Shaky. Ashamed. Frightened."

"You should feel safe, at least. The Shacklefords know

everything and won't let anything happen to you. They are being wonderful about it."

B.K. sighed and tried to sit up. "Does that mean they won't alert the troops?"

"I don't think they will. But if they do, they do. There's a kind of peace to having the biggest secrets out in the open."

"You know that I never cared about any of that unless it affects Guido and me."

Sitting on a small chair by B.K.'s large bed, Augusta removed her shoes. "This *could* affect you and Guido—if Mummie and Uncle Bryce find out, I mean. They are quite capable of turning the time-honored screws. Don't forget that they're supporting you. Of course Mummie's objections to Guido would be social, not moral."

Augusta could tell from the hesitant way B.K. looked at her that B.K. viewed Augusta's disapproval the same way.

"What do I care?" B.K. said bleakly. "I don't need a fancy East Side apartment or their allowance. I can get a job. I worry only because of the trouble it would make for you."

"Why me?" Augusta laughed. "I didn't make you pregnant."

"They'll rush over, fly in a platoon of doctors, midwives, psychologists, caseworkers . . . You'll have to meet them all at the airport, give out statements for the press, serve drinks . . ."

Augusta watched her sister's eyes close as the phenobarbital took hold. She eased B.K. down into the pillows and felt her slight body cooperate in the effort. Brushing the hair from her forehead Augusta contemplated B.K. and felt a pang of envy that her younger sister, in an important way, outdistanced her; B.K. had now experienced more of the dramas available to women.

She checked herself and knew that her own appetite for life was a highly selective one. She despised the adolescent eagerness to "experience it all." She had had quite enough of the one kind of experience and would work to avoid more of the same: severe illness, passionate fights with a lover, living by your wits, overcoming adversity, feats of physical endurance—she had no desire to test herself against such trials and she marveled at people she knew who seemed to deliberately set them up for themselves. But she recognized her reasoning as Augusta At Her Most Logical. There was still a residue of envy; B.K. had now been someplace Augusta had not.

Augusta passed through the adjoining door to her much smaller bedroom, picked up the phone and asked the embassy switchboard for Ken's hotel. He snapped up his phone on the first ring and sounded very relieved that all had gone smoothly and that B.K. was in safe hands. Augusta renewed her offer to tell the Shacklefords of his presence and get him invited to stay at the embassy.

"No, Gus. It's bad enough that they have to swallow B.K.'s love life. Why add that you are traveling through Europe with a man? If B.K. doesn't get through this soon, maybe I'll kind of *show up* in a day or two."

Augusta promised to come to his hotel at lunchtime the following day. When they hung up, Augusta undressed, put on a dressing gown and passed through B.K.'s room to the adjoining bath where she opened the tub's huge old taps. By using B.K.'s bathroom instead of her own, Augusta could luxuriate in the water and still hear if B.K. needed her.

A bottle of Floris bath oil stood on the tub's edge. Augusta read the label—Geranium—then poured a liberal dollop into the steaming water, liking the acrid, strange odor. As she lowered herself into the water, she rejoiced in the oblivion imposed by the painful heat. The ache quickly gave way to a feeling of profound relaxation, of muscles uncoiling for the first time in days, nerves dulled into insensitivity.

Even anesthetized, Augusta became more aware of her own physicality than she had been in some time. Her sister and that Italian animal. Augusta had deeply enjoyed the sex with Jeff; why did she not now crave that kind of eroticism? Why didn't she and Ken sleep together? The idea was agreeable to her. But she knew the reason they didn't. Among people like themselves—their age, their class, their probable future together—it wasn't done.

Strange that Ken didn't push for it more. Maybe there was something wrong with him. No, Augusta felt sure the same probity worked as strongly in him as in her. Ken was surely finding release elsewhere. How odd she had never thought of that before. She had to remember to ask him.

She stepped from the tub and wrapped herself in an enormous white towel as thick and soft as a fur rug. She heard B.K.—something between a cry and a groan. She pulled on her dressing gown and rushed to her bedside. B.K. was still asleep but was tossing spastically. Augusta sat on the bed and placed her hand on B.K.'s forehead. It still felt feverish. Augusta wondered if she should call the doctor.

B.K. lapsed into a calm, so Augusta decided against seeking help. She looked down on her sister and smoothed her hair. Was she losing her to currents she didn't understand? By the standards they lived among, B.K. was well into that category known as "screwed up." Barely twenty and she had dropped out of college, taken an unsuitable lover—allowing that *any* lover was suitable for girls like them—and conceived a child that no one wanted, including the two principals.

What was pushing B.K. so far from where she should be? From where Augusta was? Surely it couldn't be the Paolo catastrophe. Most of the girls Augusta knew had had their teenaged hearts broken at least once, and they had recovered. They didn't use it as an excuse to turn against the values and situations they had been brought up to.

With B.K. there was some further dislocation, but Augusta couldn't decide what it was. The agonies of their childhood had pained B.K. less than they had Augusta. Maybe that was why B.K. was more vulnerable now.

B.K. gave another cry and sat bolt upright. She opened her eyes and looked at Augusta—wildly for a moment, then with fear. She collapsed gratefully into Augusta's arms. And suddenly she was asleep again. Augusta lowered her onto the pillow.

"Don't worry, darling," Augusta murmured. "I'll save you. From Guido, from your innocence, from your anger—from death in a state bedroom."

38

Having brooded so long over whether to tell her mother about B.K.'s affair with Guido, Augusta was deflated by the Hartshornes' indifference. In Geneva her fear had been that, if they knew, they would do something. Now, back in America, with the abortion safely in the past, Augusta hoped they *would* do something. B.K. and Guido had resumed their affair, even more fervently than they had begun it. All of B.K.'s anxiety that her absence would weaken or break her hold on Guido was converted into a surge of passion the moment she saw he was still hers. The dazzling events of the elaborate summer Augusta had spread out before her were dismissed and forgotten like absurdly lavish favors from a flop party.

Augusta's alarm to the Hartshornes had fallen so flat ("Italian actor? He's not mistreating her, is he?") Augusta had been tempted to throw in the abortion to spark their interest. She had hoped for some reaction, even a promise to investigate, but the Hartshornes astonished her with their nonchalance.

She watched her stepfather pace in front of the fireplace of his Nantucket library. A portrait of Captain Joseph Hartshorne glowered down on them ("Not a whaler, mind you. He was in the China trade").

"Naturally we appreciate your telling us about B.K.'s involvement, Augusta," the ambassador said somberly. "But these things have a way of working themselves out . . ."

A gray room in Geneva flashed through her mind, a cloth-covered operating table, a shoe salesman dressed as a doctor . . .

"Your Uncle Bryce and I have something far more serious on our minds." Her mother's voice was grave, adult, a voice of state. "You know that your Uncle Bryce's name is soon to be placed before the Senate as our next ambassador to Moscow . . ."

"Yes, you told me over the phone. It's terribly exciting."

Her mother continued. "Your Uncle Bryce's appointment by President Truman has been an open secret for several weeks now. Almost from the day it was known, attempts to smear his name have appeared in the press. Vicious items. Nothing like this has ever happened before and we are at a loss to figure it out."

"Perhaps there is someone else who wants the job?" Augusta was making an effort to focus on her parents' concern.

"No. It has been established that my name is the only one the President considered. There is opposition to my appointment in the Senate, but the leader of that opposition—Arthur Vandenberg—is an old friend. He's a man of great honor who would never stoop to these tactics, nor would he permit anyone else to."

"We wanted to tell you, Augusta, so you wouldn't be distressed when you begin to see the stories."

"What sort of stories?"

"Most accuse Bryce of lavish spending to purchase important jobs for himself. They attack his competence. Even the Communist and Socialist papers stopped that sort of attack on him years ago. These slurs are appearing in popular columns like Walter Winchell and Ed Sullivan. Even Cholly Knickerbocker . . ."

A stab of anxiety passed through Augusta at this last mention.

"And some of the references are utterly unconscionable . . ." Kate said with suppressed outrage. "They have even brought in Brandon."

"Brandon?" Augusta was confused, not having thought of him in connection with her stepfather for some time.

"Oh, you know—his Bohemian existence, his Communist friends, his exotic love life."

"They don't . . ."

Ambassador Hartshorne cut Augusta off. "They don't make any specific accusations, but they imply enough for a four year old to understand."

"What has any of that to do with your qualifications as ambassador to Russia?"

"What indeed?" Hartshorne replied. "If there is one thing that characterizes all of the slings, it's that they're below-the-belt. It hits me particularly hard as I've always felt that, in the political arena, the integrity of my name was my strong suit. I've never had the glad-hander's approach, and I'm afraid my wealth precludes the man-of-the people image. The silver spoon has never been a political asset, but the public can be made to see it as immunizing its owner against the temptation to graft. But now with these attacks, the name I have been for years building as a man of public spirit, without self-interested motives, without scandal—these are the very aspects that are being impugned. It is very distressing."

Augusta was so unnerved by the suspicion that gripped her, she was barely able to contribute to the ensuing conversation about her final year at Smith and her plans for later.

When she phoned her father, asking if she might spend her final two days before returning to college with him, Augusta was flummoxed by his reply.

"It's rather inconvenient right now, my dear. *Affaire de coeur*, you know."

Never before would he have hesitated to toss an affair into the street, or at least hold it in abeyance, for a visit from either herself or B.K. On her father's promise of dinner, Augusta phoned B.K. that she wanted to spend a night with her, suddenly aware of how her New York appearances were disrupting her family's frenzied sex lives. Strange how B.K.'s enthusiasm at Augusta's visits was, if anything, greater since her affair with Guido. Perhaps it was that Augusta was the sole element of her former life B.K. wanted to keep.

Facing her father at the entrance to his apartment, Augusta was stunned at his appearance. He had put on enough weight to make his fine figure only a memory. He now looked like most other men in their late fifties. The added flesh in his face was not a wrinkle-preventing asset, as it sometimes could be in aging people. The drink and dissipation had claimed this new material for its own.

The fine profile and the wonderful dark eyes were intact but they were surrounded by a physiognomy that looked on the point of giving way to the random planes and droops of age.

Augusta thought of one of Picasso's cubist faces and wondered if the aging process was what had helped inspire his cubist break-up of form.

Augusta sensed that her father had read her reaction, but chose to ignore it.

"At last! My famous daughter. Back from the glittering capitals of Europe. I heard that not since Annie Oakley has an American had such a triumph."

How he must hate himself, she thought, for the way he has let himself go. That had always been for him the cardinal sin. He was still dressed with his customary panache—green-silk ascot, tweed jacket, fawn-colored flannels and Gucci moccasins.

He turned off a Bobby Short record, then asked Augusta what she wanted to drink. "I'm sorry I wasn't here for your triumphal return. I missed the ticker-tape parade up Park Avenue. Business has picked up considerably for me; and I had to go to London for a few days. I must have just missed you there."

He handed her a drink. "I know you have something you want to discuss, but before we get into that, let me tell you of the plan I've made for this evening. I've booked us a table at the Potiniere du Soir. Do you know it? I've grown fond of it. Quite civilized, really, and they serve till eleven—not common among Manhattan's better restaurants."

Once settled in a chair beside Augusta's spot on the sofa, he continued to put off any serious discussion. "You look particularly well. I wouldn't change a thing. The pin perhaps. It's a tad large. Was it a gift?"

"From Ken."

"Then the purity of the emotion that prompted it makes up for a slight esthetic deficiency."

"I thought so too." For a minute, Augusta felt a surge of the special empathy that flowed between her and her father. In the odd exchange both would agree to the most minute percentage point what degree of sense and what degree of deliberate absurdity had just been spoken.

Dread of the topic she planned to introduce quickly chilled

her feelings toward her father. "You know Uncle Bryce has been appointed our next ambassador to Russia?"

"Yes, I heard. I was wondering how much that cost him. Marjorie Post bought that job for Joe Davies for a rumored twenty-three thousand dollars. But that was 1936. Prices for everything have tripled since then."

"Since word of the appointment got out," Augusta ploughed on toward her accusation, "a rash of nasty items have appeared in the newspapers about him."

"I've seen one or two, I must admit," he said, making no attempt to conceal his relish. There was a pause. "What about them?"

Augusta jumped in. "Are you responsible?"

Tollover looked as though he had just been insulted by a surly waiter. For a moment Augusta thought he might strike her. Then he exploded in a loud, "HA!"

"That has to win some sort of prize for gall," he said venomously. "Did that swine put you up to coming here with that gross accusation?"

"No, I came . . ."

"Doesn't that ass realize he is playing a grown-up game for large stakes? While he struts around in nothing jobs, no one cares that he's a blithering incompetent, a rich dilettante, but now that he has the *folie de grandeur* to go after an important post, his incompetence becomes a matter of public concern. The press is simply doing its job."

Tollover jumped to his feet and paced his living room as he ranted. The impersonation of a faded film idol was now complete. "But that he—or you—would try to turn his own incompetence against *me!* That is too much. That he would try to drag me into his dirty machinations . . ."

The more he talked, the more convinced Augusta became that her father had instigated the items; his outburst was too ready, too shoaled up with prolix logic. If her father had been innocent, he would have concentrated on denying any involvement, on dispelling the suspicion. Instead he was merely using the accusation as another pretext for inveighing against

Hartshorne. Augusta had expected a bullying and was resolved to resist it.

"Daddy," she began, thinking how strange the word now felt on her lips. "Why won't you see how hurtful your hatred of Uncle Bryce is for all of us? A scandal involving him hurts B.K. and me—and of course Mummie. So much time has gone by. B.K. and I are grown up. Uncle Bryce is not important in our lives." She had almost added "anymore."

"When Mummie decided to remarry, your feeling toward him was just a wry competitiveness, nothing more. You've nurtured it into an obsessive hatred. When we all split up, you didn't want a family. You were glad to be free of us. Uncle Bryce has done nothing to you. You seem to care more about hating him than anything else. It is destructive for all of us, but mostly for you."

Once again Augusta could feel the subject of his deteriorated appearance hang in the air between them.

He glowered at her. Then took a drink from his Scotch. "If it weren't for your precious Uncle Bryce," he said calmly, "do you think you would have ever talked to me like that?" He took another swallow of Scotch and said morosely, "That's great. One daughter's going to hell with an Italian slum kid, the other's turned into an ambassador's hit man."

Augusta hadn't thought her father knew about Guido—the affair had never been discussed—but this news item was quickly wiped away by her reaction to the wrong-headedness of his thinking, the convenient pain he took in laying at the feet of his wife's second husband everything that went wrong between parent and teenaged child—independence, defiance, disaffection, disinterest. In her father's mind just one small fact—her mother's choice of husband—had shattered his fantasy of father–daughter love. The natural divisive elements of time and circumstance, the inevitable erosion that gradually develops before the eyes of everyone else, had been removed from her father's view, allowing him to wallow in the false dream of how beautiful it all could have been—better by far than it ever had been when they were together—if it hadn't been for this one bête noire.

She was marshaling her arguments to rebut this self-serving delusion once and for all when her father, as though sensing his indefensibility, suddenly derailed their combativeness. "I hardly think the evidence bears out that my dislike of your stepfather is destroying me. Perhaps you're seeing too many of these new plays—Tennessee Williams, Inge. Genteel poor families savaging each other over their grits. My life, as it happens, has never been better . . ." Augusta marveled at how quickly he could resume his old insouciance—nothing had been said, nothing had happened. Even some of his looks fell back into place, a sparkle to his eyes.

". . . I've had a bit of luck on the Street, business is popping and I have a wonderful new love affair. I'm enjoying myself thoroughly. Now, let's go to dinner. These Puerto Rican slugfests give me an appetite."

She looked at him in amazement. "Aren't we too mad at each other?" she said.

"I'm not. Are you?"

She smiled sheepishly, her pose as a lucid adult confronting a mixed-up child collapsing completely. "No."

Dinner was as pleasant as the outings her father had taken them on in the early days of the separation. He was at his most charming, his incandescence rising at the attentions of the maître d' and the waiters, and the attention of the other diners in the intimate restaurant, some of whom knew either Augusta or her father, almost all of whom knew who they both were and whispered unnecessary identifications to each other.

All of her life Augusta had admired her father's ability to put a good face on the most dreadful circumstances: his joviality on hearing one of Kate's bill-collector humiliations, optimism over hopeless business reverses, cordiality in the face of seething dislike. But for the first time she saw this ability to dissemble as an aberration, a pathological unwillingness to deal with the truth. His strength was turning into his tragedy before her eyes.

He ordered a 1948 Vourray and joked with the waiter about the inferior clientele and food at the sister restaurant across the street. Augusta had trouble keeping in mind that she believed this affable, amusing man to be guilty of an act of the most despicable vindictiveness. As the wine worked through her, the dark thought flowed from her mind, but would return resoundingly when she awoke the following morning in B.K.'s living room. Then she would feel that her father's ability to block out from his evening her bitter accusation only further established his guilt.

The increasingly surreal dinner took an unexpected turn when Augusta asked her father, one chum to another, about his new girl friend.

"I'm glad you brought that up," he said, turning earnest. "She's a wonderful woman, and I want you and B.K. to meet her one day, but . . ." He paused dramatically. "She's a bit shy. Never been involved in anything like this before—extramarital, that is. It would be better if you and B.K. phoned before dropping by."

"Don't we always?"

"Do you? I suppose you do. But just to avoid any encounters, I'm going to ask you both to return your keys for the time being . . ."

This was very odd, Augusta thought, as she rooted through her pocketbook for her keys. It was not at all like her father to give that sort of importance to a love interest. Much of his appeal was based on a policy of non-discomfiture, of haughty indifference to the lover's desires and exigencies. Whatever concessions Tollover might make were invariably abandoned when they conflicted with his daughters' slightest wants. It was such a major shift, Augusta couldn't help feeling it somehow related to the newspaper-item mystery. She would think it all through in the morning when her head was cleared of the wine and the earlier battle.

Who could this new lover be that her father would go to such pains for secrecy? Extremely famous, perhaps? Or maybe a man. She had heard rumors. Of one thing she was certain. Her father's behavior was so strange and, in a most disagreeable way, so menacing to them all, that she would no longer accept his stories but would investigate on her own.

39

"He's at the office, sweetie. Call back tonight." The exaggerated North Shore drawl on the other end of the phone was thick with sleep. Augusta hung up and looked at her watch. Ten-fifteen. She took a cab to East Fifty-first Street. If pinned down she could say she had come to return B.K.'s keys and had forgotten about the request for telephone clearance.

She had a moment's terror as she held the key to the lock. She was not so much afraid of what she would find inside her father's apartment as of what her intrusion would do to the skein of their relationship. Sunlight flooded the living room, cruelly spotlighting the residue of the previous evening: a champagne bottle upended in a silver bucket of water, ashtrays full of half-smoked, lipstick-stained cigarettes. Augusta picked up a pair of silk panties from the sofa, wondering what she planned to do with them. From the corridor to her father's bedroom a disheveled woman in a frilly peignoir emerged, pushing a great shock of blond hair up over her forehead.

"I thought I heard something," she said in a baritone growl. "Who the hell are you?"

With the hair removed from the face, Augusta recognized with a stab Gwen MacNeil. Her own dislike of her friend's mother was irrelevant, Augusta knew, but her father despised her as well. And even more important, he hated everything Gwen represented—the avidly ambitious person devoid of breeding or any instinct for refinement, but who by sheer ego-hunger parlays looks into a rich marriage, then spends her way into some sort of attention. No wonder he had tried to keep his daughter from finding out.

"If you're here for the silverware, you're out of luck. I doubt there is any." She threw herself on the sofa. "Do me a favor, will you, sweetie? Lower that blind. That fucking sun is blinding me."

[265]

Augusta closed the blinds, then turned and confronted the older woman.

"Well, well," Gwen purred. "It's little Augusta. What about that? I thought you'd be out shooting tigers with some maharaja or other."

Augusta was silent.

"Surprised to see me here?"

The vulgar bitch seemed to expect an answer. What a boring irrelevancy she was! Augusta replied offhandly, "I've never understood some of my father's tastes."

"You fucking snob! I'm so sick of hard-luck cases like you Tollovers looking down your noses at me, I decided to prove what whores you all are by buying your famous father . . ."

"What do you mean?"

"How do you think he has his bills paid up for a change? His Wall Street smarts? What a laugh! Too bad he didn't take on this sort of work when he was worth having. He's still not too bad in the sack, but the real kick is that he thinks he's so far above me, and I have him jumping through hoops. You ought to come around some night and watch him kiss my foot."

Augusta turned to leave.

"Wait a minute. I haven't finished. You and I have a little business to settle. Oh, this is good, your coming in here like this. Steal the silverware. Ha! What about the twelve hundred dollars in clothes you swindled me out of? Sandra told me all about it. The sum is one thousand, two hundred and thirty-nine, to be precise. I'd appreciate a check from your moneybags stepfather. You can make up a story he'll swallow, but don't bother. I'll tell him the truth when I feel like it. God, how I hate you superior shits. Whores and crooks."

As Augusta started toward the vestibule, Gwen followed, ranting without interruption.

"You're the crook and he's the whore! You'll probably switch roles with time, if you haven't already. And I'm the one not good enough to give you gifts! Tell me how the world looks from up there. Let's hear a report from . . ."

As the door closed behind Augusta, she thought for a minute she might faint. She made it to the lobby still reeling from shame and outrage. The Tollover nemesis a coarse showgirl in a five-hundred-dollar peignoir! Coming through the door from the street was her father. She had no idea what he was doing home at this time of day and she didn't care. She wanted to walk past him but he blocked her way.

"I phoned B.K. She said you were on your way to return her keys. I knew you were up to something."

She stood and stared at him. It was as if she had never seen him before. All the many layers had been stripped away and there was nothing left but an enemy. "You've finally hit bottom," she said through clenched teeth. "And you've managed to pull me down with you. Next Mummie and Uncle Bryce. What do you have in mind for B.K., or did you send Guido to ruin her?"

"Augusta. You're upset. It's all been a shock . . ."

She wrenched her arm from his grasp. "You disgust me," she said through the tears that she had held in since leaving Gwen. "I don't want to see you again. You've killed it."

She pushed through the door into the bright midday sunlight.

That evening B.K. had planned a dinner for Augusta's last night before returning to college. Ken had come down from New Haven and Brandon made up the fourth. Guido would be out of the apartment; he was performing that evening. As B.K. cut strips of beef for the Stroganoff she planned Augusta told her about the charged clothes.

"God, it must have been ghastly for you," B.K. said. "But does it really matter about Daddy and her? We've never exactly been enthralled by any of his girl friends."

"Oh, B.K. That woman of all women! Daddy has many failings, but he always had certain standards about people. He can have nothing but contempt for her."

Augusta realized that B.K. might not remain her staunchest ally against socially unacceptable lovers. "Don't you see, B.K. She's not that good-looking anymore. He can have only one motive."

"Her money?"

"Of course. Oh, it's all so sickening."

B.K. concentrated on the onion she was chopping. "Mummie did it; why shouldn't he?"

Augusta was stunned by the range of her sister's cynicism. "It's hardly the same thing. For one thing, I'm sure Daddy has no intention of marrying Gwen MacNeil."

"The other way round, most likely," B.K. chuckled. "Too bad, since marriage seems to be able to sanitize the most sordid alliances."

"I'm staggered to think you'd connect this with Mummie. It's so unfair. She and Uncle Bryce adore each other."

"You know damn well she wasn't about to adore a poor man."

"I don't know anything of the kind. But why should she? To prove she has character? Why are we getting sidetracked on this? Our father is going mad—disgracing himself, trying to destroy Uncle Bryce. You see it as a reason to put Mummie on trial."

"I was only trying to soften your judgment on him. But you're right. He seems to have sunk pretty low."

When Ken and Brandon arrived, over drinks they discussed the press attacks on Ambassador Hartshorne.

"So the old boy is getting a few handfuls of mud," Brandon smirked. "About time. I'm glad they dragged me into it. Removes the suspicion that I planted them. Although I'm not sure I wouldn't rather enjoy that suspicion."

"I can't believe that," Augusta said. "You can't hate him that much."

"Oh, the hate's there, all right," Brandon said blithely. "But I find the tactics too underhanded."

"And you really think your father's behind it, Gus?" Ken asked. "That's pretty shitty."

Augusta tried to be conciliatory. "He's let his resentment get out of hand. We should do something."

"How can we?" B.K. said. "We can't prove it's him."

"Just ask the papers who told them these things," suggested Ken.

"They never tell their sources," Brandon said.

During dinner Brandon cheered them with stories of an Off-

Broadway play he was finally being given a chance to direct. "It would not be my first choice, but the playwright's a friend of mine and he is alarmingly talented. The play is bizarre. One character is nailed to the proscenium throughout the entire play and he never shuts up. At least his crucifixion reduces my blocking problems."

"What's blocking?" Ken said with no interest.

"How a director—me—moves the actors around the stage. You've got to come for the first night. It may be the only one."

Ken took them all to the Stork Club. As they made their way to the table, a number of people greeted Augusta and Ken. Acknowledging the whispers as he escorted B.K. through the tables, Brandon said, "I wonder if they think I'm the sexy Italian you're involved with. How wonderful. Maybe I should perform some indignity on you. Or at least scratch my ass."

B.K. giggled. After they had ordered drinks, Sherman Billingsley joined them for a few minutes. They weathered the lugubrious honor with polite replies to his questions about their parents. When B.K. and Brandon went off to dance, Ken asked Augusta if she were all right.

"You're being wonderful, Ken. You never miss a crisis."

"Strong right arm, that's me. Your life is getting so complicated these days—with your entire family going crazy—you need someone."

Despite the banter in his voice, she replied seriously. "B.K.'s problem didn't affect anyone but herself. We were just there to help her. My father is different. He's actually working to damage us. It's horrendous."

"I can understand about the newspaper business, but aren't you overreacting to Gwen MacNeil?"

She glowered, disliking him for the first time. "You wouldn't understand," she said coldly.

"I see." His face reddened.

"I'm sorry. I only meant that our history with her goes back so far."

They discussed plans for the first Yale football weekend and a house party they had been invited to in October. "Over the Christmas holidays," Ken said, trying to reweave their bond, "we can always visit Gran at Hobe Sound."

"That would be nice."

After B.K. and Brandon returned, their table was joined by Leonard Lyons, who had been doing his nightly table-hopping in search of items for his column.

He spoke directly to B.K. and Augusta, ignoring the two males. "Your father's been behaving so strangely, I feel I must speak out. He's been trying to plant items with me about your stepfather. He's been doing it all over. I chalked it up to poor-loser and ignored it. We get that kind of thing all the time. Some guys printed the stuff. That's their business. But now he's giving out something so big I can't brush it off."

Augusta felt her heart stop. "What is it?" she said quietly.

"He says," Lyons began matter-of-factly, "that it took years of Nuremberg trials and batteries of lawyers to put Krupp, the big munitions manufacturer, behind bars. Krupp was finally serving his sentence, but then what happened? Your stepfather is appointed to the German High Commission and Krupp is mysteriously released. That much we knew. But your father has pointed out a missing link. He says that Hartshorne's law firm did business with Krupp for many years . . ."

"But what of it?" Augusta said, with failing energy for this combat. "That doesn't prove anything improper was done."

"Perhaps not, but Krupp's release has never been explained. This connection is news. We've got to print it."

"If you're going to print it, why are you telling us?" Ken said arrogantly, his tribal defenses surging forward.

Lyons addressed his reply to Augusta. "I wanted to give your stepfather a chance to deny." He handed Augusta his card. "Hartshorne knows how late I'll be up." He rose and left without saying good night.

Augusta thanked fate for the padded phone booth. She reached her mother at Tidewater Farm. Kate sounded as though she had been crying. "It doesn't matter, dear," Kate said. "Drew Pearson already has the story in tomorrow morning's paper. There's not a word of truth in any of it, but it will take ages to sort out. I'm afraid chances for the Russian post are effectively destroyed."

"Mummie," Augusta said, feeling nine years old. "It *is* Daddy."

"I knew it from the start, darling. I suppose I'm paying for my sins against him."

Augusta felt a rare surge of sympathy for her mother. "Do you think he's gone crazy, Mummie?"

"I've known for some time something like this would happen. There's a lot I haven't told you."

"What? What?" Augusta fought back the hysteria.

"Phone calls at three A.M.—a string of profanity, then abrupt hang-ups. Anonymous letters about you and B.K. Of course we never believed a word of any of it."

A woman tapped on the glass of the phone booth. Augusta was relieved for diversion from her careening emotions.

"Mummie, I . . ."

"Don't let it upset you too much, Augusta. We're all really very lucky. This will pass. I just feel so horrible for Bryce."

The group of young people left the Stork Club. B.K. was meeting Guido after his performance, so Brandon took her downtown. Ken wanted to stay with Augusta but she persuaded him she was too confused and depressed to be with anyone. His cab dropped her off at B.K.'s place on East Sixty-fifth Street and he continued with it to his aunt's on East End Avenue.

When she saw the feet in the shadow of the doorway as she came up the steps from the street, she knew with a sickening wrench that it was not a rapist or a mugger. How preferable that sort of terror would be. For the first time in his life, he looked not just dissipated but disheveled, his hair hanging down on his forehead revealing patches of gray beneath. She had not realized before that he dyed his hair. Despite the driving rain, he had no coat, only his tweed jacket, which looked soaked through.

He was very drunk.

Augusta couldn't look at him. She lowered her head and said quietly, "Let me by."

"Augusta, sweetheart, I did it for you. I wanted you to see what sort of man he was. You were so impressed. You thought he was so wonderful."

"You're despicable."

"No, no. You don't understand. I'm going to forgive you for all the time you spent with him, all of his money that you spent. Now that all that's behind us, things will be as before. We'll be together . . ."

Tollover grabbed his daughter and, holding her in a tight embrace, buried his lips in the nape of her neck. For a moment Augusta was paralyzed, her skin turning to ice beneath the heat of his mouth. Then she pushed herself free and screamed, pouring out years of stifled reactions, festering wounds, diffuse pain. While his hand tried to cover her mouth, she gulped a breath and screamed again. Lights came on in the building, windows shot up, she could hear voices. She broke free and got inside the building, praying she would hear the door latch lock behind her. A click. He was on the outside. It was over. She could take no more. She would do whatever she had to do to see that there was no more.

As soon as the Hartshornes heard what had happened, they came to New York and took Augusta in with them at a suite at the Mayfair. Kate Hartshorne was wonderful to her daughter, saying almost nothing but treating her like an extremely delicate patient. Augusta felt closer to her mother than she ever had remembered feeling. They had both suffered at the hands of the same man.

Ambassador Hartshorne had been trying to reach Tollover all day and there was no answer at his apartment and his office had no idea where he was. In the afternoon, he engaged a private detective to locate him. B.K. joined them for a dinner served in their living room. It was a glum affair with sparse conversation. The next morning the word arrived. Tollover's body had been found in Central Park. The cause of death was said to be exposure.

Part Three

Absently driving his Jaguar through the monotonous streets of a new housing development, Brandon treated B.K. to a spirited description of the Hollywood caste system. "The thing that's so fascinating is not that it exists—God knows, you hear enough about it—but how quickly you get caught up in it. In any room full of guests, the power centers are those who are making it *now*. If you are talking to a great star of movies' Golden Age, someone you never thought you would actually meet, you find yourself looking over the legendary shoulder to spot *this* year's winners . . ."

Ordinarily, B.K. would have been eager for Brandon's comments on Hollywood. His inside vignettes of the film world were refreshing after her Sussex hibernation. Today, however, she was too enmeshed in her own life to give anyone else's much attention.

As Brandon's monologue progressed, B.K. glanced at the ranch houses they were passing. She noticed incongruous stone gate posts framing a side street that led off to more ranch houses. The masonry posts signaled the former location of one estate whose acreage now constituted an entire neighborhood. Maybe that was the way the world was going; thank God she and Augusta had moved in the opposite direction.

She glanced at the smug, flat houses, calculated their cost at a hefty $80,000 and smiled at the dream-come-true they represented to most of their owners—and what a comedown living in them would have been to the former masters of this estate.

She thought about the owners of these ranch houses, people who had no doubt fought their way into this victory ground. Were they the people who demanded from their newspapers regular news of the famous Tollover sisters? Having put all their effort into joining the solid middle class, did these people now feel they had missed something important? Did that explain their insatiable appetite for bulletins on Augusta's social life, B.K.'s home life?

Or had she and her sister been elected national representatives to the shindigs on Mt. Olympus, sent there by a public curious to know what went on, but not curious enough to try for it themselves? That was probably the answer. These suburbanites had opted for more solid values, the self-righteous squares, but satisfied their other yearnings by experiencing the Great World through their chosen representatives.

But damn it, thought B.K., I've pursued these other, finer values as much as they have. I've worked at making a good marriage, raising two children, being a good friend to those dear to me. What have they got going that should make me feel less worthy?

Then she thought ruefully how she had gone after those more solid goals only after she had had her fill of jet-set gadding about, only when, for the moment, there didn't seem to be anything else to do. Perhaps it was a hedge against her later years when respectability and money were a woman's only weapons. But why be so hard on herself? She understood her own motivations, even when they were tinged with corruption. Who knew why the women in those identical kitchens did what they did?

Hardly fair to have her actions and Augusta's judged, tut-tutted and deplored by people who, if put to any sort of test, would show less decency, less selflessness and less morality. There were many aspects of B.K.'s superstrata existence that bored her, but no aspect as much as the ongoing battle, rarely waged outside of her own head, with her fans. To hell with them.

One martini in the morning and two at lunch—she now felt drunk and a little mean, mean enough to wrench up the least savory aspects of her past. What did it matter? None of it could hurt her now. Was her protection the eight-foot wall in Sussex?

Was Augusta right about the route to self-protection? Or was it simply time, the same deliverance available to everyone?

40

Careful not to wake Guido, B.K. twisted her body across the bed and pressed her cheek against the windowpane. Straining to look straight up, she could see a sliver of sky at the top of the air shaft. Blue. A clear day, perhaps not as hot as yesterday. She propped herself up against the wall and fished for a cigarette from the pack on the floor beside her. No ashtray. Empty beer can.

She looked around her new bedroom. Not really a room, a wider space in the chain of varied spaces that was Guido's East Seventh Street apartment. "A no-room apartment" he called it, and he was right—a tunnel between two front windows that would look out on Seventh Street and two rear windows looking over a cement yard.

The bright yellow enameled floors were Guido's defiance against the gray-brown shabbiness of the Lower East Side, an area which had begun to attract Villagers in search of bargain rents. On the wall of this sleeping area was a large picture of Clark Gable and another of Rocky Graziano—both pictures extracted from billboards. A white Japanese lantern covered the two-bulb ceiling fixture.

Hanging on the permanently ajar closet door was a man's brocade dressing gown that looked like a costume for Count Vronsky. Guido loved the garment and would parade around the apartment with it flying open, wearing nothing else but a pair of jockey shorts.

She looked at the smooth musculature of his swarthy back. Would she ever stop wanting him? It was a need so fixed in her, so commanding, it obviated all other considerations. Decision-making was easy; whatever kept them together was the choice. If having Guido's baby would hold him, then have it. If it would drive him away, don't.

When Uncle Bryce and her mother, somehow learning they were living together, demanded she give up Guido or give up her apartment and allowance, the choice had been laughably easy. Out of courtesy and gratitude to them, she should have perhaps waited a day before letting them know, but why, when she had known instantly what she would choose? Even her art studies, her only other interest, would be abandoned the minute they conflicted with her relationship.

In honesty, B.K. had to admit, another thing that had made it easier for her to give up her allowance was knowing of the trust fund set up for her and Augusta—twenty thousand dollars apiece—by their great-aunt Mable. But she had been dashed to learn from the lawyers that the money was not available for education, as they had believed, and could not be touched until they were twenty-five. Tom Tollover had left only a few debts. Her announced intention of finding a job, once bravado, now proved necessity.

She rarely reflected on this all-consuming dedication. It did not respond well to analysis. She and Brandon would sometimes discuss it, but her stepbrother's usually bull's-eye insights seemed oddly off the mark.

"He's your antidote to twenty years' force-feeding of upper-class fluff—Greenvale, Walker's, the Chums, white gloves, the right fork, the right scarf, the right friend. Guido is your way of blowing a gigantic fart at all of that."

Yes, perhaps. The trouble with Brandon's explanation was its negativism—Guido as a denial of her upbringing, a reaction, a protest. Would that explain the way she ached for his body against her own? The way the sound of his key in the door could quicken her pulse? The way the sight of his face on a stage full of actors could fill her with a sense of happiness and well-being?

She knew she thrilled at his irreverence, his disdain for all the forms and protocols. It made him so much more of a person than the blindly following, eager-to-please sheep she and most of her friends had always been. This had been true in grade school even as they all approached adolescence. She had read and heard much about teenage rebellion. But where had it been? In the late forties it surely wasn't in Old Westbury, or at

Walker's or, least of all, at Wellesley where everyone vied with each other to be the best little kids in the world.

Maybe it had something to do with the war. Her age group was happy just to be able to get through undisrupted by draft calls, meatless Tuesdays, gas rationing and untimely deaths. Growing up with the war looming ahead of them, to have it end just as they were about to be swallowed by its grinders made them all too aware of their luck. Rebellion was the last thing on their minds. Conformity was the price of special privilege.

The snobbery of her earlier life, what did it add up to? The right to kick people, to suspend the rules, provided the person fouled was lower on the status scale. But even after she had become the ambassador's daughter, Paolo had still felt himself far above her, had still treated her like one of the staff. Augusta believed that money and status were protection against that sort of mistreatment. She would find out she was wrong.

B.K. did not delude herself that Guido would protect her. In fact, he'd been behaving like a shit lately. Under the best circumstances, he would fit into no one's definition of "nice," but that was Guido. No pretense, no hypocrisy, no surprises.

There was another side to him that Brandon knew nothing about. And if he did, B.K. could never make him realize the degree to which this facet triggered her outpouring of emotion toward him. It was the rare glimpses he would permit B.K. of vulnerability, self-doubt, uncertainty, acknowledged weakness that no one else was ever allowed to see.

B.K. quickly came to realize that the swaggerings that had first attracted her to him were not mere poses. They were, in the Brooklyn training ground of his youth, requisites of maleness. For him to lower his sexual guard with her, and no one else—to admit his fallibility by asking her questions on grammar, etiquette, world affairs—shook his invincible macho image. And this suspension of his pose had a curious erotic effect on her, unleashed all her physicality.

She could hear Brandon if she tried explaining this: "Well, of course, if bad grammar excites you, you could go on screwing like marmots into your eighties."

No, it had something to do with Guido's making B.K. a

collaborator in his performance as a swaggering male street hero that made her such an eager collaborator in his sexual performances.

The only time she had had second thoughts about him was during the grotesque dinner with her mother and Uncle Bryce. She knew the purpose of the dinner had been to decide if an effort should be made to break them up and she had been equally sure it would be a disaster. Her allowance would be cut off, and she was resigned to that; in a sense she welcomed it. She felt hypocritical having a lover who symbolized rebellion against her class while still being supported by that class. If you're going to do it, B.K. old girl, do it. She figured that if she moved into Guido's place and got a nighttime job, she could keep up her art classes.

So as a survival crisis, the dinner had been unclimactic. Of course Guido had made a bad impression, and of course neither her mother or stepfather could stand him. What bothered B.K. was the way Guido tried to curry favor. When they started cross-examining him, instead of telling them to go to hell—which had been B.K.'s fantasy ever since the dinner had been projected—Guido had groveled.

His summary sentence had disgusted her almost as much as it had her parents. All evening he had been asking Hartshorne to push his acting career with Frank Stanton of CBS and other show-business powers among Hartshorne's friends. The graceless campaign increasingly irritated the Hartshornes. Finally, when any pretense of amiability had left the table for good, Guido had leaned toward Hartshorne and said, "Look, you don't like me because I'm nobody. *Make* me somebody and we'll all be happy."

At a moment when B.K. was giving up their support in order to stay with Guido, he was using the occasion to try and win their support for himself. It was not the unscrupulousness that bothered her, it was his ineptitude. For that discriminating judgment, she thought wryly, Augusta would have applauded her.

Would Guido remain with her? At first she had worried a lot about that. He had been enjoying himself too thoroughly as a prime-stud welcome wagon to the swarms of liberated but untested virgins who came sweeping into New York each day. Fox in the chicken coop. But in an odd way, Guido proved as locked to B.K. as she was to him. He would get frantic if a late closing at the restaurant made her arrive home a half hour later than usual. At parties he left her with others to wander off, but he never wandered out of view.

As soon as she felt she had him completely, she let herself go and allowed herself to admit that she couldn't live without him. The minute he sensed his total victory, he of course changed. He was far less single-minded about her, would flirt openly with other women at parties and, on a few pain-wracked occasions, stayed out all night.

The ensuing battles produced some ground rules for their brave new agreement: no infidelities under B.K.'s nose and none with her friends. He had convinced her that a degree of freedom was essential to their longevity. B.K. had no desire to go off with anyone else and made no pretense that she did. This was probably dumb of her, but better than feigning interest in someone else, then having Guido learn it was a ploy. Honesty, straightforwardness and devotion were her pathetic weapons in the romantic lists.

Since the dinner with the Hartshornes, Guido's mood had been irritable—especially with B.K. That the debacle was on his mind, gripped him, was made obvious by his many references to Hartshorne's "pig-headed, boy-scout attitude." His anger would even drive him to blaming B.K. for the evening's failure, claiming that had she persuaded them in advance how important he was to her, they never would have refused to push his career. They certainly wouldn't have given him the cold shoulder.

Their lovemaking had slackened off and he carped at her about small things.

B.K. was sure this black mood would pass. It had to.

Guido opened his eyes and looked at her. "How long you been awake?" he said hoarsely.

"Not long. It's a clear day for a change."

He sat up against the wall and took her cigarette. When she saw he wasn't going to caress her, she pulled her shirt from the bottom of the bed and pulled it on, an instinct telling her to withdraw her heavy artillery in the face of disinterest.

"We could take a walk over by the Hudson, maybe sunbathe on one of the piers," she said brightly.

"No, I'm going to play handball with Charlie. I thought you were going to do laundry. I haven't had a clean pair of socks for a week."

"I was going to leave it at the laundromat."

"Terrific. And have our clothes ripped off. You debutantes are so trusting." He busied himself with a blackhead on his shoulder. "How did you do last night?"

"Wonderfully. Eighteen dollars in tips. Fat Al yelled more than usual. He's more obsessed with my social background than you are. He calls me 'Brenda Frazier.'"

"He's a jerk-off. But my pal Eddie treats you right, doesn't he?"

"Oh, sure, but he's too busy behind the bar to pay much attention to anything. We all are. From about nine o'clock on, we really have to move."

"Good for you. Is coffee going?" As B.K. left for the kitchen, he said, more to himself than to her, "Maybe I should go talk to a few people today. Things aren't moving fast enough. If I stay much longer down here in the Village, I'll become Off-Broadway's longest-running promising actor." Then louder to B.K. in the next room, "You'd think at least sweet baby brother Brandon would have given me a part in that circus he's staging. I'd look good nailed to a wall in a loincloth. All that way-out poetic garbage needs bare flesh to put it over with the clientele it draws."

"Brandon didn't have that much control," B.K. said, carrying in two steaming mugs of coffee. "The producer and playwright had it cast before he was brought in."

"You'd think at least one member of your family would stoop to do something for me. Fuck 'em. The new Inge play is auditioning next week. All I need is one break like that and your parents will be trying to throw dinner parties for me."

At the restaurant that evening, B.K. looked over the crowd as she waited at the pick-up window for an order. The usual—

mostly N.Y.U. students and their dates, all respectable middle-class kids hoping to pass as dissolute Villagers. No true Villager would pay Fat Al's price for a hamburger and a stein of beer. None of her and Guido's friends would be caught dead in the place, although she often spotted them passing on the sidewalk outside. Fat Al's was a different Village from the one she and Guido frequented.

Most customers were polite and no trouble. The worst thing she had to put up with was the show-off jokers who liked to banter with the waitress to show their girl friends how in command of the world they were. Fat Al was a pain, taking a sadistic pleasure in driving his waitresses, but the other girls told B.K. to ignore him, and she was learning.

Her two hamburger platters arrived—both with french fries. She handed one platter to the cook and asked him to remove the potatoes. They never listened to special requests.

From the back of the restaurant B.K. could see through to the brightly-lit street where a sleek Jaguar SKE, top down and gleaming, parked in the no-parking zone in front of the restaurant. A young couple got out. Such glimpses of the rich, well-heeled life she had abandoned rarely caused her a pang of regret.

Costly toys like Jaguars were fine; since being with Guido, however, she had come to associate a certain level of deprivation, even squalor, with sexual gratification. She saw the luxuries of her former life as pleasant irrelevancies. She didn't particularly miss the service—maids, cooks and laundresses. She almost preferred scrounging up meals for herself and Guido which they could eat in bed, naked as dolphins.

She didn't miss the material things either. She had enough clothes to last a decade. Most of them were rarely worn now—only when Augusta was in town. If there was one thing she missed about her pampered life as the ward of a very rich man, it was the flawless beauty of his every setting. The lawns of Tidewater Farm, policed of so much as one extraneous blade of grass, stretching to the blue Chesapeake; the handsome old Nantucket house, burnished with love and money, without an anachronistic detail to mar its period perfection. Even Walker's and Wellesley were set in lovely, unmarred countryside.

But somehow this night the sight of the two wealthy young people, blithely ignoring Manhattan's traffic laws or the jeopardy of leaving the top of the Jaguar down, gave B.K. a stab of homesickness and a feeling of being cut off. When Guido got over acting sullen she would no longer feel so insecure.

The couple entered the restaurant and sat in the window at one of B.K.'s tables. Was it set up? Yes. She delivered her hamburger platters, then got two glasses of water and menus and took them to the newcomers.

"Ah, that was quick!" said the young man, a bland-looking pudding in a navy-blue blazer and open white shirt.

"B.K. My God! What a surprise!"

B.K. looked at the girl who had just spoken. Gradually the features of Sandra MacNeil emerged from the stagey makeup and dramatic shank of dark hair that coiled down one side of her neck.

"Sandra!" B.K. exclaimed. She stooped and hugged her perfunctorily.

"How wonderful to see you, darling," Sandra effused. "I was going to call you. Are you still on East Sixty-fifth? I saw Augusta in Paris and she told me a *lot* about you. I know everything and I think it is terribly exciting." She introduced B.K. to her escort.

"It's all quite a change. And ever so broadening," B.K. said.

"I can imagine," Sandra purred. B.K. was stunned by how theatrical Sandra had become, so aggressively sophisticated. B.K. still saw the little girl in a grown-up mink coat that Augusta had described from their first year at Walker's. "Listen, we've got so much catching up to do. What time do you get off? Peter and I were going on an extended tour of the night spots. We could meet you any time you say."

"Well, I was going to meet my friend . . ."

"How wonderful! I'm dying to meet him. Naturally. Just tell us where and what time."

B.K. thought for a moment. "Do you know the White Horse on Hudson? We can meet there at one, maybe one-fifteen. I'm not sure Guido will come. He might be too tired after his performance."

"Insist, sweetie. I've simply got to see how jealous I have to be."

41

Dear B.K.,

Paris is more than I hoped! You know I don't often gush about anything, but let me gush a bit. First the specifics: the job with *Vogue* is a dream and I'll always be grateful to Uncle Bryce for setting it up. I have many duties: assist the photographers on picture sessions plus various editorial odd jobs; I am also responsible for interviewing the parade of celebrities passing through Paris, the ones my boss or I feel would interest *Vogue* readers. I've only been here two weeks and already I've talked with Noel Coward and Clare Boothe Luce. And they pay me for this! Not very much, but that plus my allowance is more than enough.

And the celebrities coming up are as enticing. Everyone you've ever heard of seems to be in Paris this summer, and a good many more you haven't. The city is packed with Americans. The prices are unbelievable! Dinner for two at Tour d'Argent can be as little as twenty dollars. So you see tables full of Ohioans gorging themselves on the pressed duck, people who have never set foot in Pavillon or Chambord—or the best restaurant in Cleveland, for that matter.

Paris is an American festival and the famous Americans are not to be left out. Any night at Deux-Magots or Champs Café you will see famous French faces—Sartre, Fernandel, Jacques Fath—but far more American ones. Last night at Deux-Magots, for example, we had Lena Horne, Tony Curtis and Tennessee Williams. Paris has to be the most exciting city in the world right now, and *Vogue* puts me right at the center of it.

Speaking of visiting celebrities, guess who I ran into in the Ritz bar a few weeks back? Sandra MacNeil. She'd been visiting her parents in Cap Ferrat and had a suite at the Ritz where she gave a cocktail party for all the stray comtes and marquises her mother had fed earlier in the summer. God, she's changed! You wouldn't believe what a grande dame she's become. The way she reeled off those titles in the Ethel Walker's French that I got her through! She looked terrifiç if a bit overdressed (both times I saw her) and she seems to have a bottomless allowance. I don't know if she learned about Daddy and her mother. I assure you, I didn't bring it up.

My job has another wonderful aspect: the woman I work for, Madge Reilly. She's been with Condé Nast for years and has published several books on her own. One was about Paris just before the Occupation, which won the National Book Award for nonfiction. She knows everyone, is super bright, but has none of the hardness of self-importance of most successful career women. She is marvelous looking considering she has to be fifty—trim and compact as a tennis champion although she detests any form of physical exertion. She was married once, briefly, but has had a string of lovers. She makes the non-glamorous part of this job a joy and I'm learning more from her than I can say.

If you can stand any more good luck from me, I've snared a fabulous apartment on the Île St. Louis. It belongs to a friend of Madge's who had gone back to the States for a while. It is a fourth-floor walk-up: small living room, a tiny bedroom, and a terrace right over the Seine just big enough for two chairs and a bottle of wine. By leaning out, you can see one tower of Notre Dame. The only thing about my apartment that is not right out of a Pascal film is the concierge. She does have the required cat, but she is not the formula grouch. In fact she's most friendly and helpful and says nothing if I have a gentleman friend up for a drink. Don't get any ideas, I am too busy drinking it all in to develop a love life.

Europe is so different when you have your own apartment with your own closet full of your own clothes, and a kitchen so that you can go for days without seeing a restaurant. A tour like ours summer before last is great fun, but too rich for a steady diet. Staying in luxurious hotels and visiting beautiful homes involves a certain amount of strain, a feeling of always being a foot or two off the ground. In this little flat, I can close the door, put on a Piaf record and vegetate for hours. The city is out there if I want it, but I have a snug and comfortable sanctuary. I can't imagine ever wanting to leave.

Even if things hadn't worked out as brilliantly as they have, coming to Paris was the best thing I've ever done. If I had to go to one more party at Cottage or Fence, or their Manhattan equivalents, I think I would have died and gone straight to Ivy League heaven (which both those clubs think they are).

More than anything else, Paris is free of reminders of Daddy. I know that neither of us will ever buy a dress without thinking of him, but so many aspects of his world—North Shore accents, polo matches, country clubs, the Stork, J. Press jackets—none of these things exist over here, and if they did they would be viewed as quaint tribal artifacts.

I remember him saying he didn't care all that much for Paris. He preferred London.

This city is such a universe unto itself, drunk with postwar euphoria and exploding with new experiences and sensations, it is just the right antidote to those grim last months of his life. And it is an excellent place for me to decide what I want. Everyone tells me I can do or become whatever I choose. How can I choose if I don't know what's available? (Or who?) Smith is no better than any other college in showing the range of possibilities—probably worse in its austere New England isolation. A perfect training ground for minor regional poetesses. As a showroom for life's possibilities, I can't imagine a better place than Paris in the 1950s.

One of my motives in ranting on about my good fortune is the hope of luring you over for a visit. I know I played all my sisterly-obligation cards when I got you to go on the tour, and I know three bulls and an elephant couldn't pull you away from Guido right now, but there is always the chance of two things happening: that you and Guido will be so permanently linked, you wouldn't mind a few weeks away from each other, or that your romance cools and you require a change of scene. You know I prefer the latter only because I feel you are missing so much (another motive for this spiel). But you know, dearest

B.K., that my preference above all other considerations is whatever eventuality makes you happiest whether it's Guido, Frank Sinatra or Jack the Ripper.

Much love,
Augusta

P.S. Mummie and Uncle Bryce are after me to visit them in Bonn. Can't they see that after Paris, that's like asking me to go for a weekend in Newark? I'm urging them to come for a visit here instead. I know they want to, but the implicit argument is "my city's better than your city."

42

When Sandra invited them to Old Westbury for the weekend, B.K. was delighted. Mr. and Mrs. MacNeil were still in Europe, so they would have the house to themselves. It was the first time B.K. had gotten away from the city all summer. More than that, the invitation represented a reprieve from East Village squalor, which had lost some of its initial romance and daring. She had assumed that the posh playgrounds of her pre-Guido life were off limits while she was with him. It was exhilarating to find she could take him into that world and have him not only accepted, but fussed over and flattered.

If Sandra's hospitality opened up possibilities for B.K., it seemed to have an even more inspiring effect on Guido himself. He knew what a hit he had made with Sandra that first evening at the White Horse. Now with two socialite conquests, Guido saw himself as the pet of the upper classes.

B.K. was amused and happy at the change; his mood was better than it had been in months. They even laughed together again and made energetic love at three A.M. the Sunday morning they arrived at Sandra's from the city. Guido had been released from his Sunday performances, which meant they could spend all day Sunday and Monday and a good part of Tuesday on the shores of Long Island Sound.

The MacNeil estate was a revelation for Guido. His initial effort to take the opulence in stride collapsed into a gee-whiz wonderment. Everything fascinated him—the intercom phone system, the buzzers to summon servants, the concealed wet bars off three of the downstairs rooms, the seven cars in the garage, the recessed spotlights on the most famous paintings (he stood snapping one of the spotlights on and off, studying the effects of the different lights on a white-and-gray Utrillo).

Sandra's friend for the weekend was, B.K. gathered, a former boy friend demoted to useful escort for Sandra's complex social life. She sat on several charity committees in Manhattan and attended endless parties in connection with these socially auspicious good works. Her own parties were attracting press attention, she bragged to B.K., mainly because of the celebrated theater people she lured. Now that she had found B.K. again, she and Guido had to attend some of them; it was sure to help his career.

The first day at the estate was ideal—sunny and not hot. B.K. and Guido played tennis, swam in the pool, ate delicious wine-washed meals and contemplated how nice things would be now that Sandra had swept into their lives. B.K. had assumed that, at some point during their visit, Sandra and she would slip off for a catch-up talk about more personal aspects of their lives than the chatter about Guido's roles, B.K.'s job, Augusta's Paris life and Sandra's social plans for the coming fall (a cast party for *New Faces of 1952*, a dinner for Patrice Munsel).

But the tête-à-tête did not occur; Sandra was always the attentive hostess, but never relaxed her stance of the gay, brittle gadabout. She professed to adore Guido, and this alone made B.K. limp with gratitude. She laughed at his every line, kidded him about his gaucheries and, never having seen him act, waxed ecstatic about his future on the stage and in films. ("We *must* get him into the Actors' Studio!")

After lunch on Monday, B.K. impulsively borrowed a car and drove over to Mapleton. Guido had declined accompanying her ("If it's not as grand as this place, forget it") and planned instead to lie in the sun. The Tollovers' old house was being lived in, so she contented herself with entering the driveway, pausing for a long stare, then driving out. The place looked eerily the same; the foliage was cut back, but the house and lawns were as she remembered them. She thought at any minute she would see Kate come out the front door, looking harried, calling to them to leave for school. Frustrated at not seeing more, B.K. thought of parking on the road and walking to the fountain, but decided her nostalgia did not justify trespassing.

She drove into the village and for old times' sake had a soda at the drugstore they had frequented as children. She thought of looking up one or two old friends, but decided that Mapleton and Sandra was enough history for one dose.

As she headed back to her present life—a moody Guido, sporadic sex and a steamy, demanding job—she felt a rare sensation of loss. Was it the happy aspects of childhood—there *were* some—that Mapleton conjured up? Or was it the glittering, comfortable life Augusta kept insisting B.K. *could* have, a life that seemed so obtainable by returning to settings of earlier times, times that predated various choices? B.K. comforted herself that the sight of Guido would cure her of such wistfulness.

She arrived back to a dead-quiet house. She wandered through the rooms and then to the pool and the tennis court. She could find no one. Finally she found Sandra's date reading in the sun room. "So you're back," he said, with a voice soaked in irony. "How were the scenes of childhood?" He said Sandra had gone sailing. He didn't know where Guido was.

B.K. went to their room. Guido was lying on the bed in his bathing suit, talking on the phone. When he hung up, he turned to B.K. jauntily. "That was a Marine buddy of mine in Chicago. I haven't seen him since we did boot camp together."

"You shouldn't make long-distance calls in someone else's house."

"Are you crazy? Do you think with what this place costs to operate, they're going to notice a two-dollar call?"

"I know a little about the rich. They hate it when you help yourself."

"I've learned a little about the rich myself this afternoon," he answered. The sly tone said a lot.

"What do you mean. What's happened?"

"Your friend Sandra's quite a woman, you know?"

"I knew something happened when I walked in the door. There was kind of a smell of treachery about the place. Tell me."

"I was sunning myself at the end of the dock. She comes by in her sailboat and says, 'Get in.' I did. Three times."

"You shit! How could you? A friend of mine!"

"She's no friend of yours. You said you hadn't seen her in years. What kind of friend is that?"

"But we're all staying together. If I can't trust you in situations like this, how can we ever do anything with other people? Go anywhere?"

"We'll just have to adopt a more open policy."

"God, I hate you at times! All the concessions must be on my side. Have you given up one thing for our relationship?"

"Yes. Fun." Guido's voice took on that edge that announced the end to his willingness to be upbraided. Then, sneeringly, "You always wanted me to make it with society, didn't you?"

B.K.'s head, a tangle of outrage, was unsorting itself. She knew what Guido was and what little expectations she had for decent behavior. Sandra's betrayal was starting to dominate in B.K.'s fury. She suddenly turned and set out to find her schoolmate.

B.K. doubted Sandra was still sailing, since the point of that outing had been accomplished. She went straight to Sandra's room where she found her seated at her dressing table in a red silk robe brushing her dark hair.

"If this is why you invited us, Sandra, why did you bring me into it? You could have just sent Guido a note to the theater."

"Oh, grow up, B.K. How can you have any feeling for a

cheap slob like him? I didn't think much about it, but I may have helped to open your eyes." She turned and looked coldly at B.K. "I could get him away from you in a second. Not because I'm sexier. I can *do* more for him. He suggested we should team up." She turned back to the mirror and resumed brushing. "Me with him? What a joke! He's good for one thing. And as far as I'm concerned—one time."

B.K. wanted to break a perfume bottle and disfigure Sandra with it. She had never hated anyone so much. "God. My father was right. You and your family are scum!"

Sandra looked up at B.K.'s reflection in the mirror and smiled. "Your father seemed to have gotten over that feeling—at least as far as my mother was concerned. The only difference between your father and Guido is a few tailored suits—which my mother or some other woman probably paid for."

B.K. grabbed Sandra's shoulders and spun her around, then slapped her face with all the force she could find. Sandra rubbed her cheek and, with an askew smile, said, "Which one did I insult?" Then she turned her back on B.K. "The chauffeur will take you and your prize Italian to the station."

43 Augusta looked around the marvelous living room and felt she had arrived at an important destination. The assignment was routine, less glamorous than many she had done for *Vogue* recently. Endicott de Tristan was an important composer, one of the most important in Europe, but writing serious music, he was not a celebrity of the magnitude that *Vogue* usually celebrated. The Stuttgart Orchestra would be performing his new clarinet concerto in Paris; *Vogue*, in its lip service to the finer things, wanted to make mention.

As proof of his marginal celebrity status, Augusta realized she had no idea what he looked like. Then she laughed at herself for her new snobbish criterion: instant recognizability. She had heard one of de Tristan's symphonies at a concert of the New

York Philharmonic a few years back, but recalled only that she found it less painful than most contemporary music.

But the room. It made her like him enormously. Even if he turned out to be a lopsided dwarf with bad teeth, she would admire any man who could create a setting like this. De Tristan's house was a converted mill about twenty-five miles southeast of Paris near the village of Rambouillet. It sat in a flower-filled clearing on several heavily wooded acres. A broad, flat lawn stretched from the house to a stream that appeared to have been diverted from its original course through the building that was now the house.

The room in which Augusta waited for de Tristan was a long, low-beamed space that composed one end of the house so that it had windows on two sides and doors to a terrace on the third. The furniture was comfortable, upholstered pieces trimly slip-covered in a subdued flowered print. The room also contained many other pieces—tables, occasional chairs, cupboards, that looked sixteenth century or earlier and all were of a dark, polished wood.

The paintings were twentieth century, but of a style that somehow harmonized with the antique furniture. There was a splashy Vlaminck over the fireplace, an exquisite Modigliani oil figure of a woman's head and a marvelous pastoral, near-cubist painting that Augusta did not recognize. Several tables contained sculptures—a Degas ballerina and a Brancusi. A bronze bas-relief propped up against the wall on one table looked like a Matisse. Large vases of fresh flowers—random, exuberant mixtures—echoed the flowers outside. A grand piano stood in a bay window at the room's far end; on top of it were silver-framed photographs inscribed by Charles de Gaulle, Igor Stravinsky and Gabriel Fauré.

"I keep them there to inspire my efforts," a voice behind her said in unaccented English. She turned to see de Tristan, who had entered from a garden door. His looks were precisely what the room demanded—a handsome man in his early sixties, with a full head of trim gray hair and the figure and movements of a much younger man. He was not tall, only an inch or two taller than Augusta, and his lean, aquiline face was dominated by a strong nose that didn't mar the easy good looks.

Augusta held out her hand, which he shook in a forthright, mercifully unsexy way. He spoke again, "I am happy to meet you, Miss Tollover, I've been looking forward to your visit. And just when you arrive, I am obliged to deal with a dispute between my gardener and my cook about the upkeep of the herb garden. I'm sorry to have kept you waiting."

"I've enjoyed examining this room—so many wonderful things."

"You are kind to say so. It happens to be my favorite room in all the world. It's taken me years to assemble this hodgepodge. Come, let's sit over here. Can I offer you something?"

Augusta declined. "You have no accent."

"My mother was American. I was brought up in France and Switzerland, but always with an English governess. And I went to Harvard."

Augusta remembered Madge's briefing: his grandmother was a pharmaceuticals heiress from Providence, Rhode Island, who had married Hervé de Tristan, a poet from a socially powerful Parisian family and an intimate friend of Marcel Proust.

Because of several investments his father had made, the fortune was seriously eroded, but de Tristan had inherited enough to live, not in grandeur, but in genteel comfort. His artistic renown bridged the chasm between his wealth and that of his friends, some of whom were among the wealthiest people in Europe. He had another whole circle of friends—France's artistic-intellectual establishment. Augusta, having grown increasingly aware of the meretriciousness of *Vogue*'s monthly celebrities, had a salutory sense of being with a man of real substance.

"I am delighted that *Vogue* takes an interest in my new work," de Tristan said as he settled into a high-backed armchair and crossed his legs. "I am very pleased with it. For me, this is a rare reaction indeed. Now what can I tell you?"

As Augusta began her interview, his responses were bright, succinct and invariably good-natured—even to the frou-frou questions (preferences in wine, decoration, dinner parties) that

Vogue requested. At one point he commented on this.

"I find it remarkable," he said with a chuckle, "that my having written a few pieces of music qualifies me, in the eyes of your editors, as an expert on cuisine or on French politics."

"But, Mr. de Tristan, you are widely known as one of Europe's most cultivated men. Your music is only part of our interest. And, too, I am not a writer *on* music, the magazine doesn't have one, in fact . . ."

"Quite right. I stand flattered into obedience. Please forgive my interruption."

When Augusta concluded her questions, de Tristan clapped his hands once and said, "Ah, good, we have business out of the way, now we must wax social, maybe become friends. What will you have as an aperitif? The cook has prepared a special lunch for us."

"That's very kind, but I really hadn't expected . . .

"I must insist. By the time you get back to Paris the maître d's will be glowering at anyone coming in for lunch. And besides, I deserve some sort of reward for my cheerful acquiescence to all of *Vogue*'s . . ."

"Silly questions? Thank you for not blaming me."

"I didn't know you five minutes when I was convinced you were following company policy and not your own instincts."

"*I* stand flattered into lunch. I'd like to have whatever you drink before lunch."

"I'm very partial to Punt é Mes. Do you know it? It's bitter."

Augusta watched de Tristan remove a square of embroidered beige linen from the top of a crystal ice bucket and, using tongs, drop cubes into cut-glass old-fashioned glasses. A twist of lemon in each glass, then he poured the dark-brown fluid over the ice. The silvery clinking, then the splash of vermouth had the same salubrious effect on the senses as the first swallow of a much-needed drink.

"I must admit to an ulterior motive in agreeing to this interview. I knew it would be you and I was curious to meet you."

"But how did you know who I was?"

"A great friend of mine, Sylvia Thornton, knows your

stepfather. She told me that you were an outstanding example of young American womanhood."

"I'm not sure I can do justice to my country. I don't recall Mrs. Thornton . . ."

"*Miss* Thornton. You've never met, but Sylvia visits the States often and keeps up. We're delighted you've come to live in Paris."

"How very nice, but there seems to be no shortage here of young Americans. It appears to be another Occupation."

De Tristan was eager to know everything about Augusta's Parisian existence—no aspect of her job, apartment, or social life was too detailed for him. He quizzed her relentlessly about what she had seen of France's artistic treasures and immediately began compiling lists of things she still had to see.

They went in to lunch in the dining room, another low-ceilinged room overlooking the garden. At each place was a small silver *pot-au-feu* cup tooled with an intricate design. As a maid poured a superb Montrachet, Augusta lifted the silver lid to find a small portion of fluffy scrambled eggs with a sizable quantity of truffle bits in the center. The aroma as she lifted the lid was ethereal, unlike anything she had experienced. The eggs were so delicate, the truffles predominated.

For some reason, she asked de Tristan if he had known her father.

"Ambassador Hartshorne?"

"No, my real father, Tom Tollover."

"No, I don't believe I do. I think Sylvia knows him, but Sylvia knows everyone."

Always before when Augusta learned that a recent encounter knew her father, or knew of him, she had relaxed in the knowledge that the person then knew who *she* was. It made her feel at home, no longer at sea. Now for the first time she was relieved that her new friend knew nothing of the glamorous Tom Tollover.

But why think of her father?

De Tristan's age would naturally remind her of him—also his meticulousness about his appearance. How rare good looks become with advancing age. Few men maintained them after fifty, some lost them at thirty, yet at sixty-three de Tristan had remained a handsome man. Augusta had no idea of how he had looked when he was young, but his looks would make heads turn for another ten years.

As lunch progressed and conversation branched out, another important difference between this man and her father emerged. Augusta had always admired her father's sure knowledge of so many things of the world: the right time to visit Aiken, the correct dress for tennis matches, the proper jewelry for the theater, the precise amount of vermouth that belonged in a martini. Part of the fun and comfort of being his daughter was the cheerful certainty with which he issued his edicts. In the face of this European's vast erudition, however, Tollover's knowledge seemed frivolous and parochial. Yes, de Tristan would probably know which tie to wear to Longchamps, maybe feel strongly about it. But he also knew which Picassos changed the course of art, or could point to the spot in the Spanish Steps where the Roman builders abandoned impromptu building and continued with the world's first architectural drawings. Such were the topics that occurred and on which he sparkled so effortlessly.

He also had more grace than any man Augusta had met. He sensed precisely when her awe was running dangerously high, then would deftly undercut his impressiveness with self-deprecation—his incomprehension of most abstract art, or his failure with American idioms.

The main course arrived: a grilled turbot with a sorrel sauce, creamy and delicate. It was served with tiny carrots cooked in butter and fresh thyme. Dessert was a tart: raspberries, fuzzy and unmolested, on a bed of custard over a butter crust.

After lunch, de Tristan said he had errands to run in Paris; he would drive Augusta back. Conversation never flagged for the forty-five-minute drive. When he dropped her at the Faubourg St. Honoré Augusta had decided the day was all a day could be, de Tristan everything a man should be.

Seated behind her cluttered desk, Madge brought Augusta closer to earth. "Oh, you have to watch that guy. He gobbles up

American debutantes for breakfast. He's a notorious womanizer. I'm surprised you were so taken in, Augusta. I thought you had better reflexes of mistrust."

"Are you saying he's a scoundrel?"

"I'm saying he's a man—and a very intelligent, cunning one."

"You can't hang him for being charming," Augusta said. "I found him quite genuine. He is curious about everything. I represented something he knows little about, but which fascinated him."

"What? An attractive young woman he hasn't had?"

"A well brought up American. He says that, like all Europeans, he is intrigued by our country, but that he suspects only the most vulgar side is visible."

"That is reasonably perceptive, but just beware. Behind every intellectual enthusiasm, there is usually an unintellectual lust."

A few weeks later, Augusta was surprised to receive an invitation to dinner at Baron and Baronne Cabrol's. They were a very socially prominent Parisian couple who entertained frequently in their apartment on the Avenue Wagram. Augusta had met the baronne only once while covering an opening at Balmain; she was flattered and intrigued by the invitation.

When she arrived at the party, Augusta did not see a face she recognized among the twenty-odd formally dressed French men and women sipping cocktails in the Cabrols' large drawing room, which was dominated by a huge tapestry dramatically lit from below.

As Augusta was led around the room to meet the others, she felt a growing bleakness as she encountered one person after another who scrutinized her as though she were a Tanganyikan native supplied by the host for exotic color. Suddenly, to her delight, she found herself facing de Tristan. B.K. was the only person she would have been happier to see.

"Ah, Miss Tollover," he beamed, shaking her hand. "I'm glad to see you are meeting some of the nicer people in Paris."

She was escorted by the baronne on to the next group and was disappointed when de Tristan made no attempt to join her during cocktails. When he was seated next to her at dinner she began to smell a French rat, but found the smell exhilarating.

His conversation during dinner aimed to amuse and it succeeded. He offered a catalogue of French facial expressions for different reactions—disbelief, disgust, shock, admiration, cynical knowing; each was perfect and terribly funny. They talked about the horrors of attending parties when you knew no one. Everything they spoke about was, to Augusta, deliciously pretense-shattering. She knew she hadn't laughed as unrestrainedly since her father's death.

De Tristan asked if he might see her home. As they glided down the Champs Elysées in his large Citröen, Paris seemed a place where unhappiness could not exist. In the euphoria inspired by the wine and the evening, she voiced this observation to de Tristan.

"It is true," he said solemnly. "When Parisians get into a bad mood, the government sends them to Marseilles until they get over it."

Augusta laughed. "Why Marseilles?"

"It needs the hotel business. Also the Mediterranean and the *soupe de poisson* is famous for cheering people."

The government should send depressed French people to dine with de Tristan, Augusta thought. She had never met a man who could so quickly put others at their ease. She felt a wonderful combination of total relaxation, an absence of the least worry—and at the same time a feeling of stimulation. She never quite knew in which direction his mind would leap or if she could follow.

"Surely you will allow me to offer you a nightcap at some café."

"I love the Deux-Magots," she said.

"Any other place, I beg you. I know too many people there and I want to spend the time talking with you, not greeting friends. Let me take you to a favorite café of mine in Montparnasse. I can sit there for hours and never see a soul I know."

When they finally arrived back at Augusta's address on the Île St. Louis, de Tristan made no move to get out of the car. He turned to her somberly.

[297]

"I can't tell what a pleasure it is getting to know you, Augusta. You are a most remarkable young woman. But, intelligent as you are, I doubt you have any idea what makes you so much more interesting than European women to a bored, jaded bachelor like myself."

"You're right. I think I would like you to tell me."

He patted her hand. "With pleasure, but it will take some time and considerably more observation. I think our becoming good friends would be a fine thing. There is an outdoor chamber concert at Versailles next Friday night. Will you let me take you?"

"That would be lovely. But you must forgive me if I stay on my guard."

"Your guard?"

"You have a Don Juan reputation. I am a naive, trusting American. No match at all."

He laughed softly. "You offend me to imply that I would make advances to you. And you offend me to imply that I shouldn't. Do not think about it. I have many faults, but child molestation is not one of them."

God, thought Augusta, how difficult it is to issue the appropriate sexual signals. Everything ,is supposed to sail smoothly along exactly as both people want until, after considerable time and emotional effort, it is discovered that both people want very different things.

She loved the idea of spending time with him, but a large part of his attraction was that he held out the prospect of "the finer things" and by that she knew she meant "finer than sex." He was a delightful haven of wit, intelligence, cultivation, superb living. If there were the slightest possibility of his turning out to be a person of all-consuming sexual or emotional needs, their friendship would be a serious error. She had felt compelled to send up one chastity rocket, despite the rude noise it sent out over their evening's end.

"Would you call me at *Vogue?* I don't remember my number here." She kissed him lightly on the cheek and hopped out of the car.

[298]

44 Augusta started seeing de Tristan regularly. Soon she rarely went out with anyone else. When she had insisted to Madge that the friendship was platonic, Madge had been understanding. "We all go through periods when we only want companionship, good friendship, mental stimulation—not sex, passion and all that. Or at least I've heard we do."

De Tristan took her to the opera, museums, horse races; as they became known as a couple, they were invited to parties and weekends together. De Tristan introduced her into two Parises, both impregnable to most Americans: the old-line society and the cultural elite. She might find herself seated at dinner next to the young and handsome Duc d'Orleans, whose father, le Comte de Paris, was Pretender to the French throne. Or at an informal dinner with de Tristan's artistic friends find herself next to Max Ernst. Her French was now equal to such challenges, allowing that these intellectuals did not look to the pretty American for philosophical breakthroughs or deft ripostes. They were occasionally surprised.

Much as Augusta loved the excursions into privileged precincts, she preferred the evenings alone with de Tristan. Sometimes she would cook supper for them at her apartment, after which they would take long walks along the Seine, both of them safely immune from the romantic contagion.

They seemed to relish their friendship as it was; neither pushed for more. If Augusta had been asked why the friendship appealed to her, she would have replied that she was happier then with de Tristan than she could ever remember being. She hoped his answer would be something similar but, having such a fuzzy insight into her own motivations, she could not pretend to understand his. Whenever they parted, the kiss she gave his cheek contented him.

Occasionally they would have dinner with his old friend Sylvia Thornton. From the first meeting Augusta liked the stunning middle-aged British woman, whose spectacularly tasteful wardrobe and grooming outshone even the French women. The more she learned of Sylvia's remarkable history, the more dazzled she became by her. Sylvia had been born to a poor but genteel Midlands family during the twenties. Somehow they had found the money to send her to school in Paris. Almost from her arrival Sylvia had fallen in with a very posh crowd; at the age of eighteen, she found herself the mistress of one of France's wealthiest bankers.

Having discovered at a young age her passion for money in vast amounts, she parlayed her looks, refinement and effortless femininity into a series of affairs with enormously rich men. In the process she had amassed a sizable fortune. Although many of her lovers had wanted to marry her she preferred remaining single—perhaps because she had learned the knack of extracting princely compensations without the legal snarls of marriage and divorce. "When you emerge from a relationship with a Rothschild no richer than you went in," Sylvia said over dinner one night, "it means you never once batted your eyes and asked investment advice."

"You see, Augusta," de Tristan said, "Sylvia elicits his advice, then the cash to try it out."

Sylvia threw a piece of bread at him. "Just for that, I will let you pay for dinner, Endicott."

"If you didn't, I'd think you were truly angry with me. But please, Sylvia, all this mercenary talk in front of Augusta; she will think we Europeans have not improved since Henry James spotted our money lust."

"I'm fascinated," Augusta said.

"If you were *truly* fascinated," Sylvia jumped on her, "you could do better than I did. Your looks and carriage are tops; you are better educated than I was, and you've been around a lot more than I'd been when I started. You could have anyone you wanted, on any terms you wanted."

"Come now, Sylvia," admonished de Tristan, "you mustn't actively corrupt Augusta. Why shouldn't she just marry a charming young French or American millionaire and settle down to respectable luxury?"

"Corrupt? Respectable?" Sylvia sounded aghast. "You'll hurt my feelings. Has my life been so sordid? Whom have I hurt? I've given a lot more pleasure and caused less pain than most respectable marrieds I know. My secret is simple: stay with it just as long as both parties are happy with the arrangement, not one minute longer. The only problem with this theory is that high mobility is expensive; that's one reason I deal only with the rich."

Augusta laughed, "You are both straight out of Colette. Are you going to instruct me on snaring a Bourbon princeling? How to snip his cigar? De-bubble his champagne? They didn't have a courtesan's course at Smith . . ."

"Could *I* set up a school?" Sylvia boasted.

"Straight tuition or percent of the profits?" asked de Tristan.

Sylvia had a ravishing house on the Île St. Louis a short distance from Augusta's apartment. Although the older woman had a complicated and highly programed social life, she would occasionally phone Augusta and ask her to supper *à deux* in her splendid dining room with illuminated *vitrines* of Sèvres, gleaming parquet floors and windows open over the river.

She would always make Augusta laugh with stories about her various protectors, but she lacked the what-have-I-to-lose honesty of Madge. Sylvia's excellent mind, for years honed to think of two things at once, had lost its spontaneity. Her sly veil of deception had worn thin with time and the mechanics of her calculations were visible.

Still, she was kind to Augusta, excellent company and an encyclopedia of information on form, dress, society and everything a woman-about-Paris should know. Augusta, of course, had de Tristan for such counsel, but it was wonderful having another woman for advice. Often when the dilemma concerned de Tristan—a birthday gift, surprise dinner dishes—Sylvia was a most useful third party.

One day toward the end of Augusta's first year in Paris, she received a breathless letter from Brandon, who had been hired on as an assistant director to an American film that would have a week of shooting in Stockholm, two days of meetings with the film-lab people in London, then immediately back to New York for more work. It would be impossible for him to break away to Paris. Could she get herself to London?

Madge engineered an errand to justify Augusta's absence from the office, and gave her transportation expenses and two nights at Brown's Hotel. Suddenly she was seated across from Brandon at The Casserole, one of the many new, homosexual-inspired restaurants that had sprung up in Chelsea to cater to the British postwar fascination with seasoned food.

"I don't want you to think that I have altogether forsaken the straight world," Brandon said, "but everyone tells me that in England, the straight restaurants are still boiling meat and potatoes." They both ordered gimlets and a casserole of lamb, curry and stewed plums. "You look wonderful, Augusta, as though you've come into your own, whatever that means. Are you having a thrilling affair?"

She laughed and said she wasn't. She told him about de Tristan; Brandon could not hide his distaste for the man's age. "It's clearly withdrawal on your part, a respite while you get your thoughts sorted out before making some important amatory move."

She asked him to bring her up to date on his career. "How did the movie thing come about?"

"Two ways. First the legitimate one. That weird play I directed got wonderful reviews from most of the critics. I found their analyses instructive—it seems I had wrung from the work all sorts of jarring meanings. I was enthralled. But more important, the notice made my agent's phone ring. A lot of inquiries, but no bites." He downed his gimlet and ordered another.

"Now fade to the bedroom of Sean and Brandon," he continued. "We had fallen ill with the malady that afflicts homosexuals more than straights: lust for everyone but each other. All very amicable. About this time I met Harold Wineburg, who had directed several *succès d'estime* films that I liked a lot. I also liked Harold, he liked me, and *voilà*, I am an assistant director!" He leaned forward and looked serious. "But I insist, it would not have been possible if I hadn't had the Off-Broadway success. A lot of people would be shocked to learn the role the bed plays in even the most brilliant careers, and the ones who think they are hip to all that—the worldly-wise cynics—they'd be just as shocked to learn that it is never the whole story. The evidence I offer in my defense is the hundreds of film hopefuls who have been balled by Harold and every other power in the business and have never made it past the after-sex shower."

"You're learning a lot about filmmaking from him? And working in films is all you hoped?"

"I'm learning an enormous amount. He makes the most inspired creativity seem nothing but the commonest good sense. As for films, it can be boring as shit; at times you think it is never going to move ahead one inch. At other times it is the most exciting, exhilarating profession in the world. And I firmly believe it is attracting the most exciting talent. All through the thirties and forties, films hired the greatest actors and writers, but they went West begrudgingly, slumming for the dough. Now the talent flocks to film as its first and only choice. Many great films were made when the medium was an overdressed stepchild of the arts. Now that films are taken seriously by artists, there is no limit to what can happen."

Augusta was excited by Brandon's optimism. His looks had altered; for someone in his twenties, he was showing traces of wear. She said he looked as though he was working too hard.

"You mean I've lost my southern-poet languor? I hope so. You wouldn't believe the effect on your metabolism of being thrown at a young age into the work you most dreamed of doing—and to be having some success at it." Their main course arrived. "But enough about me, tell me more about Paris."

"I will, but first, what about B.K.? Have you seen her?"

"Yes." His manner became grave. "I had hoped to put that off till later. It will depress you, and I thought you'd had enough lately with your father's death. But B.K.'s situation is dreadful. Quite simply, Guido is treating her rottenly. He sees other women. He abuses her in front of their friends. Each time I've been with them, I've seen only two attitudes toward her from Guido: boredom and sadism."

Augusta had suspected some sort of alarm when Brandon insisted she come to London to meet him, but this was worse than she'd feared. "But what holds him to her?" she asked.

"God knows. It would be the best thing for everyone if he would just pack up and leave—although at this point I'm not sure what that might do to B.K. You see, she insists, on the few times she's let me talk about it, that this is just a phase they're going through. She's not a masochist. I know she suffers and she hates the way he's behaving. But she looks upon this as a bad patch. Each day she can endure is an investment, she feels, in their longevity.

"My own theory about why he sticks with her," Brandon continued, "is that her money from the restaurant job is what they live on. I hate to offer such a banal rationale—even for Guido—but I'm afraid that's it. Also, something in his swinish ego is gratified by having a society girl to kick. Fighting his own little class war."

"What can we do?" Augusta said forlornly.

"I don't know if we can do anything. What would you think of writing her, raving about Paris, and urging her to come for a visit?"

"I've tried that. It's hopeless."

"You know what might be the solution?" Brandon said brightly. "If Guido becomes a star. I think with the first glimmer of success, he'll drop B.K. He has a chance, you know. He's been noticed."

Brandon could see that he had depressed Augusta. She sat brooding, and had abandoned her dinner.

"I have some hot gossip," he said, "that should divert you. Guess who I ran into in an Amsterdam homosexual bar? B.K.'s Paolo."

After Brandon had given all the particulars, Augusta said, "Isn't it incredible how relatively small things, if they must be kept secret, can do the most appalling damage?"

After dinner they walked down King's Road window-shopping and people-staring. Before saying good night, Brandon summed up the B.K. drama. "Given your sister's stubborn, obsessive nature, our only hope is his dropping her. When he does, you'd better be ready to come catch her."

Augusta thought of little else but her sister in the next few days. On her first meeting with de Tristan after her return, a dinner alone at his house, she told him the whole story, with appropriate background. De Tristan was sympathetic but gently hinted that perhaps Augusta's younger sister thrived on painful situations.

"I don't believe that. B.K. is easily bullied, but she loves being treated kindly. I know." Augusta laughed sadly. "I've been manipulating her since we were in the cradle, and I've always found her easier to manage if I was kind to her."

De Tristan smiled at her. "You are just another Guido—only with a different technique. Don't worry, even if it takes an earthquake, it will resolve itself. And B.K. will recover."

Augusta contemplated him for a moment. They were sitting on adjoining chaises on the terrace after a typically wonderful meal, each with a glass of crème de menthe. How lucky she was to have such a friend. She got up and went to sit on the edge of his chair. She leaned forward and kissed him gently on the lips. For the first time since she had known him he looked startled, off guard.

"Do you want me?" she asked, her voice quiet and even.

"You are leading the witness," he said, struggling for his usual command.

She just looked at him.

Not faltering under her gaze, he said, "Of course I do, Augusta, but it would be a mistake."

"To argue about it would be the mistake. We've been close friends for six months, I've loved it just the way it was, but I am greedy, I need more from you . . ."

"You need? I can't . . ."

She kissed him again with more warmth. This time he responded. The lights from the living room illuminated his eyes. She gazed into them, stroking the wavy hair on one side of his head. Augusta was almost as surprised at her behavior as he was, but she was acting, not on a plan, but on the sudden conviction that this had to happen between them and that it couldn't have happened a moment sooner, nor could it occur if they delayed another day. She didn't know why, but she was sure of this.

She was also sure that this was the one man she wanted. Upstairs, in his bedroom, their lovemaking was restrained at first, but quickly another notch clicked on the lift she had set into motion and everything unfolded with a sublime inevitability. She had never imagined that sex between a man and woman could be so tender, so mutually giving, so free of the slightest awkwardness. She felt a major problem in her life had been beautifully, miraculously solved.

45

March 12, 1954

Dear Gus,

Your letter was wonderful and gave me a lift I haven't felt for some time. It's nice to know places like the Île St. Louis, Fauchon's and the Café Flore go right on whether or not I am there to bring them to life. I was thrilled by your news. He sounds a dream, but doesn't his age make it all rather impractical? I know I am voicing the dreary obvious, but it isn't often I get a chance to be the cool, practical sister.

What is wrong with us? Why don't we fall in love with the people we're supposed to? When I think of the nifty young eligibles that have cocked an eyebrow at us both these past few years—looks, money, intelligence, humor, manners . . . Oh, God! Here I am washing socks for an egomaniacal street bum and you are bedding down with a man old enough to be your father, if not grandfather. I'm sorry. It's just that I know my life is somewhat less than ideal and I'd looked to you to bring an idealized prince charming into the family.

Of course I am delighted for you. You are only twenty-four

and if he's sixty-three, well, you can still have the .more customary marriage and kids if you want to later.

That was pretty tactless, wasn't it? You write me about your divine new love affair and I start calculating how many good years he has left. If living in the Village has changed me, it is that kind of frank talk. No one stands on any ceremony here. If your hair needs a shampoo, someone will let you know before you've had time to tie it in a scarf. Or if your lover's off with another woman, the news flies over the back fence with a speed that should impress Western Union.

Do I sound bitter? It hasn't been that great lately. That's why I was slow answering you. I had nothing upbeat to balance all your cheer. Guido and I have been fighting a good bit. He seems very much on edge and I'm not sure why. Rotten as he's being, I never for a minute doubt our belonging with each other. If I could only make you see, Augusta, how final this is for me—or maybe you do see, now that you feel strongly about someone too. You at least can appreciate that it has nothing to do with choice, or judgment, or wisdom, or sanity. What has to be, is. And while mine isn't very good right now, I am sure that's temporary. Oh, Gus—who are these women who say "Let me see, will it be Paul or Dick or perhaps Larry?" Are they human? Are they involved in the same thing we are?

There I go, trying to drag you into my situation. You give no indication you're in as deep as I am. But at least your new romance gives us one more thing in common: we are both in love with men who will not pass muster with Ambassador and Mrs. Hartshorne. I don't mean to make them out especially difficult to please. Our romances would not be approved of by many people, but do we care? No, we do not.

A minor interlude of these days has helped darken my mood. Sandra MacNeil breezed into the restaurant exuding Arpège and old friendship. She invited me and Guido for a weekend at Roslyn. How wonderful, I thought; she doesn't mind if I wait tables or cohabit with Italians. Childhood bonds mean more than such superficial realities.

Silly me. All she wanted was a crack at Guido, which she got.

When am I going to get over being so ingenuous and trusting? I thought Paolo had cured me of that.

Please overlook all the negative stuff earlier about you and de Tristan. You sound very happy and that's the cheeriest news to come my way lately. Enjoy yourself, but keep a few of the younger millionaires on the string. (Which reminds me, Ken came in one night and took me out for a drink after work. He tried to play Dutch Uncle, but trying to make him understand why I stick with Guido would be like explaining aerodynamics to a groundhog. He meant well, I know. He is still carrying a torch, in case you didn't know.) Enjoy yourself and look forward to a longer letter when I have something more jolly to report.

Love,
B.K.

46

Augusta had thought her affair with de Tristan would close doors to her, make her too eccentric even for Paris's self-proclaimed broadmindedness. The contrary proved true. The oddity of her loving a much older man was the imperfection she needed to remove the too-good-to-be-true image.

The French, she discovered, are among the most conservative people on earth. They love audacity, but only if it is exercised within certain rigid bounds. Because of de Tristan's prominence, his mistress, had she been a forty year old, would have been an appendage to him. Being so young, Augusta became a person in her own right.

Although this was an unexpected byproduct of her liaison, Augusta found she liked it. Her ambition had lain dormant during the confused months after graduation and her father's death. Now that a vicarious success was thrust on her, she remembered how she loved such attention. As a child she had loved entering a room or appearing before the public in a competition and seeing people whisper that she was Tom Tollover's daughter. That had been suburban Long Island—this was Paris. She was becoming as known here as she had been, as a star debutante, in East Coast social circles. She began to revel in the rewards of celebrity: the encounters with the famous people of her day, the interest they showed in her, quickly finding welcoming faces at any important gathering. But more than this, she was able to hold up her lover's social and artistic preeminence as further protection against a tricky world.

Kate Hartshorne learned of the affair; perhaps feeling a break with one daughter over her lover was enough, she chose to ignore it. Or possibly, Augusta surmised, de Tristan's wealth and position made it all right.

In June, de Tristan rented a small villa perched in the cliffs above Positano. It had a grand piano, and excellent cook and casks of the good local red wine. They would hide up there for days without descending into the tourist-infested alleys of Positano.

Other times of the year they would be doggedly social, dining frequently with his colleagues from the musical world or making three- and four-day visits to the palatial retreats of his wealthy friends. In July, de Tristan announced he couldn't bear the Paris heat another day; he had phoned his friend Henry McIlhenny and asked if he and Augusta might come spend a few days at his castle in northern Ireland. It was unlike de Tristan to behave so impetuously; Augusta did not feel the heat to be so unbearable, but off they went.

The castle was in Donegal, a four-hour drive from the airport. When they arrived at the entrance gates early on a rainy Friday afternoon, they covered the five miles of driveway without seeing a soul, only a few deer. The castle looked deserted too, but they were admitted by the butler, who told them that Mr. McIlhenny was resting and that cocktails would be in the library at eight.

After the heat of Paris it was jarring to see a fire going in their rooms and large comforters at the foot of their beds. What a desolate place to have such a grand house, Augusta thought, as she joined de Tristan to find the library. When they entered, they found their host, a middle-aged, leprechaunish man, surrounded by a dozen guests in dinner clothes.

"My dears! How wonderful you could get here!" McIlhenny exclaimed.

As Augusta glanced around the room, she saw by the fire, chatting with a distinguished man with white hair, a face so familiar its incongruity in this setting was shocking. As Augusta approached, Sylvia smiled up at her. "Surprise? I know I'm supposed to be in New York, but it got so hot, I had to get away. I told Endicott not to tell you."

Augusta felt a shudder of claustrophobia. She did not like being plotted against—even for pleasant surprises.

"But this isn't my summer for weather," Sylvia went on cheerfully. "It's rained the two days I've been here—no stalking, no tennis, no boating. Poor darling Henry . . ." she said to her approaching host, "has been at his wits' end to keep us amused."

"It's been too dreadful really," said their host in a voice of hushed conspiracy, "but I rather like the rain. I take long walks. And I have forty pairs of boots in all sizes for anyone who wants to come with me. But no one ever does. Now Sylvia has cooked up the most entertaining plan for dinner. It's had the ladies busy as hornets all afternoon . . ."

"We had to do something," Sylvia purred modestly, "to keep from going mad—as hornets. I've run out of Iris Murdochs . . ."

"Sylvia!" de Tristan said, stooping to kiss her. "Isn't this great, Augusta darling? We've ambushed you." Turning to Sylvia, he said, "I've just heard your brilliant scheme for dinner . . ."

"What is this scheme?" Augusta asked.

"It's just silliness. I got all the women to pool their jewels to create a centerpiece for the table."

Excitement mounted as dinner was announced. The party entered the long dining room, circling the table to inspect the creation. Two-foot-high silver stags had been placed on a silver tray and banked with greens and white camelias from McIlhenny's greenhouses. Glistening and sparkling among the leaves were large diamond pins, emerald rings, sapphire clasps—even the most hidden jewelry reflecting back the flickering light from two large candelabra at each end.

Across the back of each stag was a broad diamond bracelet. In the horns of one animal was a panoply of jeweled rings, all flashing their gems in the soft light. The other's antlers had one necklace of pea-sized rubies woven back and forth, creating the effect of a dazzling ceremonial headress.

"It's too thrilling!" McIlhenny gasped. "I can't bear it. Lloyd's would have a fit!"

All through the delicious, merry meal Augusta kept watching Sylvia, laughing gaily across the table, her lovely, ageless face framed by the two bejeweled animals.

Later that night, after making love to Augusta, de Tristan got out of bed and stood at the window. "Come look, my dear, the moon is coming through the clouds. It might be a good day tomorrow."

She came to his side and slipped under his arm. "How lovely the lake is in this light," she said. Then after a silence: "Tell me, Endicott, why didn't you mention that Sylvia was going to be here?"

"Weren't you pleased?"

"Of course. It just seemed odd for you."

"I mustn't get too predictable. You'll tire of me ahead of schedule."

"Have you worked out a schedule?"

"No," he said. "Nature has. I'm fighting it."

Augusta did not want to banter about this. "You don't understand how I feel about you, do you?"

De Tristan was silent. Once, when he kidded her about her puppy love, she hadn't spoken to him for a week. "Unfortunately, my dear, the future does not depend on you and me, on whether or not we are wise or of good character or capable of the deepest feelings. The more intelligent we are, the more we hate thinking we lack complete control of our destinies. It is pathetic how little we have."

"You're speaking about external forces?"

"And internal ones. The external ones—like age differences—

are beyond our control. The internal ones? We have some control, but I begin to think it is like trying to control the Rhone glacier with a cigarette lighter."

She could see that as usual he would not be maneuvered into a commitment. "All right," she said, throwing herself against the pillow-banked headboard. "If you won't have me, what's to become of me?"

"You will go on being the fabulous Augusta Tollover."

"That's not a career."

"You will marry an absurdly rich, absurdly handsome young man and make him absurdly happy."

"Why rich?"

"Because, my dear, you adore money. And you should have it. You know what to do with it. For someone your age, you have remarkable style, taste, knowledge . . . Also you have need of the distance great wealth puts between you and the rest of the world."

She thought for a minute, then glanced toward him as he leaned on the windowsill facing her. "And you? Is that why you prefer being among your wealthy friends to your intellectual ones?"

"Distance from the hoi polloi? No, both groups are quite removed from the masses. I hadn't thought I preferred one to the other, but I suppose I do. I think it is because the human is a highly competitive animal. The older you grow, the wearier you become with the endless struggle for win, place or show. With my Left Bank friends—the artists, writers, musicians—their egos are firmly, desperately tied to who they *are*. The egos of my rich friends are tied to what they *have*. It may be a more superficial form of competitiveness, but it is less deadly. Look at our host. His paintings make one of the world's finest private collections. Henry is extremely proud of his Renoirs, Cezannes, Lautrecs. But it is a far less lethal form of pride than if he had painted the pictures himself. He doesn't take himself too seriously. I assure you it is much more pleasant to be around such people for long periods of time."

Augusta lowered herself into the bed and pulled the covers

up. "But you are an artist. And I'd rather be around you than anyone I know. Does that mean I have no ego?"

"You have ego all right, but it is a rare type. Yours isn't constantly reaching out to engage other egos. Yours is curiously self-contained. You take your satisfaction in what you can make yourself, what you are—not whom you can triumph over. I noticed it right away and loved you for it."

He came over and sat on the edge of the bed. "And I will tell you something else. There is such a fierce independence about you, you aren't threatened by the success of others. If you are fond of them, you rejoice in it. You'd be amazed how unusual that is. It's what would make you a superb wife for an extremely prominent man, perhaps a great one."

"It must come through a man? You don't think I could achieve prominence on my own?"

"You probably could," he said very seriously, "but even the most successful woman rarely earns the massive wealth you should have. Also, this ego of yours, which I have studied so meticulously, doesn't require that kind of success."

Later, when de Tristan returned to his room, Augusta lay awake for some time mulling over their conversation. His remarks about competitiveness struck home. She knew she would enjoy being the editor of a magazine—it was stimulating, constantly changing, fed by the main currents of the times. It also happened to be one of the most competitive fields on earth. *Vogue*'s Paris office was small, but she could see enough from the editors passing through and had heard enough stories about the New York office to know the field was cutthroat.

The more Augusta tried to think seriously about her future, the less she liked contemplating one without de Tristan. She knew he loved her. She drifted off to sleep comforting herself, as she had many times, that his insistence on treating their romance as a fleeting, ephemeral thing was his own way of handling his insecurities about their age difference. Of course, if she couldn't see through that she had no business being the lover of such a sensitive man.

47

Back in Paris, Augusta had appealed to Madge to lay out the arguments for a career rather than marriage. Madge was happy, successful, independent. Augusta wanted to hear the brief for the other side. She was disappointed.

"I've worked like a wetback all my life and it's paid off for me more than for most. I've managed to wriggle past the obstacles men throw up. But you'd be disillusioned to hear how little satisfaction I take in all that. I once bought a car with my first royalty check, a little Peugeot convertible. Mine, all mine—I'd bought it with money *I* earned. Do you know what? I didn't take half the pride in that car I took from a pearl necklace my first lover gave me. Maybe I'd been conditioned to live through men. I don't think so. Look at my life—never married, four lovers, four thousand paychecks. That's the path I chose. I've beat the system, sure, but how much joy is there in that at the end? Look at your friend Sylvia Thornton. How unfulfilled is she? Has she ever worked a day in her life? She's rich as hell. Was she oppressed? Who was exploiting whom? And the world is full of married women who've done the same thing."

"But Madge," Augusta protested, "you of all people suggesting I should spend my life dominated by a man, living in his shadow."

"Dominated? Listen, we all know field marshals and university presidents who are dominated by *silly* women. You would never be dominated. As for living in the shadows, you haven't got the stuff for that either. These things don't depend on married or not married, and they don't depend on career versus non-career. They are matters of personality. I admire Sylvia, but you, Augusta, don't have to do it her back-street way. Find a man you like who can give you the world, and wipe out all the rest of us. Careers, talent, meaningful work—it's all Presbyterian bullshit. The important thing is to dress well and have breakfast in bed."

Augusta felt more and more as though she were being pushed into a certain kind of high-powered, big-money life of international society. She knew "pushed" wasn't the right word as she had actively sought it. After all, she had fallen in love with Endicott de Tristan, not some penniless student at the Sorbonne. But so many were cheering her on, her acceptance in the silky world was so prompt and easy, she felt as though she were losing something important. She wasn't sure what. Perhaps what was slipping from her was the ability to choose the life she wanted. She was only in her mid-twenties. Couldn't she push final decisions off another five or ten years?

But what decision? No one was asking her for a commitment. Still she felt as though a commitment was happening, other doors were closing. The various people Augusta Tollover might have been were dropping out. The elimination tournament was almost over. Maybe it had been over years ago.

She had these locked-in feelings several nights later when she was to meet Endicott at a small dinner at the Baron Edmund de Rothschild's. When the baron's car arrived for Augusta, it was a beautiful summer evening, still light, mild with a sweet breeze. She settled into the soft, pearl-gray upholstery of the Rolls, but failed to take the usual comfort in the smells and feel of wealth. As the car crossed the Pont Louis Philippe to the Right Bank, she saw three tourists, American boys, walking across the bridge ahead of her. One stopped to point out the rosy sky behind the Île de la Cité rooftops. He separated from the others, ran a few steps in a crouching position then leaped into the air, arm straight up, and gracefully tipped an imaginary ball into an imaginary basket. It was not sport Augusta was seeing, but a spontaneous outburst of joy in being young, American and in Paris.

As the car passed the trio, Augusta saw with a start that the jumper was Jeff. He looked more beautiful than ever, older than when they had spent the summer together, but still boyish. He would be going into his final year of law school now, Augusta thought, then settling down with a local girl to raise a family—accepting life as it unrolled, not trying to surmount it, control it, avoid it, triumph over it.

She had an impulse to stop the car. Not to greet Jeff, but to join him, make him love her again, go off with him and his friends—camping in the Pyrenees, boating down the Danube, sleeping bags, youth hostels. She laughed at her jejune fantasy. Even the recollection of Jeff's lovemaking stirred no memory of pleasure, refreshed no appetite.

She settled back into the deep upholstery as the limousine reached the end of the bridge and turned up the Quai Hotel de Ville.

As she drove away a sad awareness wrenched Augusta. For all young Americans of a certain level of affluence, life was a bouquet of choices. This had been even truer for her. It was not just the many careers you might pursue, the many ways of living, the infinite geographic locations—it was also what kind of person to be, what values to make the foundation stones of your being. In your late teens and early twenties, you drifted along exploring, testing, trying on different roles, savoring new experience like a desultory epicure, pushing off the day when you adopted one of the paths, when you fixed the existence for life.

She knew that for her, the choice had been made, but not in the usual way. The path had chosen her. Money and power would be her metier. As for the other major choices, it was not as though she had examined them, one by one, and discarded them. They simply weren't there anymore.

Lady Shackleford had sounded very gay on the phone. She was in town for a few days shopping and wanted Augusta to lunch with her at the Ritz with a few old friends. Perhaps it was euphoria brought on by a recess from the diplomatic formality or maybe it was being in Paris without her husband, but she sounded a different woman.

As Augusta joined the group in the Rue Cambon bar, she saw that the three other guests were all women in their fifties, all

British and all expensively dressed. They were drinking champagne cocktails.

"Now Augusta," Lady Shackleford said, after introducing her to the others. "We are all being very silly today. Just wicked gossip, nothing serious. If I hear one word about the state of the world, I'm leaving the table."

Augusta smiled amiably and steeled herself for what was the last thing she was in a mood for: a giddy hen party. Even the superb Ritz food couldn't make the next two hours appealing to her. But she was so grateful to Lady Shackleford she would have met her for a sausage sandwich in the Vincennes metro station.

It was just before dessert that one of the women, aglow with Vouvray, asked, "What about Sylvia Thorton? Who is she having an affair with now?"

"It's still Endicott de Tristan."

At first Augusta felt anger at the silly bitch for not even being able to get her gossip straight, but something moved Augusta to pursue it, to correct the misinformation.

"Sylvia Thornton," Augusta put in tentatively, "is famous, I've always understood, for affairs with enormously rich men. Is de Tristan in her financial league?"

"He doesn't have to be. He's the one great love of her life. She has the others to beef up the old portfolio, but always returns to de Tristan in between."

"And during," put in the third.

Glenveagh Castle.

The look on Sylvia's face when her eyes had met Augusta's in McIlhenny's library flashed into Augusta's mind. The image confirmed what these terrible women were saying. It was a judgment on what her life had become that her destruction should be delivered by three aging harpies in Hardie Amies suits and broadbrimmed hats.

"He's been having a bit of a fling with a young American . . ."

"From San Francisco, frightfully rich . . ." said another authoritatively.

Augusta got though the lunch on automatic pilot. She phoned

de Tristan from the lobby of the Ritz. She was coming to see him, would he meet her at the next train? All the way out she could think of nothing but her constant and systematic betrayal by two of the closest friends she had in Paris. Did all their acquaintances know what the English woman knew? Why had he allowed her to be so humiliated? None of it made sense. Did she have strength to get answers?

She got into de Tristan's car and slammed the door. He looked at her for a moment, then started the motor. His eyes on the road, he said, "It's about Sylvia?"

"How could you think I wouldn't find out?"

"I don't know what you've found out—or whether or not it's true."

"That you and she have been lovers for years and still are."

He said nothing.

"How could you have let me get involved?"

"Augusta. Please. Wait till we get to the house. This is too serious to toss over the shoulder while driving."

She put her head against the seat and looked at the car roof. "That puts me ahead of where I was fifteen minutes ago."

"What do you mean?"

"At least you think it's serious."

In the drawing room, he mixed her a Scotch and soda and handed it to her, then sat down facing her. "I go back many years with Sylvia. I didn't tell you. I thought, I hoped, it was over for me. When I met you, Sylvia and I had not seen each other for six months. She had taken up with another of her lovers. This pattern had been torturing me for years. I saw friendship with you—not our being lovers, mind you—but our friendship, as a wonderful way to put Sylvia from my mind. I was taken off guard when suddenly you wanted to change our friendship to a romance. It is a small point, perhaps, but let's remember that change was *your* idea. If I had thought Sylvia and I would get back together, I think I would have mustered the strength of character to discourage you. I thought she and I were finally finished. I was wrong, and I am ashamed."

Augusta saw a glimmer of hope and seized it. "But surely this shows you what a ruthless woman she is? That she could treat you this way for so many years, and now blithely destroy my life while professing to be my friend? Give her up, Endicott. Put her behind you. We can go on from here."

He got up, walked to the bar and picked up a bottle of cognac. He held it, looking at it absently. There was a silence, then he said, "I've decided we shouldn't see each other anymore, Augusta. I've done you enough damage . . ." She only partially heard the following words as the thoroughness of her defeat penetrated and became a permanent part of her.

". . . A brilliant life, a brilliant marriage ahead of you . . ." How much more of this did she have to hear? Oh, God, why had she come out here by train? One last fling putting herself at his mercy? How could she get away?

Perhaps he saw that his fatherly wisdom was not helping. He then spoke the truth, which rang clearly in her ears and enabled her to ride back to Paris beside him in ceremonious quiet. "You have two things I really prize," he said. "Breeding and perfect skin texture. The breeding I can get from friends my own age; the skin I can buy on the Champs Elysées. I don't have to ruin your life to get both in one person."

48

Without Madge, Augusta did not know how she would have gotten through those first weeks. The other edge of the celebrity sword, the one she discovered cuts deepest, is the gossip when you make an ass of yourself. The bored *haut monde* of Paris gobbled up the juicy story like starving geese. Most of the people she and de Tristan had known together had been twenty years older than Augusta. How they must have relished a love triangle where the loser was the one under fifty.

Madge saw to it that Augusta did not have to take any assignments or attend any functions where she might run into de Tristan or his friends. They explored restaurants together, alone at first, but as Augusta recovered, they spent lively evenings with *Vogue* photographers, writers, models.

Just when Augusta had decided that life was not over for her, Ken arrived in Paris. His timing was so perfect—a week earlier and she wouldn't have seen him—Augusta wondered if he were in touch with Madge. Although Madge may have briefed him, he never alluded to her failed romance—although she knew he was aware of everything. Had he offered her direct sympathy or commiseration, it would have shattered the delicately reforming crystals of their friendship. He asked nothing, advised nothing, urged nothing—he was simply there, and for that Augusta would always be grateful.

Besides his loyalty, Ken's presence was also healing because of his Americanness, his lack of any connection with glittering international society. Every night for a week she sat across a restaurant table from him, drinking in his lack of deviousness, selfishness, vainglory, and his guileless face took on a beauty she had not seen before. Then she realized he *was* more handsome than before. It had taken her a week to notice it. He left Paris without saying or asking anything concrete. If he had intended the visit as a display of selfless love, his point was well made.

The connection with New York was riddled with static, but she could hear Brandon on the other end. "Are you O.K.? Is there some emergency?"

"I got a letter from Ken," Augusta almost yelled. "He wants to marry me and I'm thinking of accepting."

As though shocked by the announcement, the static suddenly stopped. So did Brandon.

"Did you hear me?"

"Now Augusta, I got your letter about the de Tristan business and I think that's very rough, but why rush into marriage with Ken?"

"Because he'll never give me one moment's anxiety or unhappiness."

". . . Or excitement."

"That's not a bad trade-off. I've decided I'm sick of the Great World. I don't want to play with them anymore. They play dirty." Augusta knew that her voice on the last line had slurred and made apparent—even to one a continent away—that she was not altogether sober.

"Wait a few weeks, Augusta."

The static came back now, worse than ever. "I'm promising nothing. Goodbye, Brandon. Love to you and B.K."

As she was about to hang up she heard him trying to scream something but the static was too awful. But in the quiet of her apartment, she reassembled the unlikely sentence, "Guido's in Paris."

The next day at *Vogue*'s office, Madge confirmed it. "I want you to take a cab over to Montmartre and interview Edna Williamson and her Teatro Expresso group. They've been touring Europe on a sandal strap, but they're very hot in New York right now."

Augusta brightened and jumped for her jacket. "Wish me luck, Madge. I'm in for the fight of my life!"

Augusta paid the taxi and entered the small theater. A rehearsal was in progress. She took a seat toward the rear of the darkened auditorium. Guido stood out instantly from the dozen other young Americans who milled around the stage as a director blocked a scene. Some of both sexes were as good-looking as Guido, but none moved with his insolent assurance of sexual magnetism. A self-fulfilling self-appraisal, Augusta thought. Do we have any weapon as potent as the belief in our own sexiness?

She acknowledged that he had a good bit to work with. A tight white T-shirt showed every bulge and contour of his chest and abdomen and its abbreviated sleeves revealed arm muscles that were developed to a point just short of caricature. He also managed to insinuate the parts you couldn't see. His legs never were together, but always ajar like a door that wouldn't close.

Augusta sat studying him in the dark. It had been a long time since she had heard a group speaking English, but they could have been speaking Serbo-Croatian, her mind was so completely given over to constructing the personality of this man she barely knew; her observations would be the foundation for her strategy.

As she sat watching, a further difference between him and the others became apparent. He was good. He immersed himself in performing; he was totally un-self-conscious. And there was a vitality. Even when he wasn't moving, he gave off waves of energy that almost engulfed the other performers.

She didn't know how much time passed, but suddenly the house lights went up. Her eyes never left Guido. She was sure he hadn't spotted her, but at the first break, he disappeared from the stage and was standing over her, hands on hips, half smiling.

"So you couldn't wait till opening night?" he said. "I was going to call you. I have a ticket for you." He sat down on a seat in front of her and leaned his head on one massive arm that he had rested on the back of his seat. His look was playful-but-harmless puppy.

"*Vogue* sent me to interview Miss Williamson . . ."

"Great. I'll introduce you. Make her think I set it up."

"But I wanted to talk with you."

A wariness shot through his eyes, but he smiled broadly and said, "Great. We're rehearsing tonight, but we shouldn't run past ten. Why don't you come by the theater then. We can get a drink or something to eat."

Although it was a warm summer night, Augusta suggested they sit in the nearly empty inside room of the café, whose terrace was crowded with animated French. She also liked the bright, unromantic light. The waiter came over and said in French that there would be an empty table outside shortly.

"*C'est bien ici*," Augusta said. "*Nous le préférons.*"

The waiter shrugged and took their order—steak and fried potatoes for Guido, tea with lemon for Augusta.

"Say," Guido said, "you're pretty good at that French. Ask that guy for some red wine when he comes back, will you?"

Guido launched into an account of their European tour, just as though Augusta was an old pal he hadn't seen for some time. She thought of what a bad tourist he would make. Your first trip into any foreign country is humbling, a chain of embarrassments. You had to be able to laugh at yourself, fumble in good grace. Guido would have no facility for that. She could see him bullying concierges and waiters, placing the misunderstanding and ineptitude on their side.

She let him go on for a while, then cut him short. "You know I wanted to get together to discuss you and B.K."

"I figured that," he said moodily. Then, brightening, "Go ahead. Shoot."

"First let me ask you—what keeps you together? You are so different. You like to play around. Your theater world is so fast-moving, you must meet so many attractive women . . ." Augusta knew she was saying nothing.

With a voice he would use to explain why he had given a million dollars for cancer research, Guido said, "Your sister has a lot of class. She knows a lot I don't know. We're good together. Also, we've kind of gotten used to each other."

She wanted to scream: you mistreat her, abandon her when it suits you, humiliate her, abuse her physically—but she could see that recriminations would get her nowhere. She might as well get down to it.

"Look, Guido, I want you to leave B.K. I think you are ruining her life. You want to get into films. I have some money, it is all the money I own . . ."

When she had phoned her cousin in New York that afternoon, she was crushed to learn that the famous twenty-thousand-dollar trust set up by her great-aunt Mable Wilmot had been raided by her father; each girl's share was now only five thousand dollars. A final cheat from Daddy. Please, God, let it be enough.

"It's five thousand dollars," Augusta said. "I can write you a check on my New York account. My lawyer will transfer the money from my trust and the check will be good by the time you get home."

Guido let out a loud "Ha!" then added, "I didn't think this was still being done. Listen, Gus old pal, if you'd pay five thousand dollars, think what old moneybags Hartshorne would pay. He hates me worse than you do—and is a lot richer."

"I'm *offering* this to you. You didn't come to me. If you went to him, that would be extortion. He'd have you arrested in a flash."

Augusta surprised herself with the speed with which she demolished his unexpected parry. It had not been part of her advance calculations. She could see Guido was impressed as well. His look darkened.

"You really think I'm crude, don't you?"

"Maybe at first it was snobbery that set me against you, but I would have gotten over that. It's what your affair has done to B.K. She's cut herself off from her entire world, she's become your creature . . ."

"Look, this is boring," he snapped. "I might just consider your offer. But I have one important condition."

She waited.

"You've got to make it with me."

He was chewing on a piece of steak as he said this. She wondered, absurdly, if B.K. let him chew with his mouth open.

"You accused *me* of being melodramatic . . ." she said scornfully.

He swallowed a mouthful of *pommes frites*, took a swig of wine and said, as though discussing a routine business deal, "It makes sense. You get to see what you're forcing your sister to give up. And for me, it will take the bad taste"—his voice switched from genial business dealer to snarling, hate-filled enemy—"of your stuck-up, too-good-for-anybody attitude from my mouth."

Augusta was stunned. While she grappled with this new strategy, on another level she was replaying a scene from the film of Somerset Maugham's *The Letter:* when Bette Davis's archenemy finally agrees to return the letters that will save Davis, the other woman makes her come for them in person, then pick them up at her feet. The movie was one of Brandon's favorites.

"You have every reason to despise me," Augusta said. "How do I know you won't hurt me?"

Guido flashed his knock-'em-dead smile. "That's just the chance you'll have to take."

"Another chance I must take . . ." Augusta said, taking a glass from the next table and filling it with wine from Guido's carafe. "You might be tempted to collect the money, then go back to B.K. after a time. Let me just tell you, that if you make

this deal and go back on it—or if you ever even hint of it to
B.K.—you'll find me a lot more resourceful than you might
imagine."

Guido looked at her. "Are you threatening a Brooklyn
Italian?"

"Yes."

Guido smiled. "I was thinking of sending her back to Park
Avenue anyway. She's getting fat."

Augusta started to say something angry, but the waiter
returned and handed Guido the bill and for a moment she
thought he was going to pass it to her.

"What do you say," he said, stretching his body as he reached
for his wallet, "to a nightcap at your place?"

49

After Guido's departure from Paris, Augusta
waited for the alarums from across the Atlantic. He had said he
would leave for California within a month of getting back to
New York. The check was cashed, and still no word. She
couldn't even let Brandon in on her pact, but, consumed with
suspense, had phoned him on the pretext of needing another
lecture about Ken. Finally she asked how B.K. and Guido were.

"Same old nightmare, but I think he spends less time at home
than ever. She's been over here three days this week helping me
fix up the new apartment. If he was around, she wouldn't come
near this place."

Augusta didn't know what to say. "Call me if . . . if there's
anything I can do."

Going to bed with Guido had shaken Augusta profoundly
and she was frantic to end the whole sordid business. After the
months with de Tristan, Guido's animalistic approach to the act
came as a shock, but the real shock was how much she had
enjoyed it.

Was it the hostility she felt toward Guido that propelled the
episode into a high level of excitement? Surely at work was the
curiosity often felt about the lovers of those closest to us. But

satisfied curiosity could not explain the heights, or depths, of abandon that Augusta reached that night.

No, the answer lay somewhere in the murky area of sisterly taboo. Of all the men in the world, the man her sister loved was totally forbidden. He was the one bed partner who, if he was indiscreet, could permanently mar her life.

There was still another psychic level it took Augusta several days to admit. By making love with Guido, she was challenging B.K. for the most important person in B.K.'s life, just as B.K.'s arrival in the Tollover family so many years ago had threatened Augusta's position with the most important person in *her* life.

Now, after so long a time, it was within Augusta's power to destroy the intruding sister—and this power sprang from an action aimed at saving her. Save, destroy, save, destroy—it was the steady beat of that contradiction that made Augusta realize the sex that night had everything to do with her sister and very little to do with the male body panting and sweating over her.

When she and Guido had finished and lay silent and spent in her small bedroom on the Île St. Louis, these thoughts had not yet reached her mind, they had merely energized her body. She knew only that she had reached heights she hadn't known existed. So much so that she considered Guido's suggestion of a few encores before he left Paris—to seal the bargain. She had quickly shrugged off the thought. Once had a symbolic, almost ceremonial aspect; twice would have been degenerate. Now, weeks later, all of her snarled emotions over the business began to come together into one banal and unlofty fear: she might be swindled.

And then the call came. Brandon reached her at the *Vogue* office. "Our prayers have been answered," his voice sounded harassed, breathless. "Guido's left her. But more brutally than his biggest fans would have guessed. Just took off to California and left her a kiss-off note. It's got everything but a crying baby . . ."

"How is B.K.?"

"Bad. Really quite bad. She's hysterical half the time and the rest of the time just sits and stares. You'd better come . . ."

"Of course."

"There's a Pan Am flight that leaves Paris at noon tomorrow. If you get on that I can borrow a car and meet you at Idlewild. If it's all booked . . ."

"I'll be on it."

As Brandon negotiated the heavy traffic out of the airport, Augusta talked first. "Madge says I can stay away a week, longer if absolutely necessary. I called Mummie in Bonn and had to talk her out of coming over right away too." The last time Augusta had seen her mother, Kate had been such a grande dame, bearing no resemblance to the harried young woman who used to mend their clothes and drive them to school, Augusta was surprised at her human, motherly reaction.

"I don't know what Mother can do, but I knew she and Uncle Bryce would be so relieved. And, of course, your father said he would underwrite any program that would ease *and secure* B.K.'s break-up. . . ."

Finally they were on the open highway speeding toward Manhattan. "Now tell me in more detail how she is."

"I like to think of myself as tough, convinced that all things will pass . . . But Jesus, Augusta . . ." he turned to her in desperation, "this doesn't seem to be passing. Last night was one of the worst nights of my life. She just sits and stares without talking, for hours, then suddenly bursts into tears. I finally got some Milltown down her. She makes me believe for the first time in Ophelia, Lucia and all those dames who went mad over rotten love affairs."

"You don't think she's breaking down?"

"I don't know what I think—except that I was afraid to leave her alone last night."

Brandon parked the car illegally in front of his Grove Street brownstone and got Augusta's suitcase from the trunk. "You stay here with her. I'll stay with a friend."

When she entered Brandon's large, bare living room, B.K. got up and ran to her, threw her arms around her, and sobbed into her shoulder.

"Oh, God, that you would come all this way, Gus . . ."

"Of course I would, darling. We're all going to get you through this."

Augusta was shocked at her sister's appearance. Crying for two days is hard on the best of looks, but B.K. had also put on weight—not an enormous amount, but enough to erase the exquisite definition of her mouth and cheekbones. Now puffy and with no makeup, her wonderful features had melted into the look of thousands of faceless women. Her hair was stringy and unkempt and was pulled indifferently around her head and held at the back with one clasp. She wore a loose navy-blue sweater with no shirt, sleeves pushed up to her elbows. She looked like a waitress from a Greenwich Village restaurant.

"B.K., you know how sorry I am this happened," Augusta began when they were seated and Brandon was getting them drinks. "But maybe this will show you how rotten he is. How little he cares for you or for anybody."

"Look, Gus, I love you for coming, but your attitude toward Guido, it's always been that empty snobbery Daddy worked so hard to program into us."

"No, B.K.! The opposite is true. It's because of Daddy's faults I know you should not be with Guido. Kate had a fiercely strong attraction to Daddy, she's told me, but look what came of it. A year or two of pleasure and years and years of misery for her and for us. It's a lousy exchange. Think of yourself as lucky. You've had the two good years. You're being spared the rest."

"Guido is not as bad as you make him out to be."

"I compare Guido to our father. Selfish and irresponsible as he was, he would never have dropped anyone the way Guido is dropping you."

B.K. looked away from her sister. "I'm sorry he doesn't meet your standards for chivalrous conduct. But he's good enough for me. I'm going to California and find him."

Augusta turned to Brandon. "You've been a better brother than either of us have a right to, Brandon, but would you mind leaving us alone?"

"I have to move the car anyway."

In the vestibule, he said, "Don't exorcists like audiences?"

"Wish me luck," she whispered. He kissed her forehead.

When she returned, B.K. had put her feet up on the sofa and was holding her whiskey glass against her forehead.

"In the first place, you aren't going after him, because it would be futile. You know he wouldn't have run out like this if he wanted to leave a door open."

"Guido's confused. He feels hemmed in at times, all men do. He'll get over it, then he'll want me back . . ."

"Chasing him across the country is going to help him get over feeling hemmed in? What Guido feels and doesn't feel is irrelevant. It's what *you* feel that needs repair. It was bad enough that you wanted to sacrifice your life to a creature like that when he wanted you, but now that he clearly doesn't . . ."

"You're being very cruel, Gus . . ."

"Cruel? What do you think it does to the people who love you watching you ruin yourself this way? You've been using Guido to hide from something. Somehow all the bad things that have happened to you in your life have become tied up in your mind with the kind of background we've had, that world that Daddy pretended to give us and couldn't. And then there was Paolo. You think by running from the world in which you belong, you'll escape the pain. Most of the problems of our childhood grew out of one wretched love, our parents. You're running from that into one far worse."

"STOP IT!" B.K. screamed in anger. She shot her feet to the floor and wheeled on Augusta. "Can't you see that if I am running from anything it is *you*."

"I think I'd better hear it all," Augusta said quietly, not expecting this.

"How do you think I liked trailing along my whole life in the wake of the fabulous Augusta Tollover—with Daddy, at school, when we went to Maryland . . . I'd get the crumbs left over after you swept through. I couldn't throw up without my vomit being compared to yours and found wanting. You kept pushing me—you and the others—the fabulous Tollover sisters, we can be whatever we want. Why does it have to be the fabulous Tollover sisters? Why can't it be the fabulous Tollover sister, singular, and let me go to hell my own way?

"And as for your brilliant ambitions for us both—I gave you a clear field and what did you turn up with? One aging composer who cheated on you from the start. And you accuse me of running away? When things turn sour for you, you collapse into the arms of Kendall Fesenden the Fifteenth, a prime specimen of the American upper class at its dullest! Where are your foreign princes, your oil tycoons, your great artists—the ones you promised me by the fountain? I didn't crave all that, but you did. Are all your famous looks, brains, wit, charm to be stashed away in Greenwich with this human safe-deposit box? Maybe we're both betraying what we might be, but at least Guido offers something more than forty years of chintz-upholstered boredom . . ." She collapsed sobbing into the pillows.

Augusta got up and sat beside her. B.K. let herself be picked up and cried quietly on Augusta's bosom. "I flew the Atlantic," Augusta said, "to straighten you out, not to *get* straightened out. But maybe you're right. With Ken I'm reaching out, not for a life, but for an anesthetic. What am I so afraid of?"

"Loving someone as much as Mother loved our father?" B.K. said weakly.

"No. Loving someone as much as *I* loved him."

Augusta patted her sister into an upright position then sat with her arm around B.K.'s shoulders. She reached for B.K.'s iceless Scotch. "I'll make a deal with you, B.K. I'll give up Ken, if you'll give up Guido."

"Not much of a deal, since Guido's already dumped me."

"Not much of a deal, since all I'll be giving up is a human safe-deposit box."

B.K. smiled and rubbed her cheek with her free hand.

Augusta looked at her a moment, then said, "I always wondered why it was you never resented me. And there you were, all that time, resenting away like mad."

"No, it wasn't like that, exactly. The resentment was like a permanent callus. Most of the time you forget it's there. Then you hit it wrong and it hurts like hell."

"Well, now you're responsible for me. I always wanted to climb to the summit. Daddy made me think it was possible—at the same time he made me want to move up and away from people like him, careless people who hurt everyone else. I always had the idea it would be safer up there. But I was afraid of going alone. You've set me back on that course. The least you can do is come with me."

"Will I become so famous and desirable that Guido will kill himself?"

"Easily."

B.K. pinched her waist. "Do I have time to lose some weight?"

"Of course, it will take that long for me to map the strategy. Plan our wardrobes, where we'll travel, who we'll see."

"How about those titled bozos you fixed me up with that summer in Europe? There were a couple of those I wouldn't mind seeing again."

"O.K.—for a warm-up. I've got much bigger fish in mind."

"Bolivian tin magnates?"

"Diamond mine owners."

"A pretender to a European throne?"

"Who's tired of pretending."

"An overlooked Rockefeller?"

They went·to mix themselves drinks and were dancing giddily around the room, B.K. wielding the bottle. "You take the Eastern Hemisphere, I'll take the Western," B.K. gurgled, her mouth full of Scotch.

"We'll meet twice a year to compare domains," Augusta said, returning with a refilled drink. They stood in the middle of the room and solemnly clinked glasses.

"We will rise gently higher and higher," Augusta said, pointing to the ceiling, "until we are out of everyone's reach and we can gaze down on the scrambling mortals."

"Let's find Brandon and have a celebration at Twenty-one!" B.K. said excitedly.

"A corner table," Augusta embellished. "Champagne and blinis."

"No hoods."

"No dullards."

"Only legends allowed."

Epilogue

In the administrator's office at Mapleton, the late-afternoon sun sliced across the desk and bisected the rear wall. B.K. rose from her crouching position, brushed her pants, then closed the lid of the chest.

"The head guy never showed up," Brandon said.

"Oriental mystics are terribly discreet." She looked at her watch. "Well, that's how the elephant went through her trunk. I'm going to have the whole lot shipped to Gus's house in France. God knows there's room for the stuff. It's junk, of course, good only for an orgy of nostalgia. I sometimes think the most merciful trait built into the human species is our natural tendency to forget. I'm not talking about repressing major traumas. I mean the forgetting of the hundreds of little things that happen, the minor characters who pass briefly. It's not that it's so painful, it's just too much to carry around all the time. A leaky memory is an essential blessing."

"Tell Alphonse there to rev up the motors. I have a cocktail party in Siasconset at six."

Brandon walked B.K. across the lawn, now mostly in shadow. Against the thwapping of the helicopter motor, he said, "Did you ever find out how Guido got the money to go to Los Angeles?"

"You mean Gus ransoming me for five thousand dollars?"

"She told you, then?"

"No, I ran into Guido at the Annenbergs' in Palm Springs. He told me. I was delighted to find a subject that interested us both. Now you couldn't get him to smile for five thousand dollars. That money was everything Gus got from our father. Isn't that ironic? One loser buying off another?"

"Probably the best use of his money for either of you. Or don't you agree?"

B.K. stepped up onto the helicopter and looked back at Brandon for an instant. "Oh, sure," she said distractedly. "Guido's losing his hair. And this"—she gestured toward the aircraft—"sure beats having to drive your own Jaguar."

The helicopter started to rise.

"Give Gus a big kiss for me," Brandon yelled.

B.K. smiled down at him, then yelled, "At the very next audience."